BLOOD HEIR

BOOKS BY AMÉLIE WEN ZHAO

Blood Heir
Red Tigress

BLOOD HEIR

AMÉLIE WEN ZHAO

EMBER

Originally published in hardcover in the United States by Delacorte Press, an imprint of Random House Children's Books, New York, in 2019.

Visit us on the Web! GetUnderlined.com

Educators and librarians, for a variety of teaching tools, visit us at RHTeachersLibrarians.com

The Library of Congress has cataloged the hardcover edition of this work as follows:
Names: Zhao, Amélie Wen, author.
Title: Blood heir / Amélie Wen Zhao.
Description: First edition. | New York : Delacorte Press, [2019] | Summary: A fugitive princess with a deadly Affinity and a charismatic crime lord forge an unlikely alliance in order to save themselves, each other, and the kingdom.
Identifiers: LCCN 2018043780 | ISBN 978-0-525-70779-0 (hardback) |
ISBN 978-0-525-70781-3 (ebook)
Subjects: CYAC: Ability—Fiction. | Magic—Fiction. | Fantasy.
Classification: LCC PZ7.1.Z5125 Bl 2019 | DDC [Fic]—dc23

ISBN 978-0-525-70782-0 (paperback)

Printed in the United States of America
10 9 8 7 6 5 4 3 2
First Ember Edition 2020

To 妈妈 and 爸爸, for teaching me
to view the world with kindness,
passion, and open eyes

N
W
E
S
The Silent Sea
The Kemeiran Empire
The Jade Trail
Sapphi
Port
Blue Fort
Kingdoms of the Aseatic Isles
Kingdom of Bregon

KRAZYAST TRIANGLE
SYVERN TAIGA
Salskoff
Ghost Falls
The Cyrilian Empire
Kyrov
Novo Mynsk
DZHYVEKHA MOUNTAINS
GOLDWATER PORT
ARAMABI DESERT
Crown of Nandji

1

The prison bore a sharp resemblance to the dungeons of Anastacya's childhood: dark, wet, and made of unyielding stone that leaked grime and misery. There was blood here, too; she could sense it all, tugging at her from the jagged stone steps to the torch-blackened walls, lingering at the edges of her consciousness like an ever-present shadow.

It would take so very little—a flick of her will—for her to control it all.

At the thought, Ana twined her gloved fingers tighter around the worn furs of her hood and turned her attention back to the oblivious guard several paces ahead. His varyshki bull-leather boots clacked in smooth, sharp steps, and if she listened closely enough, she could hear the faint jingle of the goldleaves she'd used to bribe him in his pockets.

She was not a prisoner this time; she was his customer, and that sweet rattle of coins was a constant reminder that he was—for now—on her side.

Still, the torchlight cast his flickering shadow on the walls around them; it was impossible not to see this place as the fabric of her nightmares and hear the whispers that came with.

Monster. Murderer.

Papa would have told her that this was a place filled with demons, where the evilest men were held. Even now, almost a year after his death, Ana found her mouth running dry as she imagined what he would say if he saw her here.

Ana shoved those thoughts away and kept her gaze straight ahead. Monster and murderer she might be, but that had nothing to do with her task at hand.

She was here to clear her name of treason. And it all depended on finding one prisoner.

"I'm telling you, he won't give you nothing." The guard's coarse voice pulled her from the whispers. "Heard he was on a mission to murder someone high-profile when he was caught."

He was talking about the prisoner. *Her* prisoner. Ana straightened, grasping for the lie she had rehearsed over and over again. "He'll tell me where he hid my money."

The guard threw her a sympathetic glance over his shoulder. "You'd best be spending your time somewhere nicer and sunnier, meya dama. More'n a dozen nobles have bribed their way into Ghost Falls to see him, and he's given 'em nothing yet. He's made some powerful enemies, this Quicktongue."

A long, drawn-out wail pierced the end of his sentence, a scream so tortured that the hairs on Ana's neck rose. The guard's hand flitted to the hilt of his sword. The torchlight cut his face, half in flickering orange, half in shadow. "Cells are gettin' full of 'em Affinites."

Ana's steps almost faltered; her breath caught sharply, and she let it out again, slowly, forcing herself to keep pace.

Her disquiet must have shown on her face, for the guard said quickly, "Not to worry, meya dama. We're armed to the teeth with Deys'voshk, and the Affinites're kept locked in special blackstone cells. We won't go near 'em. Those deimhovs are locked in safe."

Deimhov. Demon.

A sickly feeling stirred in the pit of her stomach, and she dug her gloved fingers into her palm as she cinched her hood tighter over her head. Affinites were usually spoken of in hushed whispers and fearful glances, accompanied by tales of the handful of humans who had Affinities to certain elements. Monsters—who could do great things with their powers. Wield fire. Hurl lightning. Ride wind. Shape flesh. And then there were some, it was rumored, whose powers extended beyond the physical.

Powers that no mortal being should have. Powers that belonged either to the Deities or to the demons.

The guard was smiling at her, perhaps to be friendly, perhaps wondering what a girl like her, clad in furs and velvet gloves—worn, though clearly once luxurious—was doing in this prison.

He would not be smiling at her if he knew what she was.

Who she was.

Her world sharpened into harsh focus around her, and for the first time since she'd stepped into the prison, she studied the guard. Cyrilian Imperial insignia—the face of a roaring white tiger—carved proudly upon his blackstone-enforced breastplate. Sword at his hip, sharpened so that the edges sliced into thin air, made of the same material as his armor—a half-metallic, half-blackstone alloy impervious to Affinite manipulation. And, finally, her gaze settled on the vial of green-tinged liquid that dangled from his belt buckle, its tip curved like the fang of a snake.

Deys'voshk, or Deities' Water, the only poison known to subdue an Affinity.

She had stepped, once again, into the fabric of her nightmares. Dungeons carved of cold, darker-than-night blackstone, and the bone-white smile of her caretaker as he forced spice-tinged Deys'voshk down her throat to purge the monstrosity she'd been born with—a monstrosity, even in Affinites' terms.

Monster.

Beneath her gloves, her palms were slick with sweat.

"We have a good selection of employment contracts up for sale, meya dama." The guard's voice seemed very far away. "With the amount of money you've offered to see Quicktongue, you'd be better off signing one or two Affinites. They're not here for any serious crimes, if that's your concern. Just foreigners without documents. They make for cheap labor."

Her heart stammered. She'd heard of this corruption. Foreign Affinities lured to Cyrilia with promises of work, only to find themselves at the traffickers' mercy when they arrived. She'd even heard whispers of guards and soldiers across the Empire falling into the pockets of the Affinite brokers, goldleaves flowing into their pockets like water.

Ana had just never expected to meet one.

She tried to keep her voice steady as she replied, "No, thank you."

She had to get out of this prison as fast as possible.

It was all that she could do to keep planting one foot ahead of the other, to keep her back straight and chin high as she had been taught. As always, in the blind mist of her fear, she turned her thoughts to her brother—Luka would be brave; he would do this for her.

And she had to do this for him. The dungeons, the guard, the whispers, and the memories they brought back—she'd endure it all, and endure it a hundred times over, if it meant she could see Luka again.

Her heart ached as she thought of him, but her grief was an endless black hole; it wouldn't do to sink into it now. Not when she was so close to finding the one man who could help her clear her name.

"Ramson Quicktongue," barked the guard, drawing to a stop outside a cell. "Someone here to collect." A jangle of keys; the cell door swung open with a reluctant screech. The guard turned to her, raising his torch, and she saw his eyes pass over her hood again. "He's inside. I'll be here—give me a shout once you're ready to be let back out."

Drawing a sharp breath to summon her courage, Ana threw back her shoulders and stepped into the cell.

The rancid smell of vomit hit her, along with the stench of human excrement and sweat. In the farthest corner of the cell, a figure slumped against the grime-covered wall. His shirt and breeches were torn and bloody, his wrists chafed from the manacles that locked him to the wall. All she could see was matted brown hair until he raised his head, revealing a beard covering half of his face, filthy with bits of food and grime.

This was the criminal mastermind whose name she'd forced from the lips of almost a dozen convicts and crooks? The man on whom she had pinned all her hopes for the past eleven moons?

She froze, however, as his eyes focused on her with sharp

intent. He was young—much younger than she'd expected for a renowned crime lord of the Empire. Surprise twanged in her stomach.

"Quicktongue," she said, testing her voice, and then louder—"Ramson Quicktongue. Is that your real name?"

A corner of the prisoner's mouth curled in a grin. "Depends on how you define 'real.' What's real and what's not tends to get twisted in places like these." His voice was smooth, and he had the faint lilt of a crisp, high-class Cyrilian accent. "What's *your* name, darling?"

The question caught her off guard. It had been nearly a year since she'd exchanged pleasantries with anyone other than May. *Anastacya Mikhailov*, she wanted to say. *My name is Anastacya Mikhailov.*

Except it wasn't. Anastacya Mikhailov was the name of the Crown Princess of Cyrilia, drowned eleven moons past in her attempt to escape execution for murder and treason against the Cyrilian Crown. Anastacya Mikhailov was a ghost and a monster who did not, and should not, exist.

Ana fisted her hands tightly over the clasp of her hood. "My name is none of your concern. How fast can you find someone within the Empire?"

The prisoner laughed. "How much can you pay me?"

"Answer the question."

He tilted his head, his mouth a mocking curve. "Depends on who you're looking for. Several weeks, perhaps. I'll trace my network of wicked spies and twisted crooks to your precious person of concern." He paused and clasped his hands together, his chains jangling loudly with the movement. "*Hypothetically,* of course. There are limits to even what *I* can do from inside a prison cell."

Already it felt from their conversation as though she were walking a tightrope, and a single misplaced word could send her plunging. Luka had gone over the basics of negotiation with her; the memory lit like a candle inside the darkness of the cell. "I don't have several weeks," Ana said. "And I don't need *you* to do anything. I just need a name and a location."

"You drive a hard trade, my love." Quicktongue grinned, and Ana narrowed her eyes. From the sleazy way he spoke and the glint of glee in his eyes, it was clear he found amusement in her desperation, though he had no idea who she was and why she was here. "Luckily, I don't. Let's make a deal, darling. Free me from these shackles, and I'm yours to command. I'll find your handsome prince or worst enemy within two weeks, be it at the ends of the Aramabi Desert or the skies of the Kemeiran Empire."

His drawl set Ana's nerves on edge. She could guess at how these conniving criminals worked. Give them what they wanted and they'd stab you in the back faster than you could blink.

She would not fall into his trap.

Ana reached into the folds of her worn cloak, drawing out a piece of parchment. It was a copy of one of the sketches she'd made in the early days after Papa's death, when the nightmares woke her in the middle of the night and that face haunted her through every second of her days.

In a swift motion, she unfurled the parchment.

Even in the dimness of the guard's flickering torchlight outside, she could make out the contours of her sketch: that bald head and those melancholy, overlarge eyes that made the subject appear almost childlike. "I'm looking for a man. A Cyrilian alchemist. He practiced medicine at the Salskoff Palace some time ago." She paused, and dared a wager. "Tell me his name, and where to find him, and I'll free you."

Quicktongue's attention had been drawn to the image the second she showed it, like a starved wolf to prey. For a moment, his face was still, unreadable.

And then his eyes widened. *"Him,"* he whispered, and the word bloomed into hope in her heart, like the warmth of the sun dawning upon a long, long night.

At last.

At last.

Eleven moons of solitude, of hiding, of dark nights in the cold boreal forests of Cyrilia and lonely days trawling through town after town—eleven moons, and she'd finally, *finally* found someone who knew the man who had murdered her father.

Ramson Quicktongue, the bartenders and pub crawlers and bounty hunters had whispered to her when they each returned empty-handed from their search for a phantom alchemist. *Most powerful crime lord in the Cyrilian underbelly, vastest network. He could track down a noblewoman's guzhkyn gerbil on the other side of the Empire within a week.*

Perhaps they'd been right.

It was all Ana could do to keep her hands steady; she was so focused on his reaction that she almost forgot to breathe.

Quicktongue's eyes remained fixed on the portrait, entranced, as he reached for it. "Let me see."

Her heart drummed wildly as she rushed forward, stumbling slightly in her haste. She held out the sketch, and for a long moment, Quicktongue leaned forward, his thumb brushing a corner of her drawing.

And then he sprang at her. His hand snapped around her wrist in a viselike grip, the other clapping over her mouth before she had a chance to scream. He gave her a sharp tug forward, twisting her around and holding her close to him. Ana made a muffled sound in her throat as the stench of his unwashed hair hit her. "This doesn't have to end badly." His tone was low when he spoke, his earlier nonchalance replaced by a sense of urgency. "The keys are hanging outside, by the door. Help me get out, and I'll give you whatever information on whomever you want."

She wrenched her face free from his filthy hand. "Let me go," she growled, straining against his hold, but his grip only tightened. Up close, beneath the torchlight, the hard-edged glint of his hazel eyes suddenly took on a wild, almost crazed look.

He was going to hurt her.

Fear spiked in her, and from years of training, a single instinct sliced through her mist of panic.

She could hurt him, too.

Her Affinity stirred, drawn by the warm pulse of his blood, rushing through her and filling her with a sense of power. At her will, every drop of blood in his body could be hers to command.

No, Ana thought. Her Affinity was to be used only as an absolute last resort. As with any Affinite, her power came with tells. The slightest stir of her power turned her irises to crimson and darkened the veins in her forearms—a clear indication of what she was, for those who knew how to look for it. She thought of the guard outside, of the curve to his vial of Deys'voshk, of the wicked glint of his blackstone sword.

She was so focused on tamping down her Affinity that she didn't see it coming.

Quicktongue's hand darted out and flicked the hood off her head.

Ana stumbled back, but the damage was done. Quicktongue stared at her eyes, the anticipation on his face giving way to triumph. He'd seen the crimson of her irises; he'd *known* to look for it—for the tell to her Affinity. A grin twisted his mouth even as he let go of her and yelled, "Affinite—*help!*"

Before she could fully realize that she had fallen into his trap after all, sharp footsteps sounded behind her.

Ana spun. The guard burst into the cell, his blackstone sword raised, the green tint of Deys'voshk he'd poured over the blade catching the torchlight.

She dodged. Not fast enough.

She felt the sharp bite of the blade on her forearm as she stumbled to the other side of the cell, her breath ragged. The sword had sliced through her glove, the fabric peeling open to reveal a faint trickle of blood.

The world narrowed, for a moment, into those droplets of blood, the slow curve of their path down her wrist, the shimmer of the beads as they caught the torchlight, glinting like rubies.

Blood. She felt her Affinity awakening to the call of her element. Ana ripped off the glove, hissing at the sting of the open air on her wound.

It had started—the veins running up her arm had darkened to a bruised purple, protruding from her flesh in jagged streaks. She knew how this looked; she'd stared at herself in the mirror for hours on end, eyes swollen from crying and arms bleeding from having tried to scratch out her veins.

A whisper found her in the dark.

Deimhov.

Ana looked up and met the guard's gaze just as he raised his torch.

Horror twisted his features as he backed toward Quicktongue's corner and pointed his sword at her.

Ana swiped a finger across her wound. It came away wet, with a smudge of green-tinted liquid that mingled with her blood.

Deys'voshk. Her heart raced, and memories flickered through her mind: the dungeons, Sadov forcing the bitter liquid down her throat, the weakness and dizziness that followed. And, inevitably, the emptiness where her Affinity had once been, as though she'd lost her sense of sight or smell.

The years she'd spent downing this poison in the hopes of cleansing her Affinity from her body had, instead, resulted in a tolerance to Deys'voshk. Whereas the poison blocked most Affinites' abilities almost instantaneously, Ana had fifteen, sometimes twenty, minutes before it rendered her Affinity useless. In a desperate bid to survive, her body had adapted.

"You move and I'll cut you again," the guard growled, his voice unsteady. "You filthy Affinite."

A jangle of metal, a flash of tangled brown hair. Before either of them could do anything, Quicktongue snapped his chains around the guard's neck.

The guard let out a choked gasp as he clawed at the chains that now dug into his throat. From the shadows behind him, Ramson Quicktongue's smile sliced white.

Bile rose in Ana's throat, and a wave of dizziness hit her as the poison began to work its way through her. She clutched at the wall, sweat beading on her forehead despite the cold.

Quicktongue turned to her, holding the struggling guard close. His expression was now predatory, his earlier nonchalance sharpened to the hunger of a wolf. "Now, let's try this again, darling. The keys should be hanging on a nail outside the cell door—standard protocol before a guard steps into a cell. The set for my chains are the fork-shaped iron ones, fourth down in the row. Unlock me, get us both out of here unscathed, and we can talk about your alchemist."

Ana steadied herself against the tremors in her body, her gaze darting between Quicktongue and the guard. The guard's eyes rolled back into his head, and spittle bubbled at his mouth as he choked for air.

She had known how dangerous Quicktongue was when she had come searching for him. Yet she had never expected him, a prisoner shackled to the stone walls of Ghost Falls, to get this far.

Unchaining him would be a terrible, terrible mistake.

"Come, now." Quicktongue's voice grounded her to the horrifying choice. "We don't have much time. In about two minutes, the next shift will be here. You'll be thrown into one of these cells and sold off in some work contract—and we all know how *that* goes. And I'll still be here." He shrugged and tightened his chains. The guard's cheeks bulged. "If that's the scenario you prefer, then I must say I'm disappointed."

The shadows in the room were swaying, contorting. Ana blinked rapidly, trying to steady her racing pulse against the first stage of the poison. Next would come the chills and the vomiting. And then the sap in her strength. All the while, her Affinity would be diminishing like a candle burning to the end of its wick.

Think, Ana, she told herself, clenching her teeth. Her eyes darted around the cell.

She could torture the man while she still had her Affinity. She could draw his blood, hurt him, threaten him, and get the location of her alchemist.

Tears pricked at her eyes, and she shut them against the images that threatened to crowd into her mind. Amid all her memories, one burned as brightly as a flame in the chaos. *You are not a monster, sistrika.* It was Luka's voice, steady and firm. *Your Affinity does not define you. What defines you is how you choose to wield it.*

That's right, she thought, drawing a deep breath and trying to anchor herself in her brother's words. She was not a torturer. She was not a monster. She was good, and she would not subject this man—no matter how dark his intentions—to the same horrors she had once been through.

Which left her with one option.

Before she knew it, she had crossed the room and snatched the keys from the wall, and was fumbling at the prisoner's chains. They fell with a click. Quicktongue sprang away from them and darted across the room in the blink of an eye, rubbing his chafed wrists. The guard slumped to the floor, unconscious, his breath wheezing through his half-open mouth.

A fresh wave of nausea rolled over Ana. She clung to the wall. "My alchemist," she said. "We had a deal."

"Ah, him." Quicktongue strode to the cell door and peered outside. "I'm going to be honest with you, love. I have no idea who that man is. Good-bye." In the blink of an eye, he was on the other side of the bars. Ana lurched forward, but the cell door swung shut with a clang.

Quicktongue jangled the keys at her. "Don't take it too personally. I *am* a con man, after all."

He threw a mock salute, spun on his heels, and disappeared into the darkness.

2

For a moment, Ana only stood, staring at his retreating back, feeling as though the world were disappearing beneath her feet. *Conned by a con man.* A bitter laugh wheezed from her throat. Had she not expected that? Perhaps, after all these months she'd spent learning to survive on her own, she was really only a naïve princess who couldn't survive beyond the walls of the Salskoff Palace.

Her wound throbbed, a trickle of blood and Deys'voshk winding gently down her arm, filling the air with its metallic tang.

Her Affinity stirred.

No, Ana thought suddenly, touching a finger to her wound. The drops of blood seemed to pulse at her fingertips. No, she was not just a naïve princess. Princesses did not have the power to control blood. Princesses did not murder innocent people in broad daylight in the middle of a town square. Princesses were not monsters.

Something snapped within her, and suddenly she was choking on years of built-up ire, churning with nauseating familiarity.

No matter what she did, no matter how good she tried to be, she always ended up as the monster.

The rest of the world dimmed, and then there was only the blood trickling down her arm and onto the floor in slow, singular droplets.

You want me to be the monster? Ana lifted her gaze to the corridor where Ramson had disappeared. *I'll be the monster.*

Reaching into that twisted place within her, Ana stretched her Affinity.

It was like lighting a candle. The shadows that had been pulling at her senses burst into light as her Affinity reached out to the very element that made her monstrous: blood.

It was everywhere: inside every prisoner in the cells surrounding her, splattered and streaked on the filthy walls like paint, from vivid red to faded rust. She could close her eyes and not see, but *feel* it, shaping the world around her and gradually, several corridors down, fading into nothingness beyond her reach. She sensed it coursing through veins, as powerful as rivers and as quiet as streams, or still and stale as death.

Ana stretched her hands, feeling as though she was breathing in deeply for the first time in a long time. All this blood. All this power. All hers to command.

She found the con man easily, the adrenaline pumping through his body lighting him like a blazing torch among flickering candles. She focused her Affinity on his blood and pulled.

A strange sense of exhilaration filled her as the blood obeyed, every drop in Quicktongue's body leaping to her desire. Ana drew a deep breath and realized that she was *smiling*.

Little monster, a voice whispered in her mind—only, this time, it was her own. Perhaps Sadov had been right after all.

Perhaps there was some twisted part of her that was monstrous, no matter how hard she tried to fight it.

A shout rang out in the hallway, followed by a thud, then sounds of scuffling. And then slowly, from the darkness, a foot emerged. Then a leg. And then a filthy torso. She dragged him to her by his blood, savoring the way it leapt at her control, the way he jerked like a marionette under her power.

Outside her cell, Quicktongue writhed on the ground. "Stop," he panted. A red blotch appeared on his sweat-stained tunic, soaking through the fabric and filth. "Please—whatever you're doing—"

Ana reached an arm through the cell bars and seized his collar, wrenching him so close that his face thunked against the metal. *"Silence."* Her voice was a low snarl. "*You* listen to *me.* From now on, you will obey my every word, or this pain that you feel right now"—she tugged at his blood again, drawing a low moan—"will be just the start." She heard the words as though someone else were speaking through her lips. "Are we clear?"

He was panting, his pupils dilated, his face pale. Ana tamped down any guilt or pity she might have felt.

It was *her* turn to command. *Her* turn to control.

"Now open the door."

The con man roused himself in starts and stops, shaking visibly. A sheen of sweat coated his face. He fumbled with the lock, and the cell door squeaked open.

Ana stepped out of the cell and turned to him. The world swayed slightly as another bout of dizziness hit her—yet her stomach clenched in twisted pleasure as Quicktongue cringed. Blots of red were spreading on his shirt where vessels in his skin had broken. Tomorrow these would become ugly bruises that pocked his body like some hideous disease. *The devil's work,* Sadov had called it. *The touch of the deimhov.*

Ana turned away before she could feel revulsion at what she had done. Her hand automatically darted to her hood, pulling it back over her head to hide her eyes. Her hands and forearms felt heavy, streaked with jagged veins engorged with blood. She tucked her ungloved hand inside her cloak, fingers twisting against the cold fabric, feeling exposed without her glove.

The hairs on her neck rose when she realized that the prison had gone completely silent.

Something was wrong.

The moans and whispers of the other prisoners had quieted, like the calm before a storm. And then, several corridors down, a loud clang sounded.

Ana tensed. Her heart started a drumroll in her chest. "We need to get out of here."

"Deities," cursed Quicktongue. He'd pulled himself up from the ground and sat leaning heavily against the wall, panting, the corded muscles of his neck clenching and unclenching. "Who are you?"

The question came out of nowhere; she could think of a thousand ways to answer. Unbidden, memories flipped through her mind like the pages of a dusty book. A white-marble castle in a wintry landscape. A hearth, a flickering fire, and Papa's deep, steady voice. Her brother, golden-haired and emerald-eyed, his laugh as radiant as the sun. Her aunt, doe-eyed and lovely, head bowed in prayer with her dark braid falling over her shoulder—

She pressed the memories back, replacing the wall that she'd carefully built over the last year. Her life, her past, her crimes—these were her secrets, and the last thing she needed was for this man to see any weaknesses in her.

Before she could respond, Quicktongue leapt. He moved so fast that she'd barely let out a surprised grunt when his hand clamped down over her mouth again and he spun her behind a stone pillar. "Guards," he whispered.

Ana rammed her knee between his legs. Quicktongue doubled over, but past his furious whisper-curses, she heard the sound of footsteps.

Boots thudded down the dungeon hallway, the rhythmic beat of several guards' steps. She could make out the dim light of a far-off torch, growing brighter. Voices echoed in the corridor and, judging by the sound of laughter, the guards were cracking jokes.

Ana loosed a breath. They hadn't been discovered. These guards were only making their rounds.

Quicktongue straightened and leaned into her as he pressed himself against the pillar. Huddled together, their hearts beating the same prayer, they might have been partners in crime, or even allies. Yet the glare in his eyes reminded her that they were anything but.

She tried not to breathe as the guards passed by the pillar. They were so close that she heard the rustle of their rich fur cloaks, the scuff of their boots on the grimy floor.

A sudden realization hit her. The guard. They had left him unconscious in Quicktongue's cell.

By her side, Quicktongue tensed as well, as though he'd reached the same conclusion. He hissed a curse.

A panicked shout rang out, followed by the ominous squeak of the cell door. Ana squeezed her eyes shut, dread blooming cold in her chest. They had discovered the unconscious guard.

"Listen to me." Quicktongue's voice was low and urgent. "I've studied the plans of this prison—I know the layout as well as I know the goldleaves in my purse. We both know you're not getting out of here without my help, and I need your Affinity as well. So I'm asking you to trust me for now. Once we're out of this damned place, we can go back to tearing each other's throats out. Sound good?"

She hated him—hated the fact that he had fooled her, and the fact that he was right.

"Fine," she breathed. "But if you even think of using any tricks, just remember what I can do to you. What I *will* do to you."

Quicktongue was scanning the corridor ahead, his head cocked as he listened. "Fair enough."

Beyond their pillar, one of the guards stepped into the cell and desperately shook his fallen comrade. The other two foraged farther into the depths of the dungeons with their swords drawn, torches held high. Hunting.

Quicktongue's beard tickled her ear. "When I say 'run' . . ."

The torchlight grew dimmer.

"Run."

Ana dashed from the pillar. She didn't think she'd ever run this fast before. Cells flew by on either side of her in dark streaks of color. Down at the end of the corridor, so small that she could have blocked it out with a thumb, was the sliver of light from the exit.

She dared a glance back to find Quicktongue tearing toward her.

"Go!" he shouted. "Don't stop!"

The light was bright ahead of her, the stone ground hard beneath her pounding feet. And before she knew it, she was at the stairs, careening up two at a time, her breaths ragged in her throat.

She emerged into bright, unyielding daylight.

Immediately, her eyes began to water.

Everything was white—from the marble floors to the high walls to the arched ceilings. Sunlight streamed through the narrow, high windows above their heads, magnified by the marble. This, Ana had read, was part of the prison's design. The prisoners would have stayed in the darkness underground for so long that they would be blinded as soon as they emerged from the dungeons.

And despite all of her careful reading and research, she had no way out of this trap but to wait for her eyes to adjust.

A loud clang sounded behind her. Through her tears, she saw Quicktongue twisting the key to lock the dungeon doors in place. He hurtled up the steps, three at a time, and when he reached the top, he clamped his hands over his eyes with a curse.

Beyond this hall, somewhere that Ana could not locate, shouts echoed. A faint clattering sound thrummed along the marble floors and reverberated off the blindingly white walls—the sound of boots tapping and weapons being drawn.

The alarm had been raised.

Ana looked at Quicktongue. Through the blur of her tears,

she could make out the look of pure panic that flitted across his face—and Ana realized that, despite all his cunning and bravado, Ramson Quicktongue did not have a plan.

Fear sharpened her wits, and the world shifted into focus as the smarting in her eyes faded. Corridors fanned out in all directions from them: three to her left, three to her right, three before her, three behind her, all identical, all white.

Her head pounded with the effects of the Deys'voshk; she couldn't even remember which way she'd come in. This place was a maze, designed to trap prisoners and visitors like quarry on a spider's web.

Ana seized Quicktongue's shirt. "Which way?"

He peered out from a slit between his fingers and groaned. "The back exit," he mumbled.

She drew a breath. Of course, none of her readings of Ghost Falls—which had been sparse enough to come by already—had mentioned a back exit. The front, Ana knew, had three sets of locked and guarded doors, not to mention a courtyard watched by archers who would stick them like shooting-range targets if they even stepped a toe outside. She'd taken it all in quietly as she'd followed the guard inside—back then as a visitor.

Never, in her wildest imagination, had she thought she would be running from the prison with a convicted criminal in tow and a dozen guards on her trail.

Fury spiked in her; she grasped Quicktongue by his filth-stained tunic and shook him. "You got us into this mess," she snarled. "Now *you* get us out. Which way to the back exit?"

"Second door . . . second door to our right."

Ana hauled him into a run after her. Boots pounded along one of the corridors—she couldn't tell which. At any moment, the reinforcements would be there.

They were halfway down the hallway when a shout rang out behind them. "Stop! Stop in the name of the Kolst Imperator Mikhailov!"

The Glorious Emperor Mikhailov. They flung Luka's name around so casually, so authoritatively. As though they knew anything about her brother. As though they had the *right* to command by his name.

Ana turned to face the prison guards. There were five of them, silver Cyrilian tiger emblazoned against white uniforms, their blackstone swords drawn and flashing in the sunlight. They had come fully equipped, with helmets, too; their attire glittered with the telltale gray-hued alloy.

They snarled at her, spreading out like hunters surrounding an untamed beast. There was once a time when they might have knelt in her presence, when they would have raised two fingers to their chests and drawn a circle in a sign of respect. *Kolst Pryntsessa,* they would have whispered.

That was long past now.

Ana's fingers curled over her hood, pulling it closer. She raised her other hand, wounded and gloveless, at the guards. Blood trickled down her arm in a lover's spiral, vivid crimson against the dusky olive of her skin.

Nausea stirred in the pit of her stomach, and her throat ached with revulsion. Unlike apprenticed or employed Affinites who had honed their abilities for years, Ana had only a basic and crude control over hers. Fighting this many people at once could easily mean losing control of her Affinity entirely. It had happened before—nearly ten years earlier—and it made her sick to think of it.

An archer knelt into position, the tips of his arrows glistening with Deys'voshk. Ana swallowed. "Cover me," she said to Quicktongue, and her Affinity roared to life.

Show them what you are, my little monster.

Show them.

She let her Affinity free and it coursed through her, singing and screaming and writhing in her veins. Through the haze of her frenzy, she latched on to the outlines of the five guards, their blood racing through their bodies with a combination of adrenaline and fear.

She held those bonds and gave a sharp, violent pull—

Flesh tore. Blood filled the air. Her Affinity snapped.

The physical world rushed back in a torrent of white marble floors and cold sunlight. Somehow she was on all fours, her limbs trembling as she struggled to breathe. The beige-gold veins of the marble floor spun before her eyes, the Deys'voshk running its course through her head. In less than ten minutes, the onset would be complete; her Affinity would be gone.

She leaned forward, her back arching to a fit of coughs. Crimson spattered the white marble floors.

A hand closed on her shoulder. Ana flinched. Quicktongue crouched by her side, his mouth hanging open as he surveyed the scene.

The corridor was eerily empty. Beyond the stairwell, scattered throughout the hallway, were five crumpled shapes. They lay still in pools of their own blood, the dark stains inching over the floor and creeping across her senses.

The touch of the deimhov.

"Incredible," Quicktongue murmured, looking at her with a mixture of awe and delight. "You're a witch."

She ignored the insult and slumped over the polished marble floor, panting. The use of her Affinity had drained her energy, as it always did.

"Stay here," Quicktongue ordered. Then he was gone.

Ana pushed herself onto her knees. She was suddenly too conscious of the bodies around her, cold and still in their deaths. Their blood hung in her awareness, roaring rivers turned to pools of dead water, eerily silent. The white marble gleamed in contrast to the crimson, sunlight spilling bright on the blood as though to say: *Look. Look what you've done.*

Ana curled forward, wrapping her arms around herself to stop her shaking. *I didn't mean to. I lost control. I didn't ask for this Affinity. I never meant to hurt anyone.*

Perhaps monsters never meant to hurt others, either. Perhaps monsters didn't even know they were monsters.

She counted down from ten to give herself time to stop crying and get off the floor. The blood smeared beneath her palms as she stood. She leaned against the wall and drew in deep breaths, her eyes closing to avert the sight before her.

"Witch!"

Ana started. Quicktongue stood before the second corridor to her right, a cord of rope slung over his shoulder. He waved at her and turned down the hallway, disappearing from sight.

How long had he stood there, watching her break down? She stared after him, unease filtering through the tide of her exhaustion.

"Hurry!" His voice drifted back, echoing slightly.

It took every ounce of her willpower to straighten her spine and hobble after him.

The prison was built like a maze. Kapitan Markov had educated Ana on prison designs when she was only a young girl. His face would crease beneath his gray-peppered hair when he smiled at her, and the familiar smell of his shaving cream and armor metal had grown to soothe her.

In his steady baritone, he had told her that Cyrilian prisons were labyrinths that trapped prisoners who tried to escape, so that the panic and uncertainty had them losing their minds by the time they were recaptured. The outer rings of these maze-prisons were heavily guarded, but guards on the inside were more sparse simply because they shot any prisoners who managed to wander into the outer layers.

She could only hope this back exit of Quicktongue's did not promise such a swift death.

Ahead, the con man moved with predatory grace that reminded her of a panther she'd once seen in an exotic animal show in Salskoff. She caught the wink of a stolen dagger in his hands, the sigil of a white tiger flashing on the hilt.

As though he heard her thoughts, he spared her a glance. "Tired?" he whispered. "That's the price you Affinites pay for your abilities, isn't it? Plus our friend back there gave you a pretty dab of Deys'voshk."

A guard rounded the corner, saving her the pain of thinking up a pithy comeback.

In three light steps, Quicktongue was at his throat. A flash of metal and the guard dropped, the white-tiger hilt protruding from his chest. Even through her haze of fatigue, Ana could tell that there was a trained precision to Quicktongue's movements, a science to the way he angled his blade.

Quicktongue sheathed his dagger in a practiced stroke. "Almost there," he said.

It grew dimmer, sconces fixed more and more sparsely along the walls. Marble turned into rough-hewn stone, and once or twice Ana thought it would go completely dark. She kept her Affinity flared like a torch, all the while conscious of its diminishing range as the Deys'voshk steadily took over. Even Quicktongue, whose fast-flowing blood should have been easy for her to track, wove in and out of her awareness like a phantom.

Through the rhythmic clack of their heels, another sound had emerged—faint, but growing louder, like the whisper of wind brushing through the tall frost-larches outside her windows.

The sound of . . . water.

They had to be at the back of the prison, then, where the bodies of dead prisoners were dumped along with sewage and waste. Unlike most Cyrilian prisons, which were built atop rivers for easy disposal, Ghost Falls was built atop a cliff sliced through with a waterfall, earning its name. There was even a twist to the old joke: the prisoners were stuck between a cliff and a waterfall.

A cliff and a waterfall.

Her legs felt watery. "Quicktongue," Ana gasped, and then she was shouting. "Quicktongue!"

He'd disappeared around the corner. Ana pushed herself into a run, the churning water growing louder until even her footsteps were muffled by the rushing sound.

The next hallway ended abruptly in a narrow arched door

made of blackstone. Its cold and eerie lightlessness whispered to her.

Quicktongue knelt before the door, his gray tunic a ghostly blur against the blackstone. In the semidarkness, his hands worked with the precision of the Palace physicists Ana had studied with. Something flashed between his fingers; he made a quick downward motion, and the door jarred open.

The muffled pounding sharpened into a roaring sound that reverberated between the stone walls and low ceiling overhead. Quicktongue pushed the door open, and Ana felt her stomach drop.

Beyond the blackstone door, the corridor ended abruptly, as though someone had taken a butter knife and sliced it off neatly. Two large pillars rooted the end of the hallway into the outcrop of cliffs below. The gray-blue sky of Cyrilia stretched for miles over their heads, until it met the expanse of glittering snow-covered landscape. Beneath, ice-white waters foamed and plunged downward. Ana's legs grew weak as the familiar fear of water churned within her, carved into the bones of her memory from an incident a long, long time ago. The merciless waters of a river—a very different one—had nearly killed her not once but twice many years past.

Quicktongue was already in motion. He unslung the thick length of rope he'd been hauling. With fluid ease, he looped one end of the rope around a pillar. His fingers wove some kind of complicated knot.

Deities. Ana pressed herself against the back wall and willed her knees not to buckle. *This* was the back exit Quicktongue had spoken of: the open sewer place where they dumped excrement and dead bodies.

And they were going to jump. "I'm not jumping down there with you," she yelled, edging back into the turn of the corridors, behind the blackstone door.

Quicktongue knelt by the ledge. "Not sure how far you got in your schooling, sweetheart, but here's some wisdom from the streets. Anyone who tries to jump down there will die. The impact will shatter your bones."

The waterfall plunged like a roaring beast, fading into a white mist so thick that she couldn't even see the bottom.

Quicktongue tested his knot. The rope stretched taut. "You coming, Witch?"

Ana was almost convinced he was mad. "You just said anyone who tries to jump down there will die."

Quicktongue straightened. Outlined against the misty blue Cyrilian sky, above the frothing white waters, he looked almost heroic. "I did. But, darling, we're not going to jump." He gestured to the length of rope—most of which lay coiled in a heap between them like a snake. The other end looped around the pillar. "I plan to lower us to the river below. I've done the calculations. It'll work." He grinned and brought his index finger and thumb close to each other. "It'll be a *tiny,* dainty step. Like stepping off a carriage. Except . . . off a ledge."

His eyes glinted with mirth, and she wanted to choke him. Deities, she was going to die. Behind her: guards who would imprison her and sell her into indenturement. Before her: a mad con man who was likely going to leap to his death.

"Well?" Quicktongue listed his head. With his trickster's fingers, he'd already tied the other end of the rope securely around his waist and was waggling the last length of it at her. "We've spent a good five minutes getting here. They've raised the alarm, so more guards'll be on us like bees on honey. You're wasting my time, darling."

Ana turned her gaze back to the waterfall, watching the frothing white waters pound down at speeds that would shatter bone. And suddenly, she imagined herself caught in those currents as she had been ten years ago, the foam and the waves crushing her chest and twisting her limbs and pressing at her lips and nose.

I can't.

Somewhere back in that labyrinth, above the pounding of the waterfall, shouts sounded. She pushed her Affinity out, but it had weakened to the point that all she felt were the faintest wisps of blood. The wound on her arm gave a particularly nasty throb. A few more minutes and there would be nothing left of her Affinity to fight with.

There was no turning back now.

She wanted to cry, but she knew from her years with Sadov in the dungeons that crying achieved nothing. In the face of fear, one could choose to run, or to rise.

So Ana swallowed her nausea, bit back her tears, and lifted her chin as she marched past the blackstone door. The floor was uneven and wet, and a smell—as though something, or many things, had rotted here—choked her as she ventured out farther. "I didn't come here to die, con man," she snapped as she picked her way over to him. "If you try anything, I'll kill you before the water does. And trust me, you'd beg me to let you drown instead."

Quicktongue was balancing on the edge of the white marble floor, holding on to the rope. His lips quirked as he began to strap her tightly against his chest with the last bit of rope on his end. "Fair enough."

Ana inhaled sharply as the rope cut into her back and waist. Quicktongue gave her a crooked grin. "I know I smell, love, but you'll thank me later when you're still alive."

The wind whipped against her face as she shuffled to the edge, where the ground ended and the nothingness began. Her hair tore loose from its austere knot, dark chestnut strands fluttering against an open blue sky.

Quicktongue gave the rope another tug. "Hold tight," he shouted, and despite herself, Ana wrapped both arms around his filthy tunic, keeping her face as far from his chest as possible without straining her neck.

He swung them off the ledge.

Whatever revulsion she'd felt toward Quicktongue dissolved, and she found herself clinging tightly to him as though her life depended on it.

It did.

They dangled right beneath the ledge of Ghost Falls, spiraling gently. The waterfall roared in her ears, so close that she could reach out and touch it. The length of rope connecting them to the pillar tumbled beneath them in a long loop, disappearing into the white mist.

Slowly, Quicktongue began to lower them. His muscles were taut, veins popping from his neck as he placed one hand below the other.

Ana dared a look down. The sight had her gripping Quicktongue more tightly, swallowing her panic. She might have sent a thousand prayers to her Deities, but none would have mattered. In this instant, there was only her and the con man.

Ana looked up. The mist was so thick that she could barely make out the ledge of the prison anymore. That was a good thing. "How much longer?" she screamed, barely hearing her own voice over the waterfall.

"Almost!" He was shouting, but his words were hardly audible. "We need to get to the end of this rope, or the fall will kill us."

Ana squinted up. Something—a movement in the mist—had her instinctively grasping for her Affinity. There it was: the faintest wisp, an echo of her powers, still struggling beneath the Deys'voshk.

She frowned as she sensed something through her bonds, so faint that it almost slipped past her.

A gust of wind slammed into them and Ana closed her eyes, trying to block out the dizzying swinging sensation. When she opened them again, the wind had cleared some of the mist. At the top, over the ledge of Ghost Falls, was the outline of an archer, his bow and arrow angled toward them.

"Look out!" she cried, and the first arrow whizzed over their heads.

The second struck Quicktongue.

He grunted in pain as it grazed his shoulder, slicing open his sleeve and drawing blood. Ana bit back a scream as Quicktongue's grip slipped against the slick rope. They lurched, spinning wildly, a hand's breadth from being battered to death by the waterfall. Above, the archer nocked another arrow.

Below, she saw the end of the length of rope, looping up to connect to Quicktongue's waist. The end of the rope. They had to get to the end of the rope, or they would die.

Ana reached into herself, digging until she was nothing but blood and bone. And she found it, the last remnants of her

Affinity, as faint as a dying candle, still fighting against the Deys'voshk.

Ana stretched out her hand and latched on to the blood of the archer. And pushed.

The archer tensed and swayed for a second, as though a sudden gust of wind had hit him. Ana let her hand fall. Warmth trickled down her lip and she tasted her own blood.

That was it. The Deys'voshk had won; she had no more to give.

But it had been enough to distract the archer and get them to the end of the rope.

Quicktongue let go and reached to his hip. His dagger glinted dull silver. He leaned toward Ana, his eyes narrowed, his expression sharpened to dead, lethal calm. "Don't struggle, don't move. Just hold on to me. Feetfirst, toes pointed."

She had barely processed his words, barely let a taste of fear reach the tip of her tongue.

Quicktongue raised his arm. "First step to becoming a ruffian," he said, "is learning to fall."

His blade flashed. He brought his arm down with ruthless force.

And then they were falling.

3

The river claimed them as soon as they hit it, pulling them under with vengeance in its white-furled fluxes and battering them like leaves in a gale. Ramson let the tides take him. He knew the waters, knew when to let himself go and when to push against it. The river did not yield. It was all about learning to swim with the current.

These waters were different from the wide-open seas of Ramson's childhood. In Bregon, the waters were cobalt blue, the caps flecked with sunlight. He had swum for hours, diving beneath the surface and looking up at the faraway sky in a muted blue world of his own.

In Cyrilia, the rivers were white and frothing and cold. Ramson struggled to keep his eyes open as the current flung him to and fro. The pressure in his chest grew. Water surged at his nose and mouth.

The Affinite girl was still bound to his chest by the rope. He could feel her thrashing against him, kicking and struggling as the current pummeled her.

Ramson severed the cord. The odds of survival were greater without someone weighing you down. He had been thinking only of himself when he did it, but as he watched the current drag the witch away, he supposed it might have been true for her, too.

Stay still, he wanted to tell her. *The more you struggle, the faster you drown.*

But his own lungs were aching, and that familiar sensation of weakness was creeping into his limbs. He needed to breathe, or risk becoming a part of the current forever.

Ramson kicked out. No sooner had he righted himself than the current pushed him over again. Panic bubbled in his chest.

His head felt light. Water pressed at his nose and his lips, yet part of him remembered that he could not open his mouth. His limbs were becoming heavier. His vision was a whirl of white. It was cold.

Swim, came a voice. He knew instantly whose voice it was—that calm, thin voice that had defined his childhood and haunted him every day thereafter. Here, in the roaring chaos, it sounded so close. *Swim, or we both die.*

Ramson thrust his legs behind him, arching his back. He felt the current give a little. Somewhere above him, somewhere near, there was light.

Swim.

The light grew brighter. He broke through the surface, coughing and gulping in lungful after lungful of fresh, wintry Cyrilian air, feeling the power return to his limbs.

He hauled himself onto the bank, digging his nails into the half-frozen dirt and dragging his feet across snow-covered grass. He was shivering uncontrollably, moving in starts and stops, his arms and legs jerking in awkward movements as he tried to stimulate his blood flow.

The river had borne them quite a distance; Ghost Falls was a faraway speck, barely larger than the size of his palm. His stomach flipped as he took in the height of the cliffs, the waterfall that was no more than a misty stretch ending in the river. No matter his calculations and the meticulous planning he'd done in the darkness of his cell; it had taken a miracle and a hand from the gods for them to have survived.

Not that Ramson believed in the gods anyway.

He turned his back to the prison. A snow-tipped forest stretched before him, illuminated in a haze of dusty gold beneath the late-afternoon sun. And in the distance, ice-capped mountains rose and fell as far as the eye could see.

But Ramson felt only the cold in his bones and saw only the shadows that stretched long and dark beneath the pine trees. This was Cyrilia, the Empire of the North, where autumn nights were colder than any winter day in the other kingdoms. And if he didn't find shelter before the sun set, he would die.

A cough behind him made him spin around, dagger in hand. He felt a faint twinge of surprise as he caught sight of the Affinite struggling up the bank like a dying animal. She was on her hands and knees, her head drooping, her dark locks plastered to her face and dripping water. She would not stand again. Not without his help.

Ramson turned away.

The snow muffled his footsteps as he ventured into the forest, and soon the sounds of the girl spluttering and the river rushing faded into silence. The trees grew thick enough to block out the sun, and the cold pressed into him with every step he took.

He ran through the terrain around Ghost Falls in his mind,

but a growing sensation of doubt began to stall his progress. He'd been brought here in cuffs and a blindfold, the wagon traveling for days before he'd been hauled out and thrown into his cell. As far as Ramson knew, the area around the prison was barren—a wasteland of ice-covered tundra and the Syvern Taiga, the forest that covered half of the Cyrilian Empire.

Somehow his thoughts were drawn back to the witch. It was a shame that their escape had weakened her so much. Whereas she might have been a useful ally with her powerful Affinity, she would only be a hindrance going forward. He doubted she'd even be able to stand, let alone make it out of the woods. But then again, he thought grimly, where would she go?

Something clicked in his mind, and he came to a sharp stop. Of course. How could he have been so stupid? He turned back and half staggered, half ran to where he had left the witch.

The girl had come to Ghost Falls just to see him. Which meant she had to have a way out. A means of transportation.

He found her crouching several feet from the river, her head bent, her arms wrapped around herself and moving stiffly as she tried to rub heat back into her body. She looked up at him with half-lidded eyes as he approached. In just minutes, the bottom of her wet locks had frozen to ice.

Ramson knelt by her side, clasping a hand around her neck and feeling for her pulse. She twitched but made no further move to resist.

"How do you feel?" Injecting concern into his tone, he took her cheeks in his hands. They were ice-cold. "Can you speak?"

She opened her chapped lips. They were tinged with blue. "Y-yes."

"Do you feel dizzy? Drowsy?"

"N-no." It was clearly a lie, yet as she lifted her chin stubbornly and fixed him with that glare, Ramson couldn't help but admire her resolve.

"We need to find shelter before sunset." Ramson darted a glance over the treetops, where the sun hung, obscured by the gray clouds and mist. "Where did you come from? How did you get here?"

"W-walked."

His heart almost sang at that word. That meant there had to be shelter within walkable distance. He'd made the right choice, coming back for her. "From where? Is there a town nearby?"

A shake of her head. "A d-dacha. I l-live there."

"How far?"

Her body gave a spasm, and he bundled her closer to him. Their wet clothes might as well have been ice packs, but he knew the body heat would help. Her answer came in a breath that clouded in the air. "Two hours."

Ramson glanced at the mist-covered sun that hung precariously low over the rim of the trees. For the first time, it looked like hope. He stood, adjusting his icy clothes and testing his muscles. They weren't cramping yet, which was a good sign. "Can you walk, darling?"

The witch began to rouse herself, climbing to her feet, but almost toppled over at the effort. Ramson caught her by her elbows before she fell. "I've got you." *Earn her trust, reach the shelter.* He hoisted her onto his back, immediately feeling the icy stiffness of her cloak. "Put your hands around my neck. The more skin contact, the less likely you'll get hypothermia."

She obliged, and he shifted her weight higher. Already, his

blood was flowing from the strain on his muscles. That was good.

Ramson gritted his teeth. Putting one foot before the other, he began to walk. The muffled hush of the white landscape pressed on them, broken only by the crunch of snow beneath his boots and the occasional snap of a branch as he waded deeper into the forest. The witch gave him directions, her voice uneven as she trembled from cold.

Soon they were in the heart of the woods, surrounded by tall, crowding Syvern pines and frost-larches that cast their shadows over them. A hush had settled in the air. It felt as though the forest was alive and watching, the cold creeping steadily past his clothes, under his skin, into his bones.

The witch had fallen silent, her body still against his. Several times, he had to shake her to keep her conscious.

"Talk to me, darling," he said at last. "If you fall asleep now, you'll never wake up." He felt her perk up a little at that. "What's your name?"

"Anya," she said, too quickly for it to be true.

Another lie, but Ramson pretended to nod seriously. "Anya. I'm Ramson, though you already knew that. Where are you from, Anya?"

"Dobrysk."

He chuckled. "Talkative, aren't you?" He knew the town of Dobrysk—a small, insignificant dot on the map in southern Cyrilia. Yet—despite her best efforts to mask it—she had the tinge of a northern accent in her speech, along with the faint lilt of the Cyrilian nobility. "What did you do in Dobrysk?"

He sensed her tensing up against him, and for a moment he wished he could take back his question. It had seemed like a good opportunity, in her half-frozen and semiconscious state, to find out more about her. Draw out her secrets and use them as leverage against her later. That she was an Affinite was his first—and only, for the time being—clue. Surely an Affinity as strong as hers would have merited a place among the Imperial Patrols?

The wheels in his mind turned, and he thought of the command in her tone, the judgmental look in her eyes when he'd first spoken to her, the tilt of her sharp chin. There was definitely noble upbringing in her blood—perhaps she had simply kept her Affinity hidden to protect herself. It wasn't uncommon in Cyrilia, once a child's Affinity manifested, for the ability to be kept hidden or subdued. That was the protection that power and privilege offered the rich. A safety, Ramson thought, that the poor simply could not afford.

Affinites without the means to bribe officials into silence were made to record it in a section of their identification papers. As legal citizens of the Empire, they were allowed to seek employment—yet the branding on their papers marked them as different, as other, as something to be steered clear of and, oftentimes, feared.

Cyrilia sought to control these beings with gods-given abilities with blackstone and Deys'voshk. As foreigners from other kingdoms began coming to Cyrilia, looking for opportunities in the richest empire of the world, merchants had quickly seen the chance to exploit them.

And then the brokers had appeared. They began to lure foreign workers into Cyrilia under false promises of better work and better pay, only to force them into unfavorable contracts and trap them in a distant empire with no way out. In time, the practice of Affinite trafficking had thrived, in the shadows of the laws.

Nobility or not, this girl was an Affinite, and on the run. And Ramson wanted *nothing* to do with that.

It was simply easier to look the other way.

In any case, this girl had something to hide. And if Ramson had one skill, it was to root out secrets, no matter how deeply buried.

Her stubborn silence was dragging on, so he reverted to a relatively innocuous question: "Does sunwine really taste better down south?"

They went on like that, Ramson talking and eliciting one- or two-word responses from the girl. Despite the chatter he kept up, he could feel his hands and feet turning numb and his muscles growing weary. Darkness had steadily crept in around them, and Ramson had to blink to make out which were the trees and which were the shadows.

Time seemed to go in circles, and he began to wonder whether he was going in circles himself. The unbearable cold was addling his brain; he kept looking over his shoulder, imagining the occasional crackle of a branch or crunch of snow. The Cyrilian Empire housed different dangers than those of his homeland; he'd heard of ice spirits—syvint'sya—that rose from the snows, so that lost travelers were discovered years later beneath the permafrost. Icewolves that sprang from thin air and hunted in packs. Ramson had never traveled without a globefire that burned steadily through the night to ward off the creatures of the Syvern Taiga. Now the darkness seemed to press against him.

Ramson stopped. His heart pounded in his ears . . . but

there was something else. He listened, his palms feeling empty without the reassuring warmth of a globefire ball resting in them and lighting the way. The dark tended to yield to darker thoughts.

And then he heard it, that *snap-snap-snap* of twigs and the rustle of the underbrush, several dozen paces behind him.

Someone—or something—was following them.

Fear pricked at him. Ramson ducked behind the nearest tree, and after rebalancing the witch on his back, he stilled and strained to listen over the hammering of his own heart.

There. Rustling and crackling approached, as though something large was moving through the trees. Holding his breath, he dared a look from behind the tree and felt his legs turn to cotton.

An enormous dark shape lumbered by, so close that its musty wet-animal scent wafted past him. It paused to sniff the air and let out a deep-throated growl. As it turned its head to scan the periphery, Ramson's heart sank. He recognized the massive body, the pale face, the glinting white eyes. *A moonbear.* The fearsome predator of the northern Empire was but a whisper on hunters' lips, a prayer that they themselves would never meet one.

Ramson's mind kicked into action. The moonbear relied on its eyesight and sense of hearing to hunt, which meant that as long as he remained quiet and out of sight, he had a chance at survival. Yet there was no way he could wait it out; they would freeze to death.

He felt the witch's body slipping on his back. An idea came to mind—one so ugly that he was ashamed of it, but he considered it all the same. If he threw the girl to the bear and ran, would he make it? She was already unconscious, and it was unlikely she would recover unless they reached somewhere warm soon. A part of him almost let out a half sob, half laugh, as he thought inevitably of the popular Cyrilian joke. He was, literally, caught between the Bear and the Fool.

The moonbear raised its shaggy head, its huge body coming to a standstill. It cocked its ears.

And turned toward them.

Ramson caught the tomb-white flash of its eyes and the slice of its fangs in the night. Despite the shaking in his legs, he crouched into a defensive stance. His dagger appeared in his free hand.

There was no chance in hell he would win a fight like this, cold and cramped and weighed down by an unconscious girl. Yet despite what he was—despite all the lives he had ruined and everything he had done—Ramson knew he could not live with himself if he didn't at least try.

A dozen paces away, the bushes rattled suddenly, as though a startled animal had darted into them. Ramson froze.

The moonbear's attention shifted. Its head, larger than a man's torso, slowly swiveled.

The bushes shook again. Something shot out, heading in the opposite direction. Ramson could hear the creature clumsily snapping twigs and rustling past bushes in its way.

The moonbear gave a low growl. It swung its gigantic body around and lumbered off toward the noise without another glance back.

Ramson waited for the sound of crashing and grunting to

disappear before loosing a breath. He leaned against the tree, shifting the Affinite girl's weight between his shoulders. Night had fallen, their shelter was nowhere in sight.

A twig snapped behind him. Ramson turned, his grip tightening on his dagger. And stared.

There was a silhouette standing next to the tree, outlined against the snow and moon. No, not a silhouette—a child. She raised a hand and beckoned at them.

Ramson followed. If he was going to defend himself, he figured his chances were better with a child barely half his size than with the moonbear.

The trek seemed to take forever and Ramson found himself stumbling more and more as his fatigue became increasingly unbearable. The little girl weaved through the shadows like a spirit of the forest.

Another few dozen steps passed. The snow seemed to grow silver, and the trees became solid outlines again. *Light,* Ramson realized. There was light coming from somewhere close.

Gradually, the forest parted to reveal a small wooden dacha tucked in a ring of trees. Light from one window spilled onto the untouched snow, and Ramson's knees almost buckled with relief.

Ahead of him, the child pushed open the thin wooden door and slipped inside.

A fire crackled in the hearth, and heat enveloped him like a mother's embrace. Ramson groaned as he set the witch down on the floor in front of the fire and proceeded to remove the ice-cold clothes on his back. His fingers slipped at the buttons, and he could barely summon enough energy to peel off his shirt. He fell to the ground in a half-naked heap, soaking up the warmth of the dry wooden floor.

He never wanted to get up again, never wanted to move another muscle. But eventually, he heard rustlings and small, light footsteps. Ramson opened an eye.

The child was crouched by the witch, her hands fluttering across the Affinite's body like a pair of nervous birds. He observed her dark hair that fell soft over her shoulders, the brilliant turquoise of her eyes—a color that reminded him of warm, southern seas.

A child of one of the Aseatic Kingdoms, Ramson thought, an odd chord of sympathy ringing in him. He'd been around her age—perhaps a few years older—when he'd first arrived on Cyrilian shores, starving, frightened, and utterly lost.

Yet a growing sense of foreboding made his skin crawl the longer he looked at her. As Portmaster of the largest trading post in Cyrilia, he could think of a more sinister reason for a child from a foreign kingdom to be here alone. The Aseatic region, in particular, was known for its large number of migrants looking for work opportunities in other kingdoms—especially the ruthlessly commerce-driven Empire of Cyrilia. Ramson had seen the ghost ships dock at his harbor on moonless nights, watched the figures—men, women, and children—steal through the shadows.

The Affinites would become phantoms in this foreign empire, with no identity, no home, and no one to turn to, their pleas washed away by the drag of waves beneath a cruel moon.

Ramson, too, had turned away.

The child pressed two fingers to the witch's neck. Worry rippled across her features.

Ramson took a deep breath. "Is she alive?" His voice scratched.

The tender concern shaping the child's features vanished in an instant, as though someone had shut a book. She glared at him in a remarkably similar fashion to the witch, her small mouth puckering.

Ramson tried again. "Who are you? How did you find us?"

Her eyes narrowed to slits. Ramson couldn't fathom how this diminutive person could look even fiercer than the witch. "Who are *you*?" she shot back.

"I'm a friend."

"You're lying. Ana and I don't have any other friends. But it's all right," she added smugly. "If you're bad, I'll kill you."

Ramson sighed. What was it with him and meeting murderous females today? "Look," he said. "She's shivering. It's a good sign. We need to get her warmed up slowly." He assessed the room. There was a plank of a bed pushed against the far wall, one corner of it stacked with blankets. The hearth sat across from it, fire crackling merrily in the small room. Next to the door was an old wooden table strewn with parchments and pens. "Get her some blankets and dry clothes, and let's put her by the fire. I think she's just half-asleep. Warm some bathwater for her."

The child assessed him for a few moments more, like a cat deciding whether to attack him or trust him. Eventually, she decided on the latter, and plodded off toward the wash closet in the back of the room. He heard the sound of water splashing.

And that left him with . . . only one task.

Groaning, Ramson forced himself to his knees, to his feet. He bent down and, with back-popping effort, lifted the witch into his arms. He was shaking as he crossed the room in several strides, nudging open the door to the small washroom. A lone candle burned inside, illuminating the damp wooden tub.

Gently, he lowered the girl inside. She murmured something and shivered when he moved away. He frowned as he brushed aside a lock of her dark hair, casting a suspicious glance at the sharp lines of her cheekbones and the bold dash of her mouth against her skin. She resembled the tawny-skinned Southern Cyrilians who dwelled in the Dzhyvekha Mountains on the borders of the Cyrilian Empire and the Nandjian Crown. A minority among the predominantly fair Northern Cyrilians that held most of the power and privilege across the Empire.

And . . . he had the strangest feeling that he'd . . . seen her somewhere before.

He shook his head. The cold was getting to him.

He left her with the Aseatic child and five pails of lukewarm water. He leaned against the locked door, listening to the sounds of splashing and silence. Like water, his thoughts swirled in.

Why had he saved her from the moonbear, even when she was half-frozen and useless and a deadweight to him? The Ramson Quicktongue he knew—the one the entire criminal network was wary of—kept only the strong and the useful by his side; the weak were quickly discarded or sacrificed. Yet in the darkness and loneliness of the snow-covered Cyrilian forest, the cold had changed him, squeezing all logical calculation from him until he was nothing but raw instinct.

And instinct had guided his actions tonight.

He squeezed his eyes shut. He thought he had snuffed out that small sliver of goodness within him seven years ago. He'd sworn to himself that he would never be one of the weak again, that he would never give more than he took.

He drew in a deep breath. Opened his eyes. The room came back in crystal-clear view.

He had helped the witch this far. He had given. Now it was his time to take.

4

Ana had almost drowned twice in her life.

The first time was ten years ago, on the cusp of winter. The snow had painted the world a glittering sprawl of white, sprinkled with the ruby reds and emerald greens and sapphire blues of the Salskoff Winter Market. Ornaments winked silver and gold like small ice spirits as the Imperial family passed by on their annual city Parade to welcome the arrival of their Patron Deity. Tambourines jingled, music played, people whirled around outside in flurries of white gauze and silver sash.

The excitement had even diminished the headache that had kept Ana in bed for the past few days. She held Luka's hand as they waited for their carriage to stop, for the walk through the near-fairy-tale town, heralded and beloved and showered with gifts by the citizens of their empire.

Yet as the doors opened and the smells of roast meats and spiced vegetables and baked fish rolled in, Ana felt a wave of nausea. There was something writhing beneath all the noise from the crowds, the colored ornaments and furs and jewels clasped around people's throats, the scents and sights. It pounded at her head, throbbed at her temples.

She distinctly remembered the pot of beet soup, thick and bubbling and so vividly red.

And then that thrumming energy within her exploded, a sharp crimson that drenched every corner of her vision, rushing through her veins. The hot, pulsing beat of blood swept into her world, drowning out all else.

She only remembered the aftermath. The bodies in front of her carriage, twisted on the cobblestones; the red, blooming like poppy blossoms on a canvas of colorless snow.

Ana had killed eight people that day.

The Palace alchemist, a strange bald man with overly large eyes and a quiet demeanor, had diagnosed her that very evening. She remembered the cold glint of his silver Deys'krug as he raised a trembling hand to whisper in the Emperor's ear.

An Affinite, he'd told Papa. *A* blood *Affinite.*

Papa had bowed his head, and Ana's world had crumbled.

In a window across her room, she'd seen her reflection. Face still streaked with blood and tears from the market, her hair crusted with sweat and half-covering her eyes—her monstrous red eyes. Her arms had been heavy, the skin stretched taut over swollen, jagged veins.

That day, Ana had looked in the mirror and seen a monster.

She'd tried to run after that. Past the maids who screamed at her approach; past the guards who stepped aside, bewildered and at a loss for what to do. She hadn't known where she was going; all she'd known was that she had to get away, away from the Palace, away from Mama and Papa and Luka and mamika Morganya, so that she couldn't hurt them.

The Kateryanna Bridge had loomed out of the blur of her

tears, statues of Deities watching over her like sentient guardians. The bridge was named after Mama, and Ana watched it every day from the windows of her chambers, roping over the icy Tiger's Tail river that wound around the Palace.

It was a sign. It had to be.

Tears streaked Ana's face as she lifted her gaze to the sky. *I love you, Mama,* she thought. *Carry me somewhere safe.*

Ana climbed over the stone handrail and hurled herself into the river.

The cold jarred her bones as soon as she hit the water, and the ruthless current pulled her under. Immediately, she realized that any hopes she had of being borne to distant lands by the river's waters had been foolish. The water frothed around her, pummeling her in a way that aroused a different type of terror within her: uncontrollable and tumultuous. Instinctively, she opened her mouth to scream—but water rushed in, squeezing the air from her lungs.

Panic whitened her mind, and spots bloomed before her eyes even as she fought against the water.

She hadn't wanted to die. But perhaps the Deities meant to claim her today after all.

Something gripped her across her midriff—something different from the pressure on her chest and the cold in her lungs. The world spun in a whirl of white-ice currents and mute chaos, but she realized that the current was no longer carrying her. She was being dragged up, up, and into the light.

She burst through the surface, her lungs gasping in sweet, precious breaths of air. Her limbs drifted weakly in the violent waters, but there was a firm arm around her chest and someone was pulling her toward shore with fluid, practiced strokes.

Her savior struggled at the bank and, at last, deposited her on the ice-covered ground that stretched for miles around.

Ana's blood froze as she found herself looking into her brother's eyes—eyes that burned with rage. All traces of earlier mirth had disappeared from Luka's face—and she thought she saw a trace of the prince, the future Emperor Lukas Aleksander Mikhailov.

Her brother was panting, his hair plastered to his forehead and curling at the nape of his neck. Breath plumed from his lips, pale with cold. "Brat," he snarled, and slammed his fist into the frozen ground so hard that it cracked. *"What the hell were you thinking?"*

His tone lashed across her sharper than the bite of a whip, and she flinched. Her brother—kind, gentle Luka—had *never* yelled at her like this.

She thought of the eight dead bodies blooming red in the Vyntr'makt and lowered her gaze. "I'm a monster," she mumbled, her lips numb.

Luka hunched over her, his weight propped up by his elbows. His shoulders shook, and when he lifted his gaze to hers, he was crying. In a sudden motion, he pulled her into his arms and hugged her tight. "Don't *ever* scare me like that again. You could've died."

The maelstrom of her thoughts cleared, leaving only one: the realization that Luka was afraid she'd almost died. He hadn't . . . he hadn't *wanted* her to die.

"I'm sorry." Her voice was high and broken. "I— The Vyntr'makt—"

"Hush," Luka whispered, cradling her. "It's not your fault."

It's not your fault.

She let herself go then, the torrent of grief and guilt and

helplessness, and for a few moments, his arms held her together and his words were her salvation.

When he pulled back, his eyes—she'd always thought of them as the grasses that bloomed in the Palace gardens each spring—had hardened with resolve, a burning fire, as he cupped her face with his hands. "You are not a monster, sistrika."

A flash of the alchemist's silver Deys'krug. Papa's bowed head.

The response sprang to her lips. *An Affinite.* The alchemist whispered. *A blood Affinite.*

"My Affinity—"

"Your Affinity does not define you." His gaze seared into hers; his words cut like metal striking stone. "What defines you is how you choose to wield it. You just need someone to teach you to control it."

She loved the way he said those things—*you are not a monster; you just need someone to teach you to control it*—as though they were simple truths. It was as though he believed them, and she could start to as well. "Like Yuri?" she asked, thinking of her friend, a fire Affinite several years older than she, who worked in the Palace kitchens as an apprentice to the master chef. His Affinity made him valuable.

"Right. Like Yuri." Luka pushed himself to his feet and hauled her up. They were on the bank of the river right beneath the walls of the Palace, an abandoned stretch of land. The river had borne them to the back of the Salskoff Palace; straight across from them, the Syvern Taiga began in a line of winter-colored pines.

Luka took her hand and turned away from the direction of the bridge.

"What should we do?" Dread bloomed in her as she thought of returning to the Palace, of facing her father and the reality of what she had done.

But her brother's grip tightened and he brought her fingers to his lips, kissing her bloodstained nails. His brows were creased, his eyes stormy yet gentle at once. "We'll go back through a secret passageway Markov showed me. You'll wash off in your chambers. The truth of the incident at the Vyntr'makt was lost in the crowds and the confusion. No one has to know." His jaw set and he lifted his chin slightly, in that stubborn way she knew so well. "I'll speak to Papa. I'll tell him that you need a tutor, like the ones that teach the Affinites employed at the Palace to hone their Affinities."

Yet that night, Papa had come to her chambers, his brows creased. He oftentimes came with Mama to tuck her into bed, but this time, he'd stood at the foot of her bed, the distance between them stretching an ocean.

Quietly, he'd told her that she would have to stay indoors for a while—at least until her "condition" was gone. The official story to the outside world was that the Princess was sick, and her frail health had to be preserved within the walls of the Palace.

Ana had fallen to her knees, reaching for him—and he had remained where he was, his face carved of ice. It had broken her a little more. "Please," she'd whispered. "It won't happen again. I'll never use my . . . my Affinity. I'll be your good daughter."

Papa's eyes had clouded. "It . . . isn't acceptable for you to be an Affinite," he'd said. "Especially considering your *particular* Affinity. . . . It mustn't be known widely, nor registered on your papers. We will take measures to cure your condition. It is . . . for your own good."

Ana clung to that tiniest sliver of hope. Perhaps, if she was cured, Papa would love her again.

Within a moon, Papa had hired a tutor to "cure" Ana of her Affinity. Konsultant Imperator Sadov, they called him, and from the moment Ana met him, she knew he was made of nothing but nightmares. He seemed to grow out of the shadows: a silhouette stretched tall and slim, with hair and eyes as dark as blackstone, and fingers long and sickly white. His cure centered on the theory that fear and poison would wash the Affinity from her.

And so Ana's world had shrunk to the corners of the Palace and the depths of the dungeons, where the blackstone walls sucked all light and warmth from the air, and the darkness pressed against her like a living thing.

"Most Affinities manifest slowly, as an awareness to the elements of one's Affinity," Sadov had said, his voice smooth and cold as silk. "But yours exploded, completely out of your control. Do you know why that is?"

Ana shivered. "Why, Konsultant Imperator?"

"Because you control *blood.*" He touched a finger to her chin, and it took all her willpower not to shrink back. "Because you are a monster."

By that time, Mama had fallen sick, and within a year of the Vyntr'makt incident, she passed away. The Palace courtiers had whispered that it had been a mistake for the Emperor to take a wife of one of the southern ethnicities of Cyrilia; something about her tawny skin and dark hair made her *different.*

Something that her offspring had inherited. There had already been veiled murmurs of the Prince and Princess's distinctly southern looks, which stood out among the pale-faced, fair-haired Northern Cyrilians who dominated the ruling classes of Cyrilia. With Mama's death and Ana's confinement, the rumors grew louder.

Humans, it seemed, tended to fear things that were different.

Yet it was her brother's words on that terrible day that stayed with Ana throughout those long years, in the stretches of darkness and loneliness, during Sadov's worst rages and Papa's callous coldness.

Your Affinity does not define you.

The bitter taste of Deys'voshk, burning her throat and twisting her stomach.

What defines you is how you choose to wield it.

The nauseating fear, the cold of the blackstone, the blood pulsing through the small rabbits Sadov used to test her abilities, which never diminished in the ten years after.

You are not a monster, sistrika.

She had so, so desperately wanted to believe that.

Perhaps the Deities had willed for her to live after all—and if not the Deities, then *Ana* had willed herself to live.

It was this thought that she clung to now, half-frozen and half-dead from the battering current of the Ghost Falls river. This, and the memory of her brother, like a steady, unwavering flame in her heart, guiding her onward.

For there *was* a reason for her to live, Ana realized, as she began to surface through the bouts of sleep and groggy wakefulness that claimed her in turn. Her thoughts rose through the darkness and the cold, stubbornly, willfully, as she had that day from the icy depths of the river.

Yes, there was a reason for her to live. And that was to find Papa's murderer.

The second time Ana had almost drowned, it had been beneath a bone-white moon—not unlike the one that hung above the Syvern Taiga tonight—that had carved the world in monochrome. The winter night of eleven moons past had been cast in the color of death. She had walked into her father's chambers to see him convulsing, his face leached of color, his eyes rolling into his head, the poison and the blood roaring through him like the distorted screaming of a river. She had seen his murderer, dressed in white prayer robes, bent over her papa and tipping the vial of poison.

She'd caught sight of the man's face in the moments before he ran: a peculiar yet familiar face, like that of a dead man, with bulging eyes and a bald head. In the moonlight, his Deys'krug had cut silver like a scythe. The Palace alchemist.

Alchemist. Murderer. Traitor.

He was the reason she had been arrested that night. She had been found long after he had run, still clinging to Papa's body, covered in his blood—the poisoned blood she'd tried to pull from his body to save him. In the end, she'd lost control of her Affinity, and Papa had still died, right in front of her.

And she should have died, too, accused of murdering the Emperor and of being a traitor to the Crown. Curled against the cold bars of the Palace dungeons that night, her father's blood still staining her hands, she'd never wished more that she did not exist, that she never had.

Because you are a monster.

And yet again, on that night, fate, or the Deities, or whatever perverse dictator of the courses of lives, decided to spare her. She'd woken to the rattle of keys and the creak of her cell door opening. A weathered face out of the darkness with eyes the gray of clouds, and salt-and-pepper hair.

"I've followed you since the day you were born, so don't ask me to stand aside and just watch as you die," Markov had told her.

"It wasn't me, it wasn't me," she'd babbled, clutching at him and sinking to her knees.

Markov's face softened. "I believe you. Take the tunnel and run, Princess. I'll tell them you escaped when I was escorting you here, and that you drowned in the Tiger's Tail." He stroked her tears away with his callused thumbs. "Run, and *live.*"

Live. That felt like an impossible task.

But Ana shut her eyes, and that face came to her again: moon-pale, with owlishly large eyes. The alchemist, who'd left the Palace so many years ago, after her diagnosis. It had seemed like a dream—no, a nightmare—to see him there again, a ghost of the past.

But a ghost was all the reason she had left to live. That alchemist was the reason she'd run through that secret passageway in the dungeons that night and thrown herself into the Tiger's Tail for the second time in her life; the reason she'd crawled onto the shore of the Syvern Taiga, half-frozen on the outside and dead on the inside, waiting for the Deities to claim her. Yet he was also why she'd stood again that night, staring at the Palace and the Kateryanna Bridge in the distance and vowing that she would return only when she had found him.

Yes, she did have a reason to live after all these long years, Ana realized suddenly, her thoughts sharpening into lucidity. She lived to find the owner of that face, to hunt down the person who had murdered her father and diagnosed her with this evil affliction, sealing her fate for ten years past. She lived to redeem herself, to prove that, beyond the monstrosity of her power, she could be good.

I will find you, alchemist, she thought over and over again, like a vow. *I will find you.*

5

Ana woke with a start and the ghost of a face scattering from her dreams. It took her several moments to grasp her surroundings: the crackle of a fire burning low in the hearth, the musty smell of old pinewood floors, and the scratch of a coarse cloth pillow beneath her cheek.

She remembered flashes of the evening—the cold, the dark, the scent and silver of snow, a warm bathtub. She'd made it. She'd made it back to the dacha.

Ana clutched the ragged fur blanket tighter, surprise twanging in her stomach. How had she gotten back? She remembered the fall into the river, the feeling of utter helplessness beneath the battering current, and then crawling onto an empty, frozen shore. Her clothes had been colder than ice, and she'd barely been able to move.

Can you walk, darling?

Ana blinked. The voice had come out of nowhere—out of a foggy, distant memory. There had been a forest, an ounce of warmth, and that voice had constantly, irritably dragged her from the comfort of slumber.

Fear seized her. Now she recognized the symptoms of

near-hypothermia she'd been experiencing, and how close to death she'd been. That warm darkness had been a menace . . . and the voice had saved her.

Ramson Quicktongue, she thought, her sleep-addled brain suddenly alert as she scanned the cabin. Everything was just as she'd left it. Her rucksack leaned against the wall, her belongings spread out across the small worktable. No sign of a disturbance; no sign of any intruders.

Ana loosed a breath and pushed herself into a sitting position. Someone had washed the blood off her arm, but the wound was still raw and fresh. She remembered now, a little girl with dark hair, the edges softened by the glow of candles, almost like a halo.

"May?" she called softly. The cabin was utterly still. She leaned back against the wall, trying to quell her anxiety. The con man was nowhere to be seen, either. The remnants of the Deys'voshk were still in her system; she could feel her Affinity beginning to return, drifting in and out of her reach. Trying to use it now was like trying to set fire to wet kindling.

From the wash closet door in the far corner came the sound of splashing water. The movements were too careless for May. A masculine cough confirmed her suspicions.

The con man was still here.

Ana gritted her teeth against a groan of frustration. She'd spent months searching for this man. She'd pinned all her hopes—and more—on him. And he'd fooled her, and admitted he didn't even have a clue who her alchemist was.

And now she was stuck with him.

The door to the hut creaked open. Her thoughts scattered as a child struggled in with a pail of fresh snow. As soon as May caught sight of Ana, her eyes widened and she dropped the pail, bounding to Ana's side.

Ana sighed in relief as she buried herself in May's embrace. "Hey, you," she murmured. Being with May always, in some ways, felt like being at home.

The darkness in the boreal forest had been absolute the night Ana had run into the Syvern Taiga, though it had been nothing compared to the shadows in her heart. But May had found her and brought her to shelter by the soft glow of a globefire. May had been bound by a contract then, but it hadn't stopped her from trying to save Ana, unbeknownst to her employer.

May straightened and fixed Ana with a stern gaze. Her eyes were the startling aquamarine of the ocean waters of the Aseatic Isles that Ana had once seen in a painting, sun-kissed and warm. Ana touched her forehead briefly to the child's, her lips tugging into a smile.

"Did you get the alchemist?" May demanded. Eleven moons ago, when they'd first met, she'd been much quieter, her words a featherlight whisper. Only her quick eyes had told Ana that she drank in the world and gathered it in her heart, and gave back with kindness that had never been shown to her.

"Almost." Seeing May always cleared her mind and calmed her nerves, and the word nearly felt real. "Were you all right by yourself?"

May nodded, and a copperstone appeared in her hands. "I have three cop'stones left. Do you want them back?" The copperstone caught the shine of the firelight, a small leaf engraved in the center of the coin.

Ana hesitated. She knew what these coins meant to May,

who had spent her life accumulating meager sums of money to pay off the impossible amount of the contract she'd been made to sign. In the past, Ana might have spent dozens of cop'stones on a piece of ptychy'moloko milk cake, coins flowing through her fingers like water without a care as to their value.

Meeting May had changed that.

Ana gently curled a hand around May's, tucking the coin back into the girl's fist. "We earned this *together*. Keep it, and let's buy ourselves a treat at the next town."

May slipped the coin carefully back into her tunic. "Do you think we'll find Ma-ma at the next town?" she asked.

Ana paused, studying May's face carefully, but the child's hopeful gaze didn't waver. It haunted Ana that this girl loved so easily after what she'd been through. Over time, Ana had pieced together the child's story: a long journey from the Chi'gon Kingdom, her home in the Aseatic region, with her mother in search of a brighter future, only to find those dreams shattered and her mother sent away by a separate contract.

And May had been exploited for her earth Affinity and stuck with a debt that kept growing.

With every day, the realization had grown louder and louder in Ana's head: *That could have been me.*

"We will," Ana replied. "We'll find your ma-ma even if I have to knock on every single door of this empire."

May's smile stretched, and she threw her arms around Ana, burying her face against Ana's shirt. "You won't leave again, right?" Her voice came out muffled, and when Ana looked down, she caught a pair of bright ocean eyes peering up at her shyly. "Don't go where I can't follow."

A knot formed in Ana's throat. She knew the ache of having

lost a mother at such a young age. The feeling that you had done something wrong, that you could be abandoned by those you loved all over again, never went away.

So Ana squeezed May tight in her arms and whispered, "I'm always here."

The sound of splashing water drew both of their attention to the wash closet.

May's eyes narrowed. "That strange man brought you home, and because he sort of saved your life, I told him he could have a warm bath before leaving," she said.

Ana felt her lips curling despite herself. "Smart girl," she said conspiratorially.

"He was *smelly*. And dirty."

"I know," Ana said. "He's disgusting and stupid and ugly." It was immature, but it felt good to say anyway.

The wash closet door flew open.

In a flash, Ana heaved herself from the bed and shoved May behind her. Her injured arm throbbed at the sudden motion, but all of her attention was focused on Ramson Quicktongue.

He had shaved and cleaned the grime from his face. Now she could see that he was much younger than she had guessed—perhaps only a few years older than she. His tousled sandy hair curled on his forehead, droplets of water carving a path down his chiseled cheeks. The contrast from his filthy, unkempt state earlier made him appear startlingly handsome—the type of roguish good-looking face more befitting a Bregonian marine or Cyrilian Imperial Patrol than a shady underground crook.

Quicktongue shot a smile at May. Ana imagined it had fangs. "Hello, sweetheart."

"Don't talk to her," Ana snarled. She turned and said quickly, "May, please go and take a bath."

The child grabbed the pail of snow and slipped into the wash closet. She turned and, glaring at Ramson, drew a finger across her neck before slamming the door shut. A satisfying click sounded as the door closed, and Ana's heart settled.

She rounded on Quicktongue.

He was bruising; on his wrists where the sleeves of his tunic ended, angry red patches bloomed from where she had broken blood vessels. Guilt churned in her stomach, but she pushed it down. *He* hadn't hesitated to use and betray her. Guilt was an emotion wasted on this kind of a man.

Quicktongue's mouth quirked into a smile that was both devious and charming at once. "Well, *Ana,* love," he said, and her insides turned cold. "Here we are. You asked for my aid, and I asked for a way out of Ghost Falls. If only wishes came true every day."

Ana bit back a sharp retort. This wasn't some argument she was having with Luka or Yuri. This was a calculated stance against an enemy. There was no telling what he was planning and what he was hiding from her—even his accent, she noticed, had shifted slightly from last night. She had to tread very carefully.

"I've delivered my end of the bargain," she said instead. "Now it's your turn." She clamped down on the urge to remind him of her Affinity, just to prove that she *could* hurt him if she wanted to. That she still held some shred of power over him. That her plan hadn't all gone to . . . nothing. "I don't care if you don't have a clue who he is or where he is. You're going to help me find the alchemist, and you're going to do it in two weeks. I've heard enough of your reputation, and I know you're capable of it."

He had to be. All other searches, paid bounty hunters or trackers, had led to dead ends. Ramson Quicktongue was her last chance.

Ana didn't say that.

Quicktongue raised his brows. "You've heard enough of my reputation," he repeated, as though savoring the words on his tongue. He almost looked pleased, but then his eyes narrowed. "And what makes you think I'll help you, now that I'm free as a bird?"

Conniving, backstabbing con man. If he wanted to play dirty, so be it.

She could threaten him. The thought had been lingering in her mind for a while: an ugly, twisted thing she hadn't wanted to bring into the light.

Show him what you can do, my little monster.

"You remember what I did in the prison?" The memory of crimson pooling across white marble halls flashed across her mind. It sickened her to bring it up, but she pressed on. "I could do the same to you." She took a step closer, exhilaration pushing her forward, the thrill of danger drawing her toward him. "Can you imagine how it would feel to die with blood leaking from you, drop by drop?"

"I'll admit, that hurt." He wet his lips. "But there are worse things to fear in life. Whatever torture you're thinking of, I've probably been through it. I suppose that makes it extremely difficult to threaten me, doesn't it?"

Ana drew a tight breath. He was bluffing—he *had* to be. And he was challenging her to call his bluff. His eyes crinkled as he watched her, waiting for her response. Those eyes were cunning eyes, quick and intelligent . . . but they weren't coward's eyes. They held no fear.

He would learn to fear her. Just like everybody else did.

Ana shot him her most feral grin. Her Affinity stirred. Against the remnants of the Deys'voshk, it was still weak, but growing stronger. "So many others sang the same tune at first. I had them groveling at my feet within minutes."

"You sound like you have experience."

"You know nothing of what I've been through. I'm going to ask you one more time, and I hope for your sake you'll give the right answer. Will you help me find my alchemist?"

"I will."

Ana blinked. The sinister thoughts, the twisted memories, and the pull of her Affinity dissolved. All that was left was the crackling of fire in the hearth, the splashing sounds from the wash closet, and a child's muffled humming.

"You look startled." Ramson Quicktongue raised his eyebrows.

If she had gotten her way, why did it feel like he'd won? Ana crossed her arms, her brain whirring even as she spoke. What had she missed? "I don't believe you." *What are you playing at?*

"A wise decision. I'm a businessman, after all." His gaze sharpened. "I never give anything without asking for something in return."

Anger rose in her, sharp and hot. "In return? I broke you out of that prison. I saved you from rotting in that cell. You *owe* me."

"I didn't ask you to free me. I *suggested* an exchange, but we agreed to nothing." Quicktongue spoke conversationally, as though they were bartering over the price of beets at a marketplace.

Ana was bargaining for her *life*.

"So, I don't owe you anything, Witch," he continued, picking at a fingernail. "But I'd be willing to speak the language of deals."

Her voice came out in a snarl. "You think you're in a position to ask for something?"

"Oh, I do. You've been threatening me with torture for the past few minutes. If you actually wanted to do it, you would've done it already. Clearly, you need me. So let's stop dancing around the topic and get to the bargain, shall we?"

He had called her bluff. Ana's heart hammered as she stared back at the con man, refusing to break eye contact first. Papa had always taught her that strong eye contact was a show of confidence. But even as she scrambled for a response, she found her confidence waning.

Brat. She heard her brother's voice in her head, saw the glint of intelligence in his eyes as he leaned over their game of chess. *Think.*

Luka had told her that a negotiation was like a game of chess. To succeed, one had to consider the endgame above all else. It had seemed like such an obvious lesson at the time, but Ana found herself clutching it tightly to her now. Her goal—her *endgame*—was to get him to find the alchemist, the true murderer. And now the con man wanted something more from her in return.

Why not? After all, what more did she have to lose?

Perhaps not every move needed to be a triumphant one, as long as she was moving toward her endgame.

"What is it that you want?" she asked, lifting her chin. This way, it was easy to pretend that she was a princess granting a favor, not a nobody begging for help.

"Revenge," said the con man.

"And you think *I* can help you achieve that?"

"Perhaps. You are, after all, threatening me with your power over my mortal being."

Of course—*of course* he wanted to use her for her Affinity. Ana narrowed her eyes. Luka's voice whispered to her, gently pushing her on. *Be specific. Flesh out the details.* "Tell me what your revenge scheme entails. And be specific."

Quicktongue's smile widened as though he found something delightful in her response. "All right, I'll be *specific.* I plan to destroy my enemies one by one and take back my position and what was rightfully mine. For that, I'll need an ally. Someone powerful. And by the Deities"—he gave her a look that was somehow both caressing and calculating at the same time—"you must be the most powerful flesh Affinite I've ever seen."

Flesh Affinite. Ana almost let out a breath in relief. *Flesh,* not *blood.* She'd kept her secret well, and it was imperative that Ramson Quicktongue continue to think she was a flesh Affinite. Because while there were hundreds of flesh Affinites, working as butchers or soldiers or guards, there was only one Blood Witch of Salskoff.

Ramson Quicktongue was not as smart as he thought he was.

"I won't kill anyone for you, if that's what you want."

"Kill? I never said 'kill.' I said 'destroy.' There are many ways to destroy a man besides taking his life."

The bartenders and bounty hunters had described Ramson

Quicktongue as cunning and ruthless. She hadn't understood them until now.

Ana steeled her nerves. She dictated the terms, not him. And she would never choose to harm innocent people.

Really, now? Sadov whispered in her head. *Little monster, do you think yourself so righteous? Do you really think you're above this con man, when you have so much blood on your hands—*

"No torture," Ana said loudly. "No killing. I am to decide how to use my Affinity in our alliance. I'll ensure that no harm comes to you, and that you can dispatch your enemies as you wish. If you agree to those terms, I'll pledge my alliance to you for two weeks. *After* you've found my alchemist."

He narrowed his eyes, tapping a finger on his chin thoughtfully. "Three weeks," he said. "And in return, I want three weeks to find your alchemist as well."

"We agreed on two."

"I never agreed; I considered."

"Don't get caught up in the technicalities."

"Don't be stubborn. We both know that you need me, and I need you. That's why we're still here, talking to each other in a civil fashion. Three weeks, Witch—that's only fair. Look, I'll make a Trade with you, to show you my goodwill."

He sounded sincere, which made her even warier. "A what?"

"A Trade. A con man's promise."

"You realize you just contradicted yourself, don't you?"

The corners of his eyes crinkled. "Believe it or not, there is a code of honor among the thieves of the underworld. The Trade. It's a contract of a mutually beneficial exchange. Think of it more as a . . . a type of currency, for us. Once you invoke the Trade, there's no reneging—otherwise, you face dire consequences."

"Why does that matter? You'll face dire consequences if you renege on your offer, Trade or no Trade."

The con man sighed. "Look. I'll find your alchemist," he said, and Ana felt hope rustle its wings inside her. "I'll do it in three weeks. I could track jetsam back to its ship if I wished. And in return, you'll pledge your allegiance to me for three weeks."

It sounded straightforward enough. "All right," Ana said. Her mind was working fast, searching the agreement for holes, buttoning up the last of the terms. "So you agree to my terms?"

Ramson Quicktongue looked at her in that calculating, inscrutable way of his—yet Ana sensed something else in his gaze. Something like . . . curiosity.

"Very well," he said at last, and pushed himself off the wall, tossing his washcloth on the floor. "I agree to your terms. Six weeks together, during which I keep my nose out of your business and you keep your nose out of mine. You'll have your revenge, I'll have mine, and we'll part ways with nothing but fond memories of each other." He spread his arms. "What do you say, Witch? Trade up?"

Her head was light with elation and disbelief. It felt as though a huge weight had lifted from her chest.

She had survived a jailbreak from one of the most secure prisons in the Empire and had gotten one of the most infamous crooks in the Cyrilian Empire to agree to a bargain on her terms. And, most important, within three weeks' time, she would have the true murderer of that unforgettable night.

It had taken her nearly an entire year to get here. Several moons to crawl out of the black hole that Papa's death had left in her heart; several more wasted on bounty hunters and trackers that went nowhere; a few more to find Quicktongue and form a plan to enter Ghost Falls.

She was close. So close.

Almost a year ago, Papa had been murdered, and everything in her life had fallen apart. And, in three weeks, she would be on her way back to Salskoff to clear her name.

That was her endgame.

Ana stared at Quicktongue's hand. At the crooked grin on his face. At the gleam of intent in his eyes.

"Trade up," she echoed, and grasped his palm.

6

Ramson woke long before the first light of dawn broke, its cold blue rays filtering through the tattered curtains and rimming the thin window. He leaned against the wooden walls of the shack, running his fingers over the inside of his left wrist.

A tattoo the size of his thumb occupied that spot: a simple yet elegant design of a single stalk of lily of the valley, with three small, bell-shaped flowers and a razor-sharp stem. The ink was black as night, carved so deep into his skin that it had become a part of his living flesh, just as the Order of the Lily had consumed his life. And then destroyed it.

The sight of the tattoo brought back memories as vivid as they were painful. It was as though no time and all the time in the world had passed since he had stumbled up the gleaming marble steps to Alaric Esson Kerlan's home. Kerlan was the founder of the largest business enterprise in Cyrilia. The sprawling Goldwater Trading Group held monopolies over most of the prominent industries in the Empire—timber, non-ferrous metals, weaponry, and the prized blackstone mined in the far north at Krazyast Triangle—as well as private ownership of Cyrilia's busiest trading port, Goldwater Port.

The trading port that Ramson had run, up until several moons ago.

But few associated the Goldwater Trading Group with the most notorious criminal organization in Cyrilia: the Order of the Lily, which ran underground businesses with traffickers and illegal Affinite trades. Indentured labor was the backbone of the Goldwater Trading Group, and the cheap employment contracts it purchased from its owner's criminal organization helped keep its prices the lowest in Cyrilian markets.

Amid all this was Alaric Kerlan: successful businessman who had built his commercial empire as a foreigner to Cyrilia with merely a cop'stone to his name, and ruthless Lord of the Lilies in the dark underbelly of Cyrilia.

On the day of Ramson's initiation, Kerlan had strapped him to a hard iron table in his basement and crushed a white-hot tong into the flesh of his chest. *You feel this, boy?* he'd gritted out to a screaming, half-delirious Ramson. *You'll only feel pain like this twice in your life. The first time, when you've earned my trust and passed the gates of hell into the Order of the Lily. The second time, when you've broken that trust and I throw you back into hell. So remember this moment, and remember it well. And ask yourself if you ever want to feel this kind of pain again.*

Kerlan had flung the iron tongs onto the floor and asked the stencilmaster to tattoo Ramson.

Ramson closed his hand over his wrist, blocking out the sight of the tattoo and the memory of the searing pain from the brand. In the silver-blue sheen of an impending wintry dawn, he could just make out the outlines of the two sleeping girls, huddled beneath a ragged fur blanket, their chests rising and falling with each breath.

Which meant it was time for him to move.

He stole across the dacha, carefully planting his feet near the walls where the old wooden floorboards had the least flex. He had noticed the small worktable by the door as soon as he'd stepped inside last night. Its worn surface was strewn with papers and scrolls and pens.

Life had taught Ramson that he would never allow himself to get the short end of the stick. Even as the conditions for his end of the Trade had rolled off his tongue, smooth as marbles, another plan had quickly taken form in his mind.

This girl was by far the most powerful Affinite he had seen in this empire throughout all his years of working for Kerlan's organization. He'd studied enough about Affinites to surmise that hers was likely an Affinity to flesh. He could draw up an unending list of people who would kill for her talents. Which was why she was the key to his regaining his standing in the Order of the Lily.

Alaric Kerlan was a harsh, brutal person—the type of cold-eyed, stone-cut demon of a man one needed to be to succeed in his vast criminal empire—yet he was also a logical one. He'd seen Ramson's uncanny talent for business and negotiation from the start, and trained him from running small errands to gradually managing parts of his enterprise. By age eighteen, Ramson had become a Deputy of the Order with the precious Goldwater Port under his purview. Controlling Cyrilia's largest port meant he held a hand and a generous cut in Cyrilia's lifeblood of foreign trade, from anything as harmless as Bregonian fish and Nandjian cocoa to powerful Kemeiran weaponry.

It also meant he had the power to start distancing himself from the Order of the Lily. For most of his employment under Kerlan, Ramson had been a grunt running menial tasks and conducting side schemes to raise the margins of the criminal organization. He'd heard of the blood trades they conducted, yet with the little freedom he'd had to choose his projects, he'd kept to conning rich men and swindling businessmen: taking down competitors of the Goldwater Trading Group to allow it to maintain its monopoly in the Empire.

The darkest deeds of the Order—assassinations and trafficking—had been beyond what Ramson could stomach, and he'd gone out of his way to avoid being assigned to any such tasks.

Until a year ago, when Kerlan had chosen him for a suicide mission that had resulted in him being arrested, stripped of his ranking, and thrown into Ghost Falls.

He'd failed Kerlan in many ways: botched the most important job of his life, left the Order without a Deputy, and left his betrayer to roam free for the duration of his imprisonment.

He'd fix all that; with the witch's help, he'd root out the mole in Kerlan's ranks and claw his way back as rightful Deputy of the Order, Portmaster of Goldwater Port. And when all that was done . . . he would hand her over to Kerlan. To have an Affinite as powerful as her under the Order's control would be the cherry on top of his cake.

He'd take it back—he'd take it all back. His title. His fortune. His power.

But Ramson hadn't become the former Deputy of the most notorious crime network in the Empire just by luck. He was thorough and calculating in every aspect of his job, and he made an effort to understand everything down to the colors of his associates' window curtains and bedsheets. There was nothing not worth knowing.

And if there was any due diligence to be done in this ramshackle little dacha, it had to be on the worktable.

The table was strewn with objects—a wealth of information. He palmed a few dusty globefires that had burned out, reduced to empty glass orbs filled with ashes, and carefully pushed aside some blank parchments and charcoal pencils.

The first thing he discovered was a book, its cover worn to the point that he could barely make out the title: *Ascatic Children's Stories.* Somebody had written several lines of a poem on the cover page inside; the elegant penmanship resembled that of a professional scribe.

My child, we are but dust and stars.

Ramson set the book aside.

He picked through a dozen or so blank scrolls before he hit treasure in the form of a map.

With practiced fingers, he wiggled it loose. The map unfurled with a sigh.

Like the children's book, it showed signs of wear: someone had penciled in notes all across the outline of the Empire in the same beautiful penmanship. Some of the notes were smudged with age, while others were as new as a freshly minted contract.

The notes were brief but to the point, written in formal Cyrilian. *Buzhny,* one read, directly on top of where the small town of Buzhny might have been on the map. *Inquiry; no sign of alchemist.*

Pyedbogorozhk, said another; *Inquiry for bounty hunter. Received name from trader.*

The map was gold. The witch—if this was, indeed, her map and handwriting—had written the history of her mysterious mission all over this map like a set of footprints. Ramson set it aside carefully to scan the rest of the items on the table before he returned to it.

His eyes caught on something at the corner of a page: the outline of half a face, peering out from the pile.

Ramson reached for it too eagerly. His tunic sleeves caught on a scroll. The papers slid, cascading into a graceful pool on the worktable. As though they *wanted* to be seen.

They were sketches. Dozens of them, fanning out over each other on the coarse surface of the table. He caught glimpses of a shaggy-haired dog, curled up by a fire; portions of a domed castle in what looked like a wintry landscape; a beautiful, doe-eyed woman with long locks . . .

But his eyes landed on one, fluttering at the edge of the table as though it had a life of its own. A boy, in his teens, caught in midlaugh, the joy in his eyes nearly palpable. So much care and effort had been put into this drawing, the lines traced to perfection, every detail etched into the crinkles of his eyes and the quirk of his mouth. Still, it was incomplete, only half a face. It seemed the artist had only wanted to capture the life in the moment of the laugh.

"Get away from there."

Ramson swore and spun around.

The witch was on her feet, her outline stiff with fury. In the half-lit room, he could make out the tightness of her jaw and the glint of her narrowed eyes.

"Put that down, unless you want me to rip you to shreds this instant."

Any excuses he had planned dissipated in smoke. He'd been caught red-handed before; Ramson found that the best tactic was to admit guilt and lie his way out from there. So far, he'd been lucky.

He slid the sketches carefully back onto the table. The girl's eyes followed his every move. "I'm sorry," he said, injecting as much sincerity into his tone as he could. "I was looking for a map."

"Get away from there," she snapped again, and he obeyed. She was at the table in an instant, her fingers scurrying across the papers, checking to make sure that nothing was missing. She snatched up the sketch of the boy and glared at Ramson, livid. For a second he thought she would change her mind and kill him on the spot. But then she took a deep breath and swiped a strand of dark hair from her face. As though she had wiped a slate, the fury in her expression was gone, replaced by cool sternness. "We made a Trade last night. You have a funny way of showing diplomacy."

"Well, you know what they say about diplomacy. It's the only proper way for two parties to lie to each other's faces and be happy about it."

"Don't lecture me."

Ramson raised his hands. "All right, I was prying. But as you said, we made a Trade, so what's the point of being stuck with each other for the next six weeks if we can't trust each other?"

Behind them, on the bed, May had sat up and was listening with her head cocked to one side. The witch's eyes flickered to the girl and her expression softened momentarily. "All right," she said, lowering her voice as she turned back to Ramson. "Since you mention 'trust.' Here."

Ramson took the drawing she offered him. This sketch was swathed in shadows. Whereas the others had seemed to capture moments and memories, this one had captured the subject like a portrait. He recognized the man on the page: bald, with distrustful large eyes that were set far apart from his thin nose. It was a sketch of the same man she'd shown him in prison.

Her alchemist.

This sketch bore the same painstaking detail as the other one, which had likely been destroyed in their waterfall escapade. Ramson studied the drawing more closely, taking in the man's white priest's robes and the circlet of the four Deities that hung around his neck. "This is a good start, Witch. I need you to tell me everything you know about him."

"He worked in the Salskoff Palace ten years ago. He disappeared and was back in . . . in Salskoff eleven moons ago."

He waited for more, but she clamped her mouth tightly shut. "That's it?"

"I know nothing else," she said curtly. Her eyes burned, and her hands had curled into fists as she spoke. Whoever this man was, this girl had a debt to settle with him.

He'd find out why soon enough. For now, Ramson settled on a different question. "An alchemist, you say," he mused. "Was he an Affinite?"

Many alchemists possessed unique Affinities and were hired by the upper crust of Cyrilia to lengthen and strengthen lives with their peculiar practices. Some of the most powerful alchemists, Ramson had heard, had metaphysical Affinities. Pain. Calm. Happiness. Intangibles, coveted by those who had coins to spare.

"I'm not certain," the witch said, looping a strand of her hair behind her ear. Ramson had already picked this up as a nervous tic of hers—like the way she fidgeted with her hood. "He brewed Deys'voshk and other elixirs."

Likely an Affinite, then. His mind snagged on another detail, on the Deys'krug and the prayer robes. "Was he a priest—or a devout man? Have you tried starting from there?"

"He wasn't a *devout* man," she said bitterly, and then sighed. "I've tried that. I've looked all over the Empire for him, but I haven't found a thing. The bounty hunters I hired never even got close."

"Amateurs."

She looked as though she wanted to slap him. "I wouldn't be so confident. If this man isn't standing in front of me in three weeks, I'll bleed you dry."

"Relax," he said lazily, waving the sketch in front of her. "I have a plan."

Ramson tapped his fingers on the sketch. Two sightings, ten years apart—the trail was colder than death by now. But he had two leads: First, this man used to work at the Palace.

And that the man was likely an Affinite on the run meant he might've had to reinvent his identity and reestablish himself.

But if there was one source that tracked Affinites' movements as closely as an eagle tracked its quarry, it was Kerlan's brokers. The thought of strolling into their territory was one he didn't care for. Ramson glanced at the witch and the child, unease twinging in his stomach. Could it be that they were victims of the very brokers that they needed in order to find this alchemist?

"Good." Ana launched herself from the table and marched toward the bed, where she retrieved a small satchel from beneath the furs. May glared at Ramson, and then promptly began folding the few items of clothing on the bed and slipping them into the satchel. "We leave in one hour. I assume you'll have figured out where we're going by then."

"I already have." There was only one city in the vicinity of Ghost Falls that was crawling with ruthless Affinite traffickers hungry for information and bounty. "We're going to Kyrov."

7

The morning air was crisp, the snow glittering and dusted with gold from a distant sun by the time they set out. The quiet was broken only by the huff of their breath, that clouded in the cold air, and the crunch of their boots through snow. The boreal forest stretched from the Krazyast Triangle at the northernmost tip of Cyrilia to the Dzhyvekha Mountains that bordered Nandji in the south. Here, up north, the snow never melted, but farther south, Ana knew, summer saw the tips of green grasses and conifer pines peeking out from beneath a veil of white.

Ana hoisted her rucksack farther up her shoulders, the rustle of her parchments and the clinks of her remaining globefires strangely calming. By her side, May plodded along, turning her head this way and that to whatever sensations she felt coming from the earth buried deep below. She held a freshly lit globefire between her hands, the flames inside crawling along the oil that coated the glass, warming hands and providing light during nights. They'd spent many moons traveling like this, just her and May, a globefire, the compass she held in her hands, and the eternal silence of the forest.

Which, at the moment, was being disrupted in the most irritating way possible.

"So, how did you two beautiful damas end up all the way over here?" Quicktongue's cheerful voice drifted to them from a dozen paces behind.

Ana gritted her teeth. May shot her a knowing look and rolled her eyes.

"Rather far north for a girl from the Aseatic Isles," the con man continued. A flock of pine harriers burst into flight from some shrubs ahead.

Ana was about to spin around and snap at him, but the meaning behind his words settled into her with a chill. *Everything* Ramson Quicktongue said was deliberate, every word carefully chosen—it could hardly be coincidence that he was questioning May's origin. And the last thing Ana wanted was for the con man to know about May's status: a lost Affinite with no identity and no protection.

"It's none of your business," she replied.

"Oh, but it is," Quicktongue pressed on in that tone of voice that made Ana want to strangle him. "Seeing as we're going to be partnering together for six weeks."

"Let's keep it at that. A partnership, where we don't speak to each other unless absolutely necessary."

"This *is* necessary." He was catching up to them now, his voice growing louder and more obnoxious by the second. The crunch of snow beneath his boots drew closer. "I'll have to keep you both safe, especially if we run into Whitecloaks."

Ana whirled around. His last sentence had set off a series of sparks in her head that ignited into fury. "Keep *us* safe?" she repeated, ignoring the way the compass arrow spun in her hands to readjust. "Listen, you arrogant man. May and I have survived this long by ourselves, and we don't need you to keep us *safe* or whatever you think you need to do. This was a Trade, and I will hold you to getting your part of it done. No more, no less."

She was breathing hard when she finished, and she realized she'd closed the distance between her and Quicktongue so that they were barely two steps apart. He'd stopped where he was, his face a mask frozen like the forest around them. His hazel eyes, however, watched her with the intent and cunning of a fox.

"All right," he said softly, his breath unfurling in a small plume between them. "But let me ask you this: Have you ever been to Kyrov?"

Ana thought of all that she'd read of the trade town that thrived for its proximity to the Krazyast Triangle and its commerce of coveted blackstone. The truth was, she could recite an entire tome's worth of facts about Kyrov . . . yet she had never seen it for herself.

"No," she admitted sourly. "But I've studied it."

Quicktongue's face warped into a smile, and it was not a pleasant one. "The winners write history, love. Ever wondered why the topic of Affinite indenturement is so scarcely seen in a Cyrilian textbook?"

It felt like a slap to her face. She recalled the plush carpets of Salskoff Palace, the crackle of the fireplace and the smell of leather chairs and old books in Papa's study. She and Luka had spent half their days sitting at his tall oak desk, listening to him read through Cyrilia's histories with them in his low, steady voice.

Before he'd fallen sick, Papa had personally seen to her

education. He hadn't been able to love her Affinity . . . but he had loved her, in his own way.

She really believed he had.

"If you have a point, make it," she found herself saying, though her heart wasn't in the argument anymore.

"Kyrov's a dangerous place. I'd normally caution any Affinite to stay away from it, but seeing as I'm being *held* to getting my part of the Trade done, it's a risk I'm willing to take." Quicktongue shrugged and plowed past her, snow flying in the wake of his steps. "Especially as I'm not an Affinite."

He spoke as though there could be a large city in her own empire that was dangerous for an Affinite to cross into. Ana knew corruption existed in her empire, but it wasn't as though Affinites were pulled off the streets.

The tip of the compass spun unsteadily as she turned to follow Quicktongue northeast, toward Kyrov.

Half a day's journey left, by her calculations. Somehow the forest looked less peaceful, the sunlight cold and the pines' shadows jarring as they stretched across the snow. It was only when May slipped a small hand in hers that Ana's breathing steadied slightly.

A small ball of mud rose from the ground, hovering above May's palm. With a flick of her fingers, it shot toward Quicktongue, hitting him squarely on his back.

"I know you like to hear yourself talk, arrogant man," May said as they marched past him, "but speak again and I'll aim for your face." She paused and grinned viciously. "You'd look better, too."

8

Ana's first glimpse of Kyrov was a bundle of silver-white spires that rose above the snow-covered trees. After almost a day's travel, the sun hung low in the west, painting the city in a sheen of dusky gold. When the red-brown bricks of the dacha cottages came into view, Ana thought of the gingerbread houses she used to make as a child every year in celebration of the arrival of the Deity of Winter.

Ana tugged at her hood as the dirt roads gradually turned to slate-gray cobblestones and the sounds of city life thrummed into existence. May kept close to her side, eyes wide and head turning from side to side. After they had fled from May's employer, they'd kept to small villages and abandoned hunters' cabins. The crowds and noise and smells of large towns made Ana anxious, and even now, she tried to quiet the unease roiling in her stomach as they walked.

Yet she found her eyes lingering on objects unwittingly: the traditional silver-blue of a kechyan cloak, the bright red of a damashka nesting doll, the glint of white-gold hoop earrings. She could, so clearly in her mind's eye, see these objects as she'd known them back in her world, in the Salskoff Palace. Luka, donning his Imperial kechyan with the white tiger's emblem; Papa, kneeling by her bed with her first damashka in his large hands; Mama, sitting on a settee beneath a high Palace window, her earrings catching the sun as she swept her beautiful dark hair over her shoulder.

Her throat burned with the unexpected ache of tears. She blinked and turned her attention to the nearest object of distraction: an open-door warehouse.

Sultry heat rolled out in welcome waves, and the strike of a hammer against molten metal rang against the early-evening sounds of the town. Yet in the shadows, there was something else.

A young boy with black hair and tired eyes knelt by a furnace, his palms upturned, his back bent like a hook. Soot covered his face, but even from here, his features marked him as coming from one of the Aseatic Isles. But his midnight eyes sat atop sunken cheeks, drained of life and whittled down to bone.

"You, boy!" shouted the blacksmith, his hammer pausing in the air. "The fire needs to be stronger!"

The boy's eyes flicked to the blacksmith. Hunching over, he turned his palms to the flames. They brightened, dancing bursts of gold and orange that melted into a bloodred core.

A year ago, her gaze might have swept over this scene as an ordinary aspect of daily life in her empire. Just another Affinite at work, earning his living like Yuri and the other Affinites at the Palace. She remembered how Yuri would go to town and bring back treats for her, sneaking into her chambers late at night when Markov took up his shift by her door. Yuri had been content; he'd been earning enough to feed a mother and a younger sister in some village down south.

But now, watching the Aseatic Isles boy huddle over the fire, his soot-stained face streaked with sweat and misery, she found a shadow of doubt creeping over her thoughts.

A little under a year ago, she had seen the same sadness in the lines of May's eyes, in the hollows of her cheeks, in the sag of her skinny shoulders that tried to pitch up the dirty, ill-fitting tunic she'd been given to wear. The quiet despair in the Aseatic boy's eyes cast a mirror image to May's back then.

A cold foreboding spread through her; Ana found her steps slowing. The streets were filled with people laughing, chattering, passing the blacksmith's shop without a care in the world. Had she been just like them one year past? She wanted to reach out to the boy, to speak to him, to do *something*.

A hand wrapped around her wrist, pulling her from her thoughts. The world flooded back in a whirl of colors and sounds, and she realized that Ramson Quicktongue had been saying her name. Before she could jerk away, he drew her and May into the nearest shop.

The door clicked shut behind her, a bell chimed overhead, and the smell of wood wafted over to them from a fireplace in the back.

They stood in a shop for lacquer art. Tigers and vases lined the shelves while swans and icehawks and phoenixes twirled gently before the windows, all painted with swirling patterns of leaves, snowflakes, and fruits. Instinctively, Ana wedged herself between May and Ramson, glaring at the con man. "What are you doing?"

He stooped, his eyes trained on something moving outside the windows.

Beyond the lacquered fowl figurines, on the cobblestone streets outside, a procession passed by. Three horses trotted through the streets, their riders' snowy-white cloaks flowing proudly behind. Silver tiger crests flashed on the riders' chests, and blackstone swords gleamed at their belts.

"Whitecloaks," Ramson muttered by her ear.

Imperial Patrols—the highest order of soldiers in the Cyrilian Imperial Army, they were peacekeepers, intended to monitor and quell any clashes between citizens and Affinites. Most important, though, armed with blackstone and Deys'voshk, they were trained to fight Affinites should they get out of hand.

Ana remembered visiting cities in her childhood, before her Affinity had manifested. She'd felt inexplicably safe in the presence of the Patrols' billowing cloaks and gleaming helmets outside her carriage window. She remembered thinking that the Whitecloaks would protect her from any monsters that could hurt her.

Except now she was the monster.

"Ramson," she said quietly, watching the procession. "Earlier, you said you would need to protect us from the Imperial Patrols. What did you mean by that?"

She didn't want to hear the answer. But she knew she had to.

Ramson cast her a glance, and for a moment, she thought he would make a snide remark at her. Instead, he flicked his wrist, and a single bronze copperstone appeared between his knuckles. "It all comes down to this," he said, and began flipping the coin between his fingers, making it appear one moment and disappear the next. "In a broken system, which way does the blade point?" Ramson pinched the copperstone and held it up. "Who do you think pays them more? The Empire? Or profitable businesses that rely on them to exploit Affinites in need of work?"

Ana's heart hammered; she felt as though she were in free fall, as though the ground were slowly disappearing beneath her. "But have you seen it?"

Ramson's gaze was fixed on the coin, whose edges glinted like the curved blade of a scythe. "As I said, I'm a businessman."

Her lips parted, but she had no words and no breath left to argue.

"This empire is falling apart," Ramson continued. "The previous emperor and empress died, the princess died a year ago, and the vultures are simply waiting to see how long Lukas Mikhailov lasts." He tossed the copperstone into the air; it winked in the firelight and disappeared in his palms. "It's every man for himself; the time of profiteers and reapers. You always win if you choose the winning side."

The rest of the world seemed distant and muted as she watched him turn toward the door. The Whitecloaks had disappeared. Crowds continued to mingle in the streets outside—but everything appeared different.

"Look, just do me a favor," Ramson said, "and stay away from the Whitecloaks—especially if they have a yaeger with them." The bell jingled again as he pulled open the door. "I suspect you and the kid aren't in possession of identification . . . and I'm sure you know the consequences of being caught."

Goose bumps rose on Ana's arms, and it had nothing to do with the cold wind that swept into the shop. He had to be exaggerating—he spoke as though they could be in danger, in broad daylight, in the middle of her empire. Yet asking him to elaborate meant playing into his hand and revealing a gap in her knowledge, a weakness.

Ana clamped her lips shut and followed him out.

"This is where we part ways for now," Ramson said. "The place I'm going isn't Affinite-friendly. Luckily, the Winter Market is right ahead on this road." He winked at May. "You'd like some candy, wouldn't you, love?"

May bared her teeth at him. "Ana told me to never accept candy from strangers," she said.

Ramson looked deflated.

"Wait." Ana glared at him. "You have to tell us where you're going."

"Ah, always the vote of trust from you." Ramson pointed down a side alley, away from the general flow of the crowds. "The Gray Bear's Keep. Right there, with the red-shingled roofs. Thirty minutes is all I need; I'll meet you back here."

Ana watched him saunter down the street. If he'd wanted to betray her, he could have just left her to die on the riverbank back in the Syvern Taiga. She didn't like it, but she would have to let him go for now.

"Ana!" May pointed, her voice rising in excitement. "The Vyntr'makt!"

The streets before them opened up, and for a moment, Ana thought she was gazing at one of the miniature town carvings she'd received as gifts in her childhood. Brightly colored dachas glowed dusk-gold against a late-afternoon sun, tinsel-lined tarpaulins erected over stalls displaying trinkets and food that would make a child squeal.

May did, squeezing Ana's hand and pulling her forward, weaving through the crowds. A banner with a white tiger's head rippled at the entrance. *Vyntr'makt,* it announced. And, beneath, the motto of the Cyrilian Empire: *Kommertsya, Deysa, Imperya.* Commerce, Deities, Empire.

The Winter Market—Vyntr'makt in Old Cyrilian—was a tradition across all Cyrilian towns. Each town decorated its largest square or plaza into late autumn to await the Fyrva'snezh—the First Snow, a night that marked the beginning of winter and the awakening of their patron deity.

Kyrov's Vyntr'makt rivaled Salskoff's with the richness of its food wafting from the stalls, the opulence of iridescent jewels and silks splayed across display stands, the intricacy of sacred Cyrilian figurines carved on white gold. Fish-baked bread lined bakery windows, and the outdoor stalls boasted cold cabbage soups, beef potato pies, and lamb skewers roasting with olives.

Inevitably, in the midst of all the joy, her gaze was drawn to a single pot of beet soup boiling at the side of a wooden stall. Hot vapor rose from its crimson surface, filling the air with a pungent smell.

Nausea twisted in her stomach as a familiar image flashed through her mind. Eight bodies, splayed like twisted works of art. Blood, dark and red in the snow.

Deimhov.

Monster.

". . . Ana!"

She jerked out of the memory, the crimson pools and screams fading as Kyrov's Vyntr'makt returned. May was tugging on her hand. Her eyes were fixed on a stall ahead, filled with rows of honey apple tarts, caramel fried dough, and a variety of other treats.

Ana ran through the meager sum she'd saved up. They had enough for at least two more nights' lodging and meals, and she was reluctant to spend a single copperstone over their budget . . . and yet. She thought of the first time she'd seen May, her shock at how scrawny the girl had looked. Even then, May had split her paltry rations from her employer with Ana, walking a mile in the snow each day to the barn where she'd hidden Ana and kept her alive.

She deserved all she wanted in the world.

"Let's go get one," she said, pulling May forward, but the child shook her head.

"No, *look,*" she whispered, her gaze darting between Ana and the stall. "The girl."

It took Ana a moment to realize that May was referring to the pastry vendor, a young girl barely into her adolescent years. She wore a ragged hood, her pale face and sand-colored hair peeking out from beneath.

"She's like me," May said softly, the words falling from her lips like snow, too-soon gone. She stood still, her eyes an ocean of silent memories. "Like *us.*"

Ana looked. Harder. And it hit her all at once. The pastry vendor's slouch, curling in on herself as though she wanted to disappear from this world; the air of diffidence, bordering on fear, that emanated from her. And her eyes—eyes that were wells of sadness, like May's in the dead of winter.

Except May's had always borne hope.

Before Ana could reply, May pulled away and slipped through the crowd. Ana hurried after her, just in time to see the child reach into the folds of her gray fur cloak and dig out a single copperstone. It was one of the coins Ana had told her to keep, promising they would use it to buy a treat.

Gently, May took the pastry vendor's hands and folded the coin into them. "Keep it," May whispered, pressing a small finger to her lips. She chanced a glance at Ana, and for a moment, her eyes said it all: flashes of rage and crashing waves of grief tossing and turning within. And Ana realized with gut-wrenching pain that May had seen her ma-ma in this Affinite, that she'd been looking for her ma-ma when she'd spotted this pastry vendor.

Suddenly, the pastries looked too bright, too false, and the rest of the world faded to a blur of noises and dim colors.

It was as though the world she had seen for the past eighteen years was slowly peeling away to reveal the truth of what it was. How many times had she purchased something from someone who might have been forced into a bad contract? How many overworked and exploited Affinites had she waved at in the crowds when she had traveled with her father to see her empire as a child?

Cyrilian law stated that employment under contract was fair employment . . . but it never dug into actual terms of that agreement. How an employer was to treat an employee. The terms of payment. Whether that contract had been signed willingly . . . or through coercion.

"Here," the pastry vendor said quietly. Her hands darted over the rows of pastries on display, and she plucked one up and held it out to May. "It's a ptychy'moloko. Bird's milk cake. You can have it."

Ana recognized the hush in the girl's voice, the furtive way her eyes darted around to check that nobody else caught this transaction.

May smiled as she took her first bite, and Ana would have paid all the goldleaves in the world to see her friend smile like that again. "It's good," May said, and held it out to Ana.

It was difficult to manage a smile over the cold realization that had just seeded in her chest. "It was my favorite as a child," Ana said. She thought of Yuri, his coal-gray eyes bright as he handed treats to her and Luka, steaming hot from the kitchens. "Go ahead, finish it."

May's face was radiant. "I like the hard brown layer," she said between bites.

"That's chokolad." The pastry vendor watched May with a hint of a smile warming her eyes. "It's made of cocoa from Nandji."

"Oi!"

A man in lush furs shoved through the crowd, his gaze locked on May. The pastry vendor's face had gone paler than flour.

"Did she pay?" the nobleman snarled, storming over and making as though to snatch the pastry from May's hands.

Something snapped in Ana. "Don't touch her," she growled.

Rage flickered in the man's eyes, but he turned to the pastry vendor, who was watching him with a terrified expression. "I'm going to count my books tonight, and if I find that you've been stealing . . ." He lowered his voice to a hiss. "You'll get what's coming to you, witch."

"Ana." May's voice trembled as she tugged insistently at Ana's hand, pulling her away from the stall. "We gotta go. There's nothing we can do here. Please."

Even as she followed May, Ana's step faltered. It felt wrong, in her heart, to turn and leave someone in need of help. Someone whose Affinity made them different, ostracized. Someone like her.

A cry rang out, Ana and May froze as they turned to look. And, with the rest of the crowd, they gasped as the nobleman backhanded the young pastry vendor with all his strength.

The slap resonated in the square like the crack of a whip. The pastry vendor staggered back and crashed into the stall of neatly arranged pastries.

Anger coiled around Ana, white-hot. She was the Princess of Cyrilia. There was a time when scum like him would have bowed to her, when she could have ordered his demise with a single word.

That time was past, but she could still do the right thing.

"Please, mesyr," the Affinite girl begged.

The nobleman raised his hand again.

Ana wrapped her Affinity around him. She'd only ever learned how to push or pull, but now she commanded for the blood in his body to remain still with every ounce of her strength.

For a few seconds, the nobleman was frozen, his arm raised and his expression slipping from fury to panic. He began to choke, his eyes rolling into the back of his head.

She was aware of May tugging at her cloak. She heard the gasps of the crowd as she finally let go of the nobleman's blood and his body hit the ground like a sack of potatoes. Horrible wheezing sounds came from his mouth.

"Ana," May shrieked. "We need to go, before—"

Someone screamed. As the Vyntr'makt erupted into panic, Ana realized that she had gone too far.

"May," she gasped, and the child's hand was in hers, and they were stumbling away from the collapsed nobleman and the pastry vendor.

Yet the crowd had grown oddly still, and the skin on Ana's back pricked. It took her a moment to realize that a hush had fallen over the entire square. All the vendors and townspeople were gazing at a spot behind Ana with expressions of awe and anxiety.

Slowly, Ana turned. And looked into a squad of Cyrilian Imperial Patrols.

9

The interior of the ramshackle pub was dark, lit only by the flickering flames of candle stubs on the tables. A broken wooden sign announced in crude writing: *The Gray Bear's Keep.* Ramson paused at the door only to pass a hand over the dagger he'd stolen, before stepping onto the creaky wooden floorboards. He had come to collect a debt.

It took a few moments for his eyes to adjust to the dimness, and he saw that several tables were seated, their guests bent over their drinks and speaking in hushed tones. There was an air of menace to the flames licking at the brass mantel and the clink of cups between murmured exchanges.

Several people turned to look at Ramson as he passed them by, and he found himself assessing the new outfit he had procured—for free, albeit unknown to the seller—from a nearby stall. An ordinary tunic, black vest, gray breeches, riding boots, and a nice Cyrilian fur cloak to top it all off. He looked like the perfect patron for these types of places: sleek, groomed, and utterly unmemorable.

Ramson scanned the bar. Only a practiced eye would notice the board of Affinites-for-hire posters on the far wall, the narrow staircase by the counter with a crooked *Reservations Only* sign, and the bottle of green-tinted Deys'voshk disguised amid the rows of liquor on the back shelf. This was no ordinary pub. It was an Affinite trafficking post.

Ramson stalked up to the counter and slipped onto a bar stool, ducking his head behind an expensive-looking samovar. The barman ambled over. He was of bearish height and build, with a great gray beard—one that had grown in size from the secrets he kept over his tenure at the most notorious inn in Cyrilia. Though he wore a coarse apron smudged with grease and splashed with various shades of liquors, there was no missing the flash of his gold ring as he polished a glass. "Esteemed greetings to you, noble mesyr, and might I express my delight upon your patronage of my humble pub! Igor, at your service."

"Salutations to you, my good gentleman, and might I say that the pleasure is . . . *all mine.*" Ramson lifted his head.

Igor almost dropped the glass he was cleaning. "Damn hell, man," he muttered, slipping into a lowborn Cyrilian slur.

"Damn *hells,*" Ramson corrected him, and gave a twirl of his fingers. "Brandy. And don't bother with the cheap shit."

Igor stooped slightly, peering at Ramson's face. "So it really is you. I was wondering when you'd be back."

"You were wondering *if* I'd be back."

Igor chuckled, a low, rumbling sound. "I won't deny it. The news has spread across this entire blasted empire. You've made a mess, Quicktongue." He turned, reaching into one of the shelves at the back of the bar. There was a sharp clink and the sound of liquid sloshing.

Ramson watched the barman's beefy back as he worked to prepare a drink. "I'm cleaning it up, Igor. My betrayers'll pay." He slid out his dagger. "But first things first. I'm here to collect a debt."

Igor turned, clutching a tumbler and a bottle of Bregonian brandy. Concern seeped into his murky eyes. "Look now, Quicktongue. Business's been bad, what with the Mikhailov emperor sick and the economy tankin'." He passed a hand over his bald forehead and nodded at the board in the back. Papers were pinned chaotically atop each other, some bearing crude drawings. "Sales've been slow."

Ramson was interested enough to spare a glance at the board. *Affinites-for-Hire,* the posters declared, when really, they whispered to those in the know that these were foreign Affinites whose contracts were up for sale. "I don't want your money. I want information."

"Ah." Igor's shoulders sagged with relief, and he set Ramson's drink before him. "You know my facts're worth more than my goldleaves." He paused, and his eyes slid to the dark staircase behind the counter. "Perhaps this calls for a private discussion in the Reservation Room."

Ramson stood, grabbing his glass.

Igor hesitated. "I'll be right up. I need to close out a few tabs, grab a drink for meself, then I'll be all yours. Won't be a minute."

"Take your time. I'll show myself up."

The Reservation Room was up a narrow flight of steps built into the cold stone walls of the pub. Ramson climbed them and opened a set of wooden doors to a candlelit room, well furnished with red velvet settees and an expensive oakwood table. He didn't miss the bottles of Deys'voshk lining the shelves at the back of the room, glinting in the flickering candlelight.

He shoved the thoughts from his mind and raised his drink, inhaling sharply before taking a swig. Igor hadn't cheated him. This was real Bregonian brandy: pungently bitter and subtly sweet, with a hint of roses and the zest of citrus that blossomed on the palate and lingered as an aftertaste.

Footsteps thudded up the stairs, and Igor sauntered in with a mug in each hand. He took care to shut the door behind him.

Ramson waited for the familiar click of a lock. No conversation in the Reservation Room was conducted with an unlocked door.

When it didn't come, a thread of caution tightened inside him.

With a great sigh, Igor placed the second round of drinks on the table and plopped down on one of the settees. Firelight danced on his face. "I see the wardens haven't beaten the spirit out of you. You look healthy as a young buck, just a shade paler. What's it been, four moons?"

"Three moons and twenty-one days. I've been counting." Ramson slouched back against the plump velvet cushion of his settee like a cat basking in the sun, watching Igor through heavy-lidded eyes. "They don't serve stuff like this in prison."

"Aye." Igor raised his glass. "These'd cost a good few goldleaves."

"Word on the street is that you owe me more than a *few* goldleaves." Ramson leaned forward, his brandy forgotten, and instead savored the look of utter panic that flashed across Igor's face. "I know you turned me in. Oh, don't look so pitiful, man. Have some damned balls and own up to it."

It was a wager on Ramson's part, but it was his best guess thus far. He'd been holing up for the night at Igor's pub when a squad of Whitecloaks stormed in and arrested him on a count of treason against the Crown. He'd spent his moons in prison combing through every gnarled thread of his network until he'd pinned down a theory: Igor had turned him in, but he'd been doing the dirty work for someone else. Someone close to Kerlan who'd had information about his mission.

Igor's gaze flitted nervously to the door; he wiped a sheen of sweat from his face, smearing more grease on his forehead. "Ramson, my friend, you must know—"

"*Don't* 'Ramson, my friend' me." Ramson slammed his fist on the table, finally letting himself taste a sliver of that anger that had built up inside him as he rotted away in prison. "If you want to live, you'll tell me why you did it, and you'll tell me who made you do it."

"H-he used to work for the Imperial Court." Igor's breaths came in shallow rasps, and he looked faint. "Y-you have to understand, R-Ramson—"

"There's nothing I understand better than the gods-damned sting of betrayal."

"You were sent to murder the Emperor!" Igor exclaimed. "Deities, man, your mission was impossible from the start!"

Ramson paused. This was the question he'd turned over and over in his mind back at Ghost Falls with no leads to an answer: Why had the greatest crime lord in the Empire wanted to murder Emperor Lukas Mikhailov?

He remembered the storm that night, rain lashing at the windows in fury. Kerlan's small, twisted smile, the simple cadence to his words, as though he'd just asked Ramson to pick up beet soup for dinner.

Ramson had known, that very moment, that this was the ultimate test. If he had succeeded, Kerlan would have named him successor to the Order, cementing Ramson's power once and for all. Everything he'd ever wanted in his life sat beyond that mission.

Yet Ramson had forgotten that in a gamble where you stood to win everything, there was even more you could lose.

And he'd lost.

Perhaps capture by the Imperial Court had been a kinder fate than death at Kerlan's hands.

"I was his Deputy," Ramson gritted out. "He entrusted everything to me. The mission got leaked. And I'm going to trace that leak and destroy everyone involved in it, starting with *you.*"

"Ramson, please—"

"Shut your damn mouth. The one thing I can't stand is a spineless coward." Ramson spread his hands on the polished oakwood table. His voice was a low growl when he spoke next. "The only reason you're still breathing is because I want something from you. *I need a name, Igor.*"

"Pyetr Tetsyev!" The words came out in a sharp gasp. "He came to inquire about you and paid me a sum to turn you in if you came to my pub. And a week later you showed up." Igor's mouth was small, but it worked surprisingly fast. He fixed Ramson with a pleading gaze.

"That's all I know, I swear, man. And it was a lot of money."

"Pyetr Tetsyev." Ramson rolled the name around his tongue; it had no taste of familiarity. "Who is he, and where can I find him?"

"He's under Kerlan's employment, makes Deys'voshk for him. Showed up out o' nowhere with a past murkier'n the bottom of my boot."

"Hmm." Ramson leaned back, taking a swig from his goblet and smacking his lips. Igor watched him, his watery eyes pinned on Ramson's every move. The fact that Ramson had reverted back to his drink seemed to comfort the bartender, for his expression became obsequious. "I'll need to take a trip to Novo Mynsk, then."

"To Novo Mynsk? But that's Kerlan's territory!" Igor's false concern was magnified by his relief. "You think . . . you think Kerlan will forgive you for breaking a Trade?"

Ramson sipped his brandy, feeling a familiar tug on his lips. Now came the real show. "Oh, he'll be begging me to come back. I haven't crawled out of that shithole empty-handed. I broke that Trade, but I have something better in mind for him." He gave a dramatic pause. "A potential new ally."

Igor's lips parted slightly, and Ramson could almost see him rifling through the dozens of questions running through his mind. At last, curiosity and greed won, lighting his wrinkled face. "Who?"

"The most powerful Affinite in the Empire."

Igor suddenly looked around the room, as though expecting an Affinite to leap out from behind one of the bookcases. "Where . . . ?"

"She's just around the corner, waiting for me. A flesh Affinite. She took down five trained men with a flick of a finger."

He smothered a grin as the barman's mouth dropped open completely.

"She'd be worth a fortune," Igor whispered. "Deities, no wonder Kerlan hasn't hired anyone to replace you yet. It'd be a hard match."

Ramson stored this bit of information away. Outwardly, he snorted. "Money. That's all you think about," he said, raising his tumbler of brandy. "How much d'you think you can get for a bottle of this? Ten goldleaves? Think, instead, if I grew Kerlan a vineyard. How many bottles of brandy could he make then? How many hundreds of *thousands* of goldleaves would he get each year?" Ramson downed his drink in a single gulp and set the tumbler on the table with a satisfying clink. "Think bigger, Igor, *my friend.*"

In fact, that was the theory he'd told Kerlan when the crime lord had offered him a stake in the Order's trafficking business. Ramson had refused. He told Kerlan his skills would be put to better use elsewhere—in the port, in the weapons trade, at the casinos, and just about anywhere else.

The truth, though, was he couldn't stomach it. He'd walked past Affinite children on the streets, forced into servitude, their mouths sewn shut by terror, their eyes wide with a thinly veiled plea. And he'd seen in them the ghost of a childhood friend he'd promised to never betray.

Perhaps that was why Kerlan had assigned Ramson to the suicide mission to murder Cyrilia's Emperor. Perhaps Kerlan had seen the seed of doubt that had grown in Ramson's chest throughout these years, and he'd needed Ramson to prove his loyalty to the very end.

Ramson had failed.

He shoved these thoughts from his head now, keeping the smile playing about his lips as he looked coolly at Igor. Unbeknownst to the bartender, Ramson had just bought himself insurance. Igor would sell this tidbit to all the traders that frequented his pub, and news of Ramson's imminent comeback—along with that flesh Affinite—would spread like wildfire. By the time Ramson reached Novo Mynsk, Lord Alaric Kerlan would be welcoming him with open arms. It would be a great Trade—two birds with one stone. Ramson would return with the name of his betrayer *and* introduce the witch to Kerlan in one fell swoop. Undoubtedly, Kerlan would reinstate him as Deputy of the Order and Portmaster of Goldwater.

He simply needed a suitable occasion for his appearance: one that caught this Pyetr Tetsyev by surprise. It wouldn't do to simply waltz into the Kerlan Estate—

Waltz. Something clicked into his brain. "Igor, what day is it today?"

Igor blinked. "It's the twentieth of the third moon. Of autumn," he added unnecessarily.

In ten days, it would be winter.

Each year on the first day of winter, the entire Cyrilian Empire celebrated the First Snow with festivities. And in Novo Mynsk, there was no party more elaborate than the one thrown at the Kerlan Estate by Lord Alaric Kerlan himself. The upper crust of the town would be invited—those with power, money, and connections to the criminal world.

Now, *that* would be an entrance worth remembering. Let all his enemies know that Ramson Quicktongue was back in business, and that he would hunt down every last man who stood in his way.

Ramson's smile returned, sharper than his blade. "Igor, I need two horses for the road."

"Of course, of course." Igor looked tremendously relieved. "I have two mares I can lend you."

"Good." Ramson was about to stand when he remembered something. "One more thing." He slapped a piece of paper on the oakwood table. With a clunk, he set his empty tumbler on one corner of the scroll and ran his palm over the folds, revealing the sketch of the bald alchemist with the thin nose and wide gray eyes. "Does this man look familiar to you?"

Igor froze. "Is this a joke?"

"It would be a poor joke to make. Enlighten me."

Igor jabbed a finger at the sketch, looking up at Ramson, his face twisted in disbelief. "That's Pyetr Tetsyev."

10

Ramson had to stare at Igor for a full five seconds to determine whether the bartender was lying. But the man's expression mirrored Ramson's disbelief.

Igor was many terrible things, but he was not a great liar. He was simply too much of a coward. Apply enough pressure at the right spot and he'd crack.

"Looks exactly like him," Igor babbled, frowning at the sketch. "I'll never forget the night he showed up at my door. Drenched in rain, he was, but he came straight to me. Odd sort of fellow. Said he worked at the Palace and showed me some papers. Asked me your name and where you were." He paused, seeming to realize that he was incriminating himself again, and hurriedly changed the subject. "It's a good sketch."

Questions burst in Ramson's head like stars, but he focused on a single thought: he and the flesh Affinite had the same enemy.

The enemy of my enemy is my friend.

The day was turning out to be an excellent one indeed. Everything he had planned for—his traitor, the alchemist, and his ultimate trade of the witch with Kerlan—culminated in

Novo Mynsk. Two birds with one stone was a good deal, but *three* birds with one stone was the type of deal that set a genuine smile on Ramson Quicktongue's face. "Igor, old friend. You've given me nothing but good news today."

Igor's relief was palpable as he exhaled, the lines of tension melting from his shoulders. "Thank the Deities, Quicktongue. I thought you were going to do me in for . . . for what my big mouth let on . . ."

"Consider your debts paid." Ramson stood and stretched. "You're lucky I'm feeling generous today."

Igor gave a shaky chortle. He glanced at the door again. "A toast, then," he said, standing and handing Ramson one of the two mugs he had brought up. "To paid debts and fair trades."

"Such generosity today, Igor. Usually I'm hard-pressed to get even *one* tankard of cheap ale from you." Ramson raised his polished brass mug. "To honest words and honest men." He brought his drink to his lips and inhaled the scent of the Cyrilian sunwine.

Igor had drained half of his in a single gulp. His eyes flickered toward Ramson over the rim of his goblet.

Ramson exhaled deeply. Slowly, counting his heartbeats, he lowered his cup, the smile still pasted on his face. "I'm truly honored that you chose to toast me with Myrkoff sunwine, old friend." He paused, listing his head. "And I truly believe that the Myrkoff would have tasted better without the poison you've laced it with."

Clang.

Igor's cup rolled on the ground, sunwine spilling onto the polished floorboards. The bartender darted behind his settee, face drawn and lips tight. Ramson backed into the other end of the room. He still held his cup in one hand; in another, he palmed his dagger.

"I forgot how good you are with your alcohol," the barman snarled.

"And I forgot how good you are with your façade of stupidity. I might have fallen for it." He almost had. "Who're you expecting, Igor?"

"Even if you kill me, you'll never make it out of here." The barman was eyeing Ramson's dagger. "Kerlan set the price for your head as soon as he heard of your escape. I sent my page boy to the bounty hunters the second you walked in. I only had to entertain you while they got here."

Of course word of his jailbreak had reached Kerlan. Ramson wouldn't be surprised if the crime lord had a few of the Ghost Falls guards in his pocket.

Ramson tilted his head. Flames of rage flickered inside him. But he harnessed those flames and honed them into a weapon. Just as Kerlan had taught him. "I might kill you for the fun of it. Watch you squirm as I gut you like a squealing pig."

The blood drained from Igor's face. Without warning, he let out a yell. *"He's escaping!"*

Ramson turned, reaching for the lock on the door to bolt them inside—a moment too late.

The door to the Reservation Room burst open. Two mercenaries hurled in, charging at Ramson, swords drawn.

Ramson flung his brass cup at the first man with all his strength. With a satisfying *crack,* it smashed his temple. The mercenary cried out and staggered back, buying Ramson the precious seconds he needed.

He leapt through the air and lashed out. His dagger plunged

through the mercenary's chest in a sickening crunch of sinew and flesh. In the same motion, he seized the sword from the man's loose grip and turned to parry the second bounty hunter's attack.

Metal sang as their blades clashed. Ramson grunted and flung himself out of the way as a third mercenary appeared at the door. Ramson turned to face the man squarely, sword in hand, assessing the newcomer's build, his clothing, and his weapon.

Yet no amount of fighting prowess would have prepared him for what came next. Pain exploded on the nape of his neck, shooting through his nerves and limbs and down to his fingers. Stars burst in his eyes as he crumpled to the floor.

"All yours, boys." Igor's breathing was ragged as he set aside his brass tumbler. "That'll be an extra charge for the help I gave you there at the end. Put in a good word to Lord Kerlan for me."

Ramson fought for consciousness, but the darkness at the edges of his vision was closing in. He was dimly aware of a gag being shoved into his mouth and felt the sting of ropes tightening against his wrists. As the darkness rose to claim him, he realized that Igor had outschemed him, and that when a deal seemed too good to be true, it most likely was.

11

As a small child, Ana had stood by Papa's side on the snow-covered streets of Salskoff, looking up at the Cyrilian Imperial Patrols with awe. She'd admired the way their blackstone-infused armor glittered in the sunlight and their pure white cloaks flapped against the brilliant blue sky. Even their horses had been a sight to behold: the tall valkryfs of the north, eyes the blue of ice, bred for speed and endurance and prized for their rare ability to scale snowy mountains using their split-toed hooves. She'd learned horsemanship on the backs of these creatures, and she'd dreamt of the day she would have an army of valkryfs and their masters under her command.

Imperial Patrols—heroic, majestic, and honorable.

She stared up at them now, standing in the wreckage of the pastry stall, their dark figures looming over her. Gone were their noble gazes and benevolent words. The kapitan, his white tiger's badge gleaming on his chest, snarled down, his weathered skin wrinkling like leather. Two others in his squad flanked a large blackstone-enforced prison wagon, a dozen or so paces behind.

A third man followed the kapitan like a shadow. Unlike the cloaks of the Patrols, his tunic and cloak were black, lined with gold; his hair was bleached like wheat left too long in the sun, his eyes the ice of glaciers in the Silent Sea of the North. There was something hard about his expression that made Ana clutch May's hand tighter.

"What is the disturbance?" demanded the kapitan. His cold eyes raked past Ana and May, lingered on the pastry vendor, and settled at last on the nobleman. "Mesyr?"

Ana took one slow step backward, and then another, May's hand tight in hers. If she inched back far enough, she would blend into the crowd of onlookers. There was a stall of kechyans several steps to her right that she could duck behind. The Whitecloaks would never find her. Not unless they had a yaeger—which was exceedingly rare.

"A-Affinite," wheezed the nobleman, who had pushed himself to his feet and was shakily brushing wooden splinters off his fine furs. "Filthy witches!"

Three, four steps. The kechyan stall was within reach—

"Where are you going?"

Ana's blood turned to ice. The kapitan's eyes, as emotionless as his voice, gazed straight at her.

"Stay where you are," he continued. "This is a routine check."

By her side, May was shaking, sucking in fast, shallow breaths.

Slowly, deliberately, the kapitan held out a black-gloved hand to the pastry vendor. "Your employment and identification papers."

"Ana." May was beginning to hyperventilate, her words rushing out quickly, unevenly. "We gotta go—they're bad men—"

Cold sweat slicked the nape of her neck as Ana watched

the pastry vendor fumble for scrolls in her tunic and then hold them out.

"A grain Affinite," the kapitan remarked with disinterest. He ran a cursory glance over the scrolls before tossing them to the ground.

"Ana," May pleaded. She was shrinking back, her eyes wide, her face drained of blood. "We don't have papers—"

Dread sank in Ana's stomach as the kapitan turned his lifeless gaze to her and May. She found herself rooted to the spot, her mind blank with fear and scattering any rational thoughts she might have had.

The kapitan's black gloves extended toward them. "Your employment or identification papers."

No, a part of Ana's brain screamed. *No, no, no, no, no*—

She cut herself off, drawing in a deep breath to steady her heartbeat. These were Imperial Patrols—defenders of the law, watchers of her empire. They could not mean harm.

Yet . . . she had never known them to check for employment and identification papers.

Sucking in another gulp of air, Ana fought to keep her voice level as she replied, "We don't have papers."

The kapitan's eyes narrowed, and he cut a glance to the blackstone wagon. It wasn't until then that Ana noticed the feeling of being watched, the hairs on her arms and neck prickling.

One of the Patrols gazed at her from beside the prison wagon. Clad in the same whites as his kapitan, he stood in the shadows, his eyes as piercing as daggers. A strange sensation crept through her: a subtle tugging, as though someone were pulling at invisible bonds in the same way she called on others' blood.

Yaeger, her senses screamed at her. *He's a yaeger.*

A hunter, in Old Cyrilian: a type of Affinite with the power to sense and control other Affinities. Kapitan Markov had told her these were recognized as the most powerful and rarest of Affinites, often scouted by Imperial Patrols to keep peace between Affinites and non-Affinites.

The yaeger's gaze sliced to his kapitan and the strange man dressed in black; he gave a curt nod.

The kapitan turned back to Ana. "It is unlawful for anyone to be found without proper identification documents—especially Affinites. We'll need to take you in for questioning. Our contractor can explain this to you." He cast a nod at the black-cloaked man.

"No." The sob was barely a breath from May's lips, loud enough for only Ana to hear. "Don't listen to them, Ana. He's a bad man. A broker."

A broker. Ana stared, her mind careening. The Whitecloaks, specifically, were meant to find and stop the brokers.

How had two figures on opposing sides of the law ended up working together?

Who do you think pays them more? The Empire? Or the profitable businesses that rely on them to employ Affinites? Ramson had asked.

It suddenly all clicked with the weight of a broken world: the picture she had been searching for in the dark, now blindingly bright.

Ana staggered back.

This was wrong—this was all wrong. The bad men were the Affinite traffickers and brokers that her mamika Morganya had described to her as crooked storybook villains. Not the Imperial soldiers who served her father and brother, who pledged to protect the Empire.

What kind of an empire had her father ruled?

"We are not—" Her voice shook, and whatever denial she'd been about to voice dissipated on her lips. The pastry vendor had retreated to her now-appeased employer's side, her eyes downcast, her face in the shadows, the employment contract trembling in her hands.

I am Anastacya Kateryanna Mikhailov, Ana wanted to scream, tears burning her eyes. *I am the Crown Princess of Cyrilia.*

Yet the tricky thing about truth, Ana realized, standing beneath the shadow of the Imperial Patrols with empty hands and a threadbare cloak, was that it meant nothing if it couldn't be proven.

And it struck her, in this very moment, that there was nothing at all different between her and the grain Affinite.

Dimly, she heard the kapitan issuing orders to the rest of his squad. "Prepare for lawful arrest *by force* should the subjects not comply."

The yaeger moved forward.

May screamed.

And Ana snapped.

She scooped May into her arms, swallowing a scream as she barreled through the crowd. She could sense the Whitecloaks behind them, the yaeger's control on her Affinity flowing and ebbing like waves. With his manipulation, her awareness of the blood around her flickered, throwing off her sense of balance. He was gaining on them—fast. And May was heavy.

She made a split-second decision. Ana set May down on the ground and gave the girl a hard push. May staggered. "Run," Ana ordered. "I'll be right behind you."

"No!" May screamed. "Ana—"

At that moment, the yaeger's control over her slipped. Her Affinity flared; she used that moment to latch on to May's blood. *I love you,* Ana meant to say, but she only managed, "I'm sorry."

She seized the blood in May's small body and flung the child as far back as she could.

Ana turned to face the yaeger. She was shaking, desperately grasping at her Affinity as it slid in and out of her command. The crowd around her parted in panic as the yaeger advanced on her. He'd slowed to a walk, his footsteps falling on the cobblestones like the beat of an execution drum.

Panic whitened her mind as she continued to back away.

Stop. She wanted to plead. *I am your princess. I am the Princess of Cyrilia.*

But being Princess had only meant a crown on her head and the walls of a palace to protect her from this fate.

The fate of being born an Affinite.

The yaeger was barely a dozen steps away now. She could see the chiseled lines of his face, the hard edges of his muscles like cut marble, trained to be lethal. His Affinity clamped over hers like an indomitable mental wall, and her Affinity vanished.

Still, Ana raised a trembling hand—

The ground exploded. The yaeger's face barely registered surprise before he was thrown backward, skidding across the street, cobblestones tumbling around him. A crack had split the road between Ana and the yaeger. Her confusion was mirrored on his face as they stared at the rocks and dirt that seeped out from the fissure, rising slowly into the air.

From a row of stalls behind them, a small figure stepped into the middle of the street.

May's fists were clenched, her brow furrowed in concentration. In the dead silence, her voice rang out sharp and clear across the street: "You will not hurt her."

She tilted her head. Without warning, the suspended rocks shot toward the yaeger. He grunted as a dozen fist-sized rocks slammed into him, pounding him backward.

His hold on Ana's Affinity wavered.

Ana acted. She smashed her Affinity down on the yaeger's bonds, seized him, and hurled him farther down the cobbled streets, away from May, away from *any* possibility of even reaching May. He'd have to kill Ana first

She felt a flash of triumph as he slammed onto the ground and lay there, motionless.

She didn't see the other Whitecloak until it was too late.

A shadow fell between the stalls behind May: a Whitecloak with a bow and arrow, aimed and ready.

Ana was already screaming, and even as she tore toward May, a part of her was telling herself that this was not real, not real, not real. Time seemed to slow as she ran with all the strength her body would give.

The arrow shot forward. May staggered. And then, slowly, she fell, soft and graceful as an autumn leaf.

Time had stopped. Ana was in one of those dreams where, no matter how hard she tried to run, she was moving too slowly.

Twelve paces.

Not. Enough.

From the shadows of the stalls, the black-cloaked broker emerged, the gold lining of his collar glinting in the setting sun as he bent down. May's head lolled like a rag doll's in his arms as he turned and sprinted for the prison wagon.

Fury exploded in Ana. *"No!"* she screamed, raising a hand and summoning her Affinity.

But there was nothing. Instead, she found that unfamiliar wall against her power again, unyielding and absolute.

Several paces from her, the yaeger pushed himself to his knees. Mud and blood ruined his perfect white cloak; already, bruises were beginning to blossom on his exposed skin. But Ana felt no satisfaction, only blind fury, as he lifted his eyes to meet her gaze. Her steps slowed.

A distance behind him, the broker had almost reached the wagon. May's limp form was slung across his shoulders, and Ana could make out the shine of her hair.

She glanced at the yaeger. Glanced back at May's disappearing head. And put a burst of speed into her steps.

The yaeger shot forward. His fingers latched on to her ankles and yanked. Ana flung her hands out, catching herself before she slammed into the cobblestones.

She twisted, spitting hair from her mouth and grappling for purchase on the ground. "Let me go!" she screamed, kicking at the yaeger, but his grip was steel against her legs.

Beyond the vast stretch of road, the prison wagon loomed, its doors open like the mouth of a hungry beast. The broker leaned into its shadow as he deposited a small, limp form into the wagon. May's head lolled once, and then disappeared behind the wagon's blackstone walls.

The other Whitecloak locked the doors.

Desperation as she'd never felt before twined around Ana, squeezing the air from her throat and wringing tears from her eyes. "May!" she bellowed, her voice cracking. *"MAY!"*

At her scream, someone looked back—but it wasn't May.

The broker with the sun-bleached hair turned to her. His pale eyes locked with hers. They narrowed for a moment, and then he turned and was gone.

Ana's hand closed around something hard—a piece of cobblestone, displaced by May earlier.

Picturing the broker's hateful blue eyes, Ana smashed the stone into the yaeger's face.

He let out a low groan, his grip on her legs slackening. His hold on her Affinity wavered again.

Ana was on her feet even before the yaeger rolled over, clutching his dripping nose. Dimly, she heard him shouting something at his squad, saw looks of panic flit across the Whitecloaks' faces as they mounted their horses.

She threw her Affinity out and ran, fighting the yaeger's block, her legs pumping desperately as she tried to close the gap between her and that black wagon.

The remaining Whitecloak spurred his horse, and the wagon jolted into movement, picking up speed. Only the kapitan circled toward them, bow and arrow out and cloak billowing behind him. "Kaïs!" he shouted.

The yaeger's answering call was cut short as Ana hurled her Affinity against his power. For a moment, his wall splintered; she sensed a glimmer of the bonds in the kapitan's body and grasped them—

The kapitan's eyes widened and his horse careened sharply

to one side as his body seized beneath her control. "What in the Deities—" His arrow tumbled from his grasp, and a glass vial shattered against the ground. Even from several dozen paces away, Ana could make out the green liquid oozing between the cracks of the road.

"Kapitan!" Behind her, the yaeger let out a choked cry. "You must retreat! She's dangerous!"

The kapitan hesitated, his eyes darting between Ana and his fallen soldier. Ana seized the opportunity. "Come get me, you sick bastard!" she shouted. *Make him angry. Goad him.* Anything to stop that blackstone wagon from leaving this square.

Yet as Ana flung her Affinity at the kapitan again, he seemed to arrive at a decision. With a last glance back, he turned his horse and galloped after his squad.

"No!" Ana choked. But the wagon and its flanking riders sped off through the stalls, growing smaller and smaller.

Hopelessness tightened around her throat.

She had no idea how long she ran, chasing the wagon even after it disappeared between the red-bricked dachas of Kyrov. It was only when she tripped over a loose cobblestone and fell to the ground, splitting the fabric of her gloves and cutting her palms, that she realized she was crying. And a different voice filled her head.

Don't go where I can't follow, May had asked of her.

She'd let happen what she'd sworn she'd never let happen to May. May had saved her in the moment she'd most desperately needed saving. And she had failed May.

And . . . it was *her* fault. Ana bit into her hand to stop herself from screaming, her tears mingling with blood and dust. In another life where she might have been born differently, *normally,* she would still be the Kolst Pryntsessa Anastacya Mikhailov, second heir to the throne of Cyrilia. And in that life, a kinder life, the laws would be just and the people in power would be good and the good people would win.

She pounded the cobblestones once, crimson smearing on the dusty ground. She could sense, through her Affinity, people milling around her and slowing down to look, but none stopped to help.

This was not that world, Ana thought. This world was neither just nor kind nor good, and you chose to keep fighting or to surrender.

Ana climbed to her feet, dusting off her tattered cloak as she turned to face the Vyntr'makt. Her Affinity flared with each step, the world thrumming with blood as she ran.

She found the yaeger where she'd left him. A small crowd had gathered, and several people knelt at his side with handkerchiefs and strips of gauze. How eager they were to help the monster draped in a cloak of white.

Ana focused her Affinity and flung several onlookers back, her hands raised for dramatic effect. "Leave," she snarled, her voice cutting through the shrieks of the crowd. "Leave, or I'll kill you all."

She turned to face the yaeger. Blood ran in rivulets from where she'd smashed the rock into his head, streaming down his cheeks. He glanced up at her from a bruising eye and tensed.

He was Nandjian, Ana realized with dull surprise, taking in his olive skin and dark hair. She thought of the ambassadors who had graced the Palace's Grand Throneroom during court sessions with Papa.

Had he traversed into Cyrilia of his own volition?

She felt his power descending over hers, but instead of the iron hold from before, it was softer. Weaker.

She shrugged him off easily and seized his blood, pulling him into a sitting position. He coughed, and crimson trickled from his lips. "That broker. Where is he taking her?"

The yaeger only looked at her, his mouth tightening.

Ana snapped his head back, tilting it so he could just barely breathe. For some reason, Ramson Quicktongue's face flashed before her. He wouldn't blindly threaten—he would find his opponent's weak point, find some kind of leverage . . . and push.

She knew next to nothing about this bastard, yet it was irreconcilable to her that he wore the Cyrilian tiger's badge of honor on his chest . . . and that he had let his comrade shoot an arrow at a ten-year-old. Ana wanted to rip the insignia from his armor.

"I won't ask again," she said.

His next words surprised her. "You're the Blood Witch of Salskoff," he rasped.

Ana's breath caught. In the legend, the Blood Witch had shown up in Salskoff's Winter Market on Fyrva'snezh and murdered dozens of innocent people. Vaporized them, so that there was nothing left of them afterward but blood running red rivers on the cobblestones, staining the snow. She had red eyes that gleamed with her blood magic, and teeth sharper than a tiger's. A deimhov from hell; a monster among humans.

Nobody had connected the Blood Witch to the sick princess who had been locked away in the Salskoff Palace since her childhood.

Ana tightened her grip on the yaeger's blood. "Then you know what I can do," she said quietly.

"I know you killed eight innocent people."

It was an accident. I was seven years old. The words almost—*almost*—left her lips. Instead, she said, "And I'll do it again, unless you give me what I want."

He hesitated.

Ana tilted her head to the bloodred glow of the setting sun, so that the crimson of her eyes caught the light. "Look at where we are. Look at all of these people around you—mothers, fathers, and children. They could all be dead within seconds, and it'll be because of you. You call yourself a soldier? Then protect your civilians." She tightened her grip on his blood, just to prove her point. "Tell me where he's taking the child."

A muscle twitched in the yaeger's jaw, and his eyes seemed to burn into hers for an eternity. Then he coughed once, and the fire went out. "Novo Mynsk," he said quietly.

"Where in Novo Mynsk?" she pressed. When he was silent, she lifted her chin to scrutinize the few vendors and spectators who still lingered behind their stalls. "Shall I prove the veracity of my promise? Whom shall I pick first? A child? Or her mother? And how shall I torture them so that their screams—"

"The Playpen. He's one of the Lilies. He'll employ her there as a performer."

She let go of him at once, turning away so he wouldn't see her shaking. It felt like someone else had been speaking through her lips, murmuring those cruel, barbaric words. As if Sadov's influence remained and she'd spoken his twisted thoughts.

As she drew her hood over her head, she wondered something darker—whether it was that Sadov's voice had become her own.

"Don't hurt them," the yaeger said. "Please."

The plea was soft, and she wished she hadn't heard it. Ana looked back. The yaeger was still sitting in the same spot, but something in his expression had shifted. He was begging her. And he was afraid.

Ana thought of the helplessness of the grain Affinite, of the sadness she'd seen in May's eyes when she'd first met her. And she saw an echo of that in this soldier's eyes.

Her anger dissipated like steam in the cold. "Why do you do this?" she asked instead. "You're one of them." A pause. "One of us."

"Do you think I have a choice?" His voice was raw. "In this empire, if I am not the hunter, then I become the hunted."

She would never forget the way he gazed up at her, yaeger and Affinite in one. Trapped in a corrupt system.

Your choices, Luka's voice whispered, but something in her brother's words was broken now, changed with the year she had spent away from the Palace. Choices were for those with privilege and power. When you had none, all you could do was survive.

She left before he could see how much her encounter with him had shaken her. She'd threatened to kill innocent people. She'd tortured a man.

I did it to save May, she told herself.

But perhaps all monsters were heroes in their own eyes.

12

News of the fight in the Vyntr'makt had spread through Kyrov like wildfire. Ana hurried along the streets that had only moments earlier been celebrating the arrival of winter. Now the bricks of the dachas glowed bloodred in the setting sun, and the shuttered storefronts gaped at her like empty eyes. She caught snatches of hushed conversation from the townspeople rushing home from a day's work.

Ana tugged her hood down lower and followed the steady stream of people away from the Vyntr'makt. Exhaustion was creeping over her—the bone-deep weariness that came from using her Affinity—and she needed to leave, *now,* before that squad of Whitecloaks brought back reinforcements.

She'd—miraculously—defeated one Whitecloak, but she shuddered at the thought of having to fight an entire squad. Her Affinity was a muscle, to be exercised daily, never to be pushed to the extreme for fear that she would lose control. And over the past years, Ana had exercised it too little, and recently, she'd stretched it too thin.

Inside a glass storefront, lacquered phoenixes and icehawks spun, catching the dusk light. She and May had been in that store barely half an hour ago, whispering about Whitecloaks as though they were a distant threat. She whipped her head away as she turned a corner, the ache of tears burning deep into her heart.

She was on a smaller, emptier street. Gone were the beautiful residential dachas, the decorated storefronts and polished streetlamps. Stone buildings with wooden roofs crowded close together, dilapidated and crumbling. And, at the end of the street, was a building with red-shingled roofs. A wooden sign announced in weathered gold letters: *The Gray Bear's Keep.*

Something about the inn struck her as *off*—perhaps it was the lack of music or conversation as she drew near, or the fact that, despite its shabby appearance, its doors were made of polished oak.

Her steps slowed of their own accord, and she came to a stop several buildings away. She'd just started to convince herself that she was being paranoid when the oak doors swung open and two men exited.

Ana swung herself into the shadow of a nearby doorway and peered out. There was something strange about these men, too. One, dressed in a black riding cloak and leather boots, moved with unnatural, predatory grace. Ana caught the glint of not one but two daggers on his belt as he retrieved a bulging pouch from his cloak. *A mercenary.*

The other, tall and lumbering as a bear, wore a grimy bartender's apron. He glanced around furtively before reaching for the pouch, the greed on his face unmistakable even from this distance.

The mercenary tossed the bag at the bartender. Coins clinked as the bartender snatched it from the air. He missed—or ignored—the derisive look the mercenary shot him as he pulled open the strings to examine the bag's contents.

The mercenary tilted his head to the empty street corner. Waiting.

A shiver passed through Ana. Exhausted as she was, she kept her Affinity flared.

As though on cue, a third man appeared around the corner, leading two horses. This man was dressed like the first: black cloak, black boots, and black hood obscuring his face. He turned the horses around, and as the mercenaries mounted, Ana's stomach dropped.

She'd thought the second horse carried a large sack—but she realized now that it was actually a person. A horrible, sinking feeling gripped her as the horses shifted and the captive's face came into plain view. Tawny hair, chiseled jaw, and broken nose. Ramson Quicktongue was these mercenaries' latest haul.

Panic twisted her stomach. She thought of lunging out with her Affinity right there, right now. But her bones creaked in protest, and she clutched the wall to steady herself. There was no chance she could beat three people in her current state. Besides, there could be more of them.

Yet she couldn't afford to lose Ramson Quicktongue, either.

She couldn't beat them by brute force. She'd have to play it smart. Attack from behind.

Deities, she thought. One night with Quicktongue and she was already thinking like him. The Ana of a year ago would have valued honor and faced her enemies head-on. But then, she supposed, in a world of con men, crime lords, and cutthroats, there was no honor and there were no rules to the game. You only played to win.

Ana watched the two mercenaries round the corner and held her breath, counting to ten. When she stepped out onto the street, only the bartender remained, cradling his pouch of coins.

He turned when she was several paces behind him, but by then it was too late. Ana's hand went up and he froze, pain and shock flashing across his face as he inevitably felt her control on his blood. Ana gave a tug, just for emphasis, and the pouch of gold tumbled from his hands. Goldleaves spilled onto the ground.

"You move, and I'll kill you before you can raise a pinky," Ana said. The bartender looked at her with renewed fear. "Now I'm going to let you go, because I need you to talk."

A fresh wave of fatigue washed over her when she dropped her hold on him. She needed to conserve what little strength she had left.

The bartender stood statue-still.

Ana tilted her head. "Tell me. Who were those men?"

His eyes slid to the streets around them, as though fearing the mercenaries would emerge from the shadows. Fear was good, though. Fear was a weapon, as Sadov had taught her so very well.

"Bounty hunters," the bartender said, his words slurring with a lowborn Cyrilian accent.

"And where are they taking him?"

"Kerlan," the bartender whispered, growing paler still. The name seemed to cast a shadow over him, cinching fear tight around his neck.

"Who?"

"Kerlan. *Lord* Kerlan."

"Who is that? And where is he?"

"The Head of the Order, in Novo Mynsk."

She'd meant to ask him what Order he spoke of, but her heart caught at the words *Novo Mynsk.* May was headed there.

All other thoughts scattered. Her direction was clear. "I need a horse," Ana said, taking a wager.

The bartender nodded frantically. "The stables. Choose whichever you'd like."

She rewarded him with a flat smile like the one she'd so often seen on Sadov's face. "One more thing. I'll be taking this." She scooped up the pouch of goldleaves that had been abandoned on the dirt road. She didn't feel bad for that, Ana realized, as she turned on her heels and strode toward the stables in the back. After all, the bounty hunters had paid that gold for Quicktongue, and since Quicktongue was *her* prisoner, it stood to reason that she should take the gold.

"Stay there until you can't hear my horse anymore," she called over her shoulder. "You move, and I'll bleed you dry."

The stables were surprisingly well kept. Ana selected a valkryf with a coat the color of milk, already saddled, as though the owner had expected a short stop. When she rode out of the stables at a brisk trot, the bartender was still standing where she'd left him. She kept her Affinity honed on him until she was far enough away that the glow of his blood had faded to a flicker, and then to nothing.

The sun had almost set, its light bleeding out over the expanse of the Syvern Taiga like a last breath. Storm clouds gathered over the horizon, and the air thickened with the promise of rain.

Ana stretched her Affinity out, sweeping the vicinity for the bounty hunters' trail. The Gray Bear's Keep was close enough to the edge of town that she didn't have to wade through a thick crowd of bodies before she closed in on the bounty hunters. There was no mistaking it; she sensed, blurred and distant, three figures: two with blood fast-flowing, and one sluggish, several hundred paces ahead of her.

As she steered her horse around the last dacha, she caught sight of two horsemen in the distance, speeding into the shadows of the Syvern Taiga. She suddenly wished she had some sort of weapon on her. She'd never learned to spar—or to even handle a sword—and coming into a fight with a weakened Affinity and empty hands made her feel extremely vulnerable.

But she didn't have a choice. May was gone, her alchemist still missing, and her only hope lay unconscious on the back of one of those mercenaries' horses. Ana had no weapon and no plan, but she also had nothing more to lose.

A hundred paces. She drew steadily nearer. At any moment, the mercenaries could turn and catch sight of her.

Fifty paces. She could see them clearly now, moving much more slowly than she with the unconscious con man tied to a horse.

And they saw her.

They slowed their horses and rounded the edge of the trees, hands lingering near their swords. A cold wind stirred, rattling the dry winter leaves across dead grass. Shadows flickered across the men's faces.

Ana gave her hood a tug. Her heart thudded painfully in her chest, and she found herself reaching out with her Affinity, keeping it poised as she would a blade. A sense of calm enveloped her as her Affinity settled over the blood pulsing through the mercenaries' bodies. Hers to command, if she wished.

She grasped that thought, letting it fuel her courage. "Release that man. He is my charge," she called.

The mercenary riding alone—the leader—spoke first. Even on his horse Ana could see that he was an impossibly tall man. He was the one with a black beard, the one she had watched hand the pouch of goldleaves to the bartender. She was close enough to hear his low growl. "You got some guts, lass, riding after us alone. Got a death wish, or what?"

"You must have heard by now," Ana said, "what happened at the Vyntr'makt in Kyrov?"

"What? You lost your damashka doll?" Blackbeard and his companion rasped with laughter.

Ana kept her face blank. She knew from lessons with her brother that some negotiations required placidity. Others called for firmness. And finally, in the rarest of cases, you showed your power.

Slowly, Ana slid off her glove and stretched her fingers, lifting her hand high.

She summoned her Affinity.

The mockery on the mercenaries' faces vanished, replaced by alternating horror and disgust, as the veins in her hand began to turn dark, from the tips of her fingers to her elbow.

"An Affinite," sneered Blackbeard. "You think you can threaten us just because you're one of those deimhovs? Oi, Stanys. Watch me cut this witch down."

"Need help, boss?" his companion called.

"Take the quarry to a safer place." Blackbeard turned to Ana with a malicious grin. "The witch is mine."

Anger bottled at her throat, but she forced it down, down as she thought of Luka. Her bratika had always strived for peace where possible. Ana gave it one last try. "Hand him over now, and no one has to be hurt."

Blackbeard's expression darkened. "I'll teach you all about *hurting*," he snarled, and launched his horse toward her.

Her horse shrieked at the sudden assault, springing back. Ana had just enough time to feel the shift in balance before the saddle tilted beneath her and she tumbled off. By instinct, she latched on to Blackbeard's blood and pulled.

His curse rang out, and she saw him fall just as her back jolted against the ground, knocking the wind from her. Nearby, there was a thud as Blackbeard broke his fall with a roll.

Ana sucked in a deep breath, willing her stunned limbs to work again. She heard the *schick* of Blackbeard's dagger as he drew it from its sheath. "Damned deimhov," he snarled, and sprang.

Through the haze in her mind, she grasped at her Affinity.

Blackbeard drove his blade down. A rumble of thunder muffled her scream as pain seared over her shoulder. Blood bloomed across her senses.

The mercenary's smile sliced white. Pinning her down with his body, he brought his dagger to her cheek. In the dim light, she could make out the green-tinted liquid as it formed a drop at the tip of the blade. Terror filled her. "Recognize that, you witch?" Blackbeard's tone was triumphant, mocking. "You think just because you're an Affinite, that makes you more powerful than us?"

Slowly, she was regaining control of her body; the fog in her mind was dissipating. Ana twitched a finger.

"Think again. You made a dumb choice, revealing yourself to us, deimhov. I dominate monsters like you. I *trade* monsters like you." Blackbeard brought his face close to hers. "You don't scare me."

With his other hand, he shoved a glass vial of Deys'voshk to her lips. Bitter liquid filled her mouth. She was back in the dungeons again, metal chains and straps holding her in place, the taste of the pungent poison flooding her senses. *My little monster,* Sadov whispered.

She choked now, her mind paralyzed with fear, her throat swallowing the Deys'voshk as she'd been conditioned.

Something splashed on her face. At first, Ana thought she was crying, but as another drop landed on her face, then another, she realized that it was raining.

The sky lit up with a streak of lightning, and thunder clapped as rain began to pour. A cold wind tore at her hair, urging her in angry whispers. She was not in a dungeon, this was not Sadov, and she was not the helpless, frightened girl she'd been.

And she had developed a tolerance to the Deys'voshk.

Blackbeard tossed his vial onto the grass. Lightning flashed, reflecting off the glass, an arm's length from Ana. "Still feeling powerful, you witch?" he hissed in her ear. "I don't have a particular preference for your type, but I know some people who do." He gripped her chin hard enough to bruise. Ana forced her eyes to remain on Blackbeard as her hand snaked out along the grass. "Lots've things one could do to a pretty face like yours. Lots've goldleaves one could pay." His grin widened, and his hand wandered to his belt. "But first, I'll have to try it out for myself—"

Ana's hand closed around the glass vial. With all her strength, she smashed it into his face.

The shards pierced her palm, sending sharp streaks of pain up her arm, but Ana only felt grim satisfaction as the man howled, clutching his face. Blood ran down his cheeks, and when he removed his hand, Ana saw that a shard of glass had lodged itself in his right eye.

She lashed out. Her Affinity was still there, still strong despite the mist of Deys'voshk that had started creeping across her senses. She locked on the blood dripping down Blackbeard's face, seizing that and the bonds inside his body and giving it all a single, vicious tug.

It was like uncorking a bottle of wine; blood spilled from Blackbeard's mouth at her coaxing, running through the grass in rivulets with rainwater.

Die, Ana thought, fury coiling around her, white-hot. What he had wanted to do to her, what he'd probably done to dozens of other powerless Affinites—she would make sure he was *never* able to do any of it again.

Die.

Lightning lit up Blackbeard's bloodied face, and for a moment, Ana saw the face of the broker who had stolen May, his pale-ice eyes boring into hers.

Wrath burned through her veins; she gave a violent pull. There was the wet sound of flesh ripping. Blackbeard made a choking sound as his chest tore open; for a moment he hung suspended in time, mouth agape, eyes wide, droplets of his blood glistening like rubies in the rain.

Then his eyes shuttered, and he keeled over on the grass with a dead thud.

Exhaustion smothered Ana, so suddenly that her vision blurred around the edges. Her limbs were leaden; she felt as though she were sinking into the mud. She could no longer tell whether the dizziness was from the Deys'voshk working its poisonous effect in her system or from overexertion. Perhaps it was both.

"What the—"

Twenty paces away, the second mercenary—Stanys—had dismounted. He stared at his leader in disbelief before his eyes landed on Ana. "What the hell did you do, you deimhov?"

Her head swam as she pushed herself to her feet. Blackbeard's dagger lay in the mud next to his body, discarded, but she didn't think she'd have the strength to pick it up. "Leave, or I'll kill you, too." Her voice barely carried over the rushing sound of rain.

Stanys palmed his dagger. There was a challenge in his eyes as he took a step forward. Then another. And another.

He was testing the waters, seeing how close he could get before she used her Affinity. Seeing if she still *could.*

Ana's legs trembled with the effort of standing. The world swayed as she grasped for her Affinity. *Please.* She'd hated her Affinity, the thought of using it . . . but now she needed it. There was nothing else standing between her and the blade in Stanys's hand.

Her head split with pain. Ana dropped to her knees. As she lifted her head to look at Stanys, she realized that her Affinity had reached its limit. She might as well have been trying to grasp empty air, the twisting wind.

No, she thought, shaking, her head pounding with each footfall of the approaching man.

Stanys's shadow fell over her; she could see the fur of his boots from where she knelt, the curve of his blackstone-steel blade that parted the rain. Her hands shook. Was this it?

The mercenary's dagger flashed. Lightning streaked across the sky, illuminating his blade . . . and the shadow behind.

Stanys swung his blade down.

And met metal. A shrill screech rang out in the night. A battle cry.

"Move!" Ramson shouted. With a last spurt of strength, Ana rolled away from them just as Ramson lunged forward.

Ana lifted her head and watched as Ramson Quicktongue, self-serving con man and egotistic bastard, fought for their lives.

13

The mercenary charged, dual daggers glinting like the eyes of a demon through the heavy rain. Ramson parried the blow head-on, grunting as he narrowly dodged the swipe of the second dagger. He twirled and slashed out. The tip of his sword swerved in a graceful arc—but nowhere close to the mercenary.

His opponent pounced again, twin blades unrelenting. Metal clanged as Ramson blocked one dagger. This time, the second bit him in a vicious slash across his forearm.

Grimacing, he pivoted out of the way, backing up as far as he could without drawing the man closer to the witch. Blood dripped from the wound in his arm, mingling with the rain. *Shit,* he thought, readjusting his slippery grip and shaking his head to clear the dizziness from Igor's blow earlier. *Shit.* His opponent was taller and stronger.

And Ramson was rusty.

Think, he told himself desperately. He needed to buy time.

His enemy lunged. Ramson met the twin blades with a blow of his own, slashing downward. Metal screeched. He twisted his blade sharply, using a technique he'd learned from his swordmaster, momentarily locking the two daggers together. The bounty hunter looked up at him and bared his teeth.

"Just a reminder," Ramson called over their entangled blades. "Lord Kerlan probably wants me in one piece, right?"

"I'll bring you in one piece," the mercenary snarled. "After I cut you up and stitch you back together again."

It wasn't a confirmation, but it was just as much: Kerlan was hunting him. Though Ramson would, ironically, bet his life that Kerlan wanted him back alive. If Kerlan wanted you dead, you'd wake with a dagger against your neck and your throat slit before you could even scream.

Most people, anyway. There was a reason Ramson had been Kerlan's Deputy.

As long as Kerlan still wanted him alive, Ramson had a bargaining chip.

With a grunt, Ramson turned and twisted his blade free, pivoting full circle so that he was several paces back, sword raised. "No need to be so angry over your dead partner. With him gone, you'll now have twice the reward."

"I don't give a rat's ass about him." The mercenary raised a dagger, pointing over Ramson's shoulder. "Once I take care of you, I'll make that witch feel living hell before she dies."

Ramson's blood turned stone-cold. He knew these types of men: cutthroats who'd known nothing but violence their entire lives. To Ramson, violence was a means to an end. To these men, violence had no end.

You could run, a voice inside him urged. *Leave the girl to him and take the chance to escape.*

He'd kill her. Do worse things to her.

You don't care, the voice insisted. *You made the mistake of caring before. And they ended up dead anyway.*

Logic urged him that escape was the best course of action. Calculation told him that the mercenary was taller and stronger, and that his own odds of winning were narrower than a new moon.

Yet something more powerful than logic and more compelling than calculation roared in his veins as he angled his blade at the mercenary. Ramson dug his heels into the ground. "She's mine," he snarled. "And I don't share."

With a growl, his enemy rushed forward. Ramson darted back, dodging each whip-fast slash of the two alternating blades. Swerve, duck, twirl, parry, as though he were in a deadly dance, his moves light and fluid. The lessons of his youth were coming back to him and he felt as though he had been transported to another time and place, when his swordsmaster was bearing down on him beneath the brilliant blue of a Bregonian sky

As fluid as the river, as strong as the sea.

This was just another lesson; just another dance.

Ramson leapt out of the way as the mercenary's blades slashed at him, so fast that they were a silver-gray blur in the rain. Blow after blow, the mercenary bore down, his slashes growing faster and stronger. Ramson dodged. Face, throat, chest, legs—back and back, the song of their blades rising to a crescendo.

Ramson feinted left; his opponent lunged.

Ramson slashed right; his opponent dodged.

Bit by bit, Ramson's exhaustion began to show. His limbs ached. Soon his weakness would cost him.

Ramson leapt back as the mercenary swung his blades down, but he felt the sharp sting of metal across his chest. Blood warmed his clothes. He barely had enough time to glance up when the mercenary's fist collided with his face.

Pain exploded in his jaw. Black spots filled his vision and the world spun as he reeled off balance. He plunged backward into cold, wet mud.

Gasping, he rolled to his side, reaching for his sword.

A dark shape burst from the curtain of rain, and the mercenary was on him, landing one, two, three vicious punches in his abdomen. Ramson retched; stars erupted before him.

A flash of metal. Kneeling atop Ramson, the mercenary drove his blade down.

Ramson's hands flew up. His arms screamed; his legs felt like cotton; his head was light from the breaths that he could not draw.

A savage grin split the mercenary's face as he threw his body weight into pushing the dagger down, its steely edge glinting like a wicked promise. The man was going to sink the blade into Ramson's heart. Slowly.

I'm going to die.

The tip of the dagger pressed into his rib cage, drawing blood. A strangled yell tore from Ramson's throat as he gave one final push—

And suddenly, the pressure on his chest and on his arms was gone. The mercenary's head flew back sharply, throat exposed. For a moment, he was frozen, outline rigid in the rain as though he was grappling with an invisible force. And then he toppled into the mud.

Ramson scrambled into a crouch. Even as he stumbled away, the mercenary began to rise.

But it was the figure ten paces behind the mercenary, barely an outline in the falling rain, that caught Ramson's attention.

The witch was on her hands and knees, the crimson in her eyes receding as they shifted away from the mercenary. Blood dripped from her nose and mouth. For a moment, their gazes met. And then she collapsed.

Ramson had heard of Affinites surpassing their limits. Affinities drew energy from their bodies, and overexertion could lead to unconsciousness or, in the rarest of cases, death.

For a split second, staring at the witch's still frame, he wondered whether she'd died, and how he would feel about that. She was a Trade and a valuable asset, so that would be a loss . . . but there was something more tugging at his conscience.

She'd saved him again. For the second time, he owed the witch a blood debt.

Long ago, his father—the demon who called himself his father—had taught him the meaning of blood debts, of honor, and of courage. Ramson had made himself forget almost all memories of that man. But today, with the rain roaring all around him, phantom shapes rose from the ground, whispering to him in his father's words.

Lightning flashed, outlining the mercenary's towering form amid the slashing rain. His sword gleamed wet as he turned to Ana's crumpled form.

Ramson's head spun. The ground blurred, weaving in and out of focus.

Move. Ramson gouged his nails into the mud, struggling to

regain control of his muscles. Something rough and hard dug into his palm. He lifted his hand. Half-buried in the muddy water beneath him was the coarse, wet rope that he'd easily shimmied out of while the mercenaries had been distracted by Ana.

Ramson's hands closed around the rope, thick as a vessel's anchor line.

Sudden inspiration struck.

He was weakened and exhausted, with no leverage over this mercenary in a sword fight. Yet outside of swordplay, Ramson did have one advantage.

Before he'd become a Cyrilian crime lord, Ramson had been a sailor. A blue-blooded Bregonian sailor.

He stood, gripping his sword and stretching the long coil of rope between his hands. Within a few seconds, his sailor's hands had worked the end into a bowline with a loop large enough to fit a man's head. *As fluid as the river,* he thought.

The rain fell so thickly now, it was difficult to see past a dozen paces. The roar of the deluge blocked out any other sound. He was on a ship again, in the middle of a storm, navigating with nothing but a broken compass and that boy with the thin, sharp voice by his side.

Ramson clenched his lasso, his muscles coiled tighter than a spring. "Hey, horseface!" he yelled. "Find your balls and take on someone your own size, won't you?"

The mercenary turned. A snarl split his ugly face as he palmed his daggers. "I'll snap you like a stick," he growled, and hurtled toward him.

Ramson leapt back. In an extension of the same motion, he

whipped out the length of rope, lashing it at his enemy. The motion was smooth, familiar. He'd done it a thousand times in a life long past.

The rope met its mark. Like a living thing, it whipped around the mercenary's neck.

Ramson threw his weight backward and pulled, sharply and with all his strength. The mercenary stumbled off balance, his legs tangling as he fell to the ground. His fingers scrabbled at the noose around his neck.

Ramson leaped forward, the hilt of his dagger slick but firm in his hands. He plunged it through skin and sinew and flesh, and slashed upward.

The mercenary jerked, and with a few more twitches, his struggles ceased. Blood gushed, quietly pooling around him.

Ramson sank to his knees. The rain fell steadily, already washing away the blood on his hands. He drew a deep breath, trying to still the frantic galloping of his heart and his shaking limbs.

He'd been careless; he'd almost died. Perhaps prison had made him slower, softer. He couldn't afford that again, because next time, the witch might not be there to help him.

He was cold and drenched and injured, and he would have willingly handed over half the goldleaves in his possession for a soft bed, a warm fire, and a good bottle of Bregonian brandy right then. But he needed to move—quickly. There was no telling whether the mercenaries had allies close by.

Groaning, he pushed himself to his feet.

The witch lay motionless by the trunk of a tree, but it wasn't her he looked at. Ramson paused at the body of the first mercenary. The man's mouth was open, his face frozen in a silent scream, his skin oddly colorless, as though the blood had been drained from it.

And it had, Ramson realized with sickening dread. The rainwater pooling around the body bled into crimson, the color seeping into the mud.

He'd heard a tale once: a terrible haunting that had occurred ten years back with an Affinite. The bodies, twisted like a grotesque piece of artwork. The looks of terror on the victims' faces. The lack of puncture wounds. And the blood, all the blood . . .

They'd called her the Blood Witch of Salskoff—a story a decade old, at this point, the culprit having vanished to never be seen again. Some had taken it as a sign that Affinites were growing more powerful, that darker powers graced these monsters sculpted by the hands of demons.

Ramson had thought it all a pile of waffles. But that hadn't stopped him from keeping his eye out for the powerful Affinite who had become that myth.

He'd simply never thought she'd come looking for *him*.

A cough snatched his attention. He hurried to the witch. Blood dripped from her nose. She was shivering, but she was conscious.

"Are you all right?" He touched a finger to her cheek; her skin was colder than ice. For the second time since they'd met, he examined her, running his gaze over her elegant cheekbones, the heart-shaped face and sharp chin that rendered her beautiful yet feral in appearance. She was young, too young, to be the Blood Witch of Salskoff—yet as he reached forward and tipped her face up, he caught the fading red hue of her eyes.

Something stirred in his memory again—she looked faintly

familiar, like a portrait he'd come across many years ago that had left a single, deep impression. But that was impossible.

Ramson let his hand drop. "How did you find me?"

"The Gray Bear's Keep. The bartender."

"He told you?" She nodded. Ramson cursed. "We have to move. He'll send men after us. Can you stand?"

She tilted her head in a motion that might have been a nod or a shake. "I took a horse." Her voice was barely a whisper, and she nodded toward the trees behind her. "That way."

The mercenaries' horses had fled, which left them with a single steed—the one Ana had stolen. With a resigned sigh, he straightened and went in search of the horse.

Finding the beast was hell itself, with the rain-turned-sleet reducing his vision, and his boots squelching through mud with every step. When he did see its pale outline, he almost laughed.

"A valkryf?" he asked when he led the horse back. "Igor must be cursing the Deities that you took the most valuable living creature in his tavern." The witch was curled against the tree in the same position as he'd left her. When she didn't respond, he dropped the reins and knelt by her, lifting her chin and forcing her face toward his. "Witch?" he breathed. "Ana?"

Her eyelashes fluttered. Ramson cursed. She was going to pass out again—and that would make it hugely inconvenient for him to hoist her onto the horse. "Ana," he said urgently, shaking her shoulder. "I need you to stay awake for a little while longer. Can you do that?"

Her head dipped in the faintest of nods.

He stood and suddenly realized what was wrong. The absence of curious ocean-colored eyes. "Where's May?"

Ana's face had been drawn and tired previously, but a steely spark had shown in her eyes. At the mention of May, though, whatever remaining resolve in her seemed to dissolve. Ana's face crumpled, and such raw sorrow and vulnerability crossed her features that Ramson looked away. It felt as though he was gazing at something intensely private.

A sob gurgled from her throat. "They took her." Her shoulders drooped and she wrapped her shaking arms around herself. "The Whitecloaks. I couldn't . . . I couldn't—"

"We'll get her back." He grasped the first comforting phrase that came to mind, and it was the first that wasn't intentionally a lie. "But right now, we need to move. Can you stand?"

She stirred weakly. Blood continued to drip from her nose.

Ignoring the shaking in his own limbs, Ramson bent down, wrapped an arm around her waist, and hoisted her to her feet.

They staggered unevenly to Ana's horse. It stood silently in the downpour with the quintessential patience of a valkryf.

Grunting, Ramson heaved the witch—Ana—onto the saddle. Keeping his hand on her back to steady her, he swung himself up behind her. As he took the reins in his hands, he felt a renewed sense of power surge through him despite the battered state of his body. He was alive, with a powerful Affinite beside him, riding a valkryf to shelter. Things had improved significantly since his kidnapping.

Ana shifted, reaching for something in front of her. With what seemed like tremendous effort, she lifted a large leather pouch for him to see. "I took this from the bartender," she croaked. "Since I won you from the bounty hunters, I suppose it belongs to me now."

Ramson stared at the bulging pouch of goldleaves in her hands, a laugh caught in his throat. For once, he had no interest in the gold. There were so many things he wanted to say to her, so many words at the tip of his tongue. *Thank you for coming after me. Thank you for fighting for me. Thank you for saving my life.*

But Ramson couldn't bring himself to utter any of those. Instead, he gave a raspy chuckle, tapped the pouch, and said, "I've taught you well."

14

Ana awoke slowly to the cool scent of a rain-soaked world and the crackling of a fire.

Everything hurt. She had the strange sensation that every part of her had turned to stone—heavy, cold stone—and she would never move an inch again.

Blearily, she opened her eyes. Just as reluctantly, the world came back into focus in a blur of light and shadows. She was lying on a hard stone floor. All around her, great pillars rose, curving into arched ceilings high above her head. The stone was embellished with ornate carvings, and she thought of the temples she'd frequented back in Salskoff. Men and women danced in a never-ending circle in a weaving interlude of the four seasons, from flowers to fall leaves to flakes of snow.

Spring. Summer. Autumn. Winter.

She was in a Temple of Deities, in the middle of the Syvern Taiga, judging from the whispers of the trees outside. Moonlight dripped through the cracked glass of the long windows, casting the world in silhouettes and light. At the top of the dome, circular windows formed a ring around the center. The windows were split into quadrants, each with a carving inside:

a flower, a sun, a leaf, and a snowflake. The Deities' Circle—the Deys'krug.

Light filtered through the carvings and cast them in overlapping shadows on the white marble floor. A slight wind stirred, and as always, when she found herself in a temple, she thought of her aunt. Mamika Morganya had always devoutly worshipped the Deities, kneeling in the Palace temple with her dark hair twined in a braid, her beautiful doe eyes closed. If Ana closed her eyes now, she could almost hear the sigh of her mamika's silk kechyan, the soft clinks of a silver Deys'krug around her neck.

Her heart ached as she thought of her mamika. It was her aunt who had taught her to interpret the legends of the Deities, to find a sliver of relief in a world that despised Ana and her kind.

Ana pushed herself up, drawing a deep breath and wincing as she felt a sharp pain in her midriff. One hand darted to her abdomen; the other reached out for May.

Her hand clasped empty air.

Details of the previous night came crashing back. The rain. The mercenaries. The blood. Bile rose in her throat; she rubbed her eyes to chase away Blackbeard's image, his face contorting, crimson spilling from his mouth.

Literally bled dry.

The work of the deimhov.

But . . . there had also been something else. Someone lifting her onto a horse, holding her steady throughout the night as they rode through a dark, rain-beaten forest. She'd lost consciousness at some point . . . and yet . . .

Ana touched the roughspun linen of her undertunic and

breeches, her hands automatically tugging for a hooded cloak that wasn't there. It lay strewn out across a stone by the fire, drying. Her rucksack sat nearby.

"Finally," came a familiar voice, startling her. In the shadows beneath a pillar with the carving of a leaping fish, a figure moved. Ramson Quicktongue leaned into the firelight, eyes glinting, mouth curved in that infuriating grin. "I was tired of checking whether you'd died."

Unease coursed through her. How long had he been sitting there, watching her? Last night had been a mistake—she'd overspent her Affinity and left herself defenseless. He could easily have killed her.

But . . . he hadn't.

Ana narrowed her eyes. "I'm fine, thank you for asking." Her voice came out in a rasp, as though someone were rubbing sandpaper down her throat.

Ramson chuckled and stood, clutching a waterskin. As he drew closer, she realized that the dark patches on his face were not shadows, but blooming bruises that were turning a nasty shade of purple. "Thank you for saving my life, Ramson," he recited, spreading his hands and sauntering over. "Thank you for keeping me warm and dry, Ramson. Thank you for feeding me water and making sure I stayed alive, Ramson." He paused as he reached her, and sank into a bow. "You're very welcome, meya dama."

She glared at him, but softened as he passed her the waterskin. As she guzzled down the cool rainwater, she suddenly realized how thirsty and how hungry she was. "How long was I asleep?"

"One day."

The words hit her like a punch. They had lost an entire day's time doing nothing—*nothing,* when they should have been going after those Whitecloaks who had taken May.

May.

Panic seized her. The world tilted sharply when she scrambled to her feet. She slammed into the wall, pain bursting in her shoulder. "We need to go," she gasped. "We've lost too much time, we—"

Ramson was talking over her, his voice raised. "Calm your sails. We can't leave now—"

"They have her!" Her voice rose hysterically. "They have May. The yaeger—he said they were going to lock her up—"

"Ana, stop!" His voice rang sharply in the empty temple chamber. The easy smile had slipped from Ramson's face, and his hands were raised in a placating gesture. "Stop and *think.*"

A lump rose in her throat as she thought of May, standing alone in that empty square, fists clenched. *You will not hurt her.*

Tears burned behind her eyes. She had promised to protect May forever. "All right," she said, and though her voice shook slightly, she steeled it. She was going to get May back. And she would do it Ramson's way—by thinking through it thoroughly, and coming up with a plan and ten backup plans. "Sit."

Ramson's brows twitched, but he gave a seemingly good-natured shrug and sat across from her.

"You're going to help me get her back, con man."

"Me? Deities, who would have thought?"

"I'm not playing around. I don't care if it isn't part of our Trade. I saved you from whatever fate those bounty hunters had in mind for you. Since you speak so well in the language of bargaining, let me put it this way: you owe me, and you're going to pay me back."

"Since you think you speak so well in the language of bargaining, let me tell *you* this." Ramson's eyes had taken on a playful glint, and he leaned forward as he spoke. "If you hadn't saved me, you would have lost your Trade and your precious alchemist."

She would not be distracted by the taunts he threw her way. "I left you alone for thirty minutes and you were outsmarted by a bartender and two mercenaries." Her mood perked slightly at the sullen look that flitted across his face. Ana leaned forward, mirroring his pose. They were barely an arm's length from each other. "Why did they kidnap you? Who's hunting you?"

"I told you. It's the mark of an excellent crime lord to have many enemies."

"It's also the mark of an excellent crime lord to be able to *defeat* his enemies." Ana leveled an even gaze on him. "You need me. You need my Affinity. I'm your Trade. And I'll only uphold it if you help me."

Ramson ran a hand through his hair. "If you want to save May, we may not make it in time to find your alchemist. Whose name and location I now have, by the way."

He'd stolen the breath from her again. Yet Ana found herself leaning forward, reeled in by his line. "Where is he? Why won't we make it?"

"The only way we can find him," Ramson said, "is if we arrive in Novo Mynsk before the Fyrva'snezh. There's an event that we should . . . attend."

"Novo Mynsk," she repeated breathlessly. "That's where they're taking May. They're going to make her perform at a place called the Playpen."

"Who told you?"

"The yaeger—the Whitecloak."

"Ah," Ramson said slowly. "That . . . complicates things quite a bit."

"It doesn't. Our destination is Novo Mynsk."

Ramson sighed. "There is a name you should know. Alaric Kerlan. Remember it well."

That name again. The Gray Bear's Keep bartender had said it. He'd called him "Lord," but there was something more alarming, something that hadn't clicked until now—

"Alaric Kerlan," she whispered. "You mean A. E. Kerlan? The founder of the Goldwater Trading Group?" It was a name most nobles in the Cyrilian Empire were familiar with. Ana had read entire tomes of Cyrilian history with the Goldwater Trading Group lauded as a turning point for Cyrilia's modern economy. Yet for the greatest businessman in the Empire, A. E. Kerlan remained reclusive. The most anyone knew of him was that he was a nobody who had come from the gutters of Bregon and single-handedly built a thriving trading route between the then-run-down Goldwater Port and the rest of the world.

Caution flickered in Ramson's eyes. "Yes," he admitted, "but also the most powerful Affinite broker in the Empire."

"What?" Her world tilted. Ana gripped her arm, nails digging into flesh. "You're lying." The words came out sharp as shards of glass.

The founder of the Goldwater Trading Group—the largest business corporation in the Cyrilian Empire—an Affinite broker?

"I assure you, there are plenty of times I've lied to you, but this is not one of them," Ramson answered, deadpan.

Something in her was unraveling, her image of her empire crumbling into pieces and rearranging themselves into something sinister and strange and utterly unfamiliar. "How do you know?"

It sounded like such a naïve question. Did everyone around her know?

Had Papa known?

"It's my vocation to know things," Ramson said. "Now, as I was saying, Kerlan is the complication to our plan." He reached for her rucksack and fumbled through it, producing her map. With a flourish, he held it up and pointed. "Novo Mynsk is Kerlan's territory. If May is being carted there, the broker must be under Kerlan's Order. You say she's going to perform at the Playpen? That is owned by Kerlan. And it just so happens that your alchemist is a close associate of his."

It was a struggle to bring her focus back to him. Ana tamped down the maelstrom of her thoughts, clearing her mind. She could think about her broken world later. Right now her sole objective was to save May. "So what's the complication?" she asked wearily. "We'll rescue May, and then locate the alchemist."

Ramson continued as though he hadn't heard her. "Kerlan hosts the grandest ball for the Fyrva'snezh each year. All of his associates—all the crime lords and thieves and traffickers in the Empire—will make an appearance. And that includes your alchemist." He gave her a pointed look. Her stomach tightened. "I can get us into this ball. But it's going to be difficult. Dangerous, even." Ramson's tone held a challenge. "Are you ready for that?"

She'd been waiting for this for nearly twelve long moons. Ana leveled a cool gaze at Ramson. "I am." She jabbed a finger at the map. "So that means we'll have to find May before the Fyrva'snezh."

Ramson lowered the map. "You can't have it both ways. Rescuing May at the Playpen is like knocking on Kerlan's door and signaling to him we're there. We need the element of surprise when we show up at the Fyrva'snezh."

"This is not negotiable."

"One fish in your hand is better than two at—"

"May's life is *not* negotiable!" Her voice rose to a scream.

Silence fell. Shadows danced across Ramson's face; the flames reflected in his eyes, which were narrowed. "You need to decide," he said at last. "What do you want?"

"To right my wrongs. What do *you* want?"

"I told you. Revenge."

"Revenge against *whom*?" Ana leaned closer, refusing to let go of his gaze. To his credit, Ramson didn't look away. "Why were those mercenaries bringing you to Kerlan?"

Ramson matched her stance. They glared at each other across the fire, the heat coiling around them like a living thing, embers flickering between them. "I botched a job for him. Broke a Trade. Now you see the implications?" At her silence, he sighed and stood. "Kerlan knows everything that goes on in his territory. If you try to save May, you risk losing your alchemist. Think about that." He paused on his way out. "And, Ana, remember this. You're not a Deity. You're not the Emperor. You can't save everybody. So think about what's best for yourself."

"Where are you going?" she demanded.

"To cleanse my soul."

She watched his retreating back and suddenly wished he hadn't left. Silence pressed in, and it was as though the entire temple, with its walls of stone figures, watched her.

Ana ran her eyes over the wall carvings. The figures might once have been gilded in gold and silver and lapis lazuli and emerald, but those had long been pillaged by thieves as the temple fell to abandonment. Still, it was beautiful. Reverential.

As always, she shrank back beneath the Deities' watchful gazes, all too aware of what she was. *Monster. Witch. Deimhov.* She heard the screams from that day long ago in the Salskoff Winter Market as she sat paralyzed in all that blood, affirming to the world that she was the demon everyone believed she was.

Yet another part of her—a small part—leaned forward, yearning for the light and rightness and goodness. It was the small flame of hope that her aunt had lit in her chest all those years back, with a single sentence.

It had been in a temple just like this, the moon weeping above snow-covered grounds and casting a cold light over Mama's new tomb. She'd been eight years old. Ana knelt beneath the statues of the four Deities, their expressions stern and ungiving. She traced her fingers over the marble, carved in the exact features of her mother's face, long eyelashes that cast half-moon shadows over high cheekbones, and vibrant curls that had always seemed so full of life. The only thing the marble did not capture, Ana thought as she stroked the small crook between Mama's nose and cheeks, was the rich fawn of her mother's skin when she had been alive; the healthy glow to her smile that seemed to light the world.

Ana's fingers drew the same patterns over and over on the marble's cold white face, mingling with her tears.

It had only been one moon, yet with Mama's absence, the winter that swept over Salskoff that year was cold and stark, the snows harsh and unforgiving.

"Why?" Ana's whisper had lingered in the air between her and the marble Deities, small and forlorn. "Why did you take her?"

Stubbornly, they remained quiet. Perhaps it was true that the Deities did not listen to an Affinite's prayers.

A warm hand slid over her shoulders, and Ana jumped. Instinctively, she swept a hand over her face to clear it of tears before turning around.

The Grand Countess's quiet eyes, the color of pale tea, met hers. It was a few moments before Morganya spoke. "Your mother meant the world to me," she whispered, and Ana had no doubt that was true. It was Mama who had found Morganya all those years ago in a village, her body battered from the torturers who had kidnapped her from her orphanage and beaten her. Mama had brought Morganya to the Palace, and they'd grown closer than sisters.

"Have your prayers worked?" Even after all those years, Morganya's voice had not lost the quiet, cautious timbre of the downtrodden.

Ana hesitated. "I'm not . . . They don't . . . I don't think . . ."

"You don't think they listen to Affinites' prayers." The words were uttered softly, but they cut deeper than any blade. Ana bowed her head, shame filling the silence.

Morganya tucked Ana's hair behind her ear in a way that reminded her so much of Mama that she wanted to cry. "I'll tell you a secret," the Countess continued. "They've never answered mine, either."

"But you're—" *You're not an Affinite.*

Morganya gripped Ana's chin and lifted Ana's face to meet her eyes. "There is no difference between you and me, Anastacya," she said softly. "The Deities have long sent me a message through their silence." A steely glow sharpened Morganya's gaze. "It is not *their* duty to grant us goodness in this world, Kolst Pryntsessa. No, Little Tigress—it is up to *us* to fight our battles."

Her aunt's use of Mama's nickname for her brought fresh tears to her eyes. But she spoke past the aching knot in her throat. "It's up to us to fight our battles," she repeated, her voice tiny but a little firmer.

Morganya nodded. "Remember that. Anything you want, you have to take it for yourself. And you, Kolst Pryntsessa, were chosen by the Deities to fight the battles that they cannot in this world."

It had been difficult to understand her mamika's words back then. Confined to the two windows of her chambers and the four walls of her Palace, she had found it hard to fathom that she had the choice to fight any battles at all, let alone imagine that the Deities had marked her.

But perhaps her aunt had been right, Ana now realized as she sat beneath the cool, moonlit gaze of the same silent Deities. The Deities had never answered her prayers—but perhaps all those years of silence were a message. *It is up to us to fight our battles in this world.*

Her eyes landed on the carving of a young child sitting in a field. Petals whirled around her in a phantom wind, and her eyes were crinkled with laughter. The first time Ana had woken up in that empty barn, May had crouched in the snow outside, nursing a small flower back to life. Ana thought of when she had followed May back to her employer's house; of the woman's spiteful words and sharp hands.

She thought of the broker back at Kyrov, of his cold eyes and pale hair. Of the Imperial Patrols, cloaks billowing the bright whites and blues of Cyrilia, tiger insignia roaring proudly on their chests.

Of the yaeger crouched before her in defeat, hunter turned victim.

Of May staggering, eyes wide with surprise, as the arrow hit her. Of the blackstone wagon doors swinging shut.

How had the Empire fallen to this? The Cyrilian Empire Ana had always held so fiercely and faithfully in her heart was as proud and as strong as its white tiger sigil, its laws unimpeachable and its rulers benevolent. Yet what she had witnessed the past few days told her otherwise. Sinister shadows had sprung up in the spaces between laws, preying on those without the protection of status or wealth.

Or had it always been like this? Ice crawled up her veins, and Ana thought of how quickly mamika Morganya had been dismissed the time she had brought up Affinite indenturement. Of the way the Palace courtiers had whispered about Mama's Southern Cyrilian origins. Of how Ana had been deemed a monster solely because of her Affinity.

Perhaps, Ana thought, the world had never been fair. She had only noticed too late.

But her mamika was right.

If there was to be fairness in this world, it wasn't to be granted by the Deities. And it started one step at a time.

By the time Ramson's footsteps sounded down the hallway, Ana had made up her mind. "We're going after May," she said quietly as he strolled into view, clutching two rolls of bread wrapped in a handkerchief.

Ramson sat down across from her and set the rolls on his lap. "You sound convinced." He tilted his head back and waved at the wall carvings around them. "Let me guess: being the devout dama that you are, you probably prayed to the Deities—and of course, they advised you to do the *right* thing, and not the expedient, selfish thing."

"The Deities don't answer my prayers," she replied.

Ramson gave her a crooked smile. "That makes two of us."

Ana reached forward and snatched a roll. The bread was cold and hard, but she tore through it in several bites. "Why don't the Deities like *you*? What's wrong with you?" It felt as though a huge weight had been lifted from her chest; whereas before, she would have shied away from such a daring topic of conversation, now the words flowed easily from her.

Ramson snorted. "What's wrong with me?" he repeated, ripping off a chunk of his bread. "Is that a rhetorical question? Let's see." Ramson scratched his chin, faking a look of concentration as he began to tick off his fingers. "Youngest crime lord of the Empire, selfish, calculating, backstabbing, oh, and let's not forget, sinfully handsome—need I go on?"

"Do you ever answer anything seriously?"

"I answer everything seriously."

Ana rolled her eyes and swallowed her last bite of bread. Her stomach gave a gurgle of hunger, but her thoughts turned to May. Had she eaten yet? Was she cold? "I want to leave as soon as the sun rises."

Ramson nodded. "Good idea." An unspoken, disconcerting thought flitted between them: The Syvern Taiga was where the most dangerous creatures in Cyrilia roamed at night. Ana had heard of ruskaly lights leading tired travelers astray, of giant moonbears thrice the height of a normal human, of icewolf spirits that sprang from nothing but the snow.

"It took us one full day to reach Kyrov from Ghost Falls," she mused aloud. "Novo Mynsk is almost ten times as far."

"We have a valkryf," Ramson noted. "By my calculation, it'll take us a bit over five days. That gives us four days before the Fyrva'snezh to save May, get our names on Kerlan's guest list, and find your alchemist." He sighed, and ran a hand through his hair. "We're working with very slim chances here."

"You're the most infamous con man of Cyrilia," Ana replied drily. "Slim chances are your friends. You'll make it work."

"I don't have any friends. And if Kerlan happens to learn of our Grand Theft Affinite, I'm blaming you. I'm not letting him kill *me* because of your righteousness."

"I might very well kill you first." Ana watched him pick his way over to the pile of logs. "Ramson?"

"Yes?"

She hesitated, and then the words left her in a rush. "What's his name? The alchemist. You said you had his real name."

For a moment, she almost expected him to bring up the Trade, tell her that it was a piece of information she would need to bargain for. But Ramson only looked at her and said quietly, "Pyetr Tetsyev."

Pyetr Tetsyev. She tasted the name on her tongue as she closed her eyes. *Pyetr Tetsyev.* It didn't sound like an evil name; it could have belonged to anyone—a scholar, a professor, a man she might have met on the corner of a street.

Pyetr Tetsyev. The Palace alchemist *existed.* She hadn't spent the past year chasing after a phantom; he was real. And he was close. The missing piece to her father's murder was less than a week's travel away.

And she repeated his name over and over again until she fell asleep: a chant of prayer, a vow for vengeance.

15

Unlike the open oceans and rain-slogged moors of Ramson's childhood, Cyrilia was a land frozen in perpetual winter. The forest held its eternal silence, silver dusting the branches of tall pines and occasional stretches of white snow in areas where nobody else had traveled before. His breath curled in plumes, and the crisp coldness of the air kept him alert as he steered the valkryf forward, the Affinite sitting uncomfortably close to him. Above, the misty gray skies promised snow very, very soon.

They had spent the first day of their travels hashing out their plan. He had told her the details of the Playpen, of Kerlan's estate and his ball—not all of them, of course, but the ones she needed to know—and they had finally, *finally,* after hours of persistent questioning and arguing from the stubborn girl, come to an agreement.

They set up camp the second night in an abandoned dacha at the edge of a small town named Vetzk. After ensuring that the curtains were drawn, Ramson started a fire and settled down to treat his wounds. The witch sat across from him. Curled up with her knees against her chest, she looked smaller, more vulnerable. Almost like the young girl she was.

Ramson knew she was anything but. He'd meant to ask her about her Affinity after that fight in the rain, after he'd seen that mercenary who'd been bled dry. Throughout his years working with Kerlan, he'd thought he'd witnessed everything—monstrosities, Affinities strange and twisted—but that dead mercenary had been something else altogether. Something of nightmares.

"I never thanked you for saving me," he said, breaking the silence.

She started, blinking as though emerging from a trance. For once, the defensiveness was gone from her expression. She dipped her chin in a regal gesture. "You're welcome."

"You're the most powerful Affinite I've seen," he said. "What, exactly, *is* your Affinity?"

He could see the guard going up in her eyes, the way her face closed off as though preparing for a fight. "Flesh."

It had been a clever lie—and she'd fooled him at first. The effects of the two could almost be interchangeable. Flesh Affinites, though potentially powerful, were seen apprenticed to butchers or the like. An Affinity to blood, on the other hand—well, the Blood Witch of Salskoff was the only rumored blood Affinite to have been known. Ramson pushed on. "Is that how you bled that mercenary dry? With your *flesh* Affinity?"

Her lips tightened.

"There's a story," Ramson continued, "of an Affinite who showed up in Salskoff around ten years ago." Her eyes glittered in the firelight, but she betrayed nothing. "She killed eight people with a single thought.

"They named her the Blood Witch of Salskoff. She was never seen again; her particular way of killing, of bleeding her victims dry, was unheard of for a long time." The fire crackled between them. He was walking a tightrope; a single misstep could send him plunging. Ramson chose his words carefully. "I always thought I'd have liked to meet her."

Something shifted in her gaze—suspicion, or surprise—and she looked away. "Why?"

He almost loosed a breath. "So that I could understand her. Ask her why she did it."

"She never meant to." Her voice was soft as a sigh, and as she gazed into the flames, her face was a well of sadness. "She never meant to hurt anybody."

The confession was unexpected, and struck a chord deep within him, one he'd kept buried beneath the great legend of Ramson Quicktongue he'd built for himself over the years. He knew, bone-deep, the feeling of hurting someone and being helpless to do anything about it.

And the ones you hurt tended to be the ones closest to you.

Ramson had been seven when he met Jonah Fisher, on the first day of their military training. He'd sized up the gangly, dark-haired boy who looked as though he'd been stretched from a shadow, stalking down the stone halls with a steady, slouched gait. When they announced his name, a titter ran through the boys and girls. *Fisher* wasn't a real last name; Fisher was a last name they stuck on Bregonian boys from the orphanages of Sapphire Port.

And it struck close to home.

Ramson himself had been close to inheriting that name. It had something to do with his mother not being properly married to his father, he'd gathered. But while some children like Ramson were never seen again, Ramson's father, Admiral Roran Farrald, the second most powerful man of the Kingdom of Bregon, had instead plucked Ramson from the small town of Elmford where his mother resided and elected him for placement at the Blue Fort, Bregon's elite military school. Only the most capable were selected, Affinites among them, and Ramson took this as a gesture of trust. He vowed he would never disappoint the father who remained as distant as the moon in the night sky, monochrome light cold and bright.

But children were the most perceptive of creatures, and the underhanded slights Ramson had received for most of his life were not lost on him. Neither were the whispers of *bastard* and *packsaddle son.*

The jeers of his new classmates struck a quiver of fear within him, and he joined them, making his taunts the nastiest and his voice the loudest among them.

Jonah Fisher paused. He looked around, expression bored, as though he'd rather be anywhere but there. "You got nothing better to do or what?" he asked.

The class burst into laughter, Ramson included. He'd heard people speak with Jonah Fisher's accent before, down at the fish markets and out in the poorest outskirts of Sapphire Port. Ramson was a city-bred boy, and his father had paid for his tutoring since he'd turned five. He prided himself on being the quickest thinker and fastest talker of his class.

A crack rang through the hall. It echoed and reverberated as utter silence fell.

Jonah Fisher held a sparring rod from the racks at the side of the training hall. He stood before the class, still wearing that uninterested expression. "All of you better walk your talk." His voice was calm, but an undercurrent of threat ran through his words. "Show you know how to *really* fight. Go on," he goaded, to the dead stillness of the children.

Ramson looked around. The trainer had stepped away; there were no adults nearby. Just a class of several dozen children who would one day become Bregon's elite marines. Who would fight for the top rank in his father's navy.

Packsaddle son.

He'd show them. He'd show them all that he was no *Fisher*, no *bastard*, no throwaway shunned by his own father. He was Admiral Roran Farrald's son.

He would prove it.

Ramson stepped forward. He felt all the eyes of his classmates shift to him, and the attention was wind in his sails, propelling him forward and lifting his courage. "We walk our talk here in the Blue Fort," he said coolly, grabbing a rod of his own. He'd never held one before that day; it was heavier than he'd expected, the wood rough against his palms.

Fisher cast his black eyes on Ramson. He lifted his rod in an unsettlingly familiar way. It shifted loosely in his hands, flowing like an extension of his body.

Ramson mimicked him, lifting his own rod. It swayed unsteadily, off balance. His heart hammered in his chest, and he could feel his courage evaporating as quickly as a puddle of water on a Bregonian summer day.

Jonah Fisher struck. He reminded Ramson of a bird—a common raven, dark and unkempt and unimposing, but surprisingly quick.

The rod thwapped Ramson and he stumbled back, gritting

his teeth against the pain that singed across his chest. He aimed a clumsy swing at Fisher, but Fisher pivoted easily out of the way.

Another blow to Ramson's thighs, and this time Ramson cried out. A third blow buckled his knees, and before he could even draw breath, the fight was over and he was lying on the stone floor, Jonah Fisher standing over him. Ramson was panting hard, and he could taste the salty tang of tears rising in his throat as he stared at the other boy.

What happened next was one of the biggest surprises Ramson could remember encountering in his life.

Fisher held out a hand.

There was no trace of arrogance on his pale, thin face. His features were arranged in that same bored expression, as though nothing in the world could interest him.

Ramson did the only acceptable thing he could think of. He slapped Fisher's hand aside. "I don't need your help," he snarled, pushing himself to his feet. "We're not friends. We'll never be."

As Ramson hobbled away to join his stunned class, leaving Fisher behind him, he caught sight of a figure at the doorway. A flash of suntanned skin and sandy brown hair, navy-blue tunic emblazoned with gold, sword flashing at hip.

Roran Farrald turned from the entrance and walked away.

Disappointment and shame burned in Ramson's cheeks. He threw a final glance at Fisher, who stood alone on the other side of the hall, and vowed that he would defeat this boy if it was the last thing he did.

Everything had changed with a boat, a storm, and a voice.

The Bregonians had the best navy in the world, but first and foremost, they were sailors. And every Bregonian child training for the Navy spent half their days on the seas.

It had been a nighttime drill during the second year of Ramson's training. The sky was moonless and the waters were black and cold, stirring uneasily with the growing wind.

The storm set upon them in the early hours of the morning. The winds shrieked and the waves stood higher than walls, tossing the small brig of ten Bregonian trainees like a leaf in the wind. Even years later, Ramson would wake up in the middle of the night with the feeling of being flung around in the dark, the taste of blind terror strong on his tongue.

As captain of his little brig, he'd been screaming orders from the ratlines when a wave reared from the black night and slammed into him. He remembered falling, the world a spinning tangle of masts and sails and wood. He'd crashed through the surface of the ocean, and then there had been only darkness and silence.

The first few moments were blind, terrifying disorientation. Ramson thrashed and kicked, not knowing whether he was going up or down or sideways, the world around him tossing and turning as wave after wave bore down on him. Almost all the air had left his lungs upon impact, and as the pressure grew in his chest and his limbs began to burn from oxygen deprivation, he'd sent a prayer to the gods.

An arm had closed around his middle, and he'd felt himself being lifted up and up by the currents and that arm. Ramson had thought he had been dying, until he'd broken through the surface and the world crashed back in a torrent of waves and winds and rain.

"Swim," said a calm voice by his ear. Coughing and spluttering, he'd turned to see that the orphan had his arm locked around him and was dragging him through the churning waves. The boy had turned, his black hair plastered to his pale face. In that thin, underfed face, Ramson saw true courage for the first time in his life. "Swim," the boy repeated, "or we both die."

Ramson swam.

The wrath of the ocean bore them up and down and back again like the small, insignificant lives they were, sputtering flickers of candlelight in a screaming gale. But Ramson held tight to Jonah Fisher and swam, one heavy kick after another, one tired stroke after the other. The cold made his limbs numb and drained him of his energy.

The rhythm of the waves lulled both boys into a stupor. At some point, Ramson must have closed his eyes or fallen asleep swimming. The next thing he knew, there were the unmistakable shouts of men above his head, and splashes in the water. Someone looped a rope around him and he was heaved up, limbs dangling and dripping like a wet sponge, onto the ship.

The sodden wood of the deck felt like heaven, and despite the rocking of the ship and the shouts and footsteps and hands wrapping blankets around him, he could have slept right there and then.

Ramson lifted his head, his vision blurring. "Fisher," he croaked.

In the darkness, a boy's face appeared, white against the black night, lips blue-tinged and trembling.

The question had lodged in Ramson's throat when he first saw Fisher's face looming like a ghost's out of the violent black waves. "Why did you save me?"

Fisher shrugged. "Because I could."

It wasn't a straight answer, but it was answer enough. Half-frozen, his thoughts muddled, Ramson felt shame heat his cheeks and guilt churn in his stomach. He'd treated Jonah Fisher abhorrently . . . and Fisher had saved his life.

"Thank you." The words were so quiet and the storm so loud that he didn't think Fisher heard him.

Even on the cusp of death, Jonah Fisher looked bored. But then he did something that surprised Ramson for the second time in their brief acquaintance.

Jonah Fisher smiled. It was an unsettling, awkward smile: more of a grimace, setting his peaky face at odds with his long, dripping hair and dark eyes. "Call me Jonah," he wheezed.

Ramson would soon learn that Jonah was named after the sea god's disciple, who had been reincarnated as a mystical ghostwhale. From that day on, Jonah was the brother Ramson had never known he wanted. The orphan seemed to know everything, from the politics of Bregon to secret passageways in the Blue Fort to the best ways to cheat on tests. It wasn't long before he turned his mind to other things—things that regular children learning and training at the Blue Fort did not care for. Jonah seemed especially interested in the politics of the grown-ups, of Bregonian warfare tactics, of what the latest shipments from the Aseatic Isles kingdoms contained, of new Cyrilian laws on Affinite indenturement. He snuck out to town often and would return looking occupied and distant for days.

"You should try harder at school," Ramson chided him. "How will you ever end up ranking high if you don't turn in your assignments? The girls like the cleverest and strongest recruits." He grinned. "Like me."

"The girls'll like me for how handsome I am," Jonah replied lazily.

Ramson burst out laughing. "Handsome? You look like a plucked crow, Jonah Fisher!"

"And you look like a gutted fish, with that constant dumb expression of yours," Jonah quipped. He grew solemn again, considering Ramson's question.

"I guess I don't really see the point of studying such obsolete histories when there are very real tragedies happening on our doorstep."

"Like what?"

"People are starving, when we have an abundance of food. People are dying from illness, when we have an entire warehouse storage of medicine."

"Because we're important," Ramson had said. "They chose us to become future leaders of Bregon—"

"Don't be naïve, Ramson. I used to be one of those starving people. There's nothing different between us and them."

"Well . . ." The thought unsettled Ramson, that his scheduled life of coursework and training and a future as a Navy commander could be wrong, and could affect someone so close to him. "Once we work our way to the top, once we rank as Admiral, we'll be able to change things. That's why you should do your assignments, you know. Otherwise you'll never make it."

He hadn't thought his words would have an impact on Jonah, but they did. That year, Jonah turned his attention to his studies. And, of course, he excelled annoyingly at everything he did, with an effortless grace and characteristic taciturnity.

Ramson, however, prided himself on being the better

talker—in fact, the best talker among the Bregonian Navy recruits.

"What's the point of being good at everything if you can't tell everyone you're good at everything?" he'd taunted Jonah once, when they were in their fourth year of training.

Jonah gave him a pointed look as he chewed through a mouthful of whatever kitchen pickings he'd stolen. He was still as thin as the day they'd met, and no matter how much he ate, he seemed to stay that way. "The point is that after you're done talking, Ramson of the Quick Tongue, I'll kick your ass."

That shut Ramson up.

Jonah dipped his finger in the water and traced a lazy circle. They were stretched out on a fishing barge, basking in the midsummer sun that lanced off the white-capped waves and made everything glitter hazily. The ocean sighed, the air was balmy, Ramson's stomach was full, and they smelled of sweat and salt and wet wood.

"Look," Jonah said, and Ramson groaned. Jonah had a way of being brutally honest, and Ramson got the brunt of it. "I know you do it to compensate, in some ways."

"Compensate? Thought big words were my thing, Fisher."

"Your da," Jonah continued, turning his head so that his dark eyes dug into Ramson like hooks. Ravens' eyes. Even now, he spoke with that lowborn accent; instead of changing it, he'd taken it and made it acceptable, even admirable. "You're doing all this for him."

Ramson sat up. "That's not true."

"It is," Jonah continued calmly. "He's got a daughter now, but you still think you've a chance at his title someday."

Something in Ramson coiled tighter at Jonah's mention of

his half sister. Rumor had it that she was old enough to start training at the Blue Fort in a year, and he'd yet to meet her.

Ramson doubted he ever would. "Everyone has a chance at Admiral," he snapped, and the next words left him before he could think. "Even *you.*"

Jonah's finger paused; the circles stopped, and Ramson froze. He wished he could swallow his words. The waves seemed to fall still, the wood suddenly searing beneath his hands.

"Truth is, I probably won't," Jonah said at last. Ramson glanced at Jonah, startled, but the latter continued calmly. "The world's divided into two, Ramson: the powerful, and the pawns. Orphans like me? Without a family or fortune or even a name? We'll never become anything. Power breeds power, and few without it can claw their way to the top."

The waves roared in Ramson's ears, and specks of salt stung his face. "That's not true," he managed at last. "The top Navy commander becomes Admiral. We all have a chance." *I have a chance.*

"That's what they tell you. You'll see the truth of it in a few years." Jonah shrugged. "'S all right. I've made my peace with it. I just wanted to say, you shouldn't do something for anyone else but yourself. Especially someone who doesn't give a damn about you."

Ramson's throat felt tight, Jonah's words rattling around his skull, denying the single goal he'd dedicated himself to with every extra training hour he spent at the Blue Fort, honing his skills to become the best of the best.

To become Admiral.

"I don't think—" he began, but Jonah tossed something at

him. By instinct, Ramson snatched the object out of the air. It glinted bronze, larger than his palm.

A compass.

"They say this was the only thing they found on me when I got to the orphanage," Jonah went on. "I'd no idea what it was, but I've thought about it over the years. Thing is, Ramson, you can achieve everything in this world, but if it's for someone else, it's pointless. Figure out what you want to do in this life. Live for yourself. You might be the world's strongest battleship, but you can't navigate without a compass." Jonah turned away, closing his eyes to the sun's rays. A faint trace of a smile hung about his lips as he dipped his hand in the ocean and began to make circular motions again. "Keep it, and remember this. Your heart is your compass, Ramson of the Quick Tongue."

The compass was a rusty old thing, its bronze edges darkened with age and touch. The glass was yellowing, and the small paper map inside looked as though it had been stained by tea leaves and partially burned. It still worked, though, and Ramson had tucked it into his pocket and kept it on him. He had brushed his fingers against it for luck and for courage, or just for a small reminder that he had Jonah and all would be fine in the world.

The compass traveled with Ramson until Jonah died, almost exactly one year later. Ramson remembered hurling the thing at the wall, and then picking it up to see the arrow spinning like a broken helm amid the shattered glass, faster and faster until it seemed to careen into a wild blur. And Jonah's death had left Ramson that way, broken and directionless and spinning out of control ever since.

* * *

Ramson blinked, and the traces of his memories vanished. He was back in the small dacha, the fire dying low, the Affinite girl—Ana—curled against the wall opposite him, watching him over the flickering embers. Phantoms danced around them in the shapes of light and shadows, and he suspected he wasn't the only one haunted by ghosts of the past tonight. "I'd tell the Blood Witch that I understand," Ramson said quietly. "I never meant to hurt anyone, either."

It was a half-truth. After Jonah's death, Ramson had set out ensuring that that truth never held again. He'd hurt anyone and everyone who got in his way. And even those who didn't.

Yet as Ana gave him a wide-eyed look, the curiosity on her face open like a book toward him, a part of him faltered.

What do you want?

To right my wrongs. What do you *want?*

I told you. Revenge.

It had been his motto for the past seven years, even when the molten fire of his anger had cooled to cold steel. Revenge, for what his father had done, for all the broken flaws of this crooked world.

For Ramson's own flaws, which had cost Jonah Fisher's life.

Yet as he turned a palm up against the dying light of the fire, he could almost see the ghostly outline of a compass. Jonah's words whispered in his ears. *You can achieve everything in this world, but if it's for someone else, it's pointless. Live for yourself.*

Ramson almost turned, as though expecting to see Jonah slouched against the wall next to him, watching him through those dark, half-lidded eyes.

Ramson snapped his fist shut. The ghosts vanished, and there was only the witch, sitting before him, her head tilted against the wall as she drifted to sleep.

Such easy prey. He would gain her sympathy, manipulate her into trusting him for his own gain.

That would make it easier for him to hand her—the infamous Blood Witch of Salskoff—over to Alaric Kerlan. A better Trade, the best Ramson had ever made, in exchange for a clean slate.

Yet as he settled on the hard floor, using his own arm as a pillow, he wondered why something that should have been made easy had, instead, seemingly become harder.

16

It took them five days to reach Novo Mynsk: a sprawling mass of a city in the north of the Empire. It was a city of extremes, where white marble houses and gilded roofs oozed opulence, towering over dark alleyways in which the wet smell of gutters lingered like death. The cobblestone streets were lined with glass-paned storefronts boasting lush silk kechyans, gold jewelry inlaid with precious stones of all colors and sizes, and trinkets that winked and glittered as they passed. Fur-cloaked nobles swarmed the streets, bellies and coin pouches bulging, just steps from the dark alleyways in which half-clothed beggars crouched.

Ana kept close to Ramson as they wound their way through the streets. It was late afternoon and the sun slanted over the marble mansions. Five days of travel had worn her out; she gratefully collapsed on the cold bed of the room they rented in one of the hundreds of pubs scattered throughout the city.

Ramson had purchased fresh clothes for them with a portion of the coins she had taken from the bounty hunters. After a quick meal of beef and onion pirozhky pies, Ana cleaned up and quickly slipped into the new outfit. The destination for the night: the Playpen.

The silks and chiffons slid smoothly over her skin, and Ana shivered as she turned to look at herself in the cracked glass mirror of her rented room. The clothes were extravagant—finer than anything she had worn in the past year. Ramson had mentioned that only the affluent could afford such lavish entertainment; to get in, they had to look and act the part.

Her dress, in her opinion, bordered on suggestive. The midnight-black evening gown draped over the curves of her body like the cool caress of water, pooling at her feet. The back plunged to her waist, and she was thankful for the fur drape that Ramson had bought her. Still, she felt almost naked without her hood.

Ana braided her hair and twisted it into a bun, in an attempt to reproduce some semblance of what her maids at the Palace used to style for her. She dabbed some rouge on her lips, brushed powders on her cheeks, and traced kohl over her eyes. It had been so long since she'd looked in a mirror, and dressing up felt like a strange game she was trying to play, an imitation of a past she could never again have. Her skin had grown rough over the past year, crisscrossed with tiny scars where she'd fallen or where branches or the elements had chipped at her, her lips dry and cracked.

She leaned back, and it felt as though she were staring at a ghost in the looking glass: an echo of the Crown Princess Anastacya Kateryanna Mikhailov she'd been.

A knot formed in her throat at all the possibilities of how her life might have turned out, the could-have-beens if the smallest thing had just gone differently.

Ana shoved those thoughts to the back of her mind. She pulled on a new set of black velvet gloves. Drew a deep breath. Lifted her chin.

Three sharp raps sounded on her door. And, just like that, their plan was in motion.

Ana barely recognized the young man who stood in her doorway. Ramson was clean-shaven, his hair slicked back, his sharp black peacoat fitted perfectly to his lithe figure. Dressed like that and grinning arrogantly, he could have passed for a nobleman's son or a haughty young duke, come for a night of trouble in Novo Mynsk.

They stared at each other for a heartbeat, and she wondered whether Ramson found the sight of her in fine clothing just as strange. Heat rushed to her cheeks; she grappled for something to say as she turned away. No matter how well the con man cleaned up, she couldn't make the mistake of thinking his character had changed as well. He was still dangerous: a wolf in sheep's skin. One slip of her focus, and he'd have his jaws around her neck. "You clean up nicely for a criminal."

"Darling, you'd do well to remember it's often the criminals who are the best-dressed." Ramson strode in and dumped what he had been carrying onto her bed. "Papers," he said. "Keep them on you at all times."

Anna scanned one of the papers.

"'Elga Sokov, water Affinite'?" she read skeptically. To Ramson's credit, though, the document looked authentic, stamped and signed with the proper formatting of legal documents she'd studied.

"I figured after Kyrov, it would be best for you to have proper documentation, just in case," he replied, and then pointed to a second set of items. "I also purchased masks. It's tradition at the Playpen."

Ana tucked the papers into the folds of her cloak and picked up one of the masks, holding it to the candlelight. It shimmered with silver glitter, faux-gold swirls fanning out from each of the eyeholes. The gold-painted lips stretched in a cruel, mocking smile.

Ramson held up his own mask. A thoughtful look passed over his face as he examined it. "Some think their actions are more forgivable if they hide their faces."

"You can't hide your sins from the Deities." It was a fact she had accepted for her own crimes.

"Correct." Ramson tipped the mask onto his face, fastening it with swift, surgical accuracy. "But, in this world, life is a masquerade. Everyone wears masks."

Perhaps that was true, Ana thought as she slipped on her mask.

Ramson turned to her, a hand on the doorknob. His black mask glittered with faux-gold and counterfeit jewels that looked real. "Have you ever been out for a night in Novo Mynsk, Ana?"

Something in his tone made her heart pound—a thrill of danger beneath the calmness. "No."

He tipped his head in a nod. "Then stay close to me."

The streets of Novo Mynsk had transformed. Gone were the fine window displays, the vegetable and fruit carts, the gilded carriages and pure white valkryfs. Gone were the families who strolled around in fine furs, the ring-studded merchants who rushed about their business. It was as though the city had donned a mask of its own, replacing its idyllic daytime façade with a dark and dangerous nighttime act.

Torches blazed in the streets, casting flickering shadows on groups of lurkers and revelers. The small pubs and cramped inns in the dark alleyways flared with life, roaring with bawdy singing and laughter. The scents of smoke and alcohol hung thick in the air.

Ana stayed close behind Ramson, clutching her fur cloak tight to her chest. She'd switched her rucksack for a refined purse, in which she carried all of her sketches. They were the only reminder of the life she'd had, and she had the irrational fear that if she lost them, she would lose her past.

She was grateful they had put on their masks before leaving their tavern. Women in strange animal masks and lurid gowns strolled dangerously close to her and Ramson, smiling and purring in their direction. Sallow-faced men with daggers glinting at their belts flashed their gold teeth as they waved their hands at her in salutation.

It felt as though she had stepped into a surreal underground world that was nothing like the Cyrilia she had known her entire life.

Ramson dipped his head to her, and his voice was husky when he murmured in her ear. "The Playpen is ostensibly a club with Affinite entertainers. But like most aspects of this world, it isn't what it appears to be. Merchants are known to purchase Affinite employment contracts in the back rooms."

The words haunted her as they wove through the laughing crowds, toward a club that should never have existed in the first place.

Where had it all gone wrong? She remembered, toward the later years of Papa's life, how he had grown weak and frail; how his judgment and memory had suffered from blinding, fever-induced rages; how his moments of lucidity had become sparser and sparser throughout the years.

Yet another memory gripped her. Papa, turning away from her as she begged him not to let Sadov take her again. *We will take measures to cure your condition. It is . . . for your own good.*

Ramson's hand brushed her shoulder and she jumped, her thoughts dispersing. They were in the middle of a crowded street. People pushed past her, staggering and shouting in their drunkenness, bottles of liquor flashing in the torchlight.

Ahead of them was the most brightly lit building on the street. It was built in the fashion of a Cyrilian cathedral, domes tapering into sharp spires that loomed into the night sky. Yet instead of the white marble walls and stained-glass windows depicting Deys'krug, the exterior had been built in cheap red-brown bricks and the windows were painted with figures of women twisting in grotesque dance moves—a farcical replica of a revered, holy building.

Ana realized that while she had been staring in disgust at the pub before them, Ramson, too, had not moved. He stared up at the tavern, his outline rigid. With his mask on, he felt like a stranger rather than the young crime lord she had partnered with over the past week.

He turned to her, his quick hazel eyes finding hers. There was no humor to his tone as he said, "Welcome to the Playpen." Ramson's voice took on a new layer of urgency as he repeated, "Stay close to me."

Ana did her best as they stepped through the polished mahogany doors. As her eyes adjusted to the darkness, she began to make out the silhouettes of women splayed on love seats or slouched over bars, crooning words in their patrons' ears. Candles flickered in magenta casings, casting a seductive hue around the interior of the tavern.

Were all the girls here Affinites? How many had been brought here from a foreign land with the promise of opportunity, and became indentured to this vile place?

Ramson wound his way through a maze of curved archways with beaded curtains until, at last, they reached a foyer with another set of mahogany doors. Two women were perched on a red settee, both wearing black masks with feline features and very little else. Their eyes drifted to Ramson.

One stood, smiling, and sashayed over. Ana noticed that she had whiskers painted on her cheeks, and even a fake tail attached to her backside. "If you're looking for a show, mesyr, I can give you one." Her voice was a purr as she ran a hand down Ramson's shoulder.

"I'd hate to miss that," Ramson said. "But I'm quite certain the show I seek tonight lies beyond those doors."

"Hmm," the cat-masked courtesan hummed thoughtfully. "Well, perhaps I'll have my share of you another night, then. You may proceed."

Ana loosed a breath she didn't realize she had been holding. She stepped forward, eager to leave this eerie room.

"Wait."

The second woman on the settee had spoken. Unlike the first, her voice was sharp, and her eyes pierced like daggers as she rose to her feet. They were trained on Ana.

With a growing sense of dread, Ana watched her approach. She sensed Ramson stiffening in front of her. From the corner of her eyes, she saw the first courtesan take a step back.

"What business have you?" The second woman stopped several paces from Ana. Her eyes pinned Ana like a butterfly on a corkboard. Ana's mind began speeding through all the possible answers to her question. Was it a riddle? Was there a right answer—a code—that she was supposed to give, and that Ramson had neglected to tell her? Or was there another, more sinister reason for that question?

Dread settled in her stomach when the first woman retreated to her companion's side, raising her hands toward them in a defensive stance. Two small steel blades appeared out of nowhere, hovering above her shoulders, poised to strike. *Affinite,* Ana realized, and she reached out for her own bonds.

The second woman snarled, and Ana felt a strange, cold pressure on her Affinity: familiar, yet not as strong as the wall-like blockade that the yaeger had pressed on her at the Winter Market in Kyrov. Ana stifled a gasp. The woman was a yaeger.

They had been discovered.

Ana's thoughts scrambled. Instinctively, she grasped for her Affinity, preparing for the rush of blood and power that would flow through her.

A voice interrupted her. "Deities, how thoughtless of me." Ramson sighed. In a flash, he positioned himself by her side, his hand gripping her waist as he yanked her against him. "She's mine."

Ana tried to tear away from his grasp, but Ramson gave her a light squeeze. A warning—a signal. *Let me handle this.* She stopped struggling.

"Show your contract," the yaeger growled. The pressure on Ana's Affinity did not yield.

Contract, Ana thought, swallowing and trying to steady her racing heart. Of course. Ramson had given her papers back at the hotel, and told her to keep them on her—as a precaution.

With shaking fingers, she took them out and handed them to the yaeger.

"Hmm," the woman purred, displeasure seeping into her features. She gave the papers a cursory scan, then shrugged and tossed them aside. Ana watched them flutter to the floor. "No."

"No?" Ramson repeated, but Ana's temper flared at the sight of the yaeger's nonchalance, the way she had so casually discarded Ana's papers. Those papers, Ana now knew, could mean the difference between life and death for an Affinite.

"Why not?" she demanded. "I showed you my papers!"

"Your papers are necessary to prove your status." The yaeger's eyes flashed. "But we are not obliged to let you enter, *witch*."

The insult struck her harder that it ever had, coming from the mouth of one who should have been on the same side as her. *Why?* Ana wanted to ask. *Why do you do this?*

But she knew why: the same reason that yaeger back at Kyrov's Vyntr'makt had fought against her. *If I am not the hunter, then I become the hunted.*

Ramson seemed to reach a decision. "You have the authority on these decisions?" The arrogance and disgruntlement had vanished from his tone, leaving only cold calculation.

The yaeger lifted her chin. "Yes."

"Then you'd do well to remember your place." Ramson let go of Ana and strode over to the two women, his steps lithe and powerful. His back was to Ana, but what the two women saw had them widening their kohl-rimmed eyes and staring up at Ramson with fear plainly written on their faces.

"Please, mesyr," the cat-masked woman whispered. "We never meant—we didn't know—"

"Enough." The brusqueness of Ramson's voice made Ana jump. "Open the door now."

"Yes, mesyr," said the first courtesan, while her companion stared at Ana with horror. "Thank you for your kindness, mesyr." She thrust a hand up, and a series of metallic clicks sounded within the two locked mahogany doors. They swept open, revealing a winding set of stairs lit by torchlight.

Ramson extended an arm, the shadows beneath him stretching long. "Come," he crooned. Ana hurried over, scooping up the fallen papers on the floor. She felt rigid under the stares of the two courtesans, but then Ramson's arm closed around her and they were through. The two doors clanged shut behind them, trapping them in darkness.

Only then did Ramson stop and lean against the door. His arm was still slung around her waist, as though he'd forgotten about her, and she found herself leaning into him, their hearts beating the same relieved murmur.

Ramson exhaled, his chest heaving beneath him. A second passed, and then another, then he seemed to realize their strange proximity. Ana pulled away just as he tucked his arms against his sides.

"That was close." Ramson's voice was rough as he turned to the steps. His mask flashed, his eyes glinting as they caught the strange, far-off light.

Ana glanced at his wrist, which was covered by the sleeve of his peacoat. "What did you show them?"

"A con man's tricks," he said briskly, and she couldn't tell whether he was still acting or speaking the truth. "Let's go. We don't want to be late."

As Ana looked at the stone steps that led down into the unknown, she suddenly felt cold, heavy dread settle in her stomach. Beyond those stairs was the answer to the question she had been asking herself since that day in Kyrov. Beyond those stairs was the answer she was simultaneously awaiting and dreading.

Was May alive?

Her hands darted to her chest in an instinctive sign of prayer. She had been so certain, back in the Temple of Deities, that she would be able to save May herself. Yet now she would give anything to have the Deities answer her prayers.

"Ana." Ramson had paused on the steps. For a moment, he looked as though he was struggling to find words. And then he said, "We're late."

They were, and May could be down there. She had to be.

Ana drew a deep breath and squared her shoulders. She gave a curt nod and followed Ramson down the steps, into the darkness.

17

The descent seemed to last an eternity. Torches blazed from sconces in the walls, and the stairway was silent but for the swish of Ana's skirts and the clack of Ramson's boots.

Gradually, she began to hear a faint sound: At first, it was no louder than a buzz, yet it grew in volume until it became a rhythmic, pulsing beat.

The spiraling stairs gave way to a long, dark corridor that stretched before them, where the steady pounding noise emanated like a living thing. Ramson's dark mask glittered in the torchlight. Clad in his black peacoat and hidden behind his jeweled mask, he looked like a phantasmal creature of the night.

Ana found his eyes—sharp and intelligent. Their gazes locked, a ghost of a smile flitted across his face, and he gave an almost imperceptible nod. *After you.*

Ana lifted her chin. *After me.*

The corridor turned and opened up. Beyond an arched stone doorway was a vast auditorium with a sprawling stage, lit by flickering torches. Four tall stone pillars punctured each corner of the stage, with faux-marble renditions of the Deities atop each one. Higher up, empty balcony seats encircled the auditorium.

A strange feeling—of cold, of hollowness—wrapped around her like a nearly imperceptible cloak. For some reason, this place brought back memories of darkness, of helplessness.

The drums continued to pound from somewhere behind the stage. People milled about, torchlight lancing off the precious stones on their masks. Their expensive furs rustled as they clinked glasses of wine, the gold jewelry on their arms flashing as they tipped drinks back in laughter.

"What does this show entail?" Ana whispered to Ramson as they squeezed past a tiger-masked couple. The stage, she saw as they drew closer, was built of blue-veined marble, its edges gilded. The pillars were festooned with expensive silks and silver ribbons, the sapphire curtains made of rich, heavy velvet. The stage itself seemed to have a strange, almost surreal quality to it—something Ana couldn't quite put her finger on, no matter how hard she looked at it.

"They make Affinites perform using their abilities," Ramson replied, gently cleaving apart two drunk noblewomen. His hand slipped back, locking around hers, and she nearly jumped. Her heart skittered in an unfamiliar beat. "The nobles pay for good entertainment. And it's a cover. Some never know about the contract dealings in the back."

Ana shuddered. "The Affinites, don't they ever try to run? Even the weakest could put up a good fight against a non-Affinite."

Ramson tilted his head and pointed, drawing her attention to the viewing alcoves several levels up. "In a few minutes, a marksman is going to appear in every single one of those. They have Deys'voshk-tinged arrows, and they shoot to kill." He nodded at the stage. "Look closely there."

Ana squinted and suddenly realized what had made the stage seem so strange. Behind the four pillars, walls of blackstone-infused glass almost as high as the viewing alcoves encircled the entire stage, leaving an area in the front center for a host.

Blackstone. The cold, the feeling of emptiness she'd felt as she'd stepped into this room made more sense now. The same she'd felt each time Sadov took her to that room in the dungeons.

Ramson's tone was grim when he said, "If any Affinite tries anything, they'll be shot before they can even crack the glass."

The design was cruel but efficient; no Affinity could reach past the blackstone-infused glass, which meant the Affinites were limited to the resources they were given for their performances. No wonder none of them had tried to escape.

Ana remembered pushing against the Salskoff dungeons' blackstone doors, reaching out with her Affinity and only sensing cold black nothingness. When her throat was raw from screaming and her tears were spent, she'd been reduced to huddling against them, shaking and scratching at them with bloodied nails.

She shook the memory away, focusing on a different question. "How do you know all this?"

Ramson's jaw tightened. "I've been to a few of these shows before. I've seen how it works. The people here can negotiate purchases of Affinite employment contracts as the night goes on. It's all done discreetly behind closed doors." He paused. "That's what we need to try for once we see May perform."

She pulled her hand from his, suddenly cold. Of course Ramson knew of these shows—he was a criminal, an underground crook. But she had to ask—she had to know. "Ramson," she said, and her voice was barely a breath. "Did you ever . . . were you ever one of *them*? A broker?"

"No." The word cut with truth, yet something in his eyes made her insurmountably sad as he turned them to her. "But watching it happen is another crime in itself, is it not?"

She had no answer to that. Ana shuddered and turned away just as the drumbeats came to a sudden stop. As though on cue, the crowd erupted into wild cheers. A figure strode onstage, in front of the blackstone-infused glass wall and velvet curtains within. He was a clean-cut, gold-haired man who wore his charm like his navy-blue silk waistcoat: diamond-studded and glittering and sewn to the collar with flashing gold thread. When he waved, the bejeweled rings on his fingers glimmered as they caught the torchlight. "Mesyrs, meya damas, and all other guests!" he cried in a booming voice that resonated across the entire auditorium. "Are you ready for tonight's show?"

The crowd's screams grew louder and became a chant. "Bogdan! Bogdan! Bogdan!"

"That's the Penmaster," Ramson explained.

The Penmaster—Bogdan—raised his hands, beaming. "We have an excellent program planned for you tonight! Watch a formidable Ice Queen give us a prelude to the Fyrva'snezh! A Wood Nymph grows flowers from thin air! A Marble-Maker creates stunning statues! And, don't miss it: our Steelshooter battles a Windwraith to the death! Who will make it out alive?

There's only one thing we know, and it is that *you* will all leave happy!"

The crowd erupted with cheers and applause. Ana's stomach tightened, but she stayed silent as she watched a scene that should never have existed unfold before her eyes.

Bogdan held his hands up, and the crowd fell silent.

Suddenly, the drums started again. *Boom-ba-da-boom.* Ana's pulse thundered with the beat, and she found herself holding her breath as she stared at the brightly lit stage.

The curtains exploded behind the confines of the glass. The crowds screamed as a massive cloud of mist obscured the stage from view for a moment, curling up against the glass walls and pouring over the top in plumes of white. As the vapor cleared, a figure stood in its midst. Tall, pale, and slender, with flowing ash-white locks and a dress of pale blue, she was winter incarnate.

The Ice Queen swept her palms in an arc around her. Ice spread at her feet, propelling her in a wide circle around the inside of the glass. Hair flying, dress rippling, she twisted her hands and ice shot from her wrists to the ground, anchoring her as she somersaulted through the air and landed on the other side of the stage.

The crowd erupted; the Ice Queen smirked and curtsied with all the grace of a performer.

"She looks like she's enjoying it," Ana whispered.

"She's a regular," Ramson muttered by her side, bringing his hands together in a slow clap. He was staring at the stage, his jaw clenched, his shoulders stiff. "She works with the brokers."

"Under contract?"

"Right, but . . ." Ramson hesitated, and for the first time

since they'd met, Ana watched him struggle to find words. "She's not contracted against her will, if that's what you're asking. She works *with* the brokers."

Not against her will, Ana thought, turning back as the Ice Queen spun onstage, ice blooming beneath her feet.

The audience oohed and aahed as the Ice Queen began to sculpt ice with flicks of her wrist. A splash of ice rose into the air, becoming a graceful, loping deer. Another wave crystallized into a pack of running wolves. A prowling Cyrilian tiger. A valkryf horse.

This was greater than just a show, Ana realized. This was a Deities-damned *display* of what Affinite employment *could* look like; a reassurance to those who blindly believed their own righteousness and morality while continuing to perpetuate violence and abuse against those powerless to resist it. May. The grain Affinite at Kyrov. And the Affinites who stood in the wings, waiting to be exhibited like dolls.

All of that pain and suffering, veiled behind a single glitzy show of sparkling ice sculptures and glittering outfits.

The Ice Queen slammed her hands to the ground. A column of ice thrust her into the air, growing taller and taller until it was level with the top of the glass wall—

And she vaulted over the wall, landing on two pillars of ice that shrank rapidly down toward the outside of the stage where Bogdan stood. The archers hidden in the ceiling alcoves made no motion to stop her.

The Ice Queen stepped onto the marble of the stage and took a deep bow.

"I present," cried Bogdan. "The Ice Queen!" As the crowd

thundered with applause, Bogdan took the Ice Queen's hands and brought them to his lips. She smiled coyly at him before beaming at the audience and waving.

"Next up, Wood Nymph!"

"Ramson." Ana's voice was low with urgency. "He didn't announce any earth Affinites today."

"Bogdan chooses the Affinites he wants to announce." Ramson cut her a glance. "Patience. All good things come to those who wait."

So Ana watched the show in silence. Affinite after Affinite emerged through the curtains to show their powers. Before long, the marble stage was littered with flower petals, twigs, and earth; the glass was smudged with mist, frost, and water. The crowd cheered or booed depending on the performance of the Affinite. And sometimes, for a few goldleaves, Bogdan would engage the audience, directing the Affinite onstage to obey requests from the crowd. Particularly popular performances could end with showers of goldleaves pooling at his feet.

The night wore on and there was no sight of May. Yet Ana felt a chill spreading through her. She was no different from those Affinites onstage, whose suffering the world chose to hide beneath a sham layer of paint and bright outfits. Whose existence some hated, yet continued to profit from.

We will continue to cure your condition, Papa had told her. *For your own good.*

She blinked back tears as the realization twined around her chest, leaving her breathless and reeling. Papa had only loved the part of her that wasn't an Affinite, a monster, a deimhov, in his words. He'd only wanted to save a part of her, not all of her.

Just as he'd only wanted to save the part of his empire he thought of as worth saving.

And for so long, *she* had only loved a part of herself, denying that other half, hiding the crimson of her eyes and the grotesque veins of her hands beneath hoods and gloves. For so long, she had desperately wanted to tear that other part of herself off, to make herself into something wholly deserving of love. Something that could step into the light, something worthy of the Deities' blessings.

Yet who was it . . . who had deemed the other parts of her and her empire unworthy? Who had determined that Affinites were less worthy of love, of being human, and why? Simply on the basis that they were . . . different?

And a new thought came to her, piercing the wild screams of the crowd and the pounding of the drums.

I have to fix this.

"Mesyrs and meya damas! The show you have all been waiting for." Bogdan's voice dragged Ana from her thoughts. A ripple of anticipation and thrill seized the crowd. "Our performances are over, but we never end a night without the Clash of the Deities. Welcome our Steelshooter, undefeated champion of the Playpen!"

Ana's spirits sank just as a deafening roar of approval went up from the audience, and the drums started a new beat: low, somber, and steady.

The curtains at the back of the stage drew apart. A hulking figure stepped into the light. He was monstrous, armor glinting under the torchlight and muscles bulging beneath the steel plates. A dozen white scars slashed across his bald head and his face, which looked as though it had been dragged for miles against jagged outcroppings of rock. He leered at the audience, metal flashing in his teeth.

"And now," Bogdan shouted. "A newcomer to the challenge: welcome, Windwraith!"

Boom-boom . . . da-boom-BOOM. From the shadows of the curtains stumbled another figure. At first glance, Ana thought it was a child. As she strained to see better, hoping to catch a glimpse of May's ocean-blue eyes, she realized that the new arrival was no child but actually a young woman. Her scrawny form was emphasized by her dark, formfitting shirt and breeches. She looked up, her face framed by midnight-black hair that caught the torchlight.

Kemeiran. A whisper rustled through the crowd as they pointed at the girl.

She was about to tell Ramson that they should leave, when something else caught Ana's attention. A figure, standing at the edge of the stage just in front of the velvet curtains. The pale blue of his eyes scanned the crowd, the white-blond of his hair glowing bloodred in the firelight.

The broker. The one who had snatched May from Ana's fingertips back in Kyrov.

Without thinking, Ana sprang forward, knocking hard into a group of people in front of her. A glass tumbled from someone's hands and shattered.

The man she'd bumped into turned around. He wore a gold mask with a farcical crying face, the mouth overly large and turned mockingly downward. "What—" he began.

"Get out of my way," Ana snapped. The blue-eyed broker

would disappear at any moment; she had no time. Ana reached for her Affinity—

"Excuse me, kind mesyr." A hand looped around her waist and Ramson neatly stepped between her and the man, obscuring her view of the stage. Ana twisted, but he kept his fingers locked around her waist. "Meya dama here has had a little too much to drink! A testament to the great entertainment tonight."

The nobleman's eyes flashed, but he gave an indignant snort and turned back to the stage.

"Let me *go,*" Ana snarled, yet Ramson gripped her tighter.

"What are you *doing*?" he whispered.

She shoved him back, but he held firm. "The broker," she growled, already reaching for Ramson's blood with her Affinity. "The one who took May—I saw him. Now, get *off*!" She shoved him aside with her Affinity, her anger white-hot.

Ramson stumbled back but caught himself, ignoring the strange looks of several people nearby as they moved away. His jaw was clenched; a strand of his hair fell over his mask. "And?" he challenged, his voice low. "What were you going to do?"

Something, she thought furiously. *Anything.*

Ana barreled forward but Ramson caught her, his arms wrapping around her in a viselike grip. Her head buzzed with anger and she considered ripping him from her with her Affinity, no matter the consequences.

"Think," Ramson whispered, his lips next to her ear. To any outsider, they might have been locked in a passionate embrace—but Ana was one step short of blasting him across the room. "You're here to save May. How is attacking that broker and exposing yourself going to help? At *all*?"

Ramson's words fell like cold water on the molten metal of her anger. Ana stopped fighting, her breathing ragged, as she stared up at the Kemeiran girl. She stood alone on the stage beneath the shadow of the Steelshooter. Behind her, the curtains where the broker had been standing rustled, as though stirred by a phantom wind. He was no longer there.

Ramson was right. Using her Affinity against that broker, or doing anything reckless, would only expose them and foil their plan.

Ramson's grip on her loosened, and for a moment she simply stood with his arms around her, her cheek against his shoulder, watching the stage and breathing in the clean, calming fragrance of his kologne.

The Steelshooter had retrieved four sharp throwing knives. He rolled his head, cracking the joints in his thick neck and corded shoulders.

Ramson drew back. His eyes darted across Ana's face, and she imagined he was taking in every minuscule movement of her features, drawing up what to say next to assuage her.

"It's not like this everywhere, remember," he said, his voice gentler. His hands were still around her shoulders. "In Kemeira, for example, Affinites are appointed as the Temple Masters, the protectors of each village. In Nandji, Affinites are well-respected. And in Bregon—"

Ana flung his hands from her. "Is that supposed to make me feel better?" she snapped. Onstage, the Steelshooter gave a battle-roar and charged toward the tiny wind Affinite.

Ana turned away. May was not here tonight—she might not even be anywhere close—and Ana felt sick at the thought of watching Affinites kill each other for fun.

A hot, helpless tear rolled down her cheek. As she raised a hand to swipe it away, something peculiar happened. A collective gasp rustled over the crowd.

Ana turned. The Steelshooter bellowed as he staggered to face the Windwraith, who was now on the other side of the stage, pressed against the glass. Yet her stance was a fighter's stance. Her palms were raised, one before the other, and her feet were planted shoulder width apart on the marble floor.

The Steelshooter lunged. Steel knives shot from concealed areas of his armor—

—and clattered against the blackstone-infused glass. The crowd gasped; people pointed.

The Windwraith had launched herself into the air, arms spread and legs tucked like a bizarre sort of bird. She soared over the Steelshooter's head in an elegant arc. Faster than the blink of an eye, her feet tapped lightly on the gigantic man's shoulders; she flipped a full circle and, with acrobatic precision, landed behind him.

In an extension of her landing, she whipped out her hands. Two of the Steelshooter's throwing knives glinted in her palms.

By the time the Steelshooter, blinking in confusion, turned around, it was over.

The Windwraith pounced, graceful and deadly as a jaguar. She latched on to his shoulders and slashed her hands down upon his throat.

The thump of the Steelshooter's body hitting the marble stage echoed around the silent auditorium. Red seeped onto the floor, turning the marble's veins crimson. Ana's Affinity stirred, a soft whisper at the back of her mind.

The whole thing had taken less than ten seconds.

"Mesyrs and meya damas!" Bogdan's voice boomed across the auditorium. "It appears we have a new winner and a new record! I present: the Windwraith!"

The crowd erupted into cheers and screams. The few who had placed bets on the Windwraith were waving their slips and shouting at the top of their lungs, clamoring for their gold.

Ana turned and began shoving her way to the exit. She had no strength left in her to spend even a second more in this Deities-forsaken place. As she pushed her way through the wild, drunken crowd, she couldn't help but look behind her. The audience had worked itself into a frenzy and had begun chanting the victor's name. Yet onstage, behind the blood-splattered glass wall, the Windwraith was quiet. She stood several paces from the blood pooling around her opponent's body, head bowed, arms hanging by her sides.

Ana looked away. Like the Windwraith, she felt no victory at the Steelshooter's defeat. It didn't matter that a condemned girl had fought her way out and won tonight. No matter what, a body lay cooling on the floor. No matter what, a life had been lost. And until all the stadiums and brokers had been burned to the ground, Cyrilia would keep on losing.

Ana threw one last glimpse at the gleaming marble statues of the four Deities and wondered how they could ever stand to look upon such a godless place.

18

The cold autumn air that stung his face was a blissful release from the hot, cramped chambers of the Playpen. Ramson slipped through the crowds, his eyes trained on Ana's chestnut hair, the slim silhouette of her black dress as she walked briskly. He called out to her, loudly enough to attract the attention and giggling of several drunk revelers.

He caught her wrist. By instinct, he turned, pulling her into the darkness of a small alleyway. She made a noise in her throat and grew still. "Ana," Ramson panted. Something in him twisted like a knife at the sight of her: arms crossed, shoulders hunched, as though she wanted to fold herself away.

She was unbelievably naïve—yet something in the way she viewed the world, as though it were carved of white and black, reminded him of the way he'd been before Jonah's death. And somehow a small part of him wanted to protect her.

Ramson found himself reaching out and gently tilting her chin toward him.

She stepped back, snapping out of his hold, and ripped her mask off. It landed facedown in the wet garbage of the empty alleyway.

She was crying. Tears had carved dark streaks of kohl down her cheeks, mingling with her powders. For a moment, she stared at him, and he wanted to pull her close. "That," she whispered, "was beyond inhumane. I don't have the words for it."

The heat coursing through his veins dissipated, and Ramson suddenly felt cold. "It was," he said hoarsely.

She turned her gaze to him, eyes burning like embers. "How could you associate with those people? How could you watch them do that and not feel anything?"

For all these years, he'd taken the coward's way out, refusing to sink to a level as low as the brokers under Kerlan's command. Yet standing by and doing nothing was another form of evil, he realized as he dropped his gaze to the ground. And fate had rewarded him in kind, anyway.

Ramson was silent.

Ana took a deep breath. She swiped angrily at the tears on her face and seemed to collect herself as she lifted her chin and straightened. "I just need some time by myself." Her tone was impassive and flat, the same as the first time she had spoken to him back in Ghost Falls. Somewhere, somehow in her life, she had learned to mask her emotions. And she was almost as good as he was.

Looking at her, eyes blazing, shoulders squared, standing tall and regal in her evening dress, he thought she burned like a beacon. Something stirred in him—something that drew him toward her like shadows toward the light.

Ramson stamped out that inkling of desire. "All right," he said, shrugging. "I have some matters to take care of." *Stay safe. I'll see you back at the inn.* Yet he said none of those words as he turned abruptly and walked away, leaving her in the darkness of the alleyway. The Ramson Quicktongue of Novo Mynsk, Portmaster and Deputy of the Order of the Lily, gave no reassurances and made no promises.

Ramson stalked through the streets that he knew like the back of his own hand. He'd grown up in the city as a petty thief, running errands for the Order and learning everything he could about the cruel, crooked world he had been given to work with. In time, the red-shingled rooftops of the dachas had become his safe haven, and the shadows of the grimy alleyways had grown to welcome him like an old friend.

Ramson stopped by a pub. He spoke with several hooded patrons before slipping cop'stones beneath begrimed wooden tables and shaking hands, arrangement made. He then set out for the Dams.

The Dams was less of a dam than it was a vast meshwork of tight alleys and underground tunnels that separated the poor from the rich in Novo Mynsk. It was the nest of all gangs and crime networks. An open-air sewage funnel ran along the edge of the Dams, lending the area its wet, rotting stench that clung to one's clothes if one stayed too long. It was also a convenient place to dump victims. Every few days, a body would bob along the foul green stream—corpses of nobodies or criminals that the city guards and Whitecloaks alike chose to ignore.

The streetlamps had all been smashed long ago, and the remaining shards of glass on the ground crunched beneath Ramson's polished shoes. The moon hid behind clouds that promised snow—the First Snow—in four days, and Ramson was grateful that the stink of sewage had dissipated in the cold. He walked briskly, navigating the crooked twists and turns with no more hesitation than a man would pace through his own backyard.

He stopped suddenly, at the corner of an alleyway no different from any other. Ramson leaned against the wall and melted into the shadows.

He waited.

Minutes passed. The darkness pressed at his eyes. A small creature scurried through a pile of trash behind him.

And then he heard it: the faint *clop-clop-clop* of hooves, and the squeak of carriage wheels. He knew the exact carriage that was coming this way, and he knew the passenger it carried.

Of all the crime lords that ruled Cyrilia, Alaric Kerlan was the biggest and the baddest of them all. His wide-reaching network, his insurmountable wealth, and his league of highly trained brokers and gang members made him the most feared. It thus stood to reason that Kerlan's men could stroll through the Dams clad in silks and tossing gold, and the other gangs would bow them forward and scurry after them to help pick up the coins they dropped. Alaric Kerlan's wrath was the last thing one wanted to incur.

The carriage rolled into view: gilded, swathed in lapis lazuli, and pulled by two valkryfs. On the door was a huge engraving of a lily of the valley, its stalk carved of glinting emerald and its bell-shaped flowers made of white gold.

Ramson waited until the door was right in front of him. With a light leap, he was on the carriage's folding step. The bald-headed bruiser driving in front didn't even so much as glance back as Ramson swung the door open and soundlessly slipped inside.

Bogdan half turned; Ramson slapped a hand over the entertainer's mouth. He could feel his old associate's lips parting at the start of a yelp. "Make a single noise and my assassin outside will have an arrow through your heart faster than you can piss your blue silk pants."

Bogdan blinked, and his eyes rolled to the carriage window. A shadow flashed by; the Playpen host's eyes widened comically and he shrank back, nodding.

Ramson grinned and slipped off his mask. The shadow vanished from the window. "Relax, man," he said lazily. "I haven't waded through all this shit to come and kill you."

Bogdan sniffed and sat back, straightening his bow tie and smoothing his silk collar. "I thought I'd never see you again, Quicktongue."

Ramson rolled his eyes. "If I had a cop'stone for every time someone's said that to me, Bogdan."

Bogdan straightened. "Others know you're back?" he asked carefully. "Does Kerlan know?"

"Some know. But I need him to know the truth. Or whatever can be perceived as the truth in our trade." Ramson flashed Bogdan a charming smile. "And that's why I've come to you. I'm here to collect my debt."

"Your debt," the entertainer repeated, suddenly looking like a Cyrilian nobleman who had discovered something nasty in his beet salad. Bogdan wasn't the sharpest or smartest member of the Order; he was handsome and arrogant, obsessing over small details and petty money rather than looking at the bigger picture. Once, several years ago, his arrogance had nearly cost him his life.

"My dear Bogdan, surely you didn't expect me to keep your

secret from Kerlan for all these years for *nothing*?" Ramson leaned forward, locking his fingers together. "What would our master say if he knew of the side profit you were making from the contracts you sell?"

Bogdan's expression turned ugly. "What's keeping me from calling in my bruiser on you right now, Quicktongue?" he snarled. "I hired Svyet because he bested two Kemeiran assassins—"

"Because you know that before he even stops the carriage and opens this door, I'll have slit your throat and ruined these expensive velvet cushions with your blood."

"Always the same threats, Quicktongue," Bogdan growled. "You forget that Kerlan trained me, too. Let's have a try, and see whose blood spills in this carriage."

"You want me to be a bit more creative in my threats, Bogdan? Well." Ramson shifted his gaze to Bogdan's fingers. "You've always had a fondness for rings, Bogdan. Each bearing a precious stone from all the kingdoms across the world."

Bogdan drew back suddenly, his expression tightening. He twisted his hands together, tapping his nails on the rubies, emeralds, and sapphires on each hand.

"It's a nice new one you've got there, the diamond. Looks to be an original from the Blue Caves out east." Ramson's eyes snapped back up. "How's Olyusha?"

Bogdan turned pale.

"Imagine what Kerlan might say if he found out you were bedding one of his assets." Ramson frowned, feigning a look of confusion. "My mistake, Bogdan—imagine what Kerlan might say if he found out you had *wedded* one of his assets." He gave Bogdan a knife-sharp smile. "There. Much better. Affinite and Penmaster. Funny pairing, I'd say."

Bogdan's face had flipped through alternating shades of white and red, finally settling on a purplish, barely contained rage. "You're a despicable human being," he spat.

"I'm a despicable human being who gets things done. You'd do well to remember that the next time you ask me to get more *creative.*"

Bogdan stared at him for several moments with revulsion. "Fine," he snarled at last. "Name your Trade."

Ramson smiled like a cat in the sun. People were so easy, so predictable. He hadn't *really* hired an assassin. After all, those cost more than a shiny silverleaf and were difficult to book the night of. Murders were quite the economy in Novo Mynsk. No—sometimes the belief of danger was more effective than danger itself. The shadow at the window had been some street rat he'd found skulking by one of the taverns, desperate and willing to brave the Dams for a mere cop'stone.

Besides, Ramson preferred not to spend coins on his jobs where possible. He'd found, over the years, that there was a more reliable method for purchase. Secrets were Ramson's currency when it came to these dealings.

"You will tell Kerlan that I am back," he said. With Ana's stubborn creed to save May, Ramson had had to adjust his plan. Now that the element of surprise was no longer possible—well, he would simply announce his arrival, as loudly as he could. He'd played this game with Kerlan for too many years, and he knew the rules all too well. As long as you remained one step ahead of him, as long as you kept his interest piqued, you lived. "You will tell him to expect me at his Fyrva'snezh ball. And you will tell him that I return to offer him the largest Trade of his life."

"And what is it that you are offering?"

Ramson almost hesitated a beat, but the words were out of his mouth already. "The Blood Witch of Salskoff."

Bogdan's mouth formed a small O. The hostility vanished from his face, replaced by a look of pure greed. "That's just a myth," he said, but his tone begged Ramson to prove him wrong.

"She's as real as the gold in your teeth, Bogdan. Took down five guards with a sweep of her hands."

"She'd be a *fortune*," Bogdan whispered. "Worth more than the Nandjian Fire Palace. I mean . . . how much do you think she's worth?"

How much is she worth? The question jarred him, and he suddenly felt sick. He thought of Ana now, of the bold dash of her mouth, the way she frowned when she was thinking, the way she'd stubbornly kept her face fierce at the Playpen when her eyes had betrayed her horror.

The way she shone like a torch in the darkness.

Something stirred inside his chest: something buried far beneath the wall he had built from the ruins of his heart. It was as though a block had shifted in his carefully built world, changing everything with it for the first time in seven long years, when he'd flung his past behind him and kept running and had never stopped to think about what he was doing with his life.

What do you *want?*

I told you. Revenge.

But that was no longer enough, he realized. All this time, he'd thought he held the keys to his fate when really he'd been in a cage all along. Just one of Kerlan's puppets with a fancy title, scrambling to do his bidding and cast aside when no longer needed.

Handing Ana to Kerlan meant he was still playing the hand Kerlan had dealt him.

It was time to change the game.

"She's worth more than you could ever imagine," Ramson said quietly. The wheels in his mind were already turning, skipping two, three steps ahead and fanning out in the infinite possibilities that this conversation could play into. Calculating all the scenarios in which he would win, and the conditions that would allow him to.

And as he spoke, he began to weave in details for his new plan. "I want you to listen carefully, Bogdan. You'll tell Kerlan that at this Fyrva'snezh ball, I'm going to kill my betrayer, win back my title, and hand him the most powerful Affinite known to exist."

Bogdan swallowed. "All right."

"There's more," Ramson said. "I want you to get me a list of the guests attending the event this year. You'll find a runner boy outside your home by the seventh hour tomorrow morning. Give him the list."

"That's hardly any time!" Bogdan spluttered, but at a look from Ramson, he conceded. *"Fine."*

"And you'll have me added to that list. Me, and my . . . wife. I expect my runner to hand me the invitations along with the guest list tomorrow morning. And I'll know if they've been forged, so don't get any ideas, Bogdan."

Bogdan looked as though he'd somehow eaten a mouthful of cat shit that he wanted to spit into Ramson's face. Slowly, with vein-popping effort, he swallowed and said instead, "Of course."

"If anything goes wrong and I'm unable to get into Kerlan's Fyrva'snezh, it'll be on you."

Bogdan sniffed. "Right." Sullenly, he fished from his jacket a gold engraved pen and a piece of notepaper where he kept his balances. "And what name will I be adding to the guest list?"

Ramson paused. Not "Quicktongue," the flashy, ridiculous pseudonym he'd adopted for the Order of the Lily. He needed a name that nobody but Kerlan knew, that would send a signal. A code.

The answer was so obvious that it came to him like a punch in the gut.

"Farrald," he said quietly.

Bogdan rolled his eyes as he jotted down the name.

As soon as the pen and paper vanished into one of the many pockets lining Bogdan's expensive silk suit, Ramson leaned forward. "And there's more."

"For Deities' sakes!" Bogdan threw up his hands, and then lowered his voice in an angry whisper. "You're Trading me *three* conditions for only *two* secrets."

"*Four* conditions," Ramson corrected, and plowed on over Bogdan's indignant splutters. "The best deals are never on a one-to-one ratio. Think bigger picture, Bogdan. What's the loss for me if these conditions aren't met? I'd lose the option to return to the Order, and I'd leave the Empire to start a business elsewhere. But what would the exposure of those two secrets cost *you*?" Ramson raised his brows and shrugged.

Bogdan's face was red. Ramson could practically see the

gears working in his head as he weighed the costs and benefits of the Trade. "Fine," he hissed. "But after this, I want no more dealings with you, Quicktongue. After this, I'm *done.*" The entertainer punctuated his sentence with a furious jab of his finger.

Ramson held two fingers to his chest and drew a circle. "I swear in the name of the Deities and all that is holy within me, my good man."

"Oh, cut the shit. What's the third condition?"

"There's a young girl in Kerlan's inventory; an earth Affinite. Caught by the Whitecloaks from Kyrov. Sound familiar?"

Bogdan's eyes narrowed and he frowned, presumably running through the script of his upcoming shows. "Yes," he said at last, the words lending Ramson relief. "She's due to perform in three days. Look, I can't just give her to you. Kerlan'll kill—"

"I know. I understand the rules." He'd hoped otherwise, but Kerlan ran his business tight. "I'm not asking you to *give* her to me. In three days' time, I'm going to bid for her contract. And you're going to rig the bids. In my favor."

"Hum." Bogdan scratched his chin, evidently appeased at the prospect of more money. "I suppose that can be done. I'll have to make some arrangements, but . . . fine. Very well, then." He gave a lofty sniff. "And the fourth?"

Ramson leaned in. "I want to ask about your Windwraith," he said softly, and began to unspool the words that would weave the final pieces of his plan into place. When he held out his hand to shake, his peacoat was half a pouch of goldleaves lighter, and he had one last stop to make for the night.

"Trade up," said Ramson.

"Trade up," echoed Bogdan.

They shook.

* * *

Ramson chose to walk back through the Dams. A man like him was meant to crawl in the shadows of this world, without a light and without hope for anything better. Jonah had been right, after all this time—the world that the orphans and bastard sons and street rats were born into was not one of goodness and kindness. The world was divided into the conquerors and the conquered; those with power cast aside those without, like pawns on a chessboard.

When Jonah had died, Ramson had sworn on his friend's soul that he would never be one of the pawns.

If Ramson's plan succeeded, he would no longer be a pawn in Kerlan's shadow. Kerlan would be dead, and *Ramson* would be running the show on the proverbial throne of the greatest business enterprise in Cyrilia.

All those years of watching from the sidelines, of chasing after his father's distant shadow, of whispers of *packsaddle son* and *bastard*, finally, overturned. And Jonah's legacy, fulfilled.

Live for yourself.

This is for you, Jonah, he thought, with a glance at the sky—overcast, just like that night with the storm and the boat and that calm, thin voice by his ear.

Still, even after he exited the Dams he couldn't shake the small twinge of regret that clung to him. Ana would be reunited with May, and they would go far, far away to someplace where they could be free.

Something about him changed when he was with Ana. The darkness, the scheming, the cold calculation in him faded, revealing faint traces of what he'd once been. A boy in love with the ocean. A boy who'd wanted to sail the seas forever, with the sun warming his back and the waves lapping at his hands. He'd forgotten about this boy, one who'd had big dreams and foolish hopes and had been *good.* The boy who'd become the smallest sliver of hope.

But what good was goodness itself, when the world was ruled by the cruel?

Ramson drew a deep breath, and only when he was near the tavern where he was staying did he take off his mask again. The man he had become in the Dams tonight, dead-eyed and merciless and calculating, was a side of him that he never wanted Ana to see.

19

Ramson returned to the inn in the early hours of the dawn, when the sun was just rising over the red-shingled roofs and glittering marble mansions of Novo Mynsk. Ana shut her eyes resolutely, pretending to be asleep as he unlocked the door to her room with the spare key he held. She sensed him standing at her doorway for a while, and then like a shadow, he was gone.

When she met him for a breakfast of salmon porridge and sourdough bread downstairs in the morning, something in his expression had shifted. "I have news," he said through a mouthful of food. He'd showered and changed into a clean white shirt, hanging open at his collar. He squinted, and waved a spoon at her. "Is that hood always part of your outfit?"

"Is ignorance always part of *your* outfit?" Ana snapped, and cast a glance around the inn. It was mostly empty, save for one or two weary-looking travelers nursing mugs of black ale over cracked wooden tables. Still, she kept her hood drawn tightly as she sat across from him. "Besides, shouldn't you be more cautious? After what happened with the mercenaries?"

Ramson leaned back, brandishing his spoon. "Caution's my middle name, sweetheart."

"Is that why you got kidnapped in the thirty minutes I left you alone?"

"I had that situation under control." Ramson grinned at Ana's expression. "All right, let's just say I have some insurance now. Someone high up wants me alive."

Ana dug her spoon into her thick bowl of porridge. "So what's the news?"

"May is scheduled to perform in three days. One day before Kerlan's Fyrva'snezh."

Her spoon dropped. Porridge spilled on the table. The rest of the world—the dim inn, the smell of seared fish in the air, the chipped wooden table—faded. "How do you know?"

"I know everything."

"You're absolutely certain?" Her tunic suddenly felt too tight; it was hard to breathe.

"*Yes.* When you're done interrogating me, perhaps we can finalize the plan."

Plan. She couldn't concentrate, couldn't think of anything besides May behind those blackstone wagon doors, alone and helpless and afraid.

"Don't worry so much." Ana blinked, and realized Ramson was watching her with a smile curling his lips. "The plan's simple. We're going to bid for her contract after the show. Remember I told you that's what happens in the back rooms."

Ana's mind spun. "I don't understand. Bid for her? What if we don't win?"

"We will. I called in an old favor." He finished his last bite of sourdough bread and wiped his fingers on his napkin. "If you can't win it, just rig it."

"This is not a *game,* con man," Ana snarled, her temper rising at his levity, at the thought of May sitting in a cell somewhere in that horrible place from hell. "If even *one* thing goes wrong, then May's *life* is in danger."

The grin faded from Ramson's face. He placed his spoon back in his bowl, carefully, deliberately, as though handling a weapon. "You think I don't know the difference between life and death?" he said. "I've been in this business for seven years. I started as a street rat and worked my way up to where I am today—where I *was.* One slip along the way, and I would've been dead."

Her breathing came shallow. Ramson Quicktongue had taken care to never reveal anything about himself to her, other than what was strictly necessary. Yet something had changed. She just couldn't place . . . what.

"And that's why we have backup plans," he said, and the moment was gone. "I have one for several different scenarios, and they consist of secret tunnels and underground passageways." He leaned forward, his hazel eyes bright in the morning light, tousled hair curling against his temples. "As soon as we have May, we need to be ready for the Fyrva'snezh ball." He slid something across the table at her.

A piece of parchment, with names hastily scribbled on it. Ana scanned the title. "Kerlan's Fyrva'snezh guests?" She thought of asking him how he'd procured it but knew that questioning Ramson Quicktongue's sources would lead to precisely nowhere.

"Yes." Ramson touched a finger to a single name in the middle of the list, and for a moment, all that she saw were the words blazing up at her. *Mesyr Pyetr Tetsyev.*

Ana drew a sharp breath. She gripped the parchment so hard that her knuckles turned white. "We'll need to lure him somewhere quiet. Somewhere I can talk to him and then leave, unnoticed."

Ramson's eyes glinted. "There's a secret room in Kerlan's basement. It's soundproof. I have it on good authority that no one will be standing guard during the ball." He drummed the table in a restless beat. "It's perfect. There's a tunnel leading out from the basement to the back—it's where all of the estate's supplies come in. Food, flowers, clothing . . . the like. I'll arrange for a carriage pickup. We just need to agree on the timing."

They retreated to their rooms to hash out the rest of the plans. They discussed every minute, pinpointed every position, worked through all the potential scenarios, and carefully mapped it all out.

By the end of two days, they had exhausted every detail of May's rescue and Kerlan's ball, and even Ana's diligence was wearing thin.

"There's no chance we can get her today or tomorrow?" she'd pestered Ramson.

"No," Ramson replied on the afternoon of the second day, lounging on Ana's cot. "We need to attend the show and play by the rules."

"But—"

"Do you really want to rob a man before attending his

party?" He flipped a goldleaf between his fingers; the coin caught the late-afternoon sun, flashing as Ramson made it appear, and then disappear again. "We're walking into the lion's den. There's only so much we can control. But if Kerlan wanted us dead, we'd be dead already."

"Why do you say that?" Ana looked up from the corner where she sat, straight-backed and cross-legged amid dozens of parchments with the maps and plans they had scribbled. Parcels of their supplies were stacked neatly against the wall—outfits, mostly, for the next few days. They'd spent a good portion of their coin—and the rest, well, Ana assumed she and Ramson would split it between them when the time came to part ways.

The thought filled her with a strange feeling, and she quickly looked at him again—his tousled sandy hair peeking over her pillows—to make sure he was still there.

"I've been in touch with some of his contacts. He'll be expecting us at his ball. That's why, while you corner Tetsyev, I'll be upstairs distracting Kerlan so he doesn't notice anything out of the ordinary." He flicked the goldleaf into the air and caught it; when he opened his palm again, it was gone. "He thinks I'm going to offer him a Trade."

Ana bit the end of her pen. "And what *are* you going to do?"

"Kill him? Charm him? Who knows." Ramson gave her a wicked smile, and Ana suspected he knew exactly what he was going to do. She'd learned to stop asking for answers she'd never get.

So Ana returned to her papers, focusing on the things she *could* get: May, her alchemist, and a way back to her brother.

* * *

Boom-ba-da-BOOM.

The drums beat. The torches blazed. The audience cheered. Yet tonight they struck a different rhythm in Ana's heart. Tonight they were a countdown for her as she weaved through the crowds of sleepy, intoxicated nobles.

It was the fourth night of their stay at Novo Mynsk, and the evening of May's performance. Everything hinged on tonight.

Bogdan paced the stage, his voice booming across the crowded auditorium. Was it Ana's imagination, or did a sheen of sweat coat the entertainer's brow?

The Ice Queen had finished her performance; she stood at the side of the stage outside the glass, beaming at the crowd. She was the constant on a stage of rotating Affinites, their displays filling the arena with water and rocks and fire and all other elements imaginable.

Bogdan spread his arms. "Next up, mesyrs and meya damas, we have an earth Affinite."

Every fiber in Ana's body drew taut.

"She can coax life from nothing but mud; she can make your favorite flowers bloom brighter than the stars in the night sky!"

Onstage, the curtains parted. An assistant scurried out and placed a pot at the edge of the glass wall before ducking backstage.

From the darkness of the curtains, a silhouette emerged—and Ana's world hissed into sharp focus. The Affinite shuffled forward in an oversized dark brown dress sewn with glittery red flowers, their stems curling around her body. Her shoulders were slumped, her outline smaller and bonier than Ana remembered, and her head was bent. Her lovely ocean eyes were hidden.

Ana fought down tears as May, barely half the size of the other Affinites that had appeared in the ring, stumbled onto the center of the stage. Titters started in the audience, and Bogdan gave an accommodating chuckle. "Come now, darling!" he boomed. "We haven't got all day!"

May's eyes were fixed upon a spot on the floor as she tried to quicken her pace. Her skirts twisted around her ankles; she stumbled and fell with a *thud*.

A small, distressed noise escaped Ana as the crowd jeered; she felt Ramson's hand close around her arm. His eyes glinted. "All good things—" he whispered.

—come to those who wait.

Still, Ana's rage coiled white-hot within her. She stretched her Affinity, brushing it hungrily over the blood of the crowd. How she wished to unleash her power unto these bastards—to let *them* feel pain and helplessness.

"She may be small, but she is *extremely* talented," Bogdan boasted. "She can create rocks, and she can break them apart. She can manipulate them. And she has a special *touch of life* with anything growing from the earth. My honored guests, I present to you: Child of Earth!"

A murmur rippled through the crowd. Onstage, May crouched by the pot of dead flowers. Despite everything, the expression on her face was a mix of sorrow and hope as she stretched out her hands.

For a few moments, nothing seemed to happen. And then the crowd gave a collective gasp, pointing as a lovely green hue seeped up the stalks like ink. Red blossomed into the petals. In front of their very eyes, May was breathing life back into the plant. And Ana found herself leaning forward slightly.

The gasps of the crowd, the animal masks, the torches, and the blackstone glass faded, and there was just May. She sat in the middle of a clearing, surrounded by tall, snowcapped pines. Her hands were cupped around a single white daisy, wilted from the snow and locked in the hard, frozen ground. Her eyes were closed, and she hummed softly. Ana had watched as, slowly, the daisy unfurled, its petals uncurling to face the winter sun.

It had felt like watching a miracle.

The memory dissipated as the crowds in the Playpen broke into a smattering of applause. Onstage, the Ice Queen beamed.

Bogdan spread his arms. "The smallest ones are often the most underestimated and tend to be much stronger than we anticipate." He paused theatrically, waving his hands. The rings on his fingers glittered.

"Now, does anyone have any requests for our talented Child of Earth?"

A cry immediately went up. "Have her grow a fruit tree!"

"Make her juggle rocks!"

"Ask her to make a statue from earth!"

And on and on it went, copperstones and silverstones and goldleaves clattering at Bogdan's polished black shoes while May kept her head bowed. Nausea pounded at Ana's stomach as wave after wave of jeering calls and mocking yells continued, and Bogdan shouted orders for May to comply with.

"Hey." A pair of hazel eyes, a warm hand coming to rest gently but firmly on her shoulder. "It'll all be over soon. She'll be safe, with us."

Ana looked down and realized that she had gripped the sleeve of his peacoat. She snatched her hand back.

Something caught her attention. Onstage, a leather sack the size of Bogdan's head had landed. Gold coins spilled like guts across the Penmaster's feet, glittering viciously in the firelight.

A hush fell across the crowd. Ramson straightened.

From somewhere near the stage, a clear tenor rang out. "Penmaster, I have a *very special* request to make—one that I believe the audience will very much enjoy!"

Bogdan stooped to pick up the bulging pouch of goldleaves, his mouth hanging open. Coins continued to spill like water from the overflowing bag.

"Well, *mesyr,*" Bogdan exclaimed, a slight breathlessness to his tone. "You have certainly shown your dedication to entertainment!"

Behind him, May had finally lifted her head and was watching with sharp intent. The Ice Queen's beam looked frozen, forced. In the shadows of the wings, the pale-eyed broker observed with unimpassioned interest.

A feeling of foreboding descended upon Ana. She searched the crowd for the owner of the voice, panic low but rising within her. This was wrong. The amount of goldleaves offered up was enough to feed fifty families for an entire year. It was enough to buy a small dacha.

No one in their right mind would offer up this much money for a few moments of entertainment.

Onstage, Bogdan's eyes sparkled in delight. "And how else," the Penmaster continued, his voice growing louder as he held up the pouch of coins, "are affairs conducted here at the Playpen but through gold and coin? Mesyrs, meya damas, and everyone—I say we hear out this civilian who seems set to give us the show of the night!"

As the crowd burst into thunderous applause and roared their approvals, something moved amid them. A flash of gold, a hooded figure.

As the man took a light leap onto the stage, Ana found herself gazing into a familiar golden mask.

There was no mistaking it. It was the nobleman she had bumped into on her first night at the Playpen. He wore the same mask he'd worn then, with a derisive crying face, yet it was the burning in his eyes that she remembered. That first night, she had only glimpsed him, but he had looked irate.

Something wasn't right.

"Ramson," Ana whispered, but the man had begun speaking.

"I've been to many, *many* Affinite shows," the gold-masked nobleman cried, his voice lofty, his hands raised in elegant, sweeping motions. "And I have waited for this moment for *so long.*"

Ana began to move forward. She wasn't sure why, but she found herself pushing past people with a growing urgency to reach the stage. To reach May. She heard Ramson hiss her name behind her; sensed the thrum of his blood as he began to follow her.

"We're glad to have you here, noble mesyr!" Bogdan chortled, patting his bag of goldleaves. His smile stretched from ear to ear. "Let me know any and all requests you'd like to make of this Affinite, and I can—"

"I wish for everyone gathered here to remember this glorious moment with me!" the gold-masked man crowed. With a flourish, he slipped off his hood. His hair shone red as he stepped forward, closer to the edge of the stage. He ripped his mask off, tossing it onto the ground in front of the glass.

Ana stopped in place. The face onstage was alight with triumph and the orange-red glow of the torchlight. And it was utterly familiar.

Someone's hands closed around her wrist. Dimly, she heard Ramson speaking to her. "Ana, *listen* to me—"

But she couldn't. She was staring at the man's face; it drew her back to her childhood in the Palace, when he'd brought her steaming tea and fresh pirozhky pies—but it was his words and the brightness in his eyes that had warmed her to the core.

"I know him," she said hollowly.

"You—what?"

Onstage, the red-haired man had availed himself of a torch. "My fellow *noble* guests, I want you all to remember one thing." He held the torch up, and the triumphant expression on his face twisted in hatred.

"I know him," Ana gasped. "Ramson, he's an—"

"Long live the Revolution." With all his strength, the red-haired man smashed the burning torch onto the stage.

20

Flames roared to life along the thread of oil that poured from the torch, winding along the marble floor like a shimmering, transparent serpent. For a moment, the man was hidden from view behind the wall of fire. And then he stepped through, his hands outstretched, and two pillars of flames shot from his palms into the air.

The screaming started.

Ana ran for the stage.

The crowd jostled against her as the nobles fled like frightened children, the leers on their faces replaced by unadulterated fear. But Ana's eyes were fixed on the fire Affinite.

Yuri.

She remembered the sparks in his coal-gray eyes back then, when he would slip ptychy'molokos onto her dinner trays. That warmth had grown to a raging fire—wild and untamed.

He'd planned something—she didn't know what—but the show, the gold, had all been a ruse to get him to the stage. And now May's life was in danger.

Movement in the ceiling alcoves drew her attention. The

marksmen shifted, orange torchlight glinting off their blackstone arrows.

Ana's gaze whipped to the stage. Beyond the searing flames, behind the blackstone glass, stood May, alone. The broker was gone; she thought she saw a flash of his back as he disappeared behind the curtains.

The archers nocked, and drew.

For a terrifying second, the world seemed to slow, and all that Ana heard were arrows whistling as they shot toward the stage.

Ana reached for May's blood—and again, her Affinity hit cold, empty blackstone. Panic surged in her chest—

The stage exploded. Not in blood and not in fire . . . but in ice. Crystal-white ice crackled to life above the arena, forming a hard, glittering arch over the entire stage. The arrows ricocheted off the ice and clattered to the ground.

Onstage, the Ice Queen straightened, her hands outstretched, her ash-white hair whipping in the heat of the flames. She turned, locking gazes with Yuri. And gave a single slow nod.

Together, they turned to the blackstone glass wall behind them. Fire and ice crackled into existence from thin air, whorls of silver-white and flaming red that slammed against the glass.

They were going to bring down the arena. And if that glass fell, if the stage collapsed, everyone underneath would be crushed.

Which meant Ana had to get May out before that.

"May," she screamed, searching for a glimpse of the girl behind the elements that raged against the glass. She was so close—but still not close enough to protect May.

A shock wave of heat pulsed from the stage, engulfing her. Ana threw up her arms and squinted at the bright, impossible spectacle.

Yuri channeled fire from the torches encircling the arena. Heat coursed in a powerful, blazing ring around the stage, lighting up the Playpen as the terrified audience fled for the exit. He was strong—much stronger than he'd been back at the Palace. Or had he kept the true power of his Affinity from her? To be able to manipulate that much fire, whereas most fire Affinites could barely keep a small candle going . . .

She had to get behind that glass prison. She had to get to May.

Ana stretched her Affinity, and her power roared to life, brighter than any flame. She latched on to Yuri and the Ice Queen and tugged.

Through watering eyes, she saw them stumble and crash. The raging fire and roaring ice stopped, leaving an uneven, ice-covered wall. Cracks ran jaggedly along its surface, spreading like veins.

Yuri rolled over, and his burning gaze landed on Ana. He raised his palms.

"Yuri—"

As flames exploded from his hands, something collided painfully with her stomach. Ana slammed against the edge of the stage and found herself looking into Ramson's face as he untangled himself from her. Soot smudged his cheeks. "Ana," he croaked, but she shoved him back and leapt onto the stage.

Through the gently steaming ice and gray-tinted glass stood the shadow of a small figure. The translucent barrier between them made it seem like a dream.

May raised a hand. From the flowerpot before her rose a lump of earth. With a crunching noise, it shrank, hardening into a rock. May lashed out, and the rock smashed into the blackstone glass.

Boom.

Again.

And again.

On her fifth try, there was a splintering sound. Spiderweb cracks spread along the glass; the ice emitted a series of explosive pops.

She was breaking the wall.

As Ana watched the child raise her hands and draw the rock back again, it suddenly dawned on her that May was working *with* Yuri and the Ice Queen.

May was part of the plan. She was taking a stance, fighting with the rebels to end the cruelty of the Playpen, to bring down—literally—the glass prison that had caged them.

The rock swung forward. With a final resounding crack, the glass shattered. For a moment, the shards tumbled in the air, ice and glass intermingled, a thousand pieces of glistening fragments fractaling in the blazing torchlight. And then they fell, racing toward the ground with piercing intent.

Ana dove for May.

Yuri dove for Ana.

On the other end of the stage, the Ice Queen flung her hand out. Ice rose from the ground like a solid white wave, hardening into a barrier over their heads.

Fragments of what had been the blackstone glass rained down all around them, filling the air with soft tinkling as they bounced off the ice archway overhead.

Ana's shoulder slammed onto the stage as Yuri tackled her, his hands at her throat, his teeth bared in rage. She fought back, her fingers prying at his hands, her mask hot and sweaty against her face. "Yuri," she choked. "Stop—"

"I'll have you know how it feels to die at the hand of an Affinite," he growled, lifting his hand.

"Yuri!" She ripped her mask off. "It's me!"

He froze, hand hovering above her, expression suspended between confusion and rage. And then, slowly, recognition seeped into his eyes, along with disbelief. He drew back, lifting his hands from her as though he'd been burned. "Kolst—"

"Ana!" The sweetest voice rang out, one Ana would recognize anywhere.

May knelt on the stage, barely ten paces from Ana, the astonishment on her face quickly giving way to joy.

Relief hit Ana so hard that a half laugh, half sob bubbled from her lips. "May," she cried, reaching forward.

An arrow whizzed past her and struck the marble stage.

"May!" Ana's cry turned to one of panic as another arrow lanced off the stage, a hand's breadth from her.

"Dyanna!" Behind her, Yuri gave an agonized yell.

At the edge of the stage, the Ice Queen—Dyanna—looked up, her face almost as ashen as her hair. Blood, startlingly red against her pallor, dripped from her nose.

A blur whizzed toward her. Dyanna's body jolted with the shock of the impact. She slumped onto the ground, the shaft of an arrow protruding from her back. The thick scent of blood filled the air.

"Dyanna! Dyan—" Yuri's shout broke into a choked sob. "No. *No.*"

"Yuri!" Ana seized his arm, pinning him beneath the ice barrier. "We have to get out—"

An arrow struck the ground next to May. The child's eyes widened as she looked up; she turned and began to run toward the velvet curtains.

In the shadows of the viewing alcoves above, the marksmen nocked and drew. Ana was already scrambling to her feet, even as arrows shot toward them, even as she realized that she would not reach May before an arrow found its mark.

But someone else was running toward the child. Ramson flung himself at May, skidding across the ruined marble on his nobleman's trousers and peacoat. Shattered glass and ice crunched beneath him. He rolled, bundled May into his arms, and dove for the curtains.

Whoosh. The arrow grazed his abdomen. He arched his back in pain, gave a muffled grunt, and staggered.

Ana was already running. She reached Ramson's side at the same time as Yuri; together, they hauled Ramson and May off the stage and into the darkness behind the velvet curtains.

21

Backstage, the air was musty and the scent of sweat lingered. They stumbled through the sets of drapes and down the stage into a chamber, dimly lit by several torches in sconces. Dark corridors stretched out toward their left and right. The screams of the crowd seemed to come from a distant world, as though the thick drapes had partitioned them from the chaos and granted them this temporary sanctuary.

In the semidarkness, a small voice found her. "Ana?"

A sob welled up in Ana's throat. "May," she croaked. They both moved for each other at the same time, colliding with cries of relief. Ana held on tightly. "Your hair." Tears burned her eyes. "It's all sooty."

May laughed and clasped Ana's cheeks in her hands, tracing tears away with her small fingers. "It's you. It's really you."

More tears spilled down Ana's face. She chuckled, a wet, gargling sound, and pressed her forehead to May's. "Of course it's me. I would *never* leave you."

Ahead, Yuri cleared his throat. A small flame danced in his palm, illuminating the corridor ahead. "This way."

Ana clasped May's hand, and they hurried after him. "Where are we going?"

"It's the Revolution, Ana," said May. Her eyes were bright. "Yuri's a *Red*cloak—a rebel, for the Affinites. I met the other Redcloaks when I was brought here. We're going to rescue them right now."

Behind them, Ramson coughed loudly and stumbled to a sharp stop by the stone walls. Ana's stomach clenched as he braced himself, one hand at his side where the arrow had grazed him. She could sense the blood seeping into the cloth of his tunic. "Ramson!"

"I'll be fine," he rasped. "Just our luck. Damn . . . Revolution."

"The Whitecloaks have stood by for too long and done nothing, watching us as we suffer." Yuri's fists were clenched, and he spat the words. "It's time we take matters into our own hands. We're a reminder that their cloaks are not white, but *red*—stained with the blood of Affinites. We represent the flame of hope—"

"Man, now is *not* the time for poetics," Ramson gritted out. "If we don't get out of here, the only thing red will be your blood on a Whitecloak's sword."

"We need to leave," Ana agreed, gripping May's hand tightly. *"Now."*

Yuri looked slightly put out, but it was May who spoke. "No," she said, pulling her hand from Ana's. "I won't leave without the others."

It was as though, in a week's time, May had aged years.

May's mouth was a firm line as she gazed back at Ana, but her eyes were pleading. "Yuri and Dyanna planned this, and they saved me. They've saved a lot of other Affinites. And I want to . . . I want to help, too." May reached out again, taking Ana's hands between her own. "Remember the girl who gave me a ptychy'moloko at the Vyntr'makt? I thought of her every day I was here." Her voice trembled, but Ana heard a hint of steely determination beneath. "You saved me, Ana. And I wanted to help her, and others like her. I want . . ." May drew a deep breath, and her eyes were shining as she looked up. "I want the whole Empire, every single Affinite, to know how it feels to . . . to have hope."

The spark in May's eyes and the strength in her words stirred something in Ana's chest.

Before she could say anything, a noise sounded down the corridor to their right. A rhythmic clacking that grew louder by the second.

Ramson swore. "Guards," he whispered, heaving himself up. "You, Poet. Where are the Affinites?"

"Corridor on the left," Yuri said quickly. "The room at the very end." He reached into his pocket and took out a set of keys.

"I can get them." May stepped forward and took the keys from Yuri. She turned to Ana, her eyes bright, the torches carving her small, solid shadow against a world of flickering flames. "Wait here, Ana." And then she was gone, a slip of light swallowed by the darkness.

Ana gestured at Ramson. "Go with her. Yuri and I will stay here and fend off the guards."

Ramson hesitated. "Don't die," he said.

"Don't get kidnapped," she replied.

She heard his raspy chuckle and hid a smile even as she turned to face the approaching footsteps.

She felt Yuri's gaze burning into her back. "You're alive," he breathed, and she finally let herself look at him. His eyes were wide, as though he were drinking in the sight of her. "I . . . I don't believe this."

"And you," Ana said. "You're a . . . a rebel."

The footsteps thundered, just around the corner. "Later?" Yuri said, tilting his head.

"Later," she agreed, and raised her hands.

Six guards appeared, just as Ramson had predicted. Their eyes widened as the torchlight exploded at them in two columns of flames. Ana hung back, watching in awe as the once-scrawny boy advanced on the guards, flames erupting from his palms and curling on the narrow stone walls of the corridor.

A shadow flashed to her left, on the steps leading down from the heavy velvet curtains.

Ana turned, sensing the powerful thrum of blood even before she saw the woman. Steel blades flashed as the newcomer stepped into the light, her black cat mask glittering in the torchlight.

"You," Ana said hollowly.

The woman had changed from her skimpy courtesan's outfit into tight-fitting black breeches and a shirt, but it was the same steel Affinite who guarded the doors of the Playpen every night, the one who had tried to stop Ana from entering. There was no sign of her companion, the Yaeger, as she stepped in front of Ana, blocking the path. Countless small blades lined the belt at her hips, gleaming like teeth.

Instinct screamed at Ana to hurl her Affinity at the woman, to fight with every fiber in her body.

But May's words held her back. They were the same, Ana and this steel Affinite: feared for the qualities that marked them different, and persecuted by those with power.

Ana raised her hand. "Please, don't do this."

The woman's eyes glinted. "If you're not dead by the end of the night, it'll be my life he takes."

"Who?" Ana asked, though she suspected she knew the answer.

"Lord Kerlan." The steel Affinite raised her blade. "I'm sorry."

Ana didn't give her another chance to speak. She seized the Affinite's blood and slammed her against the back wall. The Affinite's eyes widened in surprise, but she twisted, and a blade shot from her belt.

Ana dove to one side; the throwing knife lodged into the wall behind her with a *plink.* She rolled and pounced to her feet, but in that second, she lost her hold on the steel Affinite.

The second blade sliced Ana's arm; she cried out and crashed against the wall, her Affinity diverted by the warmth leaking down her arm and the sharp pain of her flesh cut open.

A third knife flashed, but Ana was quicker. She grasped the steel Affinite's blood and squeezed. The woman gave an agonized scream, which quickly cut off into a choking noise as blood began to fill her lungs.

"You don't have to do this," Ana rasped. "Come with us. Fight with us."

The steel Affinite shuddered. Her head was bent, and a puddle of blood had gathered on the floor beneath her. When she lifted her face, her eyes were bloodshot, red dripping from her nose and lips. "I . . ."

Pressure clamped down on Ana's mind, so absolute that she cried out. The world dulled as her Affinity vanished; her head throbbed against a familiar, cold wall.

A shadow parted from the velvet curtains. The yaeger

stepped into the torchlight. For the first time since Ana had seen her, though, she looked afraid.

Ana didn't know why until a silky voice caressed her like the night. "Kill her, Nuryasha."

A figure stepped partially into the torchlight, lurking behind the yaeger and the steel Affinite. But even from there, Ana could see the glint of the broker's pale, icy eyes as he regarded her.

The steel Affinite—Nuryasha—coughed blood and palmed her blade. She hesitated.

"Kill her," the broker ordered again. The yaeger's eyes narrowed. The pressure on Ana's head increased. She sank to her knees, dizzy with pain, grasping for something—anything—that would save her. One thought comforted her: that May was safe with Ramson.

Nuryasha flung the blade.

A small blur shot out from the corridor to Ana's left, crashing into her middle and knocking her aside. Ana collided with the wall, pain erupting in her back and her injured arm.

Blinking through the dark spots in her vision, she looked up.

May stood where Ana had been moments before, the sheath of a throwing knife protruding from her abdomen. A dark patch was rapidly spreading across her dress, crimson seeping into her fingers as she tried to stanch its flow with her bare hands. Her eyes were wide with surprise as she met Ana's gaze, her mouth puckered in a slight O.

She staggered and fell lightly to the ground.

Time seemed to stop, and the rest of the world dissipated until there was only the image of May's small figure slumped on the reddening floor, seared indelibly into Ana's mind. Her ears filled with a strange ringing silence as she clawed her way to the child's side; she thought she heard screaming, but nothing made sense anymore.

Ana lifted May into her arms. Had she always been this light?

"May," Ana whispered. Her hands came away sticky and dark.

The world crashed back in a whirl of smoke and blood. It took Ana a moment to realize that the yaeger's barrier on her mind had lifted.

Out of the corner of her eye, she saw Ramson shove the yaeger aside, his dagger protruding from her back. Nuryasha lay at his feet, motionless in a pool of her own blood. The broker was gone.

Ramson's eyes latched on to May, and he swore softly.

"Ana," whispered May.

"Hush." Ana clasped her shaking hands over May's, pressing against the wound. "I'll stop the bleeding, and we'll get you bandaged up."

May's chest hitched in short, shallow breaths. A dizzying amount of blood hit Ana's senses; her Affinity shuddered, and she bit back her nausea.

"My ma-ma said," May murmured, and drew another rattling breath, "'We are but dust and stars.' She told me . . . before we separated . . . to look for her in the earth and in the stars."

A sob choked Ana's throat. "No," she gasped. "We're going to find her, May—*May!*" She cradled her friend's head as her eyes fluttered. "Listen to me. Your ma-ma is waiting for you out there. Waiting to *see you.* We're going to find her together, all right?"

"I don't . . . I don't want to go." May fought for breath, tears drowning her eyes. "I want . . . to live."

Ana scrabbled at May's wound, desperately grasping at the blood and pushing it back. It leaked through her fingers and her Affinity. She'd never learned to use her power this way. For her entire life, she'd learned only to hurt and torture. She had never learned to heal.

A gut-wrenching scream tore from her throat. "I can't," she gasped. "Ramson—Yuri—someone! *Help!*"

"The Revolution." May's small fingers curled around Ana's, tugging gently, insistently. "Promise me, Ana, you'll make it better. For my ma-ma. For all the Affinites. And promise . . . you'll find her."

"I will, I will," Ana sobbed. She would have promised anything in that moment to keep May talking for a little while longer. "I'll do it, May, but I need you—"

The world spun, and May's blood poured out like sand in an hourglass, time careening in a relentless blur toward that inevitable end.

"Dust and stars," May whispered. She had started to shiver. "We are but dust and stars."

"Please, May." Ana couldn't breathe. "*Please.* Don't go where I can't follow."

May drew a long breath. "I'm always here, Ana," she whispered, and closed her ocean eyes, her words fading like a whisper of wind. "You'll find me in the stars."

22

Ana clung to May, curling her own body around the child's. Was there a word to describe grief so deep that it cleaved you apart, carved a hole inside of you and left you hollow?

Ana was dimly aware that the fighting had stopped, that the guards' bodies littered the corridor before them. Several people had fanned out around her, watching her. Warm hands grasped her shoulders. A familiar voice called her name.

A hand cupped her cheek, lifting her chin. She found herself looking into Ramson's eyes. The usual mirth had disappeared from them, leaving them a somber hazel. Gently, he brushed a strand of her hair behind her ear, his fingers lingering by her cheek. She could almost read his thoughts in the gesture. *I'm sorry.* The words trembled in the air between them.

"Ana." Yuri's voice was hollow. "I'm sorry."

Ramson whirled and slammed Yuri against the wall. "You," Ramson snarled, "have no right to be sorry."

Yuri choked, his hands flying to Ramson's wrist, but Ramson didn't let go, and Yuri didn't resist.

"If you hadn't tried your little stunt, this would never have happened. You think a revolution is a game? You think making a big show in Kerlan's backyard counts as impressive?" Ramson wrenched his hand free; Yuri staggered, rubbing his throat. "This isn't a revolution. This is a massacre. And it's about to get worse if we don't get out of here *right now.*"

Ana barely registered the words; they were beyond her. Something had been torn from inside her, left a gaping wound in her that was raw and bleeding and numb. She was one step from the abyss, just as she had been almost a year ago. "Ramson," she said.

Ramson started, and backed away from Yuri.

All around Ana, watching with expressions ranging from sorrow to fear, were Affinites. They ranged from children to grown men and women, from all over the world. They wore an assortment of glitzy, gaudy outfits still fresh from the night's performances. She counted nine of them.

Nine Affinites. Nine lives in exchange for May's. Was it worth it? How did one balance the significance of a life against another? Was there even a way to measure?

You don't, Ana thought, placing a hand on May's cheek. It was still warm.

Papa had once told her, after Mama's death, that there were two types of grief. One was the type that crushed you, that broke your soul and shattered your heart, and left you an empty shell. The other was a grief that made you stronger. You rose from it, you sharpened it, and you carried it with you as a piece of your armor. And you made yourself better.

In that way, you never truly lost that person. You carried them with you.

Ana closed her eyes and burrowed her face in the crook of May's neck. Tears slipped down her cheeks, sinking into May's hair.

Promise me, Ana, you'll make it better. For my ma-ma. For all the Affinites.

Ana drew another deep breath. The urgency to act, to move, sparked in her a smallest light in the dark. For the first time, she focused on the faces of the Affinites all around her, watching her silently. Waiting.

She pushed herself to her feet, cradling May's body against her chest. Ana searched the chamber and met Yuri's eyes; he looked down, guilt stamped onto his face as clearly as if it had been branded by a hot iron. "We need to take the tunnels out," Ana said.

"Dyanna taught us to navigate the tunnels," Yuri said, the sadness almost swallowing his voice. "She's been working with the brokers for years, preparing for this moment. We have a safe house just outside of town."

"Then we need to get moving and get to that safe house," Ramson cut in. "You just took out an entire squad of guards; it should be a while before the reinforcements come. If we're fast, we might not encounter any at all."

Yuri narrowed his eyes. "Who appointed you as leader?"

"You and your incompetence," Ramson snapped without missing a beat. "What, exactly, were you planning to do after you smashed the stage and set every guard in the area after you? Sit here and recite poetry?"

"Stop," Ana said, sharply enough for both men to turn and look at her. She drew a deep, shuddering breath, trying to clear her head. May's body was light in her arms; like this, with her eyes closed, she might have simply been asleep after a long day.

Focus, she told herself. She would not let May down. Ana turned to Yuri. "Ramson and I had planned to take the tunnels out of this place. It sounds like we are aligned."

Yuri nodded. "It's a maze down here, which can work to our advantage since any reinforcements will be spread pretty thin."

"Then what are we waiting for?" Ramson pushed himself off the wall he'd been leaning against, hand on his injured side. The bleeding had stopped, Ana sensed.

Yuri turned to the silent Affinites who waited near the wall. "Redcloaks," he said, and his voice was grave and steady. "Our time has come. Anyone who tries to prevent us from reaching our freedom is the enemy. Don't hesitate to take them down." He paused, his eyes blazing. "And I swear on my Deities and whatever gods or faith you take that I will protect all of you with my life."

It was like setting a spark to kindling. An invisible breeze seemed to stir through the Affinites, drawing them to stand taller, replacing the fear in their faces with determination.

Yuri snapped his fingers and fires sparked to life in his palms, brighter than the light of any globefire. They threw flickering shadows on the stone walls, the blood and bodies on the floor cast in monochrome. "This way," he muttered, and Ana, Ramson, and the Affinites followed.

They walked in silence but for the sound of their heels clacking against the floors and their ragged breaths. Ramson stayed close to Ana, casting her sidelong glances. She kept her gaze straight, on Yuri's flame-red hair, trying not to think of May's weight in her arms.

Gradually, the stone floors grew coarse and slippery with moss, the tunnels branching out like roots of a tree and growing narrower and narrower until they had to walk single file. Several times, Ana was seized by the sudden fear that they were lost, that they would never make it out of these tunnels, that they would die trapped in an Affinite broker's maze. She kept her Affinity extended, searching for signs of warm, coursing blood approaching.

After what seemed like hours, the air changed. It grew cooler; a far-off breeze stirred the flames on Yuri's palm and kissed Ana's cheeks. Gradually, the darkness eased around them and distant light appeared, and soon they approached a broken door, swinging off its hinges.

Yuri held it open and waited as, one by one, the Affinites took their first, tentative steps into freedom.

The stars shone a cold white light on them as they stole through the town like shadows, following Yuri through dark alleyways. The streets grew emptier, the cobblestones rougher until they faded to dust; closely intertwined red-roofed dachas turning to simple cottages with clay walls.

The Syvern Taiga loomed, a jagged wall of trees. At the edge of the forest was a single cottage, lights flaring stubbornly from its windows. As they drew closer to it, Ana could make out a wooden sign hanging on the door, declaring in lavish cursive: *Shamaïra's Shop of Spiritualism.*

The group stopped at the dacha's steps, shivering, their breathing ragged. Yuri stepped up and rapped.

The door swung open at the first knock. Arms aching from exertion, Ana stumbled inside after the other Affinites.

Warmth enveloped her. A fire crackled in a hearth behind

a slanted wooden table, and the air was heavy with the smell of incense and aromatic spices. Her first impression was that the dacha was tidy, with a distinct décor that was like nothing she'd ever seen. Bookcases lined the walls, chock-full of tomes with golden inscriptions in an elegant, curling language. A giant rug sprawled in the center of the room, intricately patterned with birds and roses hewn in rich reds and deep golds. Cushioned settees surrounded it, and atop a low coffee table in the center rested a large silver samovar.

Yuri removed his shoes and stepped into the parlor.

Ana wanted nothing more than to collapse on one of those settees and wake up to May's bright blue eyes.

"Speak and be recognized by the Mother of All Knowledge, you mortals," a low voice boomed, startling Ana.

"Shamaïra, it's me," Yuri called.

There was a strange shuffling sound, and from behind a heavy brocade curtain emerged a middle-aged woman. Her eyes were outlined in black kohl against her rich olive skin, and she wore a silken shawl over her head, draped loosely over her shoulders. It was her bold cheekbones and fierce eyes that drew Ana's attention. She was beautiful; a diminutive lioness.

"Oh, it's just you," the woman growled in the raspy voice of a pipe smoker. She paused as her gaze settled on the rest of the group. Her expression shifted and she broke into a smile as fiery as the sun. "Welcome."

"Not tonight, Shamaïra," Yuri said wearily, and tilted his head toward Ana.

Shamaïra's eyes softened. "Oh," was all she said as she strode over and placed a hand on May. Ana tensed—but the woman's touch was gentle. Her eyes found Ana's, and there was such a profound sadness in them that Ana felt the blank, unfeeling wall she had put up beginning to crack.

"A Chi'gon Affinite," Shamaïra murmured. "We shall return her soul. Could I?"

Ana tightened her grip on May. She felt as though, if she just held on for a bit longer, she could delay the terrifying reality that awaited her. The reality of a world without her friend.

"She is passed, my child," Shamaïra said softly. "And we must return her to her gods and her loved ones. It does not do for the dead to dwell in this world."

This time Ana let Shamaïra lift May from her arms, as carefully as one would hold a newborn. May's head lolled against Shamaïra's shoulder, and Ana remembered the times she had carried May after a long day of travel. She hadn't minded the weight back then.

Now that was all Ana had left: memories, and the ghost of May's weight in her empty arms.

23

Shamaïra's dacha had a garden covered in overgrown vines and potted plants of every species imaginable, some of which Ana hadn't come across even in her studies at the Palace. She pushed past the ferns, venturing deeper into the silence. The scent of fresh, overturned mud and melted snow and the mysterious fragrance of plants lingered in the cool night air. Behind the yard loomed the vast outline of the Syvern Taiga.

Ana leaned against a wooden trellis, wrapping her arms around herself. The cold crept into her bones, but she might as well have been frozen—a girl carved of ice.

She felt as though if she let herself thaw, she would lose everything.

Someone moved behind her. Ana knew that presence like it was a part of her: warmth and light and flame, the smell of the kitchen hearth and freshly baked ptychy'moloko and hot tea served in a silver samovar. She turned, and it was like gazing at a stranger. The boy she had known had been soft, cheeks round and pale from the comforts of the Palace, hair shorn short. He'd laughed easily, his eyes had sparkled, and if she closed her eyes she could see him turning from the fire in the kitchen, sweat shimmering on his forehead and soot on his face.

Now, only twelve moons later, he towered over her, muscles replacing his thin freckled arms, chin chiseled and shadowed with scruff. His hair had grown to his shoulders, swept up in a ponytail that shone like a flame when it caught the light. There was a hardness to his coal-gray eyes that had never been there before.

They watched each other for a minute, Ana looking for traces of the boy she'd known. It was as though he had become a stranger. She reached out, tentatively, to touch a cut on his neck.

Something melted in Yuri's expression. "It's me, Kolst Pryntsessa," he murmured as he caught her hands, his own rough and calloused. Ana choked down a sob as she looked at them, remembering how the creases of his fingers had always been stained white with flour.

As Yuri pulled her into his arms, she buried her face in his strong shoulders, searching for the scent of baked goods and sweat and kitchen soot. Instead, she smelled fire and smoke.

But he was still Yuri—her Yuri, the one who had sat outside her chambers during her worst nightmares. The one who'd brought trays of pirozhky pies to her just so he could crouch outside the crack of her door and whisper to her.

"Call me Ana," she whispered when she finally drew away, swiping at her tears.

"I thought you were dead," Yuri choked. He was crying, too. "The Court announced—"

"I didn't kill Papa." The words tumbled from Ana's mouth brokenly, pleadingly. "I was trying to save him—but I couldn't—"

"I know," Yuri said. "I know you, Ana. You always shared your treats with me, no matter how much you liked them. You cried over your pet rabbit for moons on end. You would never do anything like that."

His confirmation sent fresh tears to her eyes and made her feel weak and strong at the same time. "Papa was poisoned, Yuri."

"Poisoned?"

Ana nodded. "I saw a man that night—it was the Palace alchemist who left many years ago. He fed my Papa something, and I watched him die." She shuddered, and Yuri locked his arm around her firmly. "I was trying to draw the poison out." Ana closed her eyes, leaning into her friend, and the words spilled from her. "It was a slow poison, Yuri—it smelled exactly like the bitter medicine Papa was taking all along. It was never helping him to get better—it was making his illness worse. That night was the final dose."

Yuri stiffened by her side. "Deities," he cursed softly.

Ana paused at Yuri's terrified expression.

"Ana," he said, his hand tightening on her shoulder. "There's something you must know. The Kolst Imperator—your brother . . . he's sick."

Her head spun at the words. "What?"

"It's exactly what your father had. The Palace thinks it's a genetic condition passed down from him. Coughing, weakness, and confusion of mind." Yuri shuddered. "But if what you're saying is true, then he's being poisoned as well."

Coughing. Weakness. Confusion of mind. Ana grasped the trellis behind her to stop the world from spinning. The image of her father's face came to her then, pale as a tomb, blood foaming from his mouth, the whites of his eyes showing as he contorted.

Nausea twisted her stomach. "That's impossible," she said, but the words sounded hollow even to her ears. It couldn't be that Luka was being poisoned. Pyetr Tetsyev had not worked at the Palace for many years.

Unless Tetsyev had had inside help. Ana thought of that night, of how the alchemist had entered the Emperor's bedchambers without raising a single alarm.

Yet all she had were wild guesses—until she found Tetsyev himself.

All the answers she sought lay with him.

Ana clasped her hands to stop their shaking. "I'm going back to Luka. One more day, and then I ride for Salskoff." She would speak with Ramson about fulfilling her end of the Trade later. She had lost too much—she couldn't afford to lose Luka, as well. "Is my brother . . . What is his condition?"

"I left the Palace almost ten moons ago." Yuri bowed his head. "When I left . . . he still held Court sessions but spent the rest of his time in his chambers."

Ana felt sick as she thought of Luka, alone in his chambers, the poison slowly consuming his body and mind. Desperation twisted a sharp, cruel blade in her, and for a moment she thought of leaping on a horse and riding to Salskoff.

Think, Ana.

If she returned empty-handed, without Pyetr Tetsyev, she would be treated as a murderer and a traitor.

The Cyrilian Imperial law granted a fair trial, and from the laws she had carefully studied under Papa's guidance, new evidence was grounds for further investigation.

She needed Tetsyev to clear her name. Once she had her title and her innocence again, she would reveal everything and hunt down the conspirators.

"I'm going to get the alchemist, and then I'm going back," Ana repeated, and this time, her voice was steady.

Something flickered in Yuri's eyes. "You're going back? Ana," he said, and grasped her hands. "The future doesn't lie in Luka or the Palace or Salskoff. Cyrilia's rulers have stood by for centuries watching the oppression of our kind. If there's a future, Ana, it isn't there."

It felt as though the small spark of hope in her heart was slowly withering to ash. "Why not?" Ana whispered. "Once I tell Luka all of this, he'll fix it. *We'll* fix it. Together. Just like . . ." Her voice broke. "Just like I promised May."

But there was a sadness to Yuri's eyes that she had never seen before; it descended on the traces of laughter and childhood like the fall of autumn upon summer. "I've seen too much and been through more in the months since I left the Palace, Ana. These cracks in our Empire . . . they can't be fixed by one person alone. The time is past for us to rely on a benevolent ruler."

Ana snatched her hands back. She felt very cold. This boy who stood across from her, tall and distant and utterly unfamiliar, had become no more than a stranger to her.

Before she could respond, footsteps sounded.

They drew apart as Shamaïra appeared at her dacha door, her face somber. She caught Ana's eye and approached.

Ramson followed. He carried May's small body carefully. The Affinites from the Playpen trailed behind, soft-colored lamps swinging from their hands and casting light into the darkness.

Ana took the child from Ramson.

How did the people of Chi'gon bury their dead? May had left the kingdom of her birth before she could even remember much about it; the glimpses that Ana had seen of the Aseatic Isles kingdom were in the stories and songs that May's Ma-ma had told her.

It came to Ana then, with a stirring of the breeze that brought to her the loamy scent of soil. Winter, a child crouched in the snow, nursing to life a small white flower. *My child, we are but dust and stars.*

"We bury her in the earth," she whispered.

Shamaïra gave a single nod. "It is time," she whispered, "to return her home."

They buried May in the ground, surrounded by flowers and plants and the life that thrived in Shamaïra's backyard. They sprinkled flower petals around her. Shamaïra hummed a Nandjian hymn.

Ana slipped a flower—a single white daisy—between May's small hands and planted a kiss on the child's forehead. She smoothed May's hair for the last time before she stood back. Ramson and Yuri picked up their shovels, and Ana watched as May slowly disappeared into the gentle earth.

A breeze stirred between the vines and the ferns, bringing with it the fragrance of snow and flowers. May was light and life and hope; the gods would return her to the earth and the flowers and the life that carried on all around her. She would live on, in the sun that warmed the earth and the stars that made the night a little less dark.

She would live on in the eyes of every Affinite who would see hope.

They stood there for a long time, heads bowed, eyes closed. The wind whispered, the flowers murmured, and Shamaïra's hymn threaded all the way up into the sky of silent, watchful stars.

24

Ana stayed behind after everyone had filed inside to rest for the night. She knelt by the freshly turned soil, her hands resting on the small mound where May had been. She thought of the ptychy'moloko; she thought of the copper coins she'd gifted May; she thought of that light in the snow-covered darkness, the whisper of an angel in the coldest, darkest night.

The light of the stars fell around her like tears.

"I unsee you, Little Tigress."

Ana spun at the voice. Outlined by a single flickering lantern was Shamaïra. "What did you call me?" Ana whispered.

Instead of responding, Shamaïra crossed the garden in a newly donned pair of woven shoes, holding a silver tray carrying a samovar and a lamp. She gently placed both items on the ground before seating herself. The lamp shone a warm light over the earth that held May.

"It's been a long day," Shamaïra said, and proceeded to pour steaming tea from the samovar into two curved glass teacups. A small glass bowl in the center of the tray held sugar cubes. "Nandjians—we have tea for every occasion."

Ana took the teacup with a murmur of thanks. The cup

warmed her hands and was nested in a metal holder patterned in silver medallions.

"You're not the only one who's lost people in this silent war we've been waging," the woman said after she had taken a long sip from her glass. "I lost my son to the Affinite trade many years ago, and I've been searching for him ever since. Twelve years, and I've never given up. Why the hell do you think I'm still in this rotten empire, entertaining Cyrilians with fortune-telling from tea dregs and poetry? Who in their gods-damned mind would shelter rebels leading a revolution that I may never see happen?" Shamaïra's eyes burned. "Few in this world are born to pure happiness and a life of comfort. The gods know that's not what life is about. No, Little Tigress—we take what we are given and we fight like hell to make it better."

Shamaïra's words blazed in the air between them long after she was silent. The tears on Ana's face had cooled and, ashamed, she turned away and swept a quick hand over her cheeks. Her thoughts focused on two words. *Little Tigress.*

It was the nickname Mama had given her. "Why do you call me that?" she said quietly.

"I know who you are." Shamaïra's voice had the silent strength of steel. "I saw the events of that day, at the Vyntr'makt in Salskoff. The Sister showed me; she whispered to me of a great fire inside you, and a grand destiny."

Ana summoned the courage to meet the woman's gaze. "Who are you?"

"I am an Unseer, my darling." Shamaïra's smile was charming yet dangerous beneath her shawl. "There is a myriad of faiths practiced in Nandji, but my particular beliefs also lend to a form of magic. A . . . branch of what you Cyrilians call

'Affinities,' I suppose. We believe in a divine Spirit, split into two halves between a Brother and a Sister." She held up the lamp. "The Brother, the Lord of Light and Lender of Fire, rules over all that is visible to the eye and physical in this world. And the Sister"—Shamaïra set down the lamp—"is the Deity of Darkness and the First Unseeress, goddess to all things metaphysical and spiritual. My Affinity is to her; specifically, to time—both what's past, and what's to come."

Ana frowned. "You can . . . change time?" It felt ridiculous to say.

"No, my child. But I can catch glimpses of it, as one might dip a finger into a grand, sweeping river." Shamaïra put a hand to her heart. "I unsee, Anastacya."

"Then can't you unsee your son?" It felt too easy, too unfair; it felt like false hope, all over again. "Can't you find him?"

And, she thought, ashamed to say it, *can you unsee where I'm meant to go from here?*

Shamaïra laughed. "I cannot unsee without *seeing* first. Without you in front of me, I would unsee nothing." Her smile turned sad. "Without my son before me, I cannot unsee his path."

"Then you are as cursed as I," Ana said, "with your Affinity."

"All Affinities are a double-edged sword. One must simply learn to wield it." There was a brief silence as Shamaïra lifted her cup to her lips. "Drink your tea. It'll get cold."

Ana took a sip; she thought she tasted roses. "Can you tell me where to go from here?" The question stole from her lips in the barest breath.

Shamaïra set down her cup with a gentle clink. Lifting the samovar, she poured herself more, and offered to refill Ana's cup. "That's the funny thing about time, my child. It is a great river, made of an infinite number of little streams. It is your choices that define your path."

Your choices. The words stirred a gentle breeze around Ana. *Your Affinity does not define you.*

But no matter how she wished her Affinity gone or even just different, she was an Affinite. *Us,* May had whispered, back in the Kyrov Vyntr'makt and at the Playpen. *Like us.*

May and countless other Affinites were all victims of cracks in her empire. Ana would fight her way back to Luka's side with Pyetr Tetsyev's confession. She would end the Affinite trade.

Promise me.

She and Luka would fix it all, together. Crack by crack.

Ana drew a deep breath, filling her lungs with the refreshingly cold Cyrilian air. Overhead, the clouds had parted, and stars twinkled in the vast canvas of the moonless night. The scent of snowfall lingered in the air. Snow was coming, and soon. "It has been a pleasure to make your acquaintance, Shamaïra."

Shamaïra's chuckle was like the sound of metal grating. "I have a feeling this is not the end for us. Our paths will cross again, Little Tigress." She placed a hand on Ana's shoulder. "Now, my darling, the Sister tells me there is someone waiting for you in the back room. Someone you, too, wish to see."

The lamps burned low in Shamaïra's parlor when Ana stepped inside. The Affinites and Yuri had spread blankets and pillows across the floor, and most were settling in or already asleep. The air smelled pleasantly of the stew and crispy rice Shamaïra had served for dinner. In the silence, Ana could hear the creak of the windows and door as the wind rose outside. She held her breath as she parted the heavy brocade curtains that partitioned the backroom from the rest of the house. Bookshelves leaned against all four walls, crammed with old, dusty tomes and parchments. In the middle of it all sat a single burgundy settee.

Ana's heart leapt lightly when she caught sight of a familiar mop of sand-brown hair.

Ramson looked up from the settee. He paused, a rag hanging from his hands. His eyes met hers, and heat rushed to Ana's cheeks when she realized that he had taken his shirt off and had been cleaning the blood from his body. A small bucket of water sat in front of him, swirling crimson. Ana's breath hitched as she remembered that he'd been wounded by an arrow when he'd hauled May to safety from the arena.

For a moment, she wanted to turn back and crawl into the blankets Shamaïra had laid out for her. But something pushed her forward.

"Do you . . ." She gestured helplessly at his towel, at the blood still splattering his torso.

He was gazing at her, his face a blank slate, those cunning eyes forever assessing. His voice was quiet when he held out the towel and said, "All right."

Ana carefully seated herself at the edge of the settee, within reaching distance yet as far from him as she could manage. Her hands fumbled with the sodden rag as she began to dab at the splatters of blood on his skin.

He smelled of sweat and iron-tanged blood, infused with a strange mixture of a nobleman's kologne. As she'd suspected,

Ramson was all taut cord and lean muscles: sinewy enough to be strong, yet slim enough to slip through his enemies' fingers. White slashes crisscrossed his flesh—scars, perhaps from the past that he so resolutely hid from her. And his chest . . . she flinched as she looked at it—his chest bore a section of pale, marred flesh. A brand.

"Ana," Ramson said, and her eyes snapped to his guiltily, the image of the brand still lingering in her vision. He was looking directly at her, his eyes almost a bright shade of gold in the lamplight. "I'm sorry about May."

She tried to ignore the rising wind outside; tried not to think of whether May would be cold and alone.

"They stay with us," Ramson said, his voice softer than she'd ever heard it. He tapped his chest. "In here. So long as we don't forget them, or what they stand for."

Ramson was right. Nothing would ever fill the despairing absence left by loss . . . but Ana would carry with her the promises she had made May. And in that way, May would live on.

Ramson's hand closed around hers, and she almost jumped at the sudden touch. "Thank you," he said, his voice husky. He slipped the rag from her fingers and rinsed it in the water.

He took her arm and, with a gentleness she would never have expected from him, began to dab at the wound near her shoulder from Nuryasha's steel blade. She almost shivered, goose bumps rising where his fingers grasped her. For several moments, there was only the sound of water sloshing and the cool, circular trails of the towel where he wiped away the blood, droplets of liquid sliding down her skin and mingling with the traces of warmth that his fingers left.

Ana closed her eyes. She needed a distraction. Something—anything. Before she knew it, words tumbled out from her mouth—the first that she could think of. "Were you a guard or a soldier before you . . . before this?"

Ramson laughed. "Did Shamaïra teach you to see the past as well?"

"You fight like one," she said. "I've seen trained men in combat; your moves are sharp and precise, just like theirs. You have calluses on your hands. And scars on your body. They're not all from daggers—they're long, broad cuts from swords."

She hadn't meant to say this much—she'd only meant to shake some sense into herself. But, sitting this close to him, the ghost of his touches still lingering on her skin, she felt her heart opening to him. The question of his past had begun gnawing at her quite some time ago, and though there was nothing in their Trade that required them to disclose anything to each other . . . she wanted to know.

He was looking at her with that same glint in his eyes, that quirk of his lips. "I'll give you a clue," he conceded. "I was neither a guard nor a soldier, so you're wrong in that aspect. However, you're right in that I was trained for combat."

Ana frowned. He'd been a recruit of some form of organized combat group—perhaps he had never been deployed. Was he a deserter? Or had he dropped out from training to make a more lucrative living for himself? "How did you get here?"

Ramson tapped a finger to his chin. "Let's see. If I remember correctly, we came to Novo Mynsk by horse, narrowly escaped death at the Playpen, had no choice but to follow your Redcloak friend—"

"Ramson." His name was weary on her lips. She should

have known better than to expect a straightforward answer from him.

His response surprised her. Ramson lowered his gaze, a mop of hair falling into his face. "I fell in with the wrong people."

Ana leaned forward. He looked so vulnerable in this moment, bare shoulders hunched and head bowed. She wanted to reach out to touch him.

Ana stamped down that urge, and instead, the warm blaze of Shamaïra's words spilled from her lips. "Life isn't going to be all happiness and wonder. We have to take what we are given, and fight like hell to make it better. That's what Shamaïra told me—and she's right, Ramson."

Ramson was silent. Slowly, he exhaled and looked up, his eyes wide. "Noblewoman."

Ana blinked. "What?"

"You had a try at my past. Now I'm taking a guess at yours." He cocked his head, a playful smirk curving his lips. "Noblewoman. You speak a noblewoman's Cyrilian, with that singsong lilt and fully rounded vowels." He narrowed his eyes, tapping a finger on his chin, thinking. "You're incredibly educated; sometimes I feel like you've memorized an entire library. And you act like you own me, giving me orders and your little airs and empty threats—"

"They are *not* empty."

"The way you raise your chin when you regard something with disdain. I am often on the receiving end of that look." Ramson was smiling now, and something in his eyes made her feel breathless and light-headed at the same time. "When you're scared, you lift your head and throw your shoulders back, like you're telling yourself to be brave. When you're thinking hard, your eyebrows crease, just a little, right there. And sometimes, when you think no one's watching, you have a faraway, almost sad look in your eyes." His smile had vanished, and the warm spark in his eyes was suddenly ablaze—a roaring fire, threatening to consume her. To destroy her. "When you walk into a room, you have the grace and gravitas of an empress, and I swear, even the Deities must pause to look at you."

She realized that she had forgotten to breathe. Her heart raced against her rib cage, drawn by some inexplicable, magnetic pull toward him. All she could think to say was, "I'm not sure those are necessarily characteristic of a noblewoman."

"Perhaps I haven't met enough noblewomen, then," he said softly. "At least, none like you."

Her heartbeat quickened as he reached out and tucked a lock of her hair behind her ear. His touch sent heat rushing through her body. The room was too warm, the heady scent of incense intoxicating as her gaze flicked to his hand.

And caught sight of something.

"What's this?" she whispered, reaching up to trace a feather-soft touch to the inside of his wrist. A tattoo curled in the black outline of a plant with three tiny, bell-shaped flowers, simple and elegant.

A sharp intake of breath from Ramson and he snapped his arm back, rubbing his hand over the spot where she'd seen his tattoo. "It's nothing."

"Ramson—"

"We should rest. It's getting late." His face had closed off, and she wondered whether she'd imagined the last few minutes, delirious with grief and fatigue.

The room was suddenly too stuffy; the heat and the aromas and the cramped shelves were too much to bear, and she needed to leave, now. Ana stood. Her cheeks flushed with—with what? Shame? Disappointment? But what had she expected from Ramson? Had she really come into this room thinking he would spill his soul and secrets to her? That he would stop donning one mask after another for just long enough so that she could glimpse his real self again?

Or had that simply been another mask?

As Ramson stood, pulling on his shirt and turning away from her, she felt the sting of tears deep in her throat. And Ana wondered whether she had actually seen someone worth saving in that dark, dark fog, or whether it had been just a trick of light and shadows all along.

A tug of blood at the edge of her mind chased away all other thoughts. Ana flared her Affinity. Ramson's blood burned bright and hot; the other Affinites' ran steadily in the parlor as they slept.

But outside, there was something else. "Ramson." She caught his arm, and he shot her a look of surprise. "There are people—"

At that moment, three faint raps sounded on the front door, in Shamaïra's parlor. Ana sensed an Affinite getting up and reaching for the door.

A feeling of foreboding filled her. She'd barely let out a cry when she heard the front door slam open.

A scream, and the air exploded with blood.

25

Ana sprang for the brocade curtains, but Ramson caught her shoulder firmly, grunting as he pulled her back and clamped a hand over her mouth. "We haven't been discovered yet." His whisper was fast, urgent. "We need to use that to our advantage. Stay calm, assess the situation, and decide on the course of action."

Glass smashed in the parlor; shouts and screams erupted, sounding disturbingly close in the small dacha. Ana's breath caught, and Ramson carefully slid his hand through the curtains and drew one back, just a slit for them to peer through.

Past all the multicolored divans and clusters of blankets, the front door was open; a cold wind swept through the house. In the open doorway an unfamiliar man held an Affinite girl. A dagger glinted in his hands; he pressed it against her neck. "Move, and this girl dies."

It was then that Ana saw Yuri, facing the door with his back to her, his fists clenched at his sides. The rest of the Affinites clustered behind couches and divans, fear carved into their features, nightmares that Ana couldn't even begin to fathom haunting their expressions.

Nobody moved.

Suddenly, behind the intruder, from the depths of the night, a second man stepped into view. "I'm afraid I'm going to need all of you to return to the Playpen."

The man's pale blond hair caught the lamplight, and his eyes shone a bleached blue. It was as though all the color and life had been drained from him, and the sight sent a surge of fury through Ana.

It was the broker. She recalled the blackstone doors of the carriage that slammed in her face, the faint trace of May's shadow over his shoulders as he'd carried her away.

He'd stood on that stage in the Playpen, watching countless Affinites forced to perform and fight to the death.

And then he'd ordered the attack on them backstage. *Kill her, Nuryasha.*

Ana thought of May's body in her arms, so light and so helpless.

I want to live.

And now May was buried in the silent earth for eternity.

Wrath wrapped its white-hot grasp around her, and suddenly she was shaking, her anger roiling and pent-up grief spilling from her.

May would never live again.

And it was all . . . *his* . . . fault.

Ramson's arms locked around her waist, but she hurled him off with a snap of her Affinity. By the time he slammed against the settee, Ana had thrown back the curtains and stepped into the living room.

She lifted the first broker bodily into the air with barely half a thought. She was one with her Affinity; it moved at her slightest thought like a phantom arm, an extension of her body. The broker's dagger thunked to the wooden floorboards; he made a gagging sound as she seized the blood in his body, interrupting the natural flow to and from his heart.

She was all too aware that she was dressed in nothing but a slim black gown, her cloak and hood left in the backroom and her velvet gloves torn and discarded at the Playpen. The man in the air struggled, twitching like a broken puppet, his face slowly draining of color, his eyes rolling back into his head.

Ana flung him aside. He crashed into the far wall with a *crack* and lay still. Dimly, Ana heard several screams from the Affinites, saw Yuri dive for the Affinite girl and bundle her behind the settee.

Ana stepped past them.

The pale-eyed broker stood in the doorway. He held a single dagger, but it trembled in his hands as he beheld her.

She was breathing hard, her vision bleeding red, her head buzzing as she pointed a shaking hand at him. The veins in her hands had grown dark and raised from her flesh, snaking around her palms and wrists, extending to her elbows. Grotesque and gruesome, lit by lamplight for everyone in the room to see.

Ana didn't care. Her fury was a living thing, turning the world red and distorted.

The broker dropped to his knees. He shook visibly, a sheen of sweat coating his face. "P-please," he whispered. "Kerlan, he'll kill me—"

He never finished his sentence. Ana wrapped her Affinity around him and lifted him into the air. He'd killed May. She wanted, more than anything, to rip him apart, to bleed him dry drop by drop and watch him suffer—

"Ana!" She heard her name as though from a distance. Someone knocked into her from behind.

They crashed to the floor, and she found herself pinned beneath Ramson. He was panting, blood seeping from his reopened wound through the bandages on his abdomen. He slammed her hands to the floor, his full weight on her. "Control yourself," he snarled. *"Think."*

"Get off me!" she screamed.

"We need *answers.* Who sent him? How did he find us? Can we ally with him—"

"Get. Off. Me." She spat the words at him.

Ramson's eyes bore into hers; his grip tightened around her wrists. "No."

It was the trigger she'd been waiting for. Keeping her hold on the broker, she flung her Affinity at Ramson. He went still, his eyes widening and veins straining in his neck, at his temples, as she took control of his blood.

Ana threw him across the room.

She heard the thud of his body as he slammed against the far wall and crumpled to the floor. A part of her was aware of Yuri and the Affinites watching her, frozen from their hiding places behind Shamaïra's divans.

Ana ignored them and turned back to the broker. He'd crumpled to the ground, but she easily lifted him again. A strange sense of calm descended upon her as she approached him. "Do you recognize me?" It was as though someone else spoke through her, pulling words through her lips.

The man hung suspended in the air, his body arched, his eyes bulging from his head. He opened his mouth to speak. Instead, blood trickled down his chin.

"No?" Ana continued her advance. A delicious feeling gripped her. "Perhaps you'll remember the young earth Affinite you took in Kyrov. The child you put on show tonight. The one you *murdered*."

Recognition lit the broker's face. He struggled against her hold, his mouth opening and closing like that of a fish out of water. Ana was a mere arm's length away now; she could see the veins of his eyes erupting, red bleeding across the white. Blood gushed from his lips.

In that moment, she recalled the Salskoff Winter Market, the screams and the terror as her Affinity ripped the life from eight innocent people. She heard Luka's voice—the voice of reason that had guided her hand and her Affinity.

Luka would counsel forgiveness.

Looking into the broker's pleading face, Ana searched for a sliver of pity.

Instead, she found the memory of May's bright eyes dimmed to emptiness.

And another voice whispered to her then:

Monster.

Ana smiled, lifting a thickly veined hand and gripping the broker's neck. It glistened, slippery and red. The blood felt like exhilaration beneath her fingertips. "Are you afraid?" she whispered. "You should know that it sometimes takes one monster to destroy another." She pressed her face close to his, forcing his terrified gaze to meet the crimson of hers. "Remember my face as you burn in hell, deimhov."

With a twitch of her fingers, she pulled.

There was a wet ripping sound. Red poured from him like

wine from an uncorked bottle, pooling on the floorboards and forming puddles beneath Ana's boots.

As the blood drained from him, her control over the lifeless body slipped. The corpse dropped to the floor with a *thunk*.

Her Affinity receded like a tide, taking with it the red of her vision, the buzz in her ears, and her adrenaline. The broker's corpse lay at her feet, limbs bent at odd angles like a broken doll.

Ana stumbled back. Nausea flooded her stomach, and bile rose, thick and bitter, to her tongue. The rest of the parlor swam into dizzying view. Overturned settees and divans. Shattered globefires and torn books. Broken shelves. And, at the far end of the room, Ramson's body curled against the wall where she'd flung him.

A sob choked Ana's throat. The room had emptied at some point; the heavy brocade curtains leading to the backroom and the rest of the dacha were drawn back, and Yuri's gaze found her. Shamaïra stood behind him, clasping an Affinite child in her arms. The rest of the Affinites behind them.

Tears blurred Ana's vision. "I'm sorry . . . I didn't . . . I . . ." Words faltered on her lips. There was nothing she could say that would justify what she had done tonight, before the eyes of a dozen witnesses.

Because you are a monster.

She was spiraling, shrinking into memories of her eight-year-old self, the world a dizzying kaleidoscope of screams and terror. Her breaths came in shallow gasps.

Ana turned and staggered out the door.

The predawn air stung her cheeks, the cold rushing into her

bones and sucking out every last bit of warmth. The shadow of the Syvern Taiga stretched before her, and she remembered the night she'd lost everything and run into its darkness.

Tonight, she stood to lose everything again. May, the light in her life, had kept her grounded, kept her *good,* and showed her the importance of love.

She was gone.

But there was one person left, Ana realized as Shamaïra's dacha faded into a small blur of golden light.

Luka was still alive. And he needed her.

She was shaking as she continued to plunge forward. The town of Novo Mynsk dozed beneath a sky that shifted from black to a dark violet with the softest of blues fringing the edges.

Footsteps fell behind her. A familiar voice called her name.

Ana slowed. Turned.

Yuri's fire-red hair was outlined in the faraway glow of Shamaïra's dacha. "Don't go," he said.

She had a sudden memory of them as children back at the Palace. Her, after her worst rages or days of silence, screaming at him to go away. And Yuri, sitting against her door until the next morning, her tea long gone cold. It had been the little things that anchored her to the present—the sigh of his roughspun servant's tunic as he stirred on the other side of the door, the gentle knock and soft whisper that he would be back with her breakfast, the slight clink of her teacup in the early-morning silence as he left with velvet steps. The smallest reminders that no matter what she became, no matter what her Affinity made her into, there was someone on the other side of that door, waiting for her. And that she had to continue to live and to hope.

"I'm sorry," Ana said quietly.

"Stay," Yuri insisted. He held out a hand.

Ana almost took it. But in the darkness, she saw the eerie veins still pulsing from her flesh. She thought of the blood red of her eyes. The bodies of the two brokers, blood pooling around them. And Ramson, lying unconscious on the floor.

She took a step back. "It's best that I don't," she whispered.

Sorrow clouded Yuri's eyes. "I stand by what I said earlier," he said quietly. "The future lies here, with us. In the hands of the people."

"I'll fix it," Ana found herself whispering. Yet the meaning of the sentence had blurred. What, exactly, was she going to fix when she went back to her Palace? She thought of Luka and his words that had defined her entire life; of Papa, turning away from her bedside that day, and then convulsing beneath her bloodstained hands. Of red blood and white snow at the Salskoff Vyntr'makt; of the broker's skin stained crimson.

Monster.

Deimhov.

She was going to fix *herself,* Ana realized, guilt seeping into her stomach. For so long, she had held on to the idea that if she could find the alchemist and avenge the murder of her papa, then somehow *she* would be redeemed, too.

Redemption was something Ana had to earn; she needed to learn to forgive herself before she could fight for others.

Yet the Affinites of her empire could not wait for the equality that they deserved. And there already was a person who could lead them to it.

Ana took Yuri's hands. "You will make a great leader, Yuri," she said. "I pledge my heart to you, and my service to fighting for all Affinites. But first I need to fix the mistakes I've made."

Yuri pressed her knuckles to his lips. "When you're ready," he said, "send a snowhawk to Goldwater Port. I plan to establish a stronghold there, in the south. Our revolution will begin there." He drew her into his arms. "And remember that I love you, no matter what you choose."

"I love you too, my friend."

She clutched him tightly, breathing in the scent of his smoke and fire, closing her eyes and wishing she could stay like this forever.

She felt Yuri slip something around her neck; it tinkled, warm against her skin. Ana lifted it into her palm. The pendant winked at her: a small silver circle divided evenly into quarters, one for each season.

"A Deys'krug," Yuri said, taking her hand. "We will come full circle again."

"We will find each other again," Ana reaffirmed, because the possibility that this was the last time they would see each other was something she couldn't bear to voice. "Will you ask Shamaïra to take care of Ramson? Tell him I'm sorry, and that . . . I'll come find him after it's all over, to honor our Trade."

Somewhere along the way, between Shamaïra's dacha and the endless stretch of night, she'd made up her mind. Ramson's body hurtling across the room, curled up against the wall bloodied—that had been her doing.

She could not let anyone else get hurt because of her. She would find him again—or he would find her—after this was all over, and she would pay him for his help. But now she would go and find her alchemist alone.

If Yuri had questions, he didn't ask them. Instead, he only said, "I will."

Ana gently dropped his hands and stepped back. "Deys blesya ty, Yuri." *Deities bless you.* It was a phrase said not in farewell but in hope and well-wishing; a phrase reserved for the ones closest to your heart.

"Deys blesya ty, Kolst Pryntsessa." His voice was faint in the silence of the night as she turned from him and began to make her way back to Novo Mynsk. Back to the inn, where her rucksack and outfits and parchments of plans and maps lay, waiting for her. Waiting for Kerlan's Fyrva'snezh.

She sensed the spark of Yuri's blood growing farther and smaller, alone against the Syvern Taiga, watching her until her feet hit the cobblestone streets of the city and dachas sprang up all around her again. And when she looked back toward the forest, Yuri and Shamaïra's dacha had disappeared, swallowed by the infinite night as though they'd never existed in the first place.

It was dawn by the time she found her way back to the inn where she and Ramson had set up camp. Her belongings and room lay untouched beneath a faint dusting of gold light that filtered through the cracked windows. Ana latched the door, took two steps, and fell onto the small cot.

Sleep took her.

26

The sky was afire when Ana woke, groggy and dizzy and drained, as though she'd slept for days. Clouds had gathered in the west, and the setting sun lit them in brilliant shades of reds and corals and violets. When she threw open the windows, the air hung heavy with the scent of winter and promised snow.

She cleaned herself in the small wash closet at the end of the hallway, trying not to think of the blood caked on her face and hands as she scrubbed it off. It all still felt like a dream—Yuri, the Redcloaks, Shamaïra's, the brokers. And May.

No, she wouldn't think of that. She couldn't, not yet, not when tonight amounted to everything she had been working for over the past eleven moons.

She would get through the night, find her alchemist, and go from there. So Ana took all the memories from the past day and locked them away. Tonight she needed to be at her strongest and quickest and cleverest.

She rummaged through the few parcels they'd stacked against the wall until she found what she was looking for. The dress she'd purchased days ago slid over her body smoothly. It was made entirely of white chiffon, embedded with tiny beads that glittered white, silver, and blue and fell in a spiral, flowing with the translucent folds and pooling at her feet. When she looked at herself in the cracked mirror hanging on the wall, she inhaled, the dress glimmering like falling snow.

She took the boxes of fresh creams and powders and began to dress her face as she remembered the maids used to back when she was a child. Bronze creams rubbed evenly across her skin, to cover bruises and the roughness. Then a dusting of rose-scented powders to give her a shimmering look. A dark blush just under her cheekbones, and a dab of vermilion rouge on her lips.

When she stood and looked at her reflection, she felt slightly more reassured. She barely recognized the girl frowning back at her in the looking glass. That girl was made up and manicured to look like she belonged. A high dama of Novo Mynsk.

No one would recognize her tonight. She was a ghost.

Still, when Ana slid the mask she had chosen over her face, she felt her entire body relax. The color matched her dress, silver whorls tracing snowflakes around the edges. Traditionally, Fyrva'snezh did not require masks. Yet . . . the people of Novo Mynsk seemed to have a fondness for masked events.

Are all balls in Novo Mynsk masked? she'd asked Ramson several days ago.

He'd smiled at her from behind a black mask of his own. *The people of Novo Mynsk have a lot to hide.*

Ana stuffed what she had left of her belongings in a small beaded purse she'd purchased as an accessory for the ball: her sketches of Luka, her parents, her mamika Morganya, and Pyetr Tetsyev. An unused globefire. A map. When she got to the bottom of her rucksack, she paused and pulled out a single copperstone.

It was the last of the three she had given May. *Let's buy ourselves a treat at the next town.*

A knot formed in her throat. She blinked, and the phantom of May's toothy smile vanished into the impending twilight outside.

She had killed the broker who had killed May. But did one life pay for another?

Ana kissed the coin and tucked it into the bottom of her purse before strapping it to her wrist. She found the parchment with the address to the Kerlan Estate that she'd gotten from Ramson several days ago and slipped that, along with her false papers, into her purse.

Then she tossed the rest of her papers and plans into a tin bucket used for collecting bathwater, set it on fire, and watched it burn until there was nothing left but ashes.

Ana pulled on matching silver-white gloves, threw on her fur cloak, and swept one last look around her now-empty room before she left. She was ready. Ramson had secured them spots as mesyr and dama Farrald, a common Bregonian last name that piqued Ana's curiosity for a moment before she brushed it off. Ramson had his reasons for everything; now was not the time to question them. She would present herself alone as such at the door and make excuses for her husband. The rest of the plan remained the same: find Tetsyev, lure him to the basement that Ramson had made her memorize the path to on a badly drawn map, and escape through the secret passageway. Ramson had hired a carriage to take them far, far away.

Twilight had fallen outside; the last rays of the sun gave way to the violet cloak of night. Storm clouds broiled in the skies. And as the lamplighters ran down the streets, Novo Mynsk came alive with the scintillating shimmer of lights, rowdy laughter, and the distant but ever-present sounds of song and bar music. Whereas the townsfolk of Salskoff would have lit blue-papered lanterns at their windows and sat at home to witness the First Snow with their loved ones, the people of Novo Mynsk took to the streets. Ana passed throngs of revelers singing in Old Cyrilian, dressed in white robes and glimmering blue headdresses that were farcical portrayals of the Deities. They danced and laughed and drank, torchlight lancing off their masks and the coins in their hands.

Ana made quick progression through the streets, her Affinity flared and her nerves set on edge. She'd studied a map of Novo Mynsk; the Kerlan Estate was about a half-hour walk from her inn.

Gradually, the cramped cobblestone streets widened; the dachas grew in size and bloomed into cream-colored mansions; the rotten smells of liquor and sewage shifted to the sweet scent of chamomile, orchids, and roses.

Finally, Ana turned and found herself facing her destination. She drew a sharp breath.

Sprawled beneath a sky of gray snow clouds, the estate was a spread of lush lawns that stretched farther than the eye could see, interspersed with tinkling fountains and marble statues. In the midst of it sat a mansion, a cream-and-gold behemoth that gleamed with torchlight.

Guests were already arriving; carriages rolled through the open gilded gates, past liveried guards standing still as statues. Few guests arrived on foot, yet all were dressed in resplendent gowns, sleek black suits, and fur coats. They filed through the gates, masks catching the light of lanterns spread throughout the gardens that led to the mansion itself.

Ana followed the steady stream of people in through the yawning gates. The Kerlan Estate had some of the most ostentatious displays of wealth she had seen in her life. Cement paths wound through displays of the riches the garden offered: bushes of the most exotic flowers ranging from the Cyrilian iris to Nandjian desert roses, and aviaries with colorful birds of all species and origins. Ana even passed by a small habitat in which several of the rarest animals in the world resided; she thought she recognized a Kemeiran snow leopard, and a pool with what appeared to be a mystical ghostwhale of Bregon.

Unease twinged in her stomach. Alaric Kerlan, it seemed, was a collector.

As she drew steadily closer to the great mansion, she thought she saw a gray tint to its glass windows and felt a slight chill seep through her furs. She wouldn't be surprised if Kerlan's entire estate was blackstone-infused and built with the highest security detail in mind. The mansion loomed, menacing now, and Ana couldn't help but imagine that it was an enormous spider amid its vast web of spies, brokers, and criminals, spinning its secrets and gold.

Light and music spilled from the giant mahogany double doors. Guests clustered up the marble steps, and through it all, Ana caught sight of a line of guards at the front, and a man in a black-and-gold doublet holding a thick stack of parchments.

Her heartbeat fluttered anxiously, and dread slowed her steps. Blood, thrumming in the excited guests all around her, crowded her thoughts. The blackstone-infused walls seemed to hum with menace.

Farrald, she reminded herself. She was dama Farrald. There was no reason for the doorman to turn her away, especially when she already looked the part.

She'd need to *act* the part, too; she'd con her way in.

She thought of Ramson, of how he could shed one act and step into another within the blink of an eye. So Ana squared her shoulders, lifted her chin, and followed the stream of guests up the steps.

The doorman barely spared her a glance. "Name and invitation letter?"

Ana froze, feeling as though a stone had dropped in her stomach. Invitation letter. Why hadn't Ramson mentioned an invitation letter? Her mind was sifting through the past few days they'd spent planning even as she stammered, "D-dama Farrald." At no point had Ramson mentioned this crucial detail and *why not?* Her heart pounded in her temples.

Had he tricked her, after all this time?

Or had he simply played the con man's part, giving away just enough information so that she would trust him . . . but not enough so that she could leave him?

The doorman shuffled through his parchments with white-gloved hands. "Letter, please, dama Farrald."

"I . . ." Her palms were sweating in her gloves, and her tongue was dry. She'd never been a good liar. "I'm afraid I've lost it."

The doorman cast her a sympathetic look; several guests behind her whispered. "I'm sorry, meya dama. We can't accept guests without an invitation. Would you mind stepping aside? I'll send for Lord Kerlan's butler." He must have seen the panic on her face, for he added as though to reassure her: "Not to worry, this is just a necessary precaution. Lord Kerlan's butler recognizes all acquainted guests."

Ana gripped her beaded purse tightly to stop herself from shaking. Lord Kerlan's butler would *not* recognize her—and she'd be ousted, perhaps even arrested, even before she could step inside and have a hope of spotting Pyetr Tetsyev.

Think, Ana. She could almost hear Ramson's voice chiding her, his I-told-you-so expression whenever she was about to make a rash decision.

Think. What would Ramson do?

The doorman raised an eyebrow. "Meya dama, I need to ask you to please step aside while we allow other guests in."

Ana was frozen to the spot, a dozen different options running through her mind yet none viable. She could steal an invitation, come back as a different guest—but the doorman would surely recognize her and call foul play. She could . . . she could . . . "Please, mesyr, I—"

"*There* you are."

A voice cut through the night. She felt someone's presence behind her, warm and solid, and a hand pressed against the small of her back. The familiar scent of kologne that had been a part of her days for the past few weeks.

Ana's legs nearly buckled with relief.

Ramson leaned past her, his black tuxedo cutting him into lean lines and sharp edges. His eyes glinted behind his dark mask as, with a small flourish, he presented two wax-sealed envelopes to the doorman. "Mesyr and dama Farrald," he declared. "I apologize for the mix-up; I lost my wife in the crowds."

His hold on her arm was so tight it almost hurt, and the razor-sharp smile he cut her chased away any foolish thoughts that he was actually glad to see her again.

And she felt it, a new stiffness to his gestures and smiles that she'd never sensed before, no matter how frustrated they'd been with each other.

Ramson was angry. Of course he was. She'd tossed him halfway across a room and left him there.

"Please, mesyr and dama Farrald." The doorman dipped his head. "I apologize for the inconvenience." His eyes lingered on them as he bowed and gestured for them to enter.

They stepped into a vast banquet hall with a glass ceiling two stories high. Crystal chandeliers dripped warm gold light into the hallway. On either side of the hall, alcoves framed with intricate marble carvings lined the first and second floors. Guests were already lounging in plush velvet chaises or leaning over the balustrade on the second floor, chatting with drinks in hand.

Ramson's grip was tight on her waist as he steered her around the edges of the ballroom. "Surely you didn't think I'd let you leave without thanking you for that wonderful parting gift?" he muttered.

His words cut. Ramson had been cold toward her, he'd been calculating, he'd been indifferent—but he'd never been angry. Angry was new. Angry was . . . personal. "I didn't want to put you in danger anymore," she said as he led her up a spiraling set of stairs to the quieter second level that overlooked the banquet hall. "You shouldn't have come."

He snorted. "So I should've let you be caught like the fool you are?"

Irritation stirred in her. "If you'd just told me about the invitation instead of trying to play me," she hissed. "You never trusted me. And I shouldn't have trusted you."

Ramson's eyes flashed. "Since when has anyone uttered 'trust' in the same breath as my name?"

The second floor was nearly empty, with most of the guests still gathering on the first floor. Ramson cast a furtive look around. "In here," he said brusquely, parting a set of heavy red curtains to a small alcove. On the far wall of the alcove, a glass door led to a balcony outside; it was dark.

Ana stumbled in. When she turned, Ramson had removed his mask. His face was cold, clean-shaven, and sharp. He was angrier than she'd ever seen him and, from the way he clutched at his ribs, in pain. Shame weighed in her chest, but she found herself growing defensive beneath his fury. "I'm sorry, all right?" she snapped.

"You're *sorry,*" Ramson repeated, and took such a menacing step forward that she started backward. She bumped against the glass door. "And what, exactly, are you sorry for? Murdering two of Kerlan's men the night before his ball? Nearly killing me? Running off without a word and leaving me to puzzle it all out from a message from Yuri?"

Whatever remorse she might have felt burned away with her rising anger, stoked by his heated accusations. "Kerlan's men killed May and exploited Affinites for a living," she growled. "I gave them what they deserved."

Ramson slashed a hand through the air. "Yes, and in doing so, you nearly single-handedly gave us away. That doorman was watching us as we entered; I wouldn't be surprised if he alerted Kerlan's security of us. I bargained for a peaceful entry to this ball and you ruined it. You focused on the battle and lost sight of the *war.*"

They stood so close that she could grab him by the lapels and shake him until his teeth rattled. She thought back to Shamaïra's dacha, the fire burning low, the smell of smoke and incense and hope hanging between them. She'd thought there was something in him worth redeeming.

Ana pitched her voice low and cast her words to cut. "Do not speak of May as though she were a sacrifice to be made, in these battles and wars *you* seem to perceive as a game."

Ramson's eyes narrowed. "Ana, be quiet—"

"Must be so easy for you to say"—she plunged on, anger and tears threatening to choke her as they did whenever she thought of May—"having never loved anybody or anything besides yourself."

In one swift step, Ramson closed the gap between them. Instinctively, Ana shrank back, her head bumping against the glass behind her as Ramson leaned over her and braced a hand on the door behind her. He reached out with the other hand, and in that moment she had a wild premonition that he would either hurt her or kiss her—but all he did was press a finger to her lips.

"Please, shut up," he whispered, and something about the urgency of his tone startled her into silence. He was so close that she could see the cuts and scratches on his chin, the slight bend to his nose, the sweep of his lashes over his hazel eyes, wide as he looked at her right now. He leaned in. His whisper was lighter than a breath by her ear. "We're being watched."

She looked past him. Through the blur of her tears, the alcove swam into view, barely wide enough for her to stretch her arms out on either side. She was suddenly aware of the silence beyond the curtains, of the music and hubbub that seemed a world away. Of how their voices must have carried to anyone listening outside.

Ramson's hand shifted to her shoulder, his gaze locked on her as though she were something wild that could become unhinged at any moment. Ana swallowed. The deluge of her emotions vanished as quickly as it had come, tempered by the chill of fear and the need to act.

Holding his gaze, she reached out with her Affinity. It was like lighting a torch; she saw with her power the blood, hot and bright in Ramson's body before her, pulsing quickly from the strong beat of his heart. Ana reached beyond that. The second floor of Kerlan's banquet hall unfurled under the sweep of her Affinity, a darkness devoid of blood, until—

There.

A single figure stood by the staircase mere steps from their alcove, still as a stone.

Fear bloomed cold against her chest.

Ramson watched her expression, as though he already knew exactly what she was doing. "Do you sense someone?" His lips barely moved.

Ana nodded.

"Can you tell me anything else about them? What they're wearing, or what they look like?"

As though in response to his question and to her Affinity, she sensed something reaching out to her—an icy, iron force that clamped against her Affinity, blotting it out like dousing a torch.

The feeling was all too familiar, and her knees almost buckled as she thought of the last time she'd felt it. "A yaeger," she whispered.

Ramson nodded almost imperceptibly. "Just don't move. Couples come up here for . . . privacy all the time. Let him think that."

She realized that she was gripping him tightly, one hand clutching at his shoulder and the other wrapped around his back. Ramson had placed a hand on her waist, his other still warm against the skin of her shoulder. He smelled of fresh kologne, clean with just a hint of spice and mystery.

He leaned over her, his head resting against the cool glass door that led outside. "Trust me," he murmured, his breath grazing her neck. "And tell me if he moves."

Trust me.

Her heart was threatening to beat out of her chest from terror at being caught, and some other strange thrill that she couldn't even begin to understand. The fabric of their outfits rustled, and in the dim light that seeped beneath the curtains into their small space, they were a tangle of chiffon and limbs and soft, cautious breaths.

Ramson sighed, the corded muscles in his neck shifting slightly. His head was bowed, his breath warming the crook between her neck and her bare shoulders. Any closer, and . . .

Something shifted in the landscape of her Affinity. Ana perked up.

The person outside was gone.

She sensed the yaeger making his way down the stairs, his blood growing dim until it blended into the chaos of the banquet hall. "He left," she murmured.

Ana felt Ramson loose a breath against her, his hand slipping from her shoulder, the calluses scraping against her bare skin as he squeezed her arm and stood back. A lock of hair had become undone and fell in front of his eyes; for some reason, she wanted to reach out and brush it away.

His gaze snapped to her. Ana stared back, shame curdling her stomach at her earlier outburst. The anger seemed to have dissipated from Ramson, too; he only looked at her, puzzled, lips half-parted as though he was simultaneously wanting to say something and waiting for her to say something.

Ana swallowed. Heat crept up her neck; the silence was becoming unbearable. She needed to break it.

"Ramson," she found herself saying. "Don't ever tell me to shut up again."

He blinked, and his lips began to lift at the corners, until he was grinning at her. It wasn't a sly or slicing smirk; it was a full-on smile, his mouth curving, his eyes crinkling, as though he found something genuinely amusing in her. And it felt like, for the first time, they were sharing something real between them, something tender.

A warm glow stirred in her chest. Ana turned away before she could smile back.

The brass handle of the glass door twisted when she tried it. A cold breeze slipped in, and she breathed in the scent of the winter night. Ana snuck a glance at the red curtains behind them again, and the shadow of that earlier figure lingered in her imagination. She shivered. "Can we talk outside?"

A trace of a smile played around Ramson's lips. "We certainly can," he said, and pushed open the door for her. "After you, meya dama."

The veranda wrapped all the way around the Kerlan mansion. There were only a handful of guests outside, and the few lamps cast a soft glow in the night. Overhead, the skies were completely dark and overcast, and a quiet stillness hung in the air as though the earth itself were holding its breath, waiting for the arrival of the Deity of Winter.

Ana leaned against the marble balustrade, exhaling and watching her breath plume before her. She felt Ramson come up by her side; he stood, barely a hand's breadth from her. Something about Fyrva'snezh, the way the night stayed silent and the air trembled with the promise of snow, filled her with a strange sense of hope. She'd stayed behind in the Palace while her family left for the annual Parade, but at night, when the servants had gone to bed and all was silent, Mama and Papa and Luka and mamika Morganya had gathered in Papa's bedroom. They'd watched the snows fall as a family. And even after Mama's death, after the incident at the Vyntr'makt, after Papa grew ill, Luka and mamika Morganya had always been there with her.

She drew in a breath and wondered if Luka was looking out his window at this very moment. Whether he thought of her. "You know," she said softly, half to herself. "Fyrva'snezh isn't meant to be about dancing and drinking. It's about the quiet worship of the first snowfall, of the first breath of our patron Deity." She hesitated, but some part of her urged her to go on. "Back at home, we celebrate by lighting prayer candles and standing outside, waiting for the first snows to fall."

They were silent for several moments, and then Ramson spoke. "Back at home, we don't worship your Deities. We have three gods: the Sea, the Sky, and the Land." There was a rawness to his voice that she had never heard before, a quiet honesty that felt intimate.

Three gods. It all came to her then. She recalled hundreds of pages from old tomes she'd studied, of the Bregonians and their gods and values and their Navy. The Bregonian surname he had chosen for their invite letter. The slightest accent to his words, so subtle that she hadn't been able to place it. Until now.

Ana whirled toward him. "You're Bregonian." The realization felt like another puzzle piece falling into place.

Ramson's mask hung in his hands. He met her gaze, his eyes darting between hers with something like uncertainty. How could she have not guessed? She thought of the calluses on his hands, of the long scars on his back, of the way he wielded a sword better than any guard she'd seen. "You were in the Bregonian Royal Navy, weren't you?"

"I was training for it," he said quietly.

It all made sense. Bregonians lived on honor and courage; no matter who he'd become and what his history was, she'd seen glimmers of both in him. Perhaps . . . perhaps he could still be brave and honorable. Perhaps he could still change.

She stared at him, outlined in sharp-cut edges against the starless night, half-shrouded in shadows. He was a man in a mask, an enigma that she had been trying to decipher since the first day she had met him. There was still so much she didn't know about him—so much she would never know. "How did a Royal Navy recruit become a Cyrilian crime lord?"

He shook his head. "It doesn't matter." A weight seemed to settle into the lines of his shoulders, and his eyes clouded as he turned to her. "So, you know the plan. The carriage will be waiting outside the passageway for you at the tenth hour. One moment past ten, and it'll be gone."

"I know," Ana said.

Ramson dug something from the pockets of his black suit and slipped it into her hands.

A silver pocket watch. Ana almost smiled at how practical his gift was.

But his next sentence thudded like the strike of a gavel. "There isn't much time left, Ana. I suppose this is good-bye."

Ana stared at him, a sudden feeling of apprehension tightening in her stomach. She'd thought this part of the plan had been clear to her: get Tetsyev, return to her brother, sort everything out. And then, once all that was over, she would fulfill her end of the bargain.

She hadn't expected good-bye this fast.

Her carefully constructed world of possibilities and future scenarios dissolved into haze. "But—our Trade," she found herself saying, against all odds. "You haven't asked me for my end of it."

He huffed, his breath forming a whorl of mist in the air. "I don't need anything from you anymore. It all ends tonight."

Something about that phrase didn't sit right, and she struggled for a moment, trying to figure out what to say. But he was already turning, reaching to put his mask back on.

Her hands shot out. Clasped his wrists.

Ramson's gaze snapped to her; his lips parted. "What—"

"Come with me," Ana said before he could speak. "You could be good." The words tumbled from her mouth, jumbled and rushed, and she could think of nothing else to say after.

Something shifted in Ramson's expression, and it was like the fog had cleared and she was looking straight at him for the first time. There was an earnestness to his bright hazel eyes that she had never seen before when he spoke again. "When I was small, my father told me that there was no pure good or pure evil in the world. He said that humans only exist in different shades of gray." He shifted, and his fingers slid around her wrists, his touch raising gooseflesh on her arms even through her gloves. "I believed that, until I met you, Ana. So . . . thank you."

Shades of gray. Why did that ring another bell within her? Humans only existed in different shades of gray—

What defines you is how you choose to wield it. A gentle wind kissed her cheeks and brought her brother's voice back to her.

"You're right," she said quietly, holding Ramson's gaze. "The world doesn't exist in black and white. But I would like to believe that it is our choices that define us." His hands were warm and steady on hers. "Make the right choice, Ramson."

Something wet fell on her cheek, and Ramson's expression shifted to wonder. Ana felt another touch of coldness and wetness, and another, and another. And as the first snowflakes gently landed on Ramson's hair, she realized that it was snowing.

They angled their faces to the sky, at the silver flecks that twirled silently in the air and came to rest on their shoulders, on their clothes, on their faces and lips and necks. If there was a single moment she wanted to imprint in a sketch, this was it; this was a scene she wanted to remember.

Ramson let go of her hands. Through the softly falling flakes that caught in his hair and on his lashes and cheeks, he looked younger and more vulnerable than she had ever seen, hunching into his suit to ward out the cold. Something flickered in his expression, and then his eyes shuttered. "Good-bye, Ana."

Wait, she wanted to say. *Tell me your real name. Tell me who you are.* Something, anything, to get him to stay.

But she could only breathe, "Good-bye, Ramson," as she watched his retreating back disappear into a night of silently falling snow.

She turned to the balustrade, composing herself for a moment, trying to tease out the tangled, gnarled strands of her emotions. The snow was coming thickly now, whirling in a blur.

Below, on the veranda leading out to the gardens, a figure stepped into the dark, clad in robes of white. And as Ana's gaze fell to him, her heart pounded and her blood roared in her ears.

The man tilted his face to the sky, and it was like looking at a ghost.

Tetsyev was here.

27

Ramson had worn many masks in his life, donning them and shedding them like second skins. He'd always played whatever role he needed to get the job done. Tonight, as he looked at his reflection in the mirror—clean-shaven in his black tuxedo and slicked hair—he felt as though he were simply wearing another mask and preparing for another show.

Except . . .

Standing there under the softly falling snow with Ana, he'd felt unmasked and raw. Something about this girl lured out the whisper of the boy he'd once been. Something about this girl made him want to *be* that boy. And his chest was heavy with the possibility of what that might have been were he a better man who made better choices.

Come with me. You could be good.

Ana had been that choice. And in some ways, Ramson had seen it through. He'd made a detour prior to arriving at Kerlan's tonight. He'd gone to a courier's cottage in the city and sent out a snowhawk, its feathers pure as freshly fallen snow.

Tonight, at the Kerlan Estate,
by the First Snow.

He'd slipped a lock of black hair into the snowhawk's beak. The animals had an impossibly keen sense of smell, capable of tracking the scent of their prey for miles in the cold, barren mountains of Cyrilia. Once trained, they made for the best type of courier birds.

The note was out, and his plans were in motion. And Ana—she would get as far away from this estate, this city, and his world of crime and darkness as possible. She was born for good. She was meant to fight for the light. And she would carry that faint possibility—the ghost of the man he might have been—on with her.

For Ramson, it was too late for that. The man he'd become believed that there was no good or bad; there were only various shades of gray.

Tonight, he would remember that—when he murdered Alaric Kerlan.

Ramson closed his eyes. When he opened them again, the world was sharper with clear-cut calculation, and he felt a wicked calmness settle into his chest. He was Ramson Quicktongue, future Head of the Order of the Lily. The ballroom lay beneath him, a theater of people in gaudy ball gowns and glittering jewels.

Ramson slipped his mask back on. The world was his stage; tonight was just another show.

The biggest show of his life.

The large clock suspended in the middle of the banquet

hall showed seventeen minutes past nine. He had precisely forty-three minutes to find Kerlan, and to persuade him to reinstate Ramson as Deputy. He needed the words penned into the Order's official mandate.

And then, as soon as Kerlan lifted his pen from the page, Ramson would kill him.

The hilt of his small dagger pressed into his sleeve, a perfect blade no longer than his forearm. A misericord, Bregonians called it, used to deliver the final blow of mercy to an opponent. At a single flick of his finger, the contraption that bound it to his arm would eject the blade into his palm.

For the first time tonight, he took in the hallways with a sweeping glance. Memories rose, unbidden, in his mind. He could still see, on the plush red carpets, the writhing bodies of people he'd disposed of simply because they were in his way—fishermen and weapons traders and business owners who tried to cheat them. He could still hear their muffled screams through the closed doors that led to the basements below. Bit by bit, he'd helped Kerlan clear Cyrilia of anyone who stood in their way, extending the Order's underground reach like an invisible hand unfurling beneath the broken empire.

No more, Ramson thought as he strode down the halls, away from the music and dancing and light. The carpets were less worn, the walls decorated with gilded frames—paintings of far-off places, mysterious islands, and oceans that glimmered turquoise.

Ramson recognized these places. It had always haunted him that he shared a home kingdom with Alaric Kerlan, that he'd almost traced Kerlan's exact steps many years past, fleeing from their wrongdoings to establish themselves in a foreign empire.

It was as though, in a desperate attempt to free himself from becoming the demon that was his father, Ramson had run onto a path that had made him into a different kind of monster.

The chandeliers above burned brightly, almost jarringly. Kerlan always made his entrances at his parties after nine o'clock. Ramson was getting closer to Kerlan's living quarters, and he was surprised there wasn't a guard—

"Stop."

A figure peeled from the shadows of the next corridor, regarding Ramson with cold eyes. Ramson recognized him. He had a name: Felyks.

"Guests are welcome in Lord Kerlan's banquet hall," Felyks said. "His personal quarters are private."

Ramson smiled a hungry smile. "I'm no ordinary guest, Felyks," he said, and pulled off his mask.

Felyks did a double take; his eyes went round. His hand twitched for his sword, even as he backed into the wall. "Qui-Qui-Quicktongue."

Ramson gave a mock bow. "In corporeal form. You seem happy to see me." His cheery tone dropped. "I want to see Alaric."

Felyks struggled. "I—I can't let you do that," he said at last, and unsheathed his sword. "The Kerlan Estate has rules."

"Rules that I set in place," Ramson said, stepping closer to the guard. He relished the way Felyks cringed slightly. "Now let me past, or I'll be using your body as a doormat."

"That's hardly necessary," came a light, familiar voice with the crystal-clear lilt of Cyrilian nobility. A man had appeared, seemingly out of nowhere, by the turn to the next corridor. His indigo silk coat flapped lightly over his slight figure, and his gold-tipped shoes tapped rhythmically with each step as he approached.

"Hello again, Ramson," said Alaric Kerlan, his eyes twinkling. "I've come to extend you a very personal welcome."

Felyks straightened at the sight of his boss, who strolled past him as though he were a part of the wall. Ramson stood where he was, though something stretched taut within him. He felt rooted to the place as a strange helplessness descended upon him, trapping him under the presence of Alaric Kerlan once again.

"Ramson, my son." Kerlan's teeth glinted very white when he smiled. "It's been so long."

"I've counted every day." Ramson's cheeks felt frozen, his mouth stuck in a smile.

"I'm so honored." Kerlan gestured at the nearest door. "It seems I'd be an extremely bad-mannered host to not have you for tea. Please, after you."

Ramson stepped through the door to a nondescript study, walls lined with bookshelves that boasted gilded tomes and dusty books, as well as the occasional eccentric piece of decoration—or, as Kerlan preferred to call it, *exotic.* A jade-sculpted dragon from Kemeira; a curved brass lamp that looked to be from one of the southern crowns; a piece of rainbow-hued rock from the depths of the Silent Sea itself. In the corner was a large brass clock, its rhythmic ticks punctuating the silence.

Yet as Ramson took in the room around him, he was suddenly struck with a realization so stark that it left him reeling. He remembered this room well, too well—it was almost as though he had been standing in it yesterday, rain-soaked and lost and wild, a boy with nowhere to hide and nowhere to run.

After Jonah's death, Ramson had wanted nothing more than to get away from the military, from his father, from Bregon, from every single bit of the world that he'd thought of as safe and good, but that had betrayed him.

Twelve years old, he'd boarded one of the supply wagons from the military in the dead of night, with nothing on him but a pouch of coins and a name and address hastily scrawled on a piece of paper. He still remembered huddling in the back of the wagon between crates of stale vegetables and rotting meat, watching as the winking torchlights of the Blue Fort grew smaller and smaller.

The wagon driver found him curled up in the back the next morning and kicked him out. Ramson clambered to his feet alone but for the cloud-filled skies, rolling moors, and endless rain in all directions. He was lost then, without Jonah or his compass. He wanted to crawl into a water-soaked ditch and die right there in the mud, but he was too afraid, and he was too angry.

So he put one foot in front of the other, and every day, he told himself, *Just one more day. Just one more day and you can see Jonah again.*

Somehow, either by the Deities' will or by some other miracle, he made it to a town. He stumbled into a bar, holding his pouch of dimes and begging for food and water.

Later that day, a group of older boys waylaid him. They

dragged him, screaming and kicking, into a back alley, beat him, took his money and his dagger, and left him to die.

Still, Ramson did not die.

When he finally summoned the courage to hobble out of the alley, night had fallen. His lip was cut and swelling, his nose broken, and his ribs bruised, but he was alive.

This was the world as it *really* was. Not good and bright and filled with light—but rather, the gray place that Jonah had painted for him, where the strong prevailed over the weak and evil triumphed and flourished.

There was no *goodness* or *kindness* in this world. Jonah had told Ramson that—and eventually, the darkness had claimed even him.

Ramson begged the first person he saw, an old man in a horse cart, for shelter. That night, he curled up in the old man's barn, unable to sleep. He pulled out the balled-up, soaked piece of paper with the name. The ink had bled into the parchment and smudged on his fingers when he tried to smooth out the wrinkles. But he whispered the name to himself over and over again that night. A sense of purpose gathered in his heart, filling his veins with a wrathful, churning energy.

In the early hours of the morning, he stole away with the horse and the cart of the old man who had saved him. He boarded a ship that night and never looked back, even as Bregon turned into a small speck on the horizon and then was swallowed whole by the infinite dark sea.

Weeks later and an ocean away, clutching the piece of paper with that name, he found himself in front of the gilded gates of the most beautiful mansion he had ever seen.

The guard laughed when he demanded to see Lord Alaric Kerlan. "I assure you, he'll want to see me," Ramson argued in his broken schoolboy's Cyrilian.

The other guard roared with laughter. "This one'll give you a run for your pluck, Nikolay!" he chortled.

Ramson was furious. "You don't know who I am," he snarled. "You don't know how much value I'll be to Lord Kerlan. And I'll wager you that if he finds out you turned me away from his gates, you won't live to see your family the next morning."

The two guards howled with laughter.

"My, my. I certainly hope I haven't garnered that kind of a reputation among the neighbors."

Ramson spun around.

A slight man in a purple bowler hat stood before them. He was middle-aged, but he was the same height and build as Ramson, with a mop of receding brown hair and a twinkle in his eyes. Dressed in an ordinary shirt and breeches, he looked like a friendly next-door neighbor.

The guards stilled, their faces molding into casts. "Lord Kerlan," they murmured.

Ramson stared. He'd heard his father speak of how the Bregonian criminal had fled to Cyrilia and built an empire on thievery and coercion, one with almost as much power as the Cyrilian throne. Alaric Kerlan was a legend and a monster, a sinister man in the darkness with a smile that sliced.

Yet now he stood at the height of an adolescent boy, a friendly beam on his face. Could this really be the man whom his father spoke of with such bone-deep hatred, that Admiral Roran Farrald sought to bring down?

"What is it that I can do for you, boy?"

Ramson of the Quick Tongue was at a loss for words. He spluttered inelegantly, "I can . . . I can help you."

Kerlan looked amused. "What's your name, boy?"

"R-Ramson. Ramson Farrald."

Kerlan's lip curled almost imperceptibly. "A Bregonian boy, then," he said. "Invite him in, Nikolay. I'd like to hear what brought a young Bregonian so far from his homeland."

Kerlan had known whose son Ramson was—of course he had known. But Ramson's arrogance had blinded him. Half an hour later, he found himself in a room, wearing an oversized vest and breeches, with silk slippers replacing his mud-caked boots.

The room was lined with shelves that were neatly stacked with leather-bound books. When Ramson looked closely, he could see gold letters shining off their spines. A large red carpet sprawled across the middle of the floor, tucked beneath an ebony coffee table. The room wasn't filled to the roof with gold statues, but its opulence pulsed subtly in the lapis lazuli–laced designs on the table and the rare Kemeiran vases dispersed across the shelves.

"Well." Ramson jumped; he hadn't even heard the door open. Lord Kerlan drew a gold fountain pen from his breast pocket and gently shut the door behind him. "Have a seat, son. Ramson . . . was it? Would you like some tea? You look half-frozen."

Ramson numbly sat himself on the red velvet couch across from the coffee table. Lord Kerlan was still looking at him with that glimmer of amusement in his eyes, and he realized he hadn't responded to the question. "No," Ramson said, "thank you."

Lord Kerlan dipped his head. "Very well." He strode over to the coffee table, flipping his golden pen between his fingers as he did. "What can I do for you, Ramson Farrald?"

Ramson parted his lips. He had been rehearsing this line since that night in the barn, when he'd lain on the hay, unable to sleep and aching in every joint and muscle fiber. "You know my father, Roran Farrald."

Lord Kerlan had been shuffling through a stack of papers; he paused, and his eyes flicked to Ramson's face like the tongue of a snake. "I do."

Ramson leaned forward, gripping the edges of his seat so hard that his knuckles were white. "I want to help you destroy him."

That had been a lifetime ago. The boy who had been heartbroken and angry at the world had died seven years ago in a dark alley. Someone else had crawled from the mud that day and risen to take his place. He stood in this room now, calm and cold and clad in a black silk vest paid for by the blood of his trades.

But part of him knew that he wasn't any less lost than the broken boy of seven years past.

"Well." Kerlan shut the door and moved silently across the room. Ramson was used to it. Kerlan had a way with the shadows.

He stood before his coffee table, wearing his confidence like an expensive suit and carrying that same twinkle in his eyes. One only had to step closer to sniff out the stench of power clinging to him, to catch the rotting smell of greed and corruption hidden beneath layers of kologne. The Farrald boy of seven years ago hadn't seen that: to him, Kerlan had been a means to an end. A means to end his father, who had taken everything from him.

But Ramson Quicktongue saw everything.

"Sit, my son," Kerlan said, and seated himself in front of the coffee table, gesturing for Ramson to take the seat across. Behind him, the great brass clock tapped down the seconds. "I thought my runners were mistaken when they brought news of your escape. It seems like I was the one mistaken."

Ramson matched the smile playing about Kerlan's lips. "I've come a long way for you, Alaric."

"So convince me why I shouldn't send you right back."

"You don't need convincing. You haven't killed me yet, which means news must have reached you that I have something to offer. Something worth more than any Trade or deal you've made in your entire life."

Kerlan tapped a gold fountain pen against a large jeweled ring on his middle finger. "Some similar whispers might have found their way to me. My yaeger certainly did sniff something strange about that young dama."

It seemed Igor and Bogdan had done their jobs and passed the word on—exactly as Ramson had orchestrated. Ramson hid a smile and matched his former master's metal-gray stare. "Ever heard of the Blood Witch of Salskoff?" he asked. When Kerlan was silent, he continued. "I've brought her to you."

Kerlan chuckled, tapping his pen twice, precisely on the tip of his finger. "No, you haven't, Ramson. Not without something in exchange."

"I've learned from the best."

"You crawl out of prison, show up on my doorstep with no ranking, and now you want to make a Trade with me? I don't know whether I should admire your bravery or laugh at your stupidity."

"Yet still you continue to entertain me. You're known to dispose of useless guests within seconds of a meeting, Alaric. It's been over a minute, and you're still listening to me." Ramson leaned forward on the coffee table. "You want my Trade."

Kerlan's eyes crinkled in the cunning way they always did when his subordinates did something right. Ramson still shuddered to imagine what those cool gray eyes looked like when a member of the Order did something *wrong*. "Go on, dear boy."

"Reinstate me as your Deputy, and I'll use the Blood Witch to whatever ends you wish. I'll hunt down the moles in the Order. I'll bury our enemies. I'll make the Order invincible." Ramson forced a cruel grin. "She's powerful, but she's volatile. And it just so happens I've gained her trust. I know how to manipulate her, and that's closer than anyone has ever gotten to her."

Kerlan rubbed his heavy ring against his fountain pen. The sound was like grating blades on bone, and it seemed to help him think. "You failed me, boy. I gave you a mission—personally—and you failed. You know how I view failures . . . *especially* among my ranked officers."

"People learn from their mistakes. I happen to be very good at it." Ramson tried not to think of the night Kerlan had sent for him and given him the most difficult job in the seven years of his tenure at the Order. *Kill the Emperor,* Kerlan had said, in this very room. *Kill him, and if anyone finds a trace of evidence that you did it, I'll be first to volunteer you for the gallows.*

Ramson had been on his way to Salskoff when he'd been intercepted several days later. The Whitecloaks had arrested him without cause, without trial, and left him to rot in Ghost Falls.

During those sleepless nights within the grime-covered walls, when the stench of sweat and piss had become too much for him to bear, one single thought had haunted him over and over again. If he hadn't been stopped, would he have finished the job? How far would he go to remain loyal to the Order?

Kerlan was silent again, and Ramson pushed these thoughts aside. Now was not the time for useless sentiment. "I knew what failing meant for me, Alaric. Our interests were aligned. The leak came from your side. And I'm going to destroy it."

The grating of the ring stopped. Kerlan looked up at last, and he was smiling. Not for the first time, Ramson had no idea how to interpret his master's smile. He'd seen that expression when Kerlan had promoted him to Deputy. He'd also seen it seconds before Kerlan slit a man's throat.

"I had already made up my mind," Kerlan declared, and Ramson's stomach tightened. Even before Kerlan went on, Ramson's mind was racing six, seven moves ahead, mapping out the many directions this conversation could take. "I just wanted to see you fight for it. You know I like playing with my food."

Ramson glanced at the clock. Forty-eight minutes past nine. Only twelve minutes, and Ana would be out of here safely.

He needed to stall for a little longer.

"You keep looking at the time, my son," Kerlan said, and Ramson snapped his attention back. "Are you waiting for someone . . . or something?"

Cold gripped Ramson. Kerlan never spoke without deliberately choosing every word. Ramson's voice sounded distant even as he said, "I wouldn't want you to be late to your own party, Alaric."

"Ah, very well, then." Kerlan drew out a piece of parchment from one of the drawers of his desk. He began to meticulously unscrew the cap of his gold pen, each twist causing a shrill squeaking sound that sent shivers down Ramson's spine. "Shall we make this Trade? I've been looking for a replacement Deputy ever since you left. I haven't found anyone nearly as close in cleverness and ambition as you, Ramson."

Ramson bowed his head. The dagger in his sleeve shifted as he leaned back in his seat. "I'm honored, my Lord."

Kerlan gave a delicate pause. His wrist brushed the contract parchment. "Of course, you've heard the old story of the Cat and the Lion?"

Ramson frowned. "I have not."

Kerlan set his pen down, eyes crinkled in what would look like kindness to anyone who didn't know the man. "It's an old Bregonian story, son. I suppose your dead mother would never have been able to tell you."

Ramson kept his face blank.

"The Cat was the predecessor and master to the Lion," Kerlan continued. "The Lion begged the Cat to train him in all sorts of skills. 'Master,' the Lion would plead, and the Cat would take pity on him and teach him something new each day. And with each passing day, the Lion grew—quicker and cleverer and more ruthless. He wanted to overthrow the Cat—to become the ruler of the mountain.

"One day, the Lion turned on the Cat. He used his strength, his stamina, his size, and his sharper claws to fight. But the Cat was older and more cunning, you see. There was one trick he hadn't taught the Lion—and that was to climb trees." Kerlan steepled his fingers, rings flashing. "And that was how the Cat survived. He knew the danger of having an apprentice too close to him in ambition and intelligence; he knew it would be his downfall, so he'd kept one last trick to himself."

Kerlan fell silent, his gray eyes boring into Ramson, a small smile curling his lips. Ramson's throat was dry; his heart pounded and his mind raced.

Slowly, Ramson flexed his hands, feeling the bulk of his dagger against his forearm.

"And that is why," Kerlan said softly, leaning forward, smile widening, "I believe it is against my self-interest to hire a Deputy who is going to try to assassinate me in this very room."

Ramson was on his feet by the time Kerlan finished the last word. He flicked his wrist; the dagger slipped out with a *schick*, blade glinting in the lamplight. He leapt onto Kerlan's desk, drew his hand back, plunged—

And his arm went limp. The blade clattered on the surface of Kerlan's oak desk, Ramson's fingers dragging uselessly on top. For a moment, Ramson stared in astonishment at his arm. He heard Kerlan laughing.

A strange feeling crept up his entire body—it was the way he'd felt back when he'd been on the streets and hadn't eaten for days. It felt like his muscles had atrophied and given out, as though all the strength had been drained from him.

He gasped and crumpled to the floor. *Move,* he commanded his body, but his arms were still as stone on the plush red carpet, as though they didn't even belong to him.

Polished black shoes rounded the desk. Kerlan bent and slowly, deliberately, picked up the dagger Ramson had dropped. "Fine little blade," he murmured, and then his gaze dropped back to Ramson. The expression on his face almost resembled pity, but Ramson knew better. Kerlan was savoring this moment.

From the hallway outside, a woman slipped in. Her hair, so black that it caught a blue sheen beneath the lamplight, and bronze skin marked her to be from one of the Aseatic Isles kingdoms. She leaned against the wall, tall and athletic, watching Ramson like a cougar watching its prey.

"How careless of me," Kerlan sighed, tapping his temple and looking genuinely confused. "I forgot to introduce you. Meet Nita, our newest member, and Deputy to the Order of the Lily."

Ramson's head spun; it felt like his muscles had melted into water and his lungs were collapsing upon themselves. As though from a distance, he heard Kerlan continue. "I think she would be classified as a flesh Affinite, though her Affinity lies in manipulating strength. Strength in your muscles, in your organs, in your heart . . ."

Even as he spoke, pain throbbed through Ramson's chest, sending spasms of nausea shooting through him. He choked a gasp.

Kerlan chuckled. Nita smiled. And then there was the cold, hard drag of a blade on his cheeks as Kerlan held Ramson's dagger to his face.

Terror locked its grip across Ramson's throat. He'd seen Kerlan torture men; he'd stood there and handed Kerlan the scalpels.

"As I said, dear boy, I like to play with my food, so don't worry. I'm keeping you for later." Kerlan stood, brushing off his immaculate indigo suit and pocketing Ramson's dagger. His shadow fell over Ramson, blotting out the world. "I'll have to beg your pardon and take my leave for now. I do hope I've been a good enough host. But after all, I have a ball to get to—there are some rather important guests tonight, I'd say." Kerlan's teeth flashed. "And, it seems, I have a very special girl to find."

No. But Ramson's scream was trapped in his throat, his body paralyzed as he watched Kerlan's retreating back disappear into the hallway outside. And then Nita stepped forward and the pressure on his chest increased, his throat constricting, his body growing numb.

Black spots dotted his vision, and soon he was drowning in darkness.

28

The snow fell thicker now, whirling in flurries beneath each swinging lamp that lit the veranda. Their shadows swayed unsteadily as Ana hurried past them. The few guests who had been outside had retreated inside. Laughter and music and light spilled from the tall windows and open doors of the banquet hall, cloaking Ana's footsteps as she ran. Down the marble steps, past the balustrades of the veranda—and then she was on the ground floor, behind a pillar that supported the balconies.

Her heart pounded an uneven beat in her chest as she hid in the shadows, watching. It was him—it was undoubtedly him, Ana thought, taking in the white of the man's cloak, the smooth skin of his head, and the paleness of his fingers as he raised them to the skies. A silver Deys'krug flashed around his neck, and she recalled with sudden sickness that he'd worn almost the same outfit exactly one year ago, when he'd murdered Papa.

Tetsyev made a circular motion across his chest, the sign of respect to the Cyrilian Deities, and tilted his face to the sky.

Ramson had coached her on how to construct the perfect ruse—her as a messenger from Kerlan, asking Tetsyev to examine the Deys'voshk in Kerlan's basement before the newest shipment of Affinites arrived.

But lies and trickery were how Ramson would conduct his scheme. They were not, Ana realized now, how *she* did things.

Ana flared her Affinity. The garden lit up in shades of dark and light—and the flaming body of blood that was Tetsyev a dozen steps in front of her.

Ana strode forward. Tetsyev's back was to her, and the snow muffled her footsteps. Her entire body shook. Something dangerous had coiled tightly in her stomach.

Her foot slipped; she muffled her cry.

Tetsyev turned. "What—" he began, eyes widening, but Ana threw her Affinity around him and tightened her grasp on his blood. Tetsyev made a choking sound, his eyes seeking out her shadow in the night.

"Do you feel that?" Ana gave another sharp tug on his blood, making sure to keep her face tilted away from the light. Tetsyev groaned. "That's just a taste of what I can do to you. Now follow me quietly, and you'll live."

Her heart raced as she led him through the glass doors into the banquet hall, her Affinity tight as a noose around his neck. She walked a half dozen steps in front of him, but she could almost *see* his figure outlined in her mind in blood. He trailed her like a ghost, his hands clasped tightly, his steps in tune to hers.

The huge brass clock in the middle of the banquet hall struck twenty-five past nine when they slipped from the ball into the maze of corridors in Kerlan's mansion. Ana recited the directions Ramson had drilled into her—*second left, first right, fifth left*—and the map he'd forced her to memorize until she could find her way in her sleep.

The halls were eerily empty, and as they walked, the winding set of hallways grew narrower, the bare floors no longer covered in exotic carpeting. The expensive décor faded to plain marble, and walls became barren. An air of neglect hung in this section of the mansion, infused with an unnatural stillness that made her feel as though they were trespassing in forbidden territory.

When Ana swept the area with her Affinity, there was not a single guard or servant around. A feeling of unease crept up on her as they made their last turn and found themselves in front of a dead end of a passageway. An ordinary oakwood door stood before them, a round brass handle polished.

Taking a deep breath, Ana grasped the handle and began to turn it. *Two circles clockwise, five counterclockwise, then three clockwise again.* Ramson's voice seemed to whisper by her ear, and she felt the ghost of his touch as he guided her hands through the motions. *Then push.*

A clacking and whirring sound almost made her jump. It came from within the door, like a series of gears grinding open. Ana threw her weight against the door and pushed.

It ground open inch by inch, and she realized that despite its appearance, this was no ordinary door. It was thicker than the length of her forearm, and as it swung open into the light, she saw the glittering black material on the other side, and felt coldness and a sense of weakness drape over her like a suffocating cloak. *Blackstone.*

A dark smear stretched from the stones at the tips of her shoes to the stone steps leading into darkness, as though someone had dragged a long brushstroke of ink from here to the depths below. *Blood,* her Affinity screamed.

"In here," she instructed Tetsyev, and quietly, he began his descent. Ana grabbed the nearest torch from its sconce and Tetsyev drifted past her in the darkness, the white of his cloak reflecting her torchlight. Ana closed the door behind her and followed the alchemist. At the bottom of the stairs was a small room, the walls made of rough-hewn stone. A distinct set of chains stretched like a grotesque vine along the walls, and to the right of the chamber, a corridor led on into darkness.

Ana threw her shoulders back. After all this time, the man she had been searching for stood before her.

Tetsyev faced the tunnel stretching beyond the chamber, his back to her. He was so still he might have been made of stone. Ana remembered this very same outline, carved in monochrome by the bone-white moon, standing over her father's deathbed.

"Turn around," she said.

He did, slowly. His frightened gray eyes fell on her as she carefully set the torch in a sconce on the wall. "Do you recognize me?"

Beneath the flickering torchlight, Tetsyev seemed to tremble as he answered. "No."

Anger stirred in Ana, white-hot. She unlaced the ribbons of her mask and slid it off her face. "Do I look familiar now, mesyr Tetsyev?"

Tetsyev's eyes widened as they swept across her face, taking in her eyes, her nose, the shape of her mouth. "Kolst Pryntsessa Anastacya," he whispered.

"I lost that title." It was difficult to keep the snarl out of her voice. "In fact, I've lost *everything.* And you're the reason for it all." Her voice shook, and the wall she had built around that black well of grief threatened to crumble.

Ask him about Luka. Tell him you're taking him back to Salskoff. And get out.

But different words, words that she had wanted to ask for so long, that she had dreamt of over and over again, clawed at her chest. Ana turned to her father's murderer, her breathing ragged. "Why did you do it?"

Tetsyev's face was twisted away from the torchlight. "I never meant to."

The confession hit her like a physical blow. She turned away from him, her chest heaving. "You never *meant* to," Ana grated out. "So you killed my father by accident? As an *afterthought*?"

"It was no accident," Tetsyev whispered. "But I never meant to, either. I was manipulated. She took control of my mind for years . . . I had no idea what I was doing—"

A word snagged her attention. "'She'?" Ana repeated. "What are you talking about?"

Tetsyev passed a trembling hand over his face. "Deities, you don't even know."

Her heart stuttered. "Know what?"

"Kolst Contessya Morganya planned it."

For a moment, Ana only stared at him, the meaning of his words sinking into her.

Ana barked a humorless laugh. "You killed my father, and now you're trying to blame my aunt for it? You are truly . . ." Words failed her, and she slashed a hand through the air. *"Sick."*

"You're right. It isn't fair of me to blame it all on Morganya," Tetsyev whispered. "I was in it with her, at first, before it all went wrong."

"You're mad," Ana snarled.

But *mad* wasn't the word she was looking for, she realized, as the flickering orange flames carved out Tetsyev's gaunt cheekbones and faraway eyes. He didn't look mad, he looked haunted.

"Morganya and I met each other many years ago," he began softly, and Ana found herself pulled along in the flow of his words, rooted in horror and helplessness and the conviction that, against all her greater instincts, he spoke the truth. "You must know by now, Kolst Pryntsessa, that life in the Empire isn't easy for an Affinite. I had lost both my Affinite parents, and Morganya had just come out of months of captivity and abuse at the hands of non-Affinites. We were damaged, broken, but not enough that we couldn't put together the pieces and dream. We envisioned a great future, a better one, where Affinites could walk freely and would no longer be reviled. But neither of us was strong enough yet to begin to create that future. Together, we practiced our Affinities: mine, in the merging and morphing of elements, and hers, in the manipulation of flesh and mind."

Tetsyev's voice sounded distant to Ana, as though she were listening to a strange, surreal story. Mamika. He spoke of her mamika—Morganya, with soft eyes the color of warm tea, her long dark braid, her devotion to the Deities.

He spoke of her, her Affinity, and her plan . . . to murder Ana's father.

"One incident changed Morganya's life forever—in many ways," Tetsyev said, and Ana knew, with a chilling premonition, the incident he spoke of. It was the day Mama and Papa had been touring the Empire with the Imperial Patrols. They had discovered a girl, barely into womanhood, bruised and half-naked and crying, crawling out from the ruins of a dacha. "We planned it all. When the Empress took pity on Morganya and brought her to the Palace, we knew we had set in motion something great . . . and that we were going to change the world."

The next sequence of events tumbled from Tetsyev's lips, unfolding before Ana like a nightmare. "She grew close to the Empress. She was appointed the Countess of Cyrilia, first in line to the throne after the Imperial family. She hired me into the Palace. She hid her Affinity with daily doses of Deys'voshk. Years had passed, but Morganya was patient. Her goal was the throne.

"I had, by then, devised the perfect poison. It was slow-working; we had to ensure that it didn't kill the Palace taste-testers and the poisoning couldn't look suspicious. It was invisible, untraceable but for a bitter stench that we could mix into meals and pass off as medicine.

"Within one year, Kateryanna was dead, and we were one step closer to the throne."

Ana's knees were weak; she felt as though she might collapse. Images flitted through her mind—a white-cloaked alchemist, a beautiful young countess, a kind empress, a brokenhearted emperor: pieces of a story set in motion, careening toward an inevitable doom.

"But Morganya's history had left a wound in her," Tetsyev continued. "One that had festered and rotted into something twisted. I didn't realize it until it was too late that her plan wasn't to balance the scales. It was to tip them. Morganya wanted to overturn the world as it was, subjecting non-Affinites to *our* rule . . . or eliminating them."

No. No, she wouldn't accept this—she *couldn't* accept it, this story of her gentle, pious mamika as a vengeful, calculating murderess . . . and a flesh Affinite capable of manipulating minds?

Ana shook off the strange spell of his story. The world flooded back into focus, the blood in Tetsyev's body pulsing hot as she latched her Affinity to it and slammed him against the wall. "You lie," she growled.

Tetsyev was breathing hard; the whites of his eyes flashed against the torchlight. "I have been a prisoner in the lies of my own making," he rasped. "This is the first time in many years that I have told the truth."

"Liar!" she screamed as she pressed him against the wall, her Affinity turning cruel in her wrath, cutting off his circulation. "I will *kill* you."

Tetsyev scrabbled at the wall behind him. "P-please, Kolst Pryntsessa," he half-wheezed, half-sobbed. "If I am lying—if I am the only culprit—then who is poisoning your brother at the Palace?"

Luka.

At the mention of her brother, Ana's fury settled into cold dread in her chest.

"I tell the truth, Kolst Pryntsessa," Tetsyev whispered, a tear rolling down his cheek. "And you must decide what you do with this truth."

Ana flung him to the ground. She was shaking as she turned, tears blurring her world out of focus. Tetsyev's story continued, washing over her like the dull roaring of a river.

"I left Morganya after Kateryanna died." Tetsyev's voice trembled, and Ana closed her eyes. She found herself matching his story to the fragments of reality that she had known. Together they wove a broken tapestry, and somewhere within that was the truth. "I remained in hiding for years—but she found me again.

"This time, she took my mind, too."

Anything you want in this world, you have to take it for yourself, Morganya had said.

"She'd grown even stronger in the time we'd been apart. You and your brother had almost come of age, and time was running out for Morganya. She kept me imprisoned in my own mind for a year, making the poison for the Emperor this time. She came up with the plan to frame you on the night we were to administer the killing dose."

Ana knew, too well, what came next. She'd relived it in her mind a thousand times over—the single night that had altered the course of her life forever.

"I was administering the final dose to the Emperor when you burst into the chambers and seized my blood." Tetsyev's voice shifted, as though he'd finally leveled his face to her. "With your Affinity, you broke the control that Morganya had over me. You didn't know it, but you saved me."

The moonlight. The alchemist, outlined against the open windows. The sobbing, so faint it had sounded like the wind. The silver Deys'krug on his chest.

Ana turned to face him at last. In the maelstrom of her thoughts, her mind latched on to a single sentence. "What do you mean, I 'broke the control' Morganya had over you?"

Tetsyev raised his eyes to her. He sat on the ground, his white robes dirtied with grime, his frame hunched and broken. "Morganya is strong, but she is not invincible. She can control only one mind at a time. And her control can be broken. When you used your Affinity on me, it cut through Morganya's

Affinity. You broke her control over my mind; you saved me, and then you condemned me, for in the moments after the murder, I was fully myself."

She watched his pitiful face, her anger settling into cold, logical fury. "And you ran."

He lowered his head. "I am a coward, Kolst Pryntsessa. That is something I'm not afraid to admit."

Ana's mind swirled, cold clarity cutting through the chaos of her anger.

Tetsyev spoke of a decade-long conspiracy in the making, orchestrated by none other than Ana's aunt. And she was one step away from succeeding.

Ana needed to go back, with Tetsyev. Reveal everything to the Imperial Court. Sentence Morganya. Save Luka. And then, with Yuri, they would begin to reverse the wheels of a great machine that had allowed this empire to thrive at the cost of the Affinites.

But first, she needed her brother to live.

"An antidote," she said. "I need you to make an antidote to this poison."

"It exists," Tetsyev said, and Ana's knees almost buckled with relief. "I made one in case the tasters became too sick. It's kept in the apothecary's wing of the Palace, with the poison itself."

There was a cure.

Luka would live.

"You must listen to me, Kolst Pryntsessa," Tetsyev whispered in the silence that had fallen. "You face more enemies than you know. Morganya has allied herself with Alaric Kerlan and the Order of the Lily. He made a deal with her—that he would end Affinite indenturement once she took the throne, and in return, she would send him to conquer Bregon.

"I've gained Kerlan's trust," Tetsyev continued. "I served him from afar for all these years. Nearly four moons ago, Kerlan sent his Deputy to assassinate your brother."

Ana's blood ran cold.

"I foiled that attempt; I alerted the Imperial Patrols. They arrested the man and threw him in prison—but I heard he is back. And I know he's looking for me. He's here, tonight." Tetsyev gave a shaky little laugh. "Funny how the Deities like to play with fates, Kolst Pryntsessa. If you hadn't found me tonight, I would have taken my own life. I cannot live this life of lies and deceit any longer, constantly looking over my shoulder and sleeping with a poison under my pillow."

Ana heard his words as though he spoke from very far away. A roaring filled her ears, and suddenly she was back in the dacha in the Syvern Taiga, Ramson standing opposite her with a smile like a wolf.

What is it that you want?

Revenge. I plan to destroy my enemies one by one and take back my position and what was rightfully mine.

The scene changed, and she was in Shamaïra's dacha, the room swirling with intoxicating warmth and heady fumes. She remembered flipping Ramson's wrist, catching sight of the flower tattoo. It had been a lily of the valley.

The Order of the Lily.

And, just like that, it all came together. It felt as though she had been walking in a thick fog, searching for something she couldn't quite put her finger on . . . and suddenly it had shown itself.

Ramson had been working for Kerlan all along. And Kerlan was working with Morganya.

Tears stung her eyes. She thought of Ramson, the way he had looked at her beneath the falling snow, his eyes bright like a boy's.

It had been an act, every moment of it. Every piece of that man she'd seen had been a lie. And she'd fallen for it all.

But there was no time to pity herself.

Ana lifted her gaze to the alchemist. There was nothing left to do, no more pieces left to puzzle over. "I'm going back to Salskoff to stop Morganya," she said, "and you're going to come with me."

Tetsyev wiped the sweat from his forehead. "I'll be executed for treason," he whispered.

"I'll grant you mercy if you cooperate." It sickened her to say the words, when she'd waited an entire year to see this man die. But she was no longer just Ana, the frightened girl who'd stumbled into the Syvern Taiga and wanted nothing more than to have her home and her family back.

She was Anastacya Mikhailov, Crown Princess of Cyrilia, and her empire depended on her.

Tetsyev had crawled over to her, his tears tracing streaks down his cheeks. He clung to her skirts and kissed them. "Thank you, Kolst Pryntsessa," he wept. "Kind, good, merciful—"

Ana tore her skirts from his hands. "I am none of those things," she said. "I only grant you mercy because your life is worth nothing to me. But make a single mistake again, and I won't hesitate to kill you."

She turned from him in disgust and retrieved Ramson's pocket watch. She wanted, more than anything, to hurl it across the room and see it shatter into pieces.

She checked the time. Forty-eight minutes past nine.

"We leave now," she said, whirling around and snatching the torch from its sconce. Ramson had told her it took roughly five minutes to get to the end of the escape tunnel. "Follow me."

She stretched her Affinity down the tunnel as they walked, sensing for the warm thrum of blood in bodies, feeling out any traps. There was a possibility that there was no carriage awaiting her at the end of the tunnel, that Ramson had tricked her and this was a trap. Still, it was the only way out.

But the corridors were empty. There was only the sound of her and Tetsyev's breaths, their harried footsteps echoing against the stone walls. The ground grew rougher, the air wet and then dry again.

A door met her at the end of the tunnel. Moonlight filtered through its cracks. Ana snuffed out her torch and twisted the handle in the same combination as the one upstairs. It swung open.

She let out a breath of relief.

They were in the back of Kerlan's gardens, a single path cutting between tall trees that obscured mostly everything else from view. A trellis covered the entrance, overgrown with ivy and small white flowers.

A carriage stood on the grassy lawn in the shadows of the trellis. Two valkryfs pawed the ground at her approach.

Ramson had told the truth.

She turned to Tetsyev. "Get in," Ana began, but Tetsyev was no longer standing behind her.

Another man stood in his place, dressed in a black doublet. The moonlight cast a long shadow in his wake, reminding her of a different dungeon filled with the pungent smell of fear and Deys'voshk.

"Hello, Kolst Pryntsessa." Vladimir Sadov smiled widely at her, pressing his long white fingers together. "I've been waiting for you."

There was a soft whooshing sound. A sharp pain pierced her shoulder, and the world went black.

29

The darkness came and went, but the pain was endless.

Ramson tried to rein his consciousness back from the depths of sleep, but then someone shook him.

He groaned and cracked an eye open. He immediately regretted it as bright light pierced his vision and the world swayed around him.

The air held the faded stench of blood and sweat. He recognized this room, with the bleeding walls and countless chains and the cupboard with vials of unknown poisons. He was once again in the dungeons of Kerlan's estate—only this time, he was the prisoner.

His shoulders ached. He strained forward and found the familiar feeling of cuffs chafing against his wrists. Ramson sank back against the wall.

He had been here for hours, or perhaps longer—he couldn't tell anymore. His interrogator, a hulking man in a black mask, was nowhere to be seen. Ramson's eyes caught the pail of black water in the corner. A shudder ran involuntarily down his back as he remembered the suffocating feeling, the feeling of drowning.

"You're awake."

He would know that voice anywhere. Ramson swung his head to the source. "You."

"Me," Kerlan agreed pleasantly, as though he had just shown up on the doorstep of a neighbor. "I decided to take over, since my bruiser, too, needs sleep. That, and I only trust myself when it comes to these types of affairs."

Ramson knew when Kerlan was trying to unsettle him. He turned his thoughts away.

Ana.

His chest tightened, and he forced himself to breathe steadily. She should be long gone by now, untraceable in the Syvern Taiga with her carriage and her alchemist.

Ramson had no idea where she was going, or if he would ever see her again. He'd consciously refrained from asking.

Kerlan was watching him with a smile. "Thinking about your girl, Ramson? Don't worry. A friend of mine is seeing to it that she's taken care of."

Cold panic spread through his veins, and it was all that Ramson could do not to beg for an explanation. He forced his lips into a wicked snarl. "When are you going to do things yourself, Alaric, instead of sending your big musclemen—"

The blow came out of nowhere, a bolt of lightning to his head that sent him reeling. Ramson groaned and coughed, blood spattering the damp stone floor. "That felt personal, Alaric," he wheezed.

"Did it? Well, I suppose the rest of your last few days will, too. Tell me, how do you wish to die, Ramson Quicktongue?" Kerlan paused. "Or should I say—Ramson Farrald?"

It was a name he hadn't used in seven years, until tonight; a past he'd tried to bury by forging a new name and a new life for himself. Kerlan knew; and he wielded it now to inflict wounds that a blade never could.

Ransom growled, "You have no right to say that name, you son of a bitch."

"You think you'll ever be smarter than me, boy?" Kerlan hissed. "I have *always* been one step ahead of you. To me, you will forever be that poor, pathetic, sniveling beggar who crawled to my door seven years ago." Kerlan's laugh was a serrated blade as he lowered his face to Ramson's. "You could have been great, my son. By my side, you might have changed the tides of this empire. Of the *world.* But now I suppose you'll die unknown and irrelevant, your unmarked body rotting with the sewage of the Dams." He grinned. "Just like your whore of a mother."

Ramson spat at him.

Kerlan straightened, wiping the spit from his face as though he were cleaning some gravy from his cheek. "That felt personal, Ramson," he said pleasantly, and Ramson knew that was Alaric Kerlan's most dangerous tone yet. "And I suppose this will, too."

At Kerlan's signal, two members of the Order came in and shoved Ramson to his knees. The lashes of the whip nearly dragged him from consciousness. But it was when the bucket of black water came to meet his face that the real torture began.

Ramson knew the feeling of drowning well. As a Bregonian recruit, the trainers at the Blue Fort had wasted no time acquainting their pupils with the whims and wishes of the ocean. They learned to dive, to swim, to float, and to sink. They trained to hold their breaths in the ocean, to defy the need for air, and on some occasions, to nearly drown.

It was when Jonah Fisher died that Ramson realized one could never truly learn to drown.

It had happened one moon before the Embarkment, the most important examination of a Bregonian recruit's career. At twelve years old, on the brink of adulthood, each recruit went through a rigorous mental and physical examination before a panel of the Navy's most highly regarded fighters. The class was ranked, the rankings were published across Bregon, and captains of all ships in the Bregonian Navy came to select one recruit to take as an apprentice on their ship.

Exactly one moon before, Ramson had received a letter. It was from a healer in the small town of Elmford.

His mother was dying. It was something in the unhygienic water that the poor drank, the healer wrote, that caused rose-colored rashes and abdominal cramps and, in its last stages, high fevers.

His mother had asked for the healer only at the onset of the fever.

Ramson had felt the strength fade from him then, at that breakfast hall in the Blue Fort. Blue Fort recruits seldom visited home—at most once a year—but Ramson hadn't been back since his father had shown up on his doorstep and taken him away in the middle of the night.

He still remembered the look on his mother's face, a simultaneous mixture of terror and dread, as though she'd known this moment would come—her brown hair, already laden with wisps of gray from a hard life, and her hazel eyes, the ones that she'd passed to him, pleading at the door.

His father had turned from her and never looked back.

And so had Ramson.

He tore from the breakfast hall. His legs were pumping so hard that he thought he'd never stop running—past the iron double doors, through the open-air archways, until he was at the jetty, the ocean waves glimmering like jewels beneath a blistering sun. He needed to get away—to just do something mindless for a while.

Ramson dove into the ocean and swam.

When he resurfaced, a boy was sitting on the docks, waiting for him.

"Anything you'd like to share?" Jonah dangled a foot in the sea, making lazy circles.

Ramson sprawled out on the sun-warmed jetty and told him. His hair dripped with water, and the sun dried him until his body was sticky with salt. The waves lapped at him, bringing the briny scent of the ocean, and gulls circled the air, their cries drifting in the wind. It was almost cruel, how beautiful this day was.

"I know where you can get medicine for that," Jonah said, after Ramson had finished.

The waves surged, slamming against the wooden post. Ramson felt breathless. "How?"

"The Rose Fever. They called it the Poor Man's Sickness back in my town. Comes from dirty food and water." Jonah tilted his head back, his eyes narrowing like a cat's in the sun. "The Blue Fort has medicine for it. It's just too costly to send to all the towns and villages. They hoard it for the Navy. The ones *worthy* of it. It's all stored up in a warehouse facility of theirs."

Of course Jonah would know. Jonah, with his uncanny

interest in Bregonian state affairs, his research into the economy and trade and distribution of supplies.

A bud of hope unfurled in Ramson's chest. "My father," he said, scrambling to his feet. "He'll know where it is. He—"

Jonah grabbed his ankle. "Your father doesn't give a damn about your mother."

"He'll do it for me," Ramson snapped.

"Don't be naïve."

"Don't be so bitter!" Ramson shouted. "You don't understand, because you've never had a family!"

Jonah's eyes darkened; his brows furrowed. "I do understand. You're my family, Ramson. My sea-brother and my best friend. I would do anything for you."

Ramson snatched his foot back as though he'd been burned.

"Wait, Ramson," Jonah began, but Ramson had already taken off. He ran past the alder trees in the Blue Fort's courtyard to where he knew his father's office was. The Naval Headquarters was an adjoining building to the Blue Fort Academy that recruits seldom visited—Ramson would sometimes walk past with his classmates and sneak glances into the shaded courtyard and latticed windows, hoping to catch a glimpse of his father.

A figure hovered by the door; Ramson's heart ballooned at the sight of his father's sandy hair and solid frame.

"Admiral!" he called. His father never answered to anything else. "Admiral—"

His father turned, the shadows of the alder trees dappling his features. Ramson saw now that he'd been speaking to someone—the dark-haired Commander of the First Fleet. The one Ramson's father wanted Ramson to impress. If everything worked according to his father's plans, Ramson would join the First Fleet aboard Commander Dallon's ship.

Roran Farrald's face remained stoic, even when he caught sight of Ramson.

"I need to speak to you," Ramson panted, slowing when he drew within a dozen steps of his father. He added, "Please."

Roran Farrald's eyes narrowed slightly. "I'm very busy."

"Please, sir!"

"Another time." Roran Farrald was turning away, striding after Commander Dallon.

"My mother is dying!" The words burst from Ramson. "Please, she needs your help."

Roran Farrald froze. His back was to Ramson, but even beneath the shade of the trees in the courtyard, Ramson could tell his outline had gone rigid. Farther ahead, Commander Dallon watched impassively.

Roran Farrald barely turned; Ramson could just make out the profile of his face, cleanly cut and square, utterly ascetic. "And why," Roran Farrald said softly, his words slicing through the slight breeze that stirred the leaves in the yard, "would your mother have anything to do with me?"

Ramson stood there a long time after his father was gone, beneath the swaying alder trees, the leaves rattling around him in the wind, their shadows scattering over him. The bright flame in his heart turned to stone that day, and when he went back to Jonah, he spoke quietly, with measured calculation. "Show me where the medicine is."

They snuck out of their dorms that night, when the moon retreated behind the clouds.

The Naval Headquarters began at the western end of the

Blue Fort, stretching across cliffs that plunged precariously into the ocean. It was a symbol of the Bregonian Navy's dominance of the seas—and utterly off-limits to the public. Jonah had speculated that it held classified information, such as naval secrets and warfare strategies.

It was near pitch-black outside, the cool breeze briny and speckled with sand, the grass of the courtyard soft beneath their boots. They stole across like shadows, and within minutes, they were outside the headquarters.

A pair of patrols passed by; Jonah shoved Ramson behind a tree. Ramson had never felt like this: adrenaline pumping through his blood, his heart pounding as though it wished to tear from his chest. And then, a beat later, Jonah was rounding to the back of the building. Ramson watched in awe and fascination as he pushed and a door appeared in the stone wall.

"An escape tunnel," Jonah whispered. "I studied structural maps of castles. They all have these. So I found the Headquarters'."

It was dark and silent inside, and it smelled of salt. The flooring was uneven, and Ramson stayed close to Jonah. After a while, the tunnel opened up. They stumbled through an iron door, and then they were inside the Bregonian Naval Headquarters.

This section of the Headquarters was dark—but from several hallways down came the faint light of torches. They passed corridor after corridor of seemingly endless doors, the marble floor sleek beneath their velvet steps, until at last, Jonah paused in front of an iron door that looked exactly like the rest.

"In here," Jonah whispered, and pushed.

A shrill peal blasted through the silence; Ramson clapped

his hands over his ears, but the sound seemed to set off a reactionary chain. He heard the muffled sound of distant bells beginning to ring, the high-pitched alarms blending into a cacophony of screams. Jonah was shouting at him, tugging at his arms, but his knees had buckled and he sat on the floor, dizzy and paralyzed with fear.

Footsteps rang, echoing through the corridors, and torchlight blazed behind them.

"Ramson!" Jonah shouted, and with a final tug, Ramson was on his feet and they were running in the opposite direction, back to the escape tunnel—

Light blazed before them as a patrol rounded the corner; he gave a shout, and a second patrol followed him. At the sight of Ramson and Jonah, he strung an arrow onto his bow and aimed. "Halt!"

Ramson was shaking so hard that his knees knocked together.

"Hands up!"

Out of the corner of his eye, he saw Jonah comply. "Please, we're recruits from the Blue Fort," Jonah said. "We got lost—"

"And ended up in a secure facility?" A voice sounded behind them, one that raised the hairs on Ramson's neck. With dreadful premonition, he turned.

Roran Farrald stood behind them, dressed in a plain gray tunic. His face was as placid as the surface of a still lake. But Ramson had never seen such fury in his father's eyes—dark, the color of storm clouds and midnight waters. They seemed to tremble as they settled on Ramson.

"Admiral Farrald." The patrols bowed their heads in respect, but the archer kept his arrow trained on Ramson and Jonah.

"What in the *devil* do you think you're doing?" Roran Farrald's voice cracked over Ramson like a whip.

Before Ramson could reply, steps sounded; four to five men rounded the corner, and Ramson recognized all of them as high-ranking officers in the Navy. Among them, he spotted Commander Dallon.

"What the hell's going on here?" a silver-haired officer asked.

Roran Farrald's eyes blazed as he took a step forward. He looked between Ramson and Jonah, and finally, his gaze settled on his son. "You are guilty of trespassing in a top secret government facility. You are aware this is punishable by death?"

Ramson thought he would throw up. *Death.* He'd studied Bregonian law, but he hadn't thought the laws would apply to them. Surely they applied to ordinary citizens, yes, but . . . not to recruits at the Blue Fort Academy.

His father's coal-black gaze was still focused on him. "Was this your idea, boy?"

Ramson tried to speak, but fear had sewn his throat shut. He opened and closed his mouth several times, but nothing came out. More footsteps sounded; more patrols had arrived, and more Naval officers in nightclothes. The bells continued to scream.

"It was mine."

Ramson's head snapped to the boy beside him. Jonah stood in the frame of the half-open door, his shadow stretching long and thin behind him. His face was pale, but his raven-black eyes glimmered in the torchlight.

"I wanted to steal the medicine," Jonah continued. Words—the truth—pushed against Ramson's chest, needing to be said.

But another warring instinct—fear—pushed back, paralyzing him to the spot.

"For what reason?" asked the silver-haired officer.

Jonah gave only the slightest pause, indiscernible to anyone but Ramson. "I'm trading it in town. People pay good mint for that kind of stuff. I asked Ramson to come along for fun. He'd make a decent partner."

There was an uproar from the officers. "This is organized crime!" Silver Hair cried. "This young man cannot be permitted to walk free tonight!"

Yet as the officers continued to yell, only one person was silent. A strange expression had crept onto Roran Farrald's face, one that resembled . . . triumph.

"Enough," he boomed. "Guards, nock!"

"No!" The cry tore from Ramson, small and feeble and lost in the fray. He flung out a hand, pushing Jonah back, meaning to protect him.

"Let go of my son," Roran shouted, but Ramson's knees had given out and he held on to Jonah, gasps racking his chest. The bells shrieked in his ears, drilling into his head.

"Father," he cried. "Please—"

"Let go of my son!" Roran roared again.

"I'm not touching him!" Jonah yelled.

"Guards," bellowed Roran.

It happened so fast. Ramson saw the archer nock, the bowstring grow taut. And then the head of the arrow shimmered as it released, cutting through the torchlight, sleeker than a whisper.

Years later, Ramson still couldn't tell why he did it. He wanted to be brave, he wanted to be selfless, like Jonah—but in the end, in his very flesh and bone, he was made of cowardice and selfishness.

Ramson ducked.

There was a soft wet sound, like a knife slicing through an apple. Jonah made a small noise—it might have been a gasp—and slowly, quietly, like the last leaf on an alder tree, fell.

Ramson barely remembered what happened next—someone was screaming, but all he knew was that he'd dropped to his knees and scrambled to Jonah's side, shaking his shoulders, convinced that he would wake up and laugh at having tricked everyone.

Yet slowly, he realized that the screaming was coming from him. Jonah lay still, his body wobbling like that of a puppet as Ramson shook him. And all Ramson saw were Jonah's midnight eyes, open wide as though in surprise, and his black hair spread across the floor like raven's feathers. Nothing made sense—Jonah, lying there, blood pooling silently on the floor, arrow shaft protruding from his chest, when he had been alive and yelling seconds ago.

The image stayed in Ramson's head, carved into his memory, as his father and the officers murmured in grave tones, as he was dragged out by the guards. The moon was impossibly bright, and a wind howled through the alder trees, whipping his face.

They took him to a room that was at once familiar and unfamiliar. The maroon walls were lined with portraits of a happy family, the young daughter laughing as her auburn curls shimmered. The cherrywood desk was clean and cold to the touch, everything in the room arranged to a sterile tidiness, devoid of warmth.

His father's office.

The door shut; a mug of something warm and strong-smelling was shoved into Ramson's hands.

"Chocolate and brandy," Roran Farrald said in his cool baritone. "Drink up."

Ramson leaned over the mug and threw up.

"Grow a backbone," he heard his father say. "Are you going to vomit every time you see a man die?"

"Why am I not dead?" Ramson whispered.

"The orphan confessed. He manipulated you. You will be punished, but the bulk of the blame lies with him. And he has been lawfully sentenced."

"Lawful—" Ramson's hands shook, and he raised his gaze to his father. "I'm the one who asked to steal the medicine," he whispered. "I told you that my mother was sick—"

Roran Farrald's gaze was colder than steel when he cut across Ramson. "Jonah Fisher was prosecuted for illegal trespassing into a government facility, perpetuation of organized crime, manipulation of a minor—"

"You know that's a lie." Tears pooled in Ramson's eyes. "It was my fault." He heard, again, Jonah's steady voice, taking blame for a crime that Ramson had committed. Saw, again, the glint of firelight on the arrowhead, the ricochet of the bowstring, the fletch spinning through the air toward him.

And he'd ducked.

"I killed him." The words tumbled from his mouth, broken, numb.

"No," Roran Farrald growled, and his large hand clasped Ramson's chin tight enough to bruise. His gaze scorned. "You are so *weak,* you foolish boy. Can't you see? You must learn

from this, if you wish to get anywhere in this world. Friendship is weakness. There are only alliances, made to be broken when it serves your gain." He lowered his voice. "There is something to be gained from every tragedy, every loss. You and I both know that Fisher would have beaten you in the Embarkment. Fisher's death comes at a convenient time for you. Now you will be ranked—"

The mug exploded against the wall behind Roran. Hot chocolate and brandy dripped down like blood. Ramson was on his feet, his hands shaking. The rage that had been simmering within him had boiled over, and he found himself screaming at his father. "My best friend—my sea-brother—is *dead*, and all you care about is some blasted examination?"

"Men like me—like *us*—cannot waste time on *friendships* and *love*."

"My mother—"

"Is dead," Roran finished calmly.

Ramson was spitting, choking on his own fury, but he wanted his father to feel his pain—to feel *something*. Wildly, he grasped at words to twist into his father's heart like knives. "Is that why you wouldn't help her? Because she was a waste of time to you?"

His father only looked at him with that cold, calculating gaze. "How do you think I got to where I am?" Roran said quietly, the painful truth of his words crackling in the air.

It couldn't be. It *couldn't* be. The world spun. Ramson's hands fumbled at the wall behind him, struggling for purchase.

Roran stepped backward and turned away. "I cleansed myself of those weaknesses—of friendships, of love—because

I knew there were more important things." Ramson made a choked sound. "Power, and my *kingdom,* boy. Those were what I gained when I made the choice. And I would make it all over again."

When his father turned around, eyes dull black, face blank as death, Ramson saw a reflection of what he was to become. A demon of a man, unfeeling and half-crazed, willing to destroy anyone and anything in his way. Willing to murder an innocent child. Willing to let a woman he'd once loved die.

Roran Farrald straightened, tucking his hands behind his back, ever the Admiral, the soldier, the fearless leader. "That is the price that men like us must pay, boy. That is the price."

Ramson Farrald didn't show up at training the next day. The soldiers and scouts that his father sent found no trace of him; it was as though, overnight, he had vanished, and they were searching for a ghost.

Men like us.

With each stinging lash, each suffocating moment in that pail of dark water, the truth grew clearer. Ramson had run to Alaric Kerlan, Bregonian-noble-turned-crime-lord, the man his father had sought for years to destroy, in hopes of using him against his father. *Your opponent's hatred is a sword; wield it. His hope is your shield; turn it against him.* One of his father's favorite battle mantras, used to destroy him. The irony had felt like a success in itself.

But how many people had Kerlan sent to this very dungeon to be chained, beaten, and tortured? How many Affinites had his Order sentenced to a life of servitude? And all the while, Ramson had managed his businesses and ports at his side, run his blood trades, and been a good lapdog.

He had purged himself of friendship, of love, of any feelings of empathy or guilt. He had forged countless alliances, and broken them just as easily whenever it served his gain. He had backstabbed good men, conned bad men, stolen from thieves, lied to liars.

That is the price that men like us must pay.

He had become the demon he'd seen in his father that night; he had become the shadow to the monster that was Alaric Kerlan. And, despite the different sides of the war they fought on, Ramson now saw the similarities in men like them. Ruthless. Self-serving. Oath-breaking. Amoral. Merciless.

Men like us.

No, Ramson thought wildly in a moment of sudden lucidity. *Not me.*

But it was Ana's face that came to him first, the fierce jut of her chin, and the way she chewed on her lip when she was thinking. Hadn't he helped her? Protected her when she was weakest, saved her from those mercenaries?

Because she was your Trade, a voice inside him jeered. *You used her to get to Kerlan; you cast her aside when you'd finished with her.*

He still remembered the last words she'd said to him. *I would like to believe that it is our choices that define us.* And as he was forced into the pail of water over and over again, as Kerlan's whip landed mercilessly on his back, Ramson clung to those words.

It is our choices that define us.

"Now it's time for my favorite trick." Kerlan's voice rattled through Ramson's half-conscious thoughts. He forced his eyes open. His back was on fire, his body on the brink of giving up. Yet despite the exhaustion that slugged at his brain, his senses perked with fear.

Kerlan had started a fire in the hearth. A single rod was perched on the floor, the iron at the end roasting in the flames.

Ramson jerked at his bonds. The chains rattled, solid as ever. He clamped his teeth against the feeling that his heart would burst from his chest. He would not give Kerlan the satisfaction of hearing him scream.

Kerlan smiled. "There we go. A dose of fear. What I'd give to see that look on your face over and over again, you incorrigible boy. Perhaps I'll keep you alive for longer. No," he said to the bruiser, who had moved to stuff a gag in Ramson's mouth. "I want to hear him beg."

Fear flooded Ramson's chest and he was drowning again, his throat closing on him, his limbs heavy and frozen. Ramson gripped his shackles so hard that he felt a nail tear. "I'll eat dog shit before I beg you, Kerlan."

Kerlan reached for the hot iron rod. "I said it once, didn't I, boy? You'll only feel pain like this twice in your life. The first time, when you've earned my trust and passed the gates of hell into the Order of the Lily. The second time . . . when you've broken that trust and I throw you back into hell." He blew on the hot iron; it glowed, bright yellow at the center, red at the edges. "I hope you enjoy hell, my son."

Ramson's courage and clarity dissolved. *Not a monster . . . your choices . . . Ana.*

A single moment flared into lucidity in his mind: a night sky black and bright, snow swirling around them as she held his hands and whispered to him that he could be good, that he could make the right choice. And when he'd let go, the course of his life had splintered into what might have been and what now was. He'd left with words unspoken that night, the ghosts of their echoes swept away in the silent snows.

She was broken, damaged, just as he was—only she still believed in goodness, and tried to be strong and kind. Drowning beneath the weight and the blood of their own pasts, she still chose to reach for the light, whereas Ramson had turned to the dark.

Your heart is your compass, Jonah whispered.

If he had a choice again, what would he choose?

When the hot iron came, Ramson gave in.

30

The world swayed around her, sending streaks of pain up her skull. Reluctantly, Ana surfaced from her sleep. Pale light danced across her eyelids, and the sound of creaking filled the air. Something cold chafed against both of her wrists.

Her eyes flew open. Moonlight streamed through a small glass window high on the far wall, illuminating a ceiling of wooden rafters. The floor beneath her tilted from side to side, in rhythm with the creaking. She was in a carriage.

"Ah, you're awake."

Ana's heart leapt into her throat. In the corner by the door, draped in darkness, was the silhouette of a man. She tried to move, but her arms remained attached to the wall by her side. Manacles peered out from the layers of chiffon and silk of her gown. She was shackled in place.

Panic fogged her mind. She grasped for her Affinity, for the instinctive feel of blood thrumming through her and all around her, but found nothing. Deys'voshk. She recognized the haze, the lingering sense of nausea.

The man leaned forward, his long fingers clasped together. His face was pale, with eyes so black it was like staring into an abyss. The face brought back memories of dark dungeons and cold stone walls and the bitter tang of blood in her mouth. Ana recoiled.

Sadov smiled. "Hello again, Kolst Pryntsessa."

She was breathing too hard to think; her hands shook against their shackles. She tasted traces of Deys'voshk on her tongue, bitter and acidic. Heard his whispers. *Monster.* Ana grasped the first words that came to mind. "Where are you taking me?"

"Salskoff Palace." He looked at her as though she were a prized gem. "Kolst Imperatorya will be pleased to see you again."

Her Imperial Majesty. There was only one person he could be talking about. Morganya. Ana's head spun; memories of her gentle aunt alternated with Tetsyev's story of a cold, calculating murderess.

But Morganya was not Empress. "My brother," Ana said. "My brother is Emperor. And he will be glad to see me."

Sadov's lips curled. It was the same soft smile he carried when he brought her to the darkest parts of the Palace dungeons. "Have you not heard, Princess? In five days' time, your brother will announce his abdication due to ill health and appoint the Kolst Contessya Morganya as Empress Regent of Cyrilia."

Five days. Her stomach felt hollow. She knew Luka was sick from the poison—but five days. That was even less time than she'd feared.

"Within weeks, your brother will be dead, and Morganya will become Empress of Cyrilia."

"No!" Ana lunged, her chains clanging as she struggled against them.

"I've missed your spiritedness, Pryntsessa," Sadov crooned. "You have no idea how long I have waited for this moment. I suppose Pyetr told you all about what Morganya and I have been planning?"

Pyetr—Pyetr Tetsyev. How much of what he'd told her had been truth? And how much had been lies? Was he still working with Morganya? Had he only told her Morganya's plan to set her up?

I tell the truth, Kolst Pryntsessa. And you must decide what you do with this truth.

She closed her eyes as the hopelessness of her situation crashed into her. May was dead; her brother was dying. Yuri and the Redcloaks were gone. Tetsyev had vanished. Ramson had betrayed her.

"Oh, don't look so heartbroken, Princess." Sadov leaned forward and trailed a finger across her cheek. His touch sent cold revulsion down her spine. "You can join us." Ana lifted her gaze to his, and she found true madness in those eyes. "For so long, Affinites have lived under the thumb of non-Affinites. We are graced with these abilities, yet we are reviled, controlled by weak humans who use blackstone and Deys'voshk against us. Why should we not have our revenge? Why should we not exploit them?"

We. She stared at Sadov in disbelief, the realization hitting her. "You're an Affinite."

Sadov's thin lips peeled back in a grotesque grin. "Oh, yes."

Ana was shaking, memories of his long white fingers reaching from the darkness of the dungeons, fear twisting her stomach until she could barely breathe. "You control the mind, just like Morganya."

Sadov tilted his head, looking like a teacher fishing for an answer from a pupil. "Almost correct, Kolst Pryntsessa. My Affinity resonates with emotions. Specifically, with fear."

Fear. He was a fear Affinite. Ana thought back to the inexplicable terror that threatened to drown her each time she descended the steps of the dungeons. The way her palms grew clammy and her throat closed up and her legs turned to cotton no matter how much she steeled herself to face the horrors.

It had been Sadov all along, playing with her mind. "But you . . . you fed me Deys'voshk. You tortured me." Her voice trembled.

"I did it to make you stronger," Sadov crooned, his eyes bright. "Deys'voshk builds your resilience; it poisons your body, but it forces your Affinity to fight back. I liken it to an infection, and your Affinity must drive it from your body. That is how the Countess and I grew our powers over the years. We constantly suppressed our Affinities and forced them to grow stronger."

Ana felt sick. "Why?"

She already knew the answer. "So you can fight with us." Sadov reached out, tipping her chin. "Join us, and together, we will resurrect this world from the ashes. We will rule, as we deserve, and we will purge the world of the unworthy."

Ana stared into her torturer's eyes—wide and burning with fervor. This was not a game; it was not a lie. Sadov actually believed what he was telling her. "You're mad."

The fire in Sadov's eyes flickered and went out. He leaned back, smooth and cold again. "The Countess said you might resist. Too righteous, she said." He threaded his fingers together and narrowed his gaze. "It matters little. You will join us, whether of your own free will or by force."

"I will never join you." Her voice was a low snarl. "You speak of mass murder across my empire. And I would die before I let that happen."

"Pity," Sadov said softly. "My other victims spoke just as bravely before they gave in to my Affinity. You don't know yet, Pryntsessa, how it feels to experience true hopelessness. I will show you."

The carriage darkened. Sadov's eyes had become bottomless pits, and she was falling, falling endlessly, with no way out.

Around her, the shadows morphed, growing claws and swarming at the windows, reaching for her. Ana bit back a scream. Her pulse raced, her heart was going to burst from her chest, her arms and legs had frozen and there was nothing she could do against the terror that was going to engulf her—

Then, just like that, it vanished. The monsters outside became the silhouettes of leaves, and the fear drained like water from a tub, leaving her hollow and empty. Sweat coated her forehead and her limbs; her palms were slick as she pushed herself up. A single, strangled sob escaped her.

Sadov leaned forward like a fascinated child. "Ah, how does it feel?" he whispered.

Ana spat in his face. "I will never stop fighting," she said. The carriage shook as it rolled over a bump on the road. Several branches snapped over the roof. "You will never win if you think fear is the way."

Sadov wiped his face and looked at her with an ugly expression. "You've lost," he said. "You think you won over Pyetr Tetsyev? He was with us the entire time. We needed him on our side until the young Emperor Mikhailov was dead."

The knowledge that Tetsyev had betrayed her settled into

her chest with dead certainty. And Ana knew, inevitably, that the next time she came face-to-face with that alchemist, she would kill him.

"You think that pathetic con man is coming for you?" Sadov continued, growing more delighted. "He's dead. There is no one coming for you, Kolst Pryntsessa."

He's dead. Despite everything she'd learned about Ramson, the words twisted in her heart like a dagger. She thought of Fyrva'snezh, standing with him outside and watching snow swirl slowly, silently from the skies.

How much of it had been real?

It didn't matter. Sadov was right—nobody was coming for her. So she would have to fight her way out by herself. Like she always had.

"I don't need anyone else," she snarled.

The carriage jerked to a halt as a loud thump sounded on the roof. Both Ana and Sadov turned their heads to the small window above. A cobweb of cracks ran across it, fracturing the moonlight from outside.

A shadow flashed. The carriage swayed. A second thump sounded and the glass split into more fissures, the cracks reverberating through the carriage. Ana had the sense to duck as, with a final resounding smash, the window exploded into a thousand glittering pieces and fell upon them like rain.

As the glass settled, Ana lifted her head. Shards slid off her hair and shoulders and clinked onto the floor. Someone—or something—had stopped the carriage and smashed the window.

In the corner, she heard Sadov groan, the sound of glass crunching beneath him.

A shadow flitted above. Ana craned her neck. There was

nothing but the swaying of trees and the barest glimpse of the moon hanging overhead like a silver scythe.

She felt the intruder before she heard him: a brush of fabric against her wrist, a rustle at her ear. She turned, and stifled a gasp.

The intruder was a child—a scrawny, preadolescent boy—wearing formfitting clothes. He circled the walls of the carriage, melting in and out of the shadows, and at last came to a standstill beside her.

Before she could draw breath to speak, the boy's hands were at her wrists, and she heard the faint jangle of keys. They sounded like small, ringing chimes. His touch was featherlight, his fingers cool and soft as they deftly worked her shackles. Left hand. Right hand. Ankles.

Ana scrambled to her feet, pressing herself against the wall, hands curling into fists.

The boy took a step back and, with all the grace of a dancer, knelt before her. The pool of moonlight pouring in from the broken window above framed him like one of the performers in the Palace's Crystal Theater. Graceful. Poised. Controlled.

"Meya dama." A female voice, quiet, steady, and sweet as silver bells. The intruder looked up. It was a girl: a girl with a small, slender face and wide, dark eyes. Her black hair was cropped just beneath her chin, curling under with a hint of waves. She could not have been much older than Ana.

Kemeiran, Ana realized with surprise. A second realization hit her, harder than the first. She'd seen this girl, many nights ago, beneath the sultry glow of torches and the low rumble of battle drums. "The Windwraith," she breathed.

The girl straightened. Before she could speak, a groan sounded from the other end of the carriage. Sadov stirred.

The barest movement, and blades glinted in the Windwraith's palms. Yet as Sadov's eyes focused on them, Ana knew with sickening premonition what would come.

The wall of fear that hit her was crippling: dark and utter terror that gripped her stomach and paralyzed her. She crumpled to the ground, images flickering through her mind. Ramson lying in a pool of blood in the banquet hall. Papa's body convulsing, blood spurting from his mouth. Eight bodies, strewn across the cobblestones, twitching as life faded from their eyes.

Dimly, she heard a *thump* as the Windwraith hit the floor. The barest whimper escaped the girl's throat, her face shadowed with whatever nightmares haunted her.

Sadov inched toward them, clutching his side from the blow the Windwraith had dealt him. He raised a hand, and moonlight lanced off the blade he held.

He was going to kill the girl.

Ana threw herself in front of the Windwraith. Sadov paused, hesitation flashing in his eyes. "Get out of the way," he snarled, "or I'll kill you both."

The slightest of movements behind her, and suddenly, wind blasted across the carriage, throwing Sadov to the floor. Ana reached out for something to hold on to, but the Windwraith's arms were already wrapped tightly around her center.

They held each other as the squall around them rose to a scream, slamming Sadov against the carriage door. Another blast and the door flew open, and Sadov tumbled out of sight.

The wind died; the world quieted.

Ana untangled herself from the Windwraith, her heart still racing. She looked to the other girl, who had picked herself up without a sound. Tears streaked her face, and she clutched the wall with one hand, a dagger in the other as her chest hitched with small, shallow breaths.

"Are you all right?" Ana asked, her gaze fixing back on the open door. Beyond, the forest stretched out in alternating patterns of shadow and moonlight.

"Yes." Her voice was as faint as a breath of air. "Who is he?"

"It's a long story." Ana bent to pick up a shard of glass, holding it like a weapon. "We need to go after him. Can you move?"

The girl gave a swift nod. Her steps were light, like the rustle of a small bird's wings, as she darted past Ana and hopped out the carriage door. Ana followed.

Her feet landed in soft, freshly fallen snow. Outside, the six guards that had ridden with the carriage lay dead, glassy-eyed beneath the shifting treetops. Dull metal blades protruded from their necks and chests. The snowfall had stopped and the skies had cleared, showing a bright moon and a blur of stars dotting the midnight sky. Sadov was nowhere to be seen.

The Windwraith pointed. A trail of footsteps led away from the carriage, into the darkness of the trees beyond. "I can go after him. He can't be far."

Ana closed her eyes. If she could just use her Affinity to sense where Sadov was right now . . .

But the Deys'voshk had already fully worked its way through her system, and the dosage that Sadov had given her could take as long as a day to wear off.

Ana shook her head. "He has an Affinity for fear. It would be dangerous for you to go by yourself."

The Windwraith nodded. She flitted among the guards' bodies, plucking knives and rations from them. For the first time, Ana realized that she was still in her ball gown, her beaded purse hanging from her wrist. The cold stung her skin and she wrapped her arms around herself.

"Here." The Windwraith held out a bundle of clothes.

Ana hesitated. She'd heard so many stories of the Kemeiran Empire growing up—of how the far-eastern kingdom raised deadly assassins and deployed them as spies to serve its brutal regime. Distrust toward the nation was rooted deep in the bones of every Cyrilian. Papa had warned her of them, her tutors had taught her to be wary of them, and Luka had told her of the long war between the two empires.

Yet . . . this girl's countenance, her quiet uncertainty, the naked fear that had seized her, all indicated otherwise. She had saved Ana's life.

The enemy of my enemy is my friend.

Ana reached out and accepted the clothes. "Thank you," she said. There were a million questions she needed to ask this girl. "How did you find me?"

The girl looked startled; she fixed her gaze on Ana. "It was part of the deal."

The sentence sounded all too familiar. "Deal?" The word rushed from her in a breath.

"Yes." Another sharp nod, and then a slight crease of confusion in the girl's brows. "My contract was purchased after my battle with the Steelshooter at the Playpen. He came and collected me that night." Her eyes turned soft. "He wouldn't tell me his name. He said I had a choice: I could make a Trade with him and gain my freedom right there."

Ana could barely breathe.

"He asked me to protect you when the time came. Then he freed me, and told me to wait for him in Novo Mynsk until he sent word with a snowhawk." The Windwraith's hand darted to her hair. "He called on me this evening, so I came."

Despite what Tetsyev had told her—despite all the evidence to the contrary and all the facts that screamed against her greater instincts, Ana knew instantly that it was Ramson. Ramson had sent this girl.

The air was suddenly too cold, each breath piercing Ana's lungs like broken glass.

Kerlan only kept him alive long enough for me to get there.

Ramson hadn't been good—and perhaps some part of him had wanted to change that. In a world of grays, he had made a choice. And that choice had saved her life tonight.

She blinked back tears. She couldn't afford to think of Ramson, or to try to piece together the full story of why he'd done the things he'd done, made the choices he'd made . . . not now, not when Luka would be forced to abdicate in five days leaving Morganya to begin her reign of bloodshed and terror.

Five days was barely enough time to make the journey but she had to get to Salskoff. She would return to the Palace, even without Tetsyev, and she would accuse Morganya of treason against the Empire.

She had proof already. The antidote was in the apothecary's wing, along with the poison. And Luka—Luka would listen to her. He would believe her.

Suddenly, the night seemed a little less dark.

The girl was untying the horses from the carriage when Ana made her way over. "What's your name?"

"Linnet," the girl whispered, as though tasting a strange word on her tongue. "My name is Linnet."

Ana drew a deep breath. Her next words were a gamble,

but it was a gamble she had to take. She had nothing left to lose. "My name is Anastacya Kateryanna Mikhailov," she said. "Crown Princess of Cyrilia. And . . . I need your help. Please."

Linnet listed her face to the sky, closing her eyes briefly in the silver fluorescence of the moon. "My people believe in fate. That man freed me from my indenturement so that I could protect you; and you saved my life from that Affinite. The gods have joined our fates, and now I must complete the circle. I will be the blade in your hands and the wind at your back." She paused, and resolve shaped her expression. "Call me Linn."

31

There was a pale-eyed ghost in the darkness with him.

Ramson moaned. It was the only sound he could make.

The ghost peered at him, candlelight shifting on its face. Ramson had seen the face somewhere, but he could not remember where.

"Stop. I'll tell you anything," he slurred. And then a new thought occurred to him. "Am I dead?"

Slowly, feeling was coming back to his body. His limbs were on fire. His head felt as though it had been used as a battering ram. And his chest—*Deities,* his chest . . .

"Not yet, Ramson Quicktongue," the ghost said. He was hooded, and he was prodding at Ramson in the most painful, irksome way.

"I suppose not," Ramson mused. "Death would feel better, and I'd be in the company of some honey-eyed girl instead of an ugly old hagbag."

The ghost gave him what resembled a sullen expression. He was starting to look extremely familiar, but Ramson could not think beyond the aching of his head as to who this was.

"Where am I?" he asked instead. It was too dim to see.

"The Kerlan Estate. In the dungeons."

The Kerlan Estate. Ramson pushed at his muggy consciousness, wincing at the effort. The memories came back to him in a slow, painful trickle. He looked at the man-ghost, suddenly wary. "Who are you?"

The man looked up at him from beneath the hood. Bulbous eyes, thin nose, bald head.

And then the name clicked.

"Tetsyev," Ramson croaked. "What do you want? What are you doing to me?"

"I am healing you," Tetsyev said calmly. "Though if you insult me again, I might change my mind."

Ramson then noticed the strange smell of herbs and chemicals, and the feeling of cold gel all over his body. He looked down at his chest and winced.

His skin resembled a bloody slab of meat, sliced in a dozen different directions. And on his chest, almost where his heart would be, was a shiny patch of flesh, seared over his old brand. The insignia of the Order of the Lily.

He remembered the iron, white-hot before his eyes. The insurmountable fear as it was pressed to his chest. The unspeakable pain, and the welcomed darkness that followed.

His resolve wavered, and the feeling of helplessness that washed over him was nearly enough to drown him. "Why are you healing me?" he asked, and despite all of his efforts, his voice trembled. "Preparing me for another torture session?"

Tetsyev stepped back and squinted at Ramson's chest. A bowl of translucent salve glistened in his hand. "No," was all he said.

Ramson was shivering, and he struggled to keep his voice

steady. Memories of cold black water poured down his throat and filling his lungs were enough to break his resolve. He could still taste bile on his tongue, feel the searing pain of iron burning his flesh. "Please," he said hoarsely. "Just kill me."

Tetsyev raised an eyebrow. "No," he repeated, and shuffled away to the nearest shelf. When he returned, he was holding a roll of bandages. Slowly, the bald man began to wrap the gauze around Ramson, pausing only to tuck corners or adjust a strip slightly. He remained silent.

At last, Tetsyev leaned away, casting another critical eye upon Ramson. He nodded, and began fishing around in his robes. Ramson caught a flash of metal.

No, he wanted to beg. *Please.*

But Tetsyev reached toward his shackles. There were a few clicks, and then Ramson fell forward, no longer held up by the chains on the wall. His limbs flailed behind him uselessly. When he hit the ground, it felt as though his bones would shatter. He gave a choked sob.

"Get up," Tetsyev said. "The Kolst Pryntsessa is waiting."

His brain felt like mush, and it was difficult to grasp what the alchemist was saying. Ramson waited for the involuntary tremors in his muscles to stop, for the blood to recirculate, for the feeling of cold to drain away. Slowly, in fits and starts, he pushed himself into a sitting position. The wounds on his chest protested with a dull, throbbing pain. He had an inkling that he was meant to feel much weaker than he actually did.

"The salve facilitates the healing of the flesh," Tetsyev said, as though he had heard Ramson's thoughts. "I injected another serum in you that speeds recovery of the muscles."

Ramson leaned against the wall, drawing deep, shaky

breaths. He flexed his hands, turned over his arms. Before—minutes, hours, or days ago, he'd lost count—he had felt as though every inch of his flesh were on fire and peeling from his bones. The pain was still there, but dull and fading. "Why are you doing this?"

"I'm repenting. Perhaps it is too late to save my soul, but I must try. I must make my choice."

"Wonderful," Ramson wheezed. "The Deities will reward you handsomely for saving my life."

"It isn't *your* life I'm saving. It's the Princess's."

"Even better," Ramson wheezed. "A noble life bears more weight in the eyes of the Deities, I'm sure."

Tetsyev sighed. "I lived an entire life of regrets," he whispered, and his words struck an odd chord of resonance in Ramson. "And I am making the choice to amend my mistakes." He cast a sorrowful eye upon Ramson. "Kolst Pryntsessa Anastacya needs us. She needs *you.* So, what choice will you make, Ramson Farrald?"

Choice. Ramson's mind was still foggy with pain, but the word brought back memories of a girl. *Our choices define us.* "The Princess," he repeated slowly, and just like that, his muggy world clicked into sharp focus.

Ana. Princess Anastacya.

Memories ignited like sparks before his eyes. The sense of familiarity he'd felt looking into her face back at the abandoned dacha near Ghost Falls. That same face had been painted in dozens of his childhood textbooks, by the side of the Emperor and Empress and Crown Prince of Cyrilia. And it had vanished from the public eye when she'd allegedly fallen sick and slowly faded from everyone's memories over the years. He recalled the sweet noble's lilt in her Cyrilian. The tilt of her chin, the command in her tone, the gravitas of her presence.

Ana was the Crown Princess of Cyrilia, the younger sister of Emperor Lukas Aleksander Mikhailov, and the heiress to the Cyrilian Empire and its sick, dying Emperor.

"I see you've finally pieced it all together." Tetsyev looked amused.

Ramson's head spun. But . . . no. "That's impossible," he said faintly. "She died a year ago. Executed for treason."

"No. One year ago, I murdered the late Emperor Aleksander Mikhailov." Tetsyev's voice shook. "Princess Anastacya . . . was framed for it that night. She was accused of murder, but she tried to run and drowned before the trial. Or so the story goes."

Ramson clutched his chest, his breaths coming short as he stared at Tetsyev. *The alchemist.* He heard Ana's voice in his head, the urgency to her tone when she spoke of him. And when he'd asked—many times throughout their journey—she hadn't relented a word as to *why* she was after him.

"You murdered her father and then framed her for it?" With sickening realization, he thought back to the number of times he had threatened her with her alchemist, dangling her quarry before her and forcing her to comply to his terms. And all along, *this* was the reason she sought him.

Tetsyev's voice was raw with regret. "It is more complicated than that."

Ramson thought of his own choices. The story was always more complicated. But that didn't justify anything. Neither did it change anything.

"Please, listen to me. We haven't much time." Tetsyev's tone was pleading. "Countess Morganya has been plotting to overthrow the Mikhailov line for years. The Princess is on her way to Salskoff now, to stop her." Tetsyev knelt before Ramson. "I begged Kerlan to let me heal you. I convinced him to drag it out, to make you live longer and suffer more.

"I saved you for a reason. The Princess needs help. This *empire* needs help. And she cannot do it alone." Tetsyev's face had settled as he watched Ramson, and resolve flickered in his eyes. "Even if you won't go, I will. For so many years, I have been robbed of the power to make a choice. I am making that choice now." He stood, straightening his reedy frame and adjusting his white alchemist's cloak. A silver Deys'krug circlet hung over his neck, half-hidden beneath his worship robes. "I'm going after the Princess. And I'm going to help her."

Your choices, whispered a small voice. Jonah's voice. *Your heart is your compass.*

He'd known for some time now, felt the irrepressible tug on his chest toward her. With each smile, each frown, each word, she'd drawn him in, slowly, irrevocably. And that slow, smoldering flame had roared to life beneath a winter sky of snow, glowing brighter than anything else in his life. She was the bearing to his compass, the dawn that his ship had been chasing for so long over an empty horizon.

My heart is my compass.

Ramson's mind cleared. In the darkness of the dungeons, he could barely make out the retreating outline of the alchemist, the white flashes of his cloak as he hurried in the direction where the escape tunnel lay.

"Wait," Ramson said.

32

Ana awoke to silence, snow, and stars. A cold draft stirred through the broken windowpanes of the dacha she and Linn had found. The fire in the hearth had gone out. From the soft, silver-blue glow of light beyond the tattered curtains, she could tell that it was still night. Dawn lingered, just out of reach.

Yet something had shifted in her senses. It took her a moment to realize that her Affinity was back.

Relief flooded her, and she sat up in the rugs and furs she and Linn had piled together for a makeshift bed. The girl was nowhere to be seen, but the soft whickering of their horses near the door told Ana that her companion would not be gone for long.

Ana clutched her head in her hands. She always felt off balance when her Affinity returned; it was like being able to see again, darkness slowly giving way to patches of light and blurred movement.

It had been a day since they'd ridden from the Kerlan Estate and escaped Sadov in the Syvern Taiga. In the semidarkness, she could still taste the nauseating fear that had coated her tongue, the hiss of Sadov's voice from the shadows.

In five days' time, your brother will announce his abdication due to ill health and appoint the Kolst Contessya Morganya as Empress Regent of Cyrilia.

The world drew into sharp focus. She had four more days to get to the capital of her empire.

She reached under the pile of blankets until her fingers grasped the beaded purse that had been tied to her wrist when Sadov had abducted her. Now ragged with dust and blood, it still held the last of her belongings.

Ana dug out a globefire and shook it. The chemical powders inside the orb rattled, and eventually, a spark caught on the oil coating the inside of the glass. Light lanced across the small cabin, and she held it close as she rummaged through her purse.

Her map was still in there, tattered and stained. Holding the globefire over it, she found the name of the village they'd passed last evening before settling into this empty dacha: Beroshk.

With her thumb, she traced the distance to Salskoff, and calculated.

Exactly four days of travel by horse. Her stomach tightened. They would just make it; they needed to be on their way soon.

She shifted her position, and the remaining contents of her purse spilled out. A copperstone and a silver pocket watch glinted in the light of the globefire. The sight of these objects brought back memories that ached like fresh wounds.

She held a purse full of things that belonged to people who, no matter how hard she tried, she would never be able to bring back.

Ana hurled the purse across the room.

The door opened behind her, bringing a breath of cold wind. Ana turned to see Linn clutching a satchel to her chest. Her knives were strapped to her waist, her movements sharp and lithe.

Ana looked away, ashamed to be seen crying.

Without a word, Linn crossed the room and plucked the scattered belongings up and carefully tucked them back into Ana's purse. She hesitated, her eyes searching Ana's face. "These seem precious to you," she said.

Ana wiped her tears, reeling back the dark well of her grief. "What's the use of holding on to these things if the people who owned them are gone?"

Linn laid the purse by Ana's mess of blankets. "Do you know what I have learned?"

"What?"

"Only loss can teach us the true worth of things." Linn's clothes rustled as she knelt before Ana and grasped her hands. "There is nothing we can do but go on, one day at a time. We live in their memory, taking the breaths they cannot draw again, catching the warmth of the sunlight that they were meant to feel."

The knot in Ana's chest loosened a little; she brushed the back of her hand against her cheek, wiping away her tears.

Linn held out her hands. "Come. There is something I want to show you."

Linn opened the cabin door and disappeared. Ana followed, and when she reached the open doorway, the cold and the sight before her stole her breath.

Outside, the sky was aglow with currents of hazy blue lights that shifted and ebbed like gentle waves, their soft glow reflected on the dark tree lines of the Syvern Taiga. A smattering of stars glittered like silver dust caught in between. And, from time to time, a wave would break away and dip down, down, down, until it disappeared beyond the trees of the Syvern Taiga.

"The Deities' Lights," Ana whispered. She had read of these

in her studies, had craned her neck at her bedroom window for a glimpse, but the walls of the Salskoff Palace had always stood too tall. "They're . . . beautiful."

Linn grasped her hand and pointed. "Look."

A cold wind brushed past them, and the entire forest seemed to whisper in response. At the edge of the trees, snow swirled from the ground as though stirred by phantom fingers. Ana watched as one of the drifts of snow swept into the air, twirling faster and faster until it took the shape of a deer. Beneath the blue glow of the Deities' Lights, the silver conjuration looked ghostly as it took a graceful step forward.

"Ice spirits," Linn whispered, hushed excitement in her tone.

Another gust of wind scattered snow that took the shape of a running fox, and then there was a bounding rabbit, and a soaring eagle plunged into a weaving sky that looked alive.

Half-fascinated, half-afraid, Ana took a step back. "Linn, these spirits can be dangerous."

Linn shook her head. "Only some. When I was with the brokers, they often made us sleep outside as punishment. The ice spirits kept me company." She turned to Ana, and the lights and snow reflected silver in her dark eyes. "I wanted to show you because I think there is good and bad in everything, Ana. And it is the good of this world that makes it worth saving."

Ana closed her eyes. The silence, the lights, and the snow made everything seem dreamlike, and she wanted for this night to never end. "When Ramson freed you, you could have taken your freedom without choosing the Trade. Why didn't you?"

Linn placed her hands together and clasped her fingers to form an oval. "Action, and counteraction," she said patiently. "My people believe that every action has a counteraction. Yin and yang; moon and sun; night and day. Ramson saved me, therefore I saved you." She said this simply, confidently, as though it were as easy as differentiating between black and white.

Ana wrapped her arms around herself. In the absolute quiet, it felt like they were the only two beings alive, and the confession unfurled with a plume of her breath in the frosty air. "I'm afraid, Linn."

"That's good." Linn gazed into the distance, where the ice spirits frolicked in their ever-shifting forms beneath the blue light of the Deities. "My mother told me that is when we can choose to be brave."

"It doesn't make it any easier."

Linn cast her eyes down and smiled. "Want to know a secret?"

Ana found herself smiling back. "Sure."

"I am afraid, too." The words were a whisper in the wind. "But . . . there is something I want, a feeling stronger than my fear."

"What is it?"

"Freedom." Overhead, the shadow of a hawk soared beneath the shifting blue lights in the sky. Its screech pierced the night. "My traffickers stole my freedom and my voice. They led me to believe that there was nothing I could do. That there was no hope." Linn's eyes were closed. She drew a breath and turned her face to the shimmering lights outside. "I have waited so long to make a choice of my own. For every Affinite freed, like me, there are thousands of others still trapped in this system, invisible in the shadows. I choose to fight for them, for *me*. Which do you choose?"

Ana's voice was hoarse when she said, "I choose to fight."

Linn's eyes flew open, and Ana could swear someone had cast in them all the stars in the night sky. "Good. Now, I have something to show you."

Back in the dacha, Linn handed Ana a rolled-up piece of parchment. "I found this at the marketplace."

Ana unfurled the poster, and the world around her seemed to crumble to ashes.

It was a portrait of Luka. He looked older than she had last seen him a year ago—or perhaps it was the way the artist depicted him. His jaw had strengthened and his shoulders had broadened, yet one thing that hadn't changed was the radiant smile that lit his face. The artist had painted him with a fur-rimmed silver cloak, a tiger's clasp at his throat, and the white-gold Crown of Cyrilia sitting perfectly on his head.

Gently, she ran a hand over his face, tracing the bump of his chin and the spot where his dimple should be. The artist hadn't captured that. She let her gaze linger on him a few moments more before dropping to the line of gold text emblazoned beneath.

Kolst Imperator
Lukas Aleksander Mikhailov
to announce the abdication of his throne
and the crowning of
Kolst Contessya Morganya Mikhailov
on the fifth day of the first moon
of Winter.

Ceremony to take place at the
Salskoff Palace Grand Throneroom.

Ana's teeth clenched. At least Tetsyev hadn't been lying to her about that part. Four days—they would arrive on the cusp of Coronation evening.

She would get there, or she would die trying.

Hold on, Luka, she thought. *I'm coming.*

"He's beautiful," Linn breathed, her gaze on the snow-dampened portrait of Luka. "I had always pictured Emperor Mikhailov to be . . . well . . . monstrous."

The words stirred a spark of anger within Ana. "Why?"

"Growing up in Kemeira, we were taught of the cruelty of the Cyrilian Empire, of the way Affinites are treated here." There was no hostility on the girl's face. She peered down at the portrait, brows creased, as though she were genuinely reflecting. "And after I came here, I learned how your people view us: as ruthless, cold-blooded warriors. I suppose we are all heroes in our own eyes, and monsters in the eyes of those who are different."

Ana thought of the Vyntr'makt in Kyrov, of how the yaeger had looked at her, like she was the monster. "It is not often brought up in Cyrilian textbooks or classes, but I know the other nations view Affinites differently," she said instead.

"Yes," Linn said. "In Kemeira, we are the Temple Masters. We serve with whatever Affinity the gods granted us. I trained with the Wind Masters to hone my Affinity, to protect my kingdom."

A chill crept through Ana. "You were trained by the Wind Masters?" The Kemeiran Wind Masters were only spoken of in hushed whispers throughout the Empire. They were the deadliest assassins in the lands, rumored to have mastered the secrets to flight. They were men and women of wind and shadows, unseen and unheard. It was said that the only time one saw a Wind Master was before he or she slit one's throat.

"I was trained to serve Kemeira; I was trained for a grander destiny. I thought I would find that." Anguish flitted across her face. "I boarded a Cyrilian ship in hopes that I would find my brother and return home. But when I landed, they took my belongings and my identification papers. They told me I would be arrested unless I signed an employment contract. I didn't know that I would lose my freedom that day." Linn hung her head. "The Wind Masters trained me for a grand fate, a great destiny. I do not know what that is yet, but I think . . . I think you might be a part of it." Linn drew a breath and lifted her eyes, courage seeming to settle on her shoulders. "My people believe in fate. So I will follow your path, Ana . . . in search of my destiny."

Ana reached out and squeezed Linn's hands. "You will carve your own path," she said. "And you will build your own destiny."

Linn's lips curled; a smile broke across her face, lovely and full of hope.

For the next three days, they traveled from dawn to dusk, bundled in furs and cloaks, their thick-hoofed horses keeping up a steady pace. Snow continued to fall from gray skies, and the world was a whirl of white. They made sure to arrive at villages or towns prior to nightfall, and crept out of snowed-up inns when the last of the Deities' Lights were still fading from the sky, and the ghostly glimmers of ice spirits disappeared with the first cracks of the day.

At night, they ran through their plans. They would arrive

just in time for the Coronation—so they would need to unveil Morganya's conspiracy before Luka abdicated.

The Coronation would be the only time the Palace had a large enough number of people going in and out that they could enter without detection. Ana knew how these events worked; there would be a line of guest carriages for miles out. Guards would be posted at the Kateryanna Bridge, checking guests and tickets.

Their only chance was to intercept a carriage and swap places with the guests inside.

Ana would reveal herself once she was inside the palace and reunited with Luka. She would tell her brother and the Court everything, while Linn went to the apothecary's wing to find the poison and the antidote, which would be evidence of her claims.

On the fourth and final day of their travels, there was a stillness in the air. The snow had stopped. The sun dusted the world in gold, and their horses' steps were quiet in the soft layers of snow.

When Ana steered her horse between two tall pines, she found herself at a cliff's edge. She gave a sharp tug on the reins, and when she looked up, a hundred emotions filled her.

The sun was rising over white-tipped mountains, transforming the snow-covered earth into a glittering canvas of corals and reds and pinks. Wisps of clouds streaked the waking sky, stained with the fiery orange rays of the sun. Tundra rolled out in every direction as far as the eye could see, interspersed with white pines and jagged mountains. And so far in the distance that it almost—almost—blended into the landscape were the shimmering white steeples and red-tiled roofs of Salskoff.

Home.

Winds—fresh and cold and scented like winter—caressed her cheeks, stroking her shoulders and the nape of her neck. Her hood tumbled from her head and her hair danced in the breeze.

Home. As she stared at the Palace in the distance—*her* Palace—a sense of doubt shadowed the longing that grasped her heart. There had been simpler times, when the halls rang with her and Luka's laughter, when she would huddle by the door of her chambers at night and whisper to Yuri over a mug of hot chokolad. When Mama and mamika Morganya had sat together by her bed, stroking her hair until their murmurs faded into dreams.

But it was impossible to think of the Palace without thinking of the cracks that had spread over the years. Papa, turning away from her. Sadov, smiling at her pain. All this, built on the fabric of corruption that had allowed for the nobility to profit from the pain of Affinites.

Home would never again carry the same meaning for her, Ana realized. And as she straightened in her saddle, Shamaïra's words whispered to her in the winter wind. *No, Little Tigress—we take what we are given and we fight like hell to make it better.*

Ana opened her eyes. She was the heiress of the Mikhailov line, the Little Tigress of Salskoff, and she was coming home.

33

In ten years, nothing and everything about her city had changed.

Walking through the moonlit and snow-dusted streets, hidden under her thick hood, Ana almost felt as though she were in a strange dream. The memories she had of Salskoff were all from her childhood, before she had been confined to the Palace. The dachas that she'd so fondly nicknamed "gingerbread houses" as a child were still there, smoke piping cheerfully from chimneys; the marketplaces that she and Luka had frequented (under Kapitan Markov's sharp-eyed stare) sat festooned in decorative silver sashes; tall arches with marble statues of the Deities and the Cyrilian white tiger stood proud and regal over town squares and main streets.

At this time of year, the town was alight with festivities. Silver banners of the Cyrilian white tiger hung from every door, paper snowflakes fluttered between lampposts, and candles flickered softly on each doorstep as Salskoff welcomed their patron Deity of Winter. Most of the town had likely congregated at local pubs by the Tiger's Tail river where they could see the Palace, awaiting news of the abdication and Coronation.

Ana and Linn had changed into modest, fur-lined woolen gowns to blend in at the Coronation, Ana's a dark shade of green and Linn's navy blue. Under the moonlight, the Kemeiran carved a slender figure, but Ana knew beneath the furs and layers of her skirts were daggers, strapped to her ankles, arms, and waist.

They selected an empty side street that led straight to the main riverside promenade. Even from afar, Ana could tell the promenade was clogged with traffic. The lights of lampposts lanced off gilded carriages and caught on the snow-white coats of valkryfs every so often.

Ana and Linn needed somewhere quiet and dark, away from prying eyes.

Ana was glad for the cloak of night as she and Linn huddled against a corner, beneath the awning of a closed store. With a flick of her wrists, Linn summoned winds that extinguished the nearby lamps, plunging the area into darkness.

They waited. Minutes passed. And then, from far off, drawing closer, was the unmistakable sound of hoofbeats and carriage wheels.

Before Ana could even blink, Linn was gone, stealing toward the carriage like a shadow. She flitted to the back and, with acrobatic precision, slipped through the door.

Silence. Ana's heart pounded out the moments. Her palms sweated. The carriage trundled on, the driver oblivious to what was happening inside.

And then the door swung open soundlessly. Linn's head

popped out. She held up a hand and cut a sharp signal through the night with a finger. *One.*

There was only one passenger inside the carriage. They needed a second invitation.

Ana motioned at Linn. *You go. I'll find another.*

She could make out, in the near-total darkness, the way Linn's silhouette tensed with consternation. Ana shook her head again and waved her hand. *Go.*

A slight pause, and then Linn vanished inside. The door shut without so much as a tap.

The whole affair had taken less than a minute.

Ana melted back into the shadows, watching the carriage bearing Linn roll toward the riverside promenade that led to the Palace.

It wasn't long before another carriage appeared.

Following Linn's strategy, she ducked behind the carriage as it rolled past and hopped onto the back. Linn had made it look effortless, but a jolt of the carriage nearly sent Ana flying, and her hands scrabbled for purchase.

Holding steady, Ana caught a breath and stretched her Affinity, scarching the inside of the carriage. One body, blood warm and pulsing.

Ana opened the carriage door and swung herself inside. She had wrapped her Affinity around the woman's neck even before she closed the door behind her. The unfortunate noblewoman twisted in her seat, choking, her face rapidly turning red.

Ana covered the woman's mouth with her hand to stop her from making noise. She pulled at the woman's blood until her eyes rolled back into her head and she slumped against her seat.

The carriage continued forward; from the outside, it would look as though nothing were amiss.

Laying the noblewoman on the carriage floor, Ana searched through the silky folds of her gown until she found what she was looking for: the invitation letter, folded in a gold-foiled envelope and scented like roses.

Though she knew the woman wasn't dead, Ana still felt a bit guilty, looking at the unconscious figure at her feet. She parted the velvet drapes and gazed out the window.

Her heart flipped. They had turned onto the riverside promenade, and across the river, the Salskoff Palace drew into sight.

Her home was still the most beautiful thing she had ever laid eyes on. The Palace walls rose impossibly high before them, the cream-white color of bricks glittering with snow and ice. Beyond the crenellated walls, the cupolas and spires of the Salskoff Palace punctured the sky, the moonlight rendering them ghostly. Specks of light flickered among the haze of gray and white, breathing life into the palace of snow and stone.

She was home.

The Kateryanna Bridge was decked with banners and silver decoration. Torches blazed on either side as statues of the Deities looked down upon them, faces aglow. Ana sent a silent vow to her parents, tracing a Deys'krug on her chest. Tonight her mother gave her courage; her father gave her the strength to correct the wrongs he hadn't.

At the end of the bridge, just outside the great gilded gates to the Palace grounds, stood a line of blue-cloaked Palace guards. Ana's stomach twisted and she shrank back slightly. But as her eyes roamed farther down the line of carriages, she saw something that nearly made her heart stop.

To the side of the bridge barely a dozen paces away, watching the procession of carriages like hawks, were Sadov and the yaeger from the Kyrov Vyntr'makt.

As though sensing her gaze on him, the yaeger's head snapped to her. He'd found her.

The yaeger murmured something to Sadov and began to make his way to her carriage. As the familiar pressure descended on her mind and her awareness of blood winked out like a candle, Ana knew it was too late.

She flung open the door and stumbled onto the cobblestones. Shouts filled the air all around her; boots clacked over the bridge, and she heard swords being drawn. And then hands seized her roughly from behind, hauling her back and slamming her against the bridge's railing.

Instinctively, she grasped for her Affinity to fling off the guards holding her—and hit the yaeger's impenetrable wall.

Ana lifted her head. And met Sadov's eyes.

"Ah," he said softly. "I've been expecting you."

Ana tugged on her Affinity again, but the wall remained. Next to Sadov, the yaeger's eyes narrowed.

She had walked right into their trap.

Linn. Ana darted a glance at the line of carriages proceeding steadily down the bridge, disappearing into the gates of the Palace. Either Linn's carriage had gotten through, or it still stood waiting to reach the bridge—buying her plenty of time to run.

At least Linn would be safe.

"Let me go," Ana snarled at the guards, twisting against their hold. "I am the *Crown Princess.* I demand to see my brother."

Around her, several guards' eyes widened, but Sadov stepped in front of her. "I knew you'd be back," he gasped, loud enough for everyone to hear. "You've returned to finish what you'd intended from the start: to murder your brother just as you murdered your father."

"No!" Ana yelled, lunging at him. The pressure in her mind increased, and she sagged to the ground.

Sadov's eyes were cold. "My yaeger has identified you as a dangerous Affinite. You must be subdued."

From the folds of his cloak, he retrieved a familiar vial and raised it to her, like a toast. The Deys'voshk winked in the blazing torchlight.

The guards held Ana firm against the railing of the bridge. Beneath, the Tiger's Tail frothed and churned.

There was no way out—not unless she could get far enough from the yaeger to regain the use of her Affinity. Ana took in the guards surrounding them in all directions. She gave another useless tug at her captors. This time, though, Sadov closed the gap between them and took her chin in his hand. His nails dug into her cheeks, and Ana knew what was to come even before his black eyes latched on to hers.

The first wave of Sadov's fear manipulation hit her, scattering all logical thought. Ana's knees gave way. Her body was paralyzed; she slumped against her restraining guards, gasping for breath, the wet cobblestones of the bridge spinning before her.

"Let her be," she dimly heard Sadov say to the guards, who released her and took a step back. Ana slumped on the ground, shaking so hard that tears dripped from her eyes. "I can control her."

Between the ebb and flow of fear, she clung tightly to one thought; a feeling, an instinctive calling from a memory ten years past.

There was only one way out.

As another spasm of fear shot through her, Ana doubled over and gagged.

"Come here, my little monster," Sadov crooned. "Be good, and obey me. Take the Deys'voshk, and we shall bring you to the future Empress. She wants to be your ally, not your enemy."

Despite the trembling in her muscles, Ana grasped the railing of the bridge and heaved herself to her feet. The railing dug into her lower back as she leaned against it, her hair clinging to her sweat-slicked face. Sadov's Affinity pressed into her, and she remembered her nightmares of tumbling over the bridge and into the Tiger's Tail. Images of the vicious white whorls flooded her mind, and she closed her eyes against the feeling of being tossed around in that violent storm.

I am afraid.

And it was Linn's voice that came to her then, like a blade cutting through the mist of her fear. *That is when we can choose to be brave.*

Ana was sobbing so hard that she thought she would break. Her hands tightened around the railing.

With the lightest tip of her weight backward, she flipped herself over the Kateryanna Bridge and plunged into the yawning depths of the icy Tiger's Tail.

34

When Ramson saw her fall, he was standing beneath a lamppost on the riverside promenade by the Kateryanna Bridge, waiting for Tetsyev's signal that he had been cleared to enter the Palace.

Princess Anastacya is going to stop Morganya, the alchemist had said. *And we must get to her before Morganya's forces do.*

Only the Countess and her forces had found Ana first.

He hadn't believed his eyes when he'd seen her on the bridge—but, he'd realized, it was utterly Ana to attempt something so brazen and ridiculously foolish with stubborn pride. He'd watched the altercation unfold on the bridge with a growing sense of dread, his mind already racing five, ten steps forward and mapping out all the different scenarios in which this could play out.

He'd just never expected for her to jump.

And Ramson did the only thing he could think of. He dove after her.

He had the sense to take a deep breath before he hit the river like a bag of rocks. The water dragged him under, buffeting him this way and that and pulling him down to its depths.

He couldn't see, couldn't hear, couldn't breathe, his world tossing in every direction possible. And, inevitably, the river's wrath pulled him back to the stormy night that had changed the course of his life forever.

He was eight years old again, and he was drowning in the black waters of that storm that had almost claimed his and Jonah's lives. But the real nightmare was that image of Jonah's crow-black eyes, gaping and unseeing, seared into Ramson's memories.

Terror choked Ramson. The darkness was absolute. He had no direction.

No, he thought, and the phantoms of his mind dispersed. By whatever means he'd met Jonah—coincidence, fate, or the Deities—it wasn't Jonah's death that his friend would have wanted him to remember.

It was what Jonah had taught him when he was alive.

Swim. The voice came to him, so real that Ramson opened his eyes. But instead of a pale-faced, dark-haired boy, there was a girl in front of him: a brave, selfless, and stubborn girl who had worked her way into his heart, by Jonah's side.

He would not lose her.

Not again.

Swim, came the voice, but this time, it was his own.

Ramson kicked out. The currents were dragging her away, down to where it grew darker. She thrashed, her gown puffing out around her, pulling her down.

A sharp pain cut across his forearm and he flinched, lashing out to grab whatever it was that had bit him.

An arrow.

Another whizzed past him, and another. Archers. Those bastards were *really* intent on killing them.

The best way, Ramson knew, to escape archers was to swim deeper. The arrows decelerated within a yard of hitting the surface of water; he and Ana stood a better chance of surviving if they remained underwater and let the river carry them far enough.

He swam toward Ana. Her arms flailed erratically, but her movements grew weaker. One more kick, and he wrapped his arms around her and pulled her deeper.

They needed to stay submerged until the archers thought them dead—but there was another problem: they needed to breathe.

Ana opened her mouth. Bubbles drifted up; he felt her spasms against his chest. The lessons drilled into him from Bregon's Blue Fort ran through his mind. Her lungs were expanding, drawn by the irresistible desire for oxygen. Water was rushing in. Soon she would lose consciousness. And after that, her heart would stop.

His own lungs burned with the need for air, and his legs grew weaker with every kick. As a recruit for the Navy, he was trained to handle water and resist the yearning to draw in breath. He'd trained in the iciest waters in the middle of winter, building up his tolerance.

But even a Navy recruit could not defy the odds of nature.

Arrows be damned—they would drown first if they stayed like this.

Ramson kicked out. *Up, up.* But which way was up? His head spun, and the currents slapped harder, grew frothier.

Was that light? He needed to breathe. He needed to find out which way was up. Bubbles—he needed bubbles. They would lead him up. But letting out even the tiniest breath might drown him faster.

Ramson struggled against the darkness clouding his vision and opened his mouth.

And burst through the surface. Cold air rushed into his lungs, and he sucked in deep, blissful mouthfuls. Then, panting, he turned to Ana.

Her head bobbed in the water. Her mouth was open, but her eyes were closed; he couldn't tell if she was breathing.

Crushing down his terror, Ramson tucked her chin over his shoulder and made for shore.

The swim to the bank was arduous in itself; the river stretched over a hundred yards wide, and the shore seemed to draw farther away with each kick. Ramson swam with the current, focusing on keeping his and Ana's head above the water.

At long last, he reached the frozen bank and hauled himself and Ana up through the mud and snow. Far off, no larger than the palm of his hand, the lights of the Kateryanna Bridge shimmered hazily. His muscles begged for rest; it would have been so easy to lie down for a few minutes.

But Ramson turned to Ana. His hands shook from more than just the cold as he touched a finger to her lips.

Not breathing. He'd expected it, but hope did foolish things to a man's head.

Ramson knelt by her side and placed his hands on her chest, one over the other. And then, counting the beats silently, he began to pump. *One, two, three, four . . .*

He wanted, more than anything, to beat the ground with his fists and scream, but Ramson forced himself to count a steady rhythm to his compressions.

Five, six, seven . . .

There was a painful lump twisting in his chest, hot and cold at the same time, threatening to crack him open. Ana was limp beneath his hands, her eyes closed and her lips sealed.

Eight, nine, ten.

Ramson lowered his face to hers, prying open her mouth. One, two breaths. Logic steeled him through the white fog of panic in his mind, and he watched her chest for movement.

Ten compressions. Two breaths. Ten compressions. Two breaths. It had become a prayer of sorts, a chant that numbed him to the core. He was doubled over on his knees, his hands clasped before him. And this time, Ramson begged. He begged his three gods, the ones he had fervently hated and refused to believe in for years. He begged the Cyrilian Deities, the ones he'd dishonored by desecrating their empire. He begged anything and anyone that would listen.

Ten compressions. Two breaths. *Please. I'll do anything.*

She coughed, then sputtered, and when she opened her eyes, the world itself seemed to move again. Even as she rolled over and threw up on the snow, he reached for her, and when her hacking coughs were reduced to gasps, he gathered her in his arms and pressed her tightly to him. As she clasped him in her embrace, Ramson realized that it was he who had needed saving all along.

His cheeks were warm with tears as he buried his face in the crook of her shoulder. Finally, Ramson thought as he let her hold him, he understood a bit of what his father had meant when he'd said that love was a weakness.

35

Ana was dreaming. Ramson held her, his outline silvered by the moon against the darkness, his arms twined around her as though he never wanted to let go. Pressed against him, through the fabric of their clothes, her heart beat in time with his.

Yet . . . she could sense the cold that numbed her entire body, the water dripping from Ramson's hair onto her neck, the goose bumps on his neck as she pressed her cheek against it. And, by her side, a roaring sound steadily grew louder.

Bit by bit, cold breath by cold breath, the world seeped back in. The untouched snow blanketing the ground. The river rushing before them. The castle walls behind them. They'd washed up to the inner riverbank at the rear of the Palace—a place impossible to get to unless you swam through the river.

Ana pushed Ramson away with a gasp. He fell back and coughed, but his eyes never left her. His voice was hollow when he said, "I thought you were dead."

"I thought *you* were dead," she choked, staring at him. "Sadov said—Kerlan—"

And then the truth of what he had done—what he was

meant to have done—hit her all at once. The Order of the Lily. The assassination attempt on Luka.

"Before you say anything," Ramson said quietly, "just know that I know everything, Kolst Pryntsessa."

"As do I." Ana snatched his left wrist, where she'd seen the tattoo of that curled stem, those three small flowers. Ramson flinched. Her gaze cut to his. "I know you were working with Kerlan. I know he sent you to kill my brother. So tell me why I shouldn't throw you back into the river right now." She was shaking, her limbs growing numb from the cold. She needed to move—but she also needed to know.

Despite the fact that he was shivering as well, Ramson managed a half smile. "Because I'd just swim back out again?" Ramson twisted his hand, trapping hers in his grip. His eyes flicked to hers, hesitant but hopeful, water clinging to his lashes. "I know I've made some terrible choices in my past, Ana. I fell in with the wrong people. I've been running in the wrong direction ever since." He swallowed, his throat bobbing, and traced a thumb over the inside of her wrist. "But then I met a girl who told me that it is our choices that define us. And I . . . I want to make the right choice. If it's not too late."

She had no idea what to say to that. No idea whether she was falling for some new trap he'd planted for her. She thought she'd seen a glimpse of the boy Ramson had once been, standing there beneath the first snows of winter with her—but perhaps that had been a lie, too.

Ana snatched her hand back and pushed herself to her feet. The river had borne them quite a ways. In the distance, the torches of the Kateryanna Bridge shimmered like forgotten stars. She could barely make out people gathered on the bridge, smaller than the size of her fingernails. She was glad for the walls of the Palace, looming over them and obscuring them in shadow. "I need to go, Ramson."

"Then I'll go with you."

"No," Ana said, already moving forward one step at a time. The cold dragged at her. Her gown was weighed down with water that would soon become ice in these conditions.

"Ana. Kolst Pryntsessa," Ramson corrected, and his hand caught hers. He stepped in front of her. All traces of mirth were gone from his face when he said, "I didn't come back for a princess. I came for the girl I met in a high-security prison. Who jumped down a waterfall with me. Who fought by my side for the past few weeks." He reached out, and she held as still as she could when he cupped a hand to her cheek. "The girl who's not afraid to stand up to me. Who threatens to choke me with my own blood. The girl who's so much stronger than most people I know, but hides both her smiles and tears for when no one else is around."

"Then tell me this." She lifted her gaze. "Would you have killed Luka if you'd had the chance?"

He hesitated. Water trickled from his hair, threading a path down his neck. "I don't know."

Ana pulled away. He'd saved her—she owed him her life. But did that make up for whatever crimes he'd committed before?

Your choices, Luka whispered, and she suddenly saw herself reflected in Ramson's clouded hazel eyes. *She* had killed; *she* had tortured—and yet didn't she still want another chance? Didn't she still wish, resolutely, desperately, that above all the crimes she had committed and the people she had killed, her choices would define who she was?

Her mind was a whirl of emotions, of indecision. But the cold pressed at her, and time seeped through her fingers. The Coronation would start soon. She had to move. She had to make a choice.

"A friend told me that there is good and bad in everything," Ana found herself saying. "It is the good that's worth saving. I hope you have enough of that left in you, Ramson."

She heard him exhale as she turned away. Ana tilted her head back, judging the distance from the Kateryanna Bridge to where they stood. Behind them, the Syvern Taiga rose, a dark outline blotting out the stars.

She knew where she was. "There's a passageway to the dungeons up ahead," Ana said quietly.

Ramson shook his head. "It'll be locked. Trust me, I've studied the Salskoff Palace extensively."

"Not this one." Her breath frosted in the air as she waded through the snow. They were at the bottom of the riverbank, the Tiger's Tail so close that one slip would send them back to the clutches of the terrifying waters. The bank sloped steeply upward to the edge of the Palace wall. Ana thanked the Deities that they were far enough to be hidden from view from the archers who would shoot anyone who approached the walls.

The cold weighed her down, robbed her of breath. Her hair, her gown, her skirts, and her shoes dripped water, and she was shivering so hard that talking felt impossible.

Ramson seemed to realize the danger they were in as well. Too long in the cold, drenched with icy river water, and their body temperatures could plummet below functional levels. His tone was devoid of its usual humor when he spoke next. "How far are we?"

"Almost," she whispered. And—*there.* She spotted it, that thin crack along the Palace wall, large enough to be noticeable from this distance, but innocuous-looking. Someone had made it a long time ago.

Which meant . . . her passageway was . . .

Right here.

Ana crouched, running her fingers along the edge of the riverbank. And, surely enough, hovering just above the frothing waters was a hole, half-submerged in the Tiger's Tail.

"Genius," Ramson said. He was on his knees, peering at the tunnel entrance. "Whoever designed this escape route held the Imperial family's swimming skills in high esteem."

"It's not an escape route. It used to be a dumping place for bodies, hundreds of years ago when executions still took place in our dungeons."

"I didn't realize princesses were intimately familiar with the waste disposal plans of their palaces."

"I'm not." Markov's salt-and-pepper hair and lined face came to her. "When I was arrested for Papa's murder, one of my guards helped me escape. This was the only way out of the dungeons."

Something flashed in Ramson's eyes—pity? sympathy?—but it was gone the next moment. He held out his arms. "I'll help you this time."

Ana gripped the slope of the riverbank, her fingers digging into frozen mud. "I'll help myself," she murmured, and, before she could think twice, swung herself down.

For a single moment she hung suspended over the edge of

the riverbank and just above the river. Water roared in her ears, so terrifyingly close. Her skirts and her feet skimmed the surface, and she swung forward by momentum. Her feet touched wet rock; her hands scrabbled for purchase.

And then she was in the tunnel, clinging to the grooves in the wall, her heart beating so fast that she thought she would throw up.

Ramson swung in just seconds later. He swore as he slammed into the wall just below her.

The tunnel slanted up, and Ana thought of the bodies that had been shoved down and discarded into the river below. It was a tunnel built for getting out of the Palace, not for going in.

Ana put one hand above the other, feeling for the grooves in the wall, and began to climb.

The cold clenched her body like a living thing. Her muscles felt like stone. More than once, she lost her grip and slipped, resulting in a single, terrifying second when she thought she would plummet back into the river.

"Will you stop kicking mud in my face?" came the whisper from behind.

Ana gritted her teeth. "Death threat, remember?"

"Charming. I was going to be a gentleman and tell you that I'd catch you if you fell."

"And I was going to be a lady and tell you that I'd kill you if you spoke."

They continued their climb, bickering between them, and each pithy retort distracted Ana from the seemingly impossible task of each painful pull upward. The roaring of the river had faded to a hum, and there was only darkness and the quiet *drip, drip, drip* of water onto the stones all around them.

And suddenly, they came upon the door: a square piece of stone made to resemble part of the dungeon's wall on the other side. With numb fingers, Ana latched on to the ridge at the edge of it and pulled. The door gave way with a loud grating noise.

Ana heaved herself up and climbed to her feet. She had always thought the dungeons to be freezing, but the dry air felt warm to her skin. Ramson slid the door shut behind them, locking them in.

"The Palace was built with hidden hallways for servants' to use." Ana tried to inject confidence into her voice, but she was whispering. "Yuri used to take me through them, so I know them well. We'll dry off and get a fresh change of clothes at one of the servants' stations, and then . . ." She grimaced. "We storm the Coronation."

Ramson didn't miss a beat. "After you."

It was painful to force her half-frozen limbs into movement again. Memories pressed at her in the darkness: Sadov, his shadow looming, his long white fingers clasped in expectation. *Little monster . . .*

Ana flared her Affinity and held it before her like a blazing torch that chased away the darkness. She sensed the blood around her. It was in every single inch of the dungeons: smeared on the walls, dried and cracked on the rusting shackles.

Nothing. Besides traces of blood, there was nothing here but her own fear.

Ramson's ragged breathing followed her. Gradually, the darkness became punctuated with orange flickers of a torch somewhere far off. They drew closer, and Ana's Affinity sensed blood flowing warm through two bodies.

She and Ramson paused around the corner. The entrance to the main section of the Palace was right in front of them.

The two men guarding the door barely had a moment to react as she fixed her Affinity upon them, holding them in place. Ramson proceeded to calmly take the cuffs on each guard's belt and chain the men to cell doors, gagging them with their own shirts.

"That was easy," he whispered, joining her at the door.

"There used to be more prisoners and guards down here," Ana said. Praying that there was nothing on the other side of the door, she opened it a crack.

A spiral of stairs led up to the ground floor of the Palace, letting out in a hallway next to the servants' living area. There would be a doorway into their rooms right next to the dungeon entrance. She'd seen Yuri emerge from it dozens of times, peering at her as Sadov led her down. The sight had given her comfort back then.

Ana and Ramson shut the door behind them and stole up the twisting staircase.

They emerged into an empty hallway. The dungeons were at the back of the Palace, and on a night like this, most Palace occupants had no reason to be there. They hurried down the familiar marble floors and silver-lined walls of her childhood until they reached a pedestal with a Kemeiran vase. Next to it, the thinnest of crevices ran up along the wall. A secret door—one of the many around the Palace—that led to the hidden servants' hallways.

Ana threw her weight against it and pushed. The door gave way, and she slipped inside, just as she'd seen Yuri do so many times.

They were in a narrow hallway lined with shelves that were stacked with white linens and clean tablecloths, ready to be transported to their destinations.

They found a rack of guest gowns and tunics and shivered as they shed their wet clothes. Ana sighed as she dried herself with a soft cotton towel. She slipped on a gown that fit her—crimson, in a neat, simple cut. She dried her hair as best as she could, running her fingers through the snarls to smooth them so she wouldn't look too out of place. And, as she waited for Ramson to finish changing, Ana finally let herself touch a hand to the cream-colored walls. This was real. She was home again.

Ana drew a deep breath. When she reopened her eyes, it felt as though she had shed the skin of the lost girl who hated herself and feared the world. She stood straighter, squared her shoulders, and lifted her chin.

She was the Crown Princess of Cyrilia and the Blood Witch of Salskoff in one, and tonight, she would take back her empire.

"Kolst Pryntsessa." Ramson stood by the door in a fresh navy-blue doublet, his hair still wet and tousled, curling at the nape of his neck. "Are you ready?"

The halls were blessedly empty when they stepped out, yet with each twist and turn of the path, Ana reached out farther with her Affinity, expecting at any moment to happen upon guards or servants or other guests.

As they turned to the corridor that led to the Grand Throneroom, Ana gave a soft gasp. She'd been so tense that she hadn't paid attention to where they were going.

A grand hallway materialized before her as though from a dream, with sweeping marble balustrades and crystal chandeliers that cast the whole place in golden light. Pillars rose as high as the arched ceilings, statues of Deities and angels poised atop as though they had just alighted from the heavens. The Hall of Deities.

"Hello again, old friends."

Ana and Ramson spun around. The voice had made Ana's blood freeze even before she caught sight of the speaker.

Dressed in an immaculate suit of deep violet, a gold fountain pen glinting at his breast, a man stood beaming at them from ten paces away. It wasn't until she heard Ramson's sharp intake of breath and caught sight of the plant with the small bell-shaped flowers pinned to his lapel that she realized who it was.

Alaric Kerlan, the Head of the Order of the Lily, spread his hands in a magnanimous gesture.

"Ah, what spectacular company we have. The Princess and the con man." Alaric Kerlan stood ten paces away from them, his smile stretching from ear to ear. "I've been waiting for you."

36

Ana crouched into a defensive stance, her Affinity flaring as she took in Kerlan and the three bodyguards at his back. One of them looked large enough to snap a person in two, his muscles bulging like the exaggerated proportions of a Deity. The others—a man and a woman—were neither large nor intimidating. Which meant they were likely Affinites. Their eyes latched on to Ana.

"Three against two," Ramson said with a resigned sigh. "You do know how to fight fair, Alaric."

Faster than a whip, Ramson flung his hand out, and a dagger flashed silver in the air. In the split second she had to process this, Ana hurled her Affinity at his target—the woman—and held her in place. The woman barely had time to widen her eyes in shock when Ramson's dagger struck her squarely in the stomach.

The woman sank to her knees and fell forward, blood pooling onto the pristine marble floor beneath her.

A shout sounded nearby; Ana turned to see a squadron of Palace guards pouring in from the direction of the Grand Throneroom.

Kerlan looked up from the body of the woman. His expression was calm, but his eyes burned.

"Fortunately, I play dirty." The cocky grin on Ramson's face disappeared as he shouted, "Again, Ana!"

Ana was about to throw her Affinity forward when she felt that cold, impenetrable wall in her mind. Her Affinity snuffed out. Ramson's knife clanged on the floor as Kerlan's second Affinite leapt out of its path.

Ana turned, knowing already what she would see.

The Nandjian yaeger stood behind them, his eyes burning into hers. Sweat shone on his skin as he stepped forward and drew his sword.

Ana swore. To their left, palace guards advanced from the direction of the Grand Throneroom. To their right, the yaeger blocked the way out. And in front of them, Kerlan's male Affinite flexed his arms. A nearby marble column tore from the wall with a great, reverberating crack. Behind him, Kerlan smiled.

"Ramson, my son," Kerlan called. "I had hoped to save you for my own special treat. Give up the witch and save your own skin. It's what you do best."

Ana sank to her knees as the pressure on her mind increased from the yaeger's power. Out of the corner of her eye, she saw him advance, his heels clicking on the marble floor. From the other end of the hallway, the Palace guards drew closer, their swords flashing silver.

A shout cut through the air; Ramson knocked into her with such force that her breath caught. Pain burst through her shoulder as they slammed into the ground and skidded.

Ana looked up just in time to see a marble pillar smash onto the spot where they had been a heartbeat ago. Bits of chipped marble and rock exploded in all directions.

Her back hurt; she and Ramson were a tangle of limbs between the silks of her gown. He pushed himself up and hauled her to her feet. "Ana." He cupped her cheek, his voice low, urgent. "The Coronation. You need to go."

"You can't win here alone." Her voice was harder than she meant for it to be, only so that it wouldn't shake.

"If you stay here, you lose your brother and your empire." His tone was harsh.

Ana hesitated.

She'd doubted Ramson and his intentions, up until this very moment. He was putting his life on the line for her.

Ana only wished she hadn't realized so late.

But Kerlan was laughing, the marble Affinite was lifting another pillar, the Palace guards were almost upon them, and the Coronation was beginning. She had a choice to make, and that choice was not Ramson.

Ana seized a fistful of his shirt, pulling him to her so that they were a breath apart. Through the haze of sweat and blood, Ramson's eyes found her. "Don't you dare die on me, con man," she whispered before she let go. And then she was on her feet and running down the Hall of Deities.

The squad of Palace guards marched toward her, blue cloaks flapping behind them, blackstone-infused swords gleaming beneath the chandeliers. She kept running until she felt the yaeger's mental block slip from her mind, his presence behind her flickering out.

She slowed, ten paces from the Palace guards. And it hit her that she recognized them—most were familiar faces who had served her just one year ago.

They seemed to recognize her, too; several guards slowed, uncertainty and disbelief warring over their faces. Their leader came to a stop, his sword steady in his hands, his eyes betraying his hesitation.

"Lieutenant Henryk," Ana said steadily.

His eyes widened. "It is you, Kolst Pryntsessa." He stood his ground, whereas a year ago, he would have knelt at her feet.

Ana tilted her head. "Where is Kapitan Markov?" When he didn't answer, she took another step forward. "Where is Markov, Henryk?"

Henryk's mouth tightened. "I have my orders to arrest you, Kolst Pryntsessa."

"Whose orders?"

"The Kolst Contessya." His tone was firm, his face belying no emotion. "Please, come quietly. I do not wish to hurt you."

"I believe you," she said, and lifted a hand. "I'm sorry, Lieutenant. I have to get through."

The six guards fell to their knees as her Affinity tightened around them, their swords clattering to the floor. Lieutenant Henryk was the last to fall. He lifted his head to meet her eyes. His mouth opened and closed, as though he were struggling to say something to her.

Ana stepped past the kneeling guards, her steps ringing loud and clear as she approached the doors of the Grand Throneroom. Another dozen steps and the grand mahogany doors with the white tiger handles loomed before her.

Fatigue descended over her like a heavy cloud. She steeled

herself, reining in her shaking muscles. Chin high, shoulders back. Just as Luka had always taught her.

Ana grasped the sigil of her empire and pushed the doors open.

Before her Affinity had manifested, she'd been in the Grand Throneroom on multiple special occasions. Papa and Mama would sit on the two white-gold thrones atop the dais at the end of the long hall, while she and Luka perched on the seats reserved for them at either side. After her incident, Papa had never brought her back in—yet the grandeur of the room had never left her memory.

Blazing chandelier light illuminated a wide hall with a stretch of pale blue carpeting that extended all the way to the dais at the other end. The domed ceilings bore frescoes of the Deities in all shapes and forms, accompanied by reverent angels and mythical animals.

Below, in the room, fifty pairs of real, live eyes stared at Ana. On the gilded seats on either side of the hall reclined the Empire's most powerful noblemen and noblewomen. The expressions on their faces ranged from confusion to shock.

But Ana's gaze was set on the thrones straight ahead and the figures seated in them. It was difficult not to notice Morganya first, draped across the throne in a fine gown of shimmering blue and silver, her black hair cascading like a waterfall. She seemed to have grown even more beautiful since Ana last saw her. The glowing chandelier light brought out her high cheekbones, full lips, and soft, doelike eyes. For a moment, Ana could imagine running into her arms and burying her face in her mamika's silky dark hair. This woman, her aunt, the murderer of her parents.

And then Ana turned her gaze to the figure next to Morganya. He also leaned against his throne—but unlike Morganya, whose position exuded power and dominance, he looked as though he were barely holding on to life itself. His face was emaciated, his skin the color of ash, his cheeks sunken.

Most painful to look at were his eyes, and only when they met her own did a crippling realization course through her.

Her brother's once-beautiful, spring-grass eyes were empty. Ana was gazing at a ghost. And it broke her heart.

"Stop where you are!"

Ana spun to face the command. Four Palace guards approached, hands at their scabbards. Their expressions were cautious but stern. In her gown, she probably looked the same as any other frantic guest to them.

"You can't be here, meya dama. We've closed off the Grand Throneroom to guests to protect our Empress from infiltration—"

The guard's message was cut short as Ana seized his blood and flung him to the side of the grand hall. Screams went up as he crashed into Imperial Councilmembers and guests alike, knocking them from their seats.

Ana reined in her Affinity and turned her gaze back to the dais. Morganya sat straighter now, focusing on Ana as though noticing her for the first time. Eight more guards stepped from posts behind the dais, surrounding the thrones in defensive stances. Their swords sang as they slid them from their scabbards.

Ana took a step forward. It was now or never.

"My name is Anastacya Kateryanna Mikhailov," she said, and her voice carried across the hall as she walked, ringing beneath the frescoed deities and carved angels. "Daughter of Aleksander Mikhailov and Kateryanna Mikhailov. Crown Princess of

Cyrilia." She threw a hand up, pointing. "I am here to stop the coronation of the Grand Countess, on account of her crimes of murder and treason against the Crown of Cyrilia."

Gasps and murmurs filled the room. Suddenly, the guests were leaning forward in their seats, craning their necks to get a better look at Ana. Even the guards at the dais, trained to remain stoic, gaped openly at her.

On his throne, Luka stared at Ana without the slightest hint of recognition.

"Stand down."

Morganya's smooth, melodic voice had soothed Ana on the worst of her nights, easing her to sleep like the mother she'd lost so long ago. The thought made her sick now.

The line of guards protecting the Countess acted immediately, lowering their swords and parting uniformly like a set of stage curtains. On the dais, Morganya stood graciously, the lead actress of this preposterous play. Her eyes scanned Ana up and down. Narrowed.

And then her face softened. Crumpled. "Anastacya?" Morganya whispered, gripping the arms of her throne. *"Ana?"*

Murmurs erupted on either side of the aisle as Ana continued to make her way toward the thrones. *It's her. It's the lost Princess. The mad Princess. The dead Princess.*

Ana trained her eyes on her aunt. "Do you deny the crimes of which I accuse you?" she called, raising her voice over the din that had filled the Throneroom.

"Ana?" Morganya shook her head, disbelief and bewilderment seeping into her expression. "I don't understand. What are you talking about?"

"Was I not clear enough?" Ana took another step forward,

steadily closing the gap between her and the dais. "In that case, allow me to make myself clear. I accuse you of assassinating my mother, the former Empress Kateryanna Mikhailov"—the crowd's murmurs grew to a low buzz—"assassinating my father, the former Emperor Aleksander Mikhailov"—a collective gasp from the crowd—"and plotting the murder of my brother, the Emperor Lukas Aleksander Mikhailov." The Imperial Councilmembers were now clamoring to get a better view of her, while the guests looked on in horror, their eyes darting between her and Morganya. *"Do you deny it?"*

Morganya was shaking her head, her expression slowly morphing into horror. "You . . . what are you talking about?" Her voice rose to a terrified squeak as she pointed a finger at Ana. "*You* murdered your father!"

"You framed me," Ana snarled.

Morganya's terror vanished as suddenly as it had come, in the blink of an eye. Her expression became serpentine smooth, calculatingly cold. "Enough," she growled. The transformation was stark—and it was now clear that everything Morganya had ever said or done had been an act all along. "I don't know how you got past the Palace guards, but one thing is clear: you are dangerous." Morganya snapped her fingers. "Guards. Seize her."

"No!" Ana shouted, but the guards were moving toward her rapidly, swords raised, the blackstone of their blades glittering.

Ana turned and found those now-dull green eyes, still gazing at her. "Luka," Ana cried. "Luka, please—it's me!"

The guards closed in. Slowly, Ana backed away.

She could easily take them with her Affinity. But that would only paint her as the monster this crowd thought her to be. This was not a fight; this was a performance.

She needed to show them that she came in peace; she needed to use her words to fight.

"Stop," Ana said, and the guards hesitated. She lifted her gaze to meet Morganya's. "Will you deny that you are an Affinite, with an Affinity to flesh and thought?" Another collective gasp swept through the Throneroom. "That you have manipulated the former Palace alchemist into concocting the poisons that killed my parents? That you are, at this very moment, manipulating my brother, the Emperor?"

"This is *madness,*" Morganya cried, and Ana was glad to hear a note of distress in her voice. Her eyes, however, burned with promised retribution. "Guards! Seize her! We will continue with this coronation!"

"Kolst Contessya Morganya," Ana said steadily. "With accusations against you, you cannot be crowned Empress until they're cleared. This is Cyrilian law—this is our law."

"She's right." Another voice spoke up. An Imperial Councilman stood, and the room fell silent. His gray-flecked hair was neatly combed, his face lined with age and wisdom that somehow made him appear more powerful. Ana recognized him as Councilman Dagyslav Taras. He'd been Papa's closest friend and councilor, and it was said that he had been in the running for Imperial Advisor before Sadov was chosen. "It is the law, Kolst Contessya."

"You forget, Taras!" Another Councilman stood, Northern Cyrilian–blond hair buzzed to an inch of his scalp. A long scar slashed across his nose. The fierceness of his expression was warriorlike, and Ana recognized him from that alone. Maksym Zolotov, Cyrilian-army-commander-turned-Councilman. He turned his heated gaze straight to Ana. "The Princess—or *former* Princess—still carries charges of murder and treason with her. Her accusations cannot stand."

Ana stared back at him, and Zolotov had the grace to look away. Inside, though, she felt the sharp sting of betrayal. In her years of confinement, she'd skulked around the Palace, watching these Councilmembers from afar. She'd memorized their names, noted the ones she'd liked best, and Zolotov had been among those. He'd struck her with his courage, his loyalty, and his straightforwardness. To have him speak against her hurt.

Taras gave Zolotov a piercing look. "You are not incorrect, Maksym. The Princess's status casts doubt unto her accusations. Yet by Cyrilian law, there is no rule dictating that those under indictment cannot accuse others."

They would not speak for her, nor would they speak against her. They interpreted the law.

Taras turned to the thrones. "When there is no law in our system for this situation, we must defer to the Emperor." He paused. "Kolst Imperator?"

Finally—*finally*—Ana let her gaze slide over to the figure to the right of Morganya. Her brother was watching this with no more reaction than a person might watch rats scuffling on the streets. "Luka," she called out again. "Luka, please, look at me. It's the truth. I have evidence—I swear on my life. She's poisoned your body and poisoned your mind, Luka." The last words came out in a dry sob. "Please. Listen to me."

"You ran when you were charged with murder," a Councilman shouted. "Is that not an act of guilt?"

"I ran because I was innocent, and I knew I had to seek proof to convict the true murderer." Ana's gaze never left her brother. "Luka. Please." Her voice sank to a hoarse whisper. "You know me, bratika. You know I love this empire too much. *Believe me.*"

Luka's gaze flickered, settling on her with a haunted look that Ana would never forget. These were the eyes of a man with a dead soul.

Her heart cracked.

Luka opened his mouth. His voice, when it came from him, was barely a whisper. "We will continue with the coronation."

"No!" Ana lunged forward. "No, Luka—she has you under her control—"

"Guards, detain her!" Morganya sounded confident again; she stood before her throne, gripping the arms. Guards swarmed forward, but Ana pushed them back with her Affinity; she was aware that archers had poured into the room and trained their arrows on her back, waiting for the command to fire. "We need Deys'voshk. I know what she can do with her Affinity—I've seen it with my own eyes. Vladimir! Vladimir!"

"Kolst Contessya, allow me."

Ana froze at the soft, smooth voice. Next to the Councilmembers seated closest to the throne stood a figure dressed in white alchemist robes. Tetsyev touched a hand to his Deys'krug as he gazed up at Morganya.

Morganya's expression softened. "Go on, Pyetr." Her eyes shone with a secret triumph.

Tetsyev turned to Ana.

"Traitor," Ana spat. It was no longer anger that gripped her. Certainty settled in her chest. If she was to die, she would at least take this murderer with her.

Yet as Ana grasped his bonds with her Affinity, something else came to her. Another memory, of a dungeon, and a weeping, frightened man.

Morganya is strong, but she is not invincible.

How much of what Tetsyev had told her that night had been the truth?

She can control only one mind at a time. And her control can be broken. When you used your Affinity on me, it cut through Morganya's Affinity.

Could it be? That her Affinity could cancel out Morganya's Affinity, break her aunt's hold over Luka for just a small while?

She hesitated. Perhaps everything Tetsyev had told her had been a lie. Yet . . . She thought of his eyes, the remorse in his voice, the words he'd whispered in the dark. She hadn't been able to shake off the feeling that he'd spoken the truth that night.

It was worth a try.

Ana threw her Affinity to Luka and gave the gentlest pull.

Even from here, she could sense the wrongness to his blood, the amount of the foreign substance in it. It was sluggish and cold whereas it should have been thrumming and warm. Her heart ached, but she pulled again.

As she concentrated her Affinity on her brother, she was faintly aware of guards seizing her, crossing their swords over her, the blackstone-infused metal cold against her throat.

For the third time, Ana pulled.

Luka blinked. Gave a small gasp.

Ana's heart soared as his eyes found hers. *Truly* found hers. They looked brighter, more alert, as though he had just woken from a long, long slumber.

Please, Luka. Wake up.

"Stop," Luka said.

The entire Court turned to look at him with wonder. Tetsyev blinked, and turned in his tracks. "Kolst Imperator . . . ?"

But the brightness in Luka's eyes was fading again; he looked even more lost as he leaned back, exhaling as though he had spent all of his energy. Flatly, he said, "We must get on with the coronation."

Ana's heart sank. Morganya was looking directly at her; a corner of her aunt's lips curled in the shadow of a smile.

"I, Lukas Aleksander Mikhailov—"

"No!" Ana shouted, but the look her brother gave her was stern—like the ones Papa used to give them.

Everything was going to hell.

"Silence her," Luka commanded the guards. His gaze then snapped directly to her: bursting with life and confidence and the power of an emperor. "Quiet, brat."

Brat. She stared at her brother, her heart thumping so hard in her chest that she thought it might burst free.

Luka drew himself straight with the small amount of energy he had left. His voice was dull as he recited, "I, Lukas Aleksander Mikhailov, announce the temporary abdication of the throne to the Cyrilian Empire for reasons of personal health."

Morganya's face was aglow in triumph.

"In the event of my abdication or death, I hereby crown the heir to the throne of Cyrilia." Luka suddenly focused on Ana with such intensity that it took her breath away. "I name the Crown Princess Anastacya Kateryanna Mikhailov as heir and future Empress to the Cyrilian Empire."

37

Ramson was going to die.

The ground rumbled beneath his feet as he dove out of the way of another crashing marble pillar, slamming against the opposite wall. His breaths were coming in ragged gasps, and blood trickled down the side of his face.

He shook his head, clearing the double vision. *Focus.* Ana was still in there. She needed him to hold Kerlan and his cronies here.

He'd held the yaeger at bay so far—when the tall man with those glacial eyes had taken off after Ana, Ramson had jumped in front of him to stop him. He'd been fighting a losing battle even before the marble Affinite joined the party.

Ramson gripped his daggers, pushing himself to his feet and swiping a hand across his nose. It came back bloody.

Three to one. Kerlan's big bodyguard wasn't an issue. That brute was made for throwing around his weight and bullying chained victims in confined spaces, not for actual freestyle sparring. And his prerogative, judging from the way he hovered near his master, was to protect Kerlan. It was the other two he had to watch out for.

He glanced at the yaeger, whose swords were out. Ramson was about to spring at him when he caught a sharp movement to his right.

The marble Affinite flung his hand out, and two fist-sized balls of marble shot from the ground. Ramson ducked behind a nearby pillar, feeling it shudder as the two projectiles smashed into it.

A sudden coldness touched his arm. A piece of marble debris snapped around his wrist. Within the blink of an eye, it twisted and closed over itself like a handcuff, and the ground jerked from beneath him. Ramson was flung bodily across the hall—or rather, the marble around his wrist hurtled so fast that his arm felt like it was going to be ripped from its socket—and the world blurred around him.

Ramson crashed against the wall. Pain flared through his body, but Kerlan was keeping him alive, torturing him. Panting, Ramson tried to heave himself up. It was just like Kerlan, to know that he had Ramson outnumbered and overpowered, and to savor his victory by quashing Ramson's hope bit by bit.

The marble on his wrist was moving again. It dragged him along the ground, toward where Kerlan and his bodyguard stood. Ramson reached out for anything to grab onto, but his traitorous, marble-manacled wrist persisted.

Out of the corner of his eye, he saw the body of the female Affinite he'd struck earlier, crumpled in the hall. The yaeger stood on the other side of the corridor. His eyes narrowed briefly before he turned and took off down the hallway.

No, not toward Ana, Ramson thought. He strained against the manacle, but it was no use.

"Well, my son." Kerlan's eyes twinkled pleasantly as he

looked down at Ramson from beneath the shadow of his huge bodyguard. "Had enough yet?"

Ramson coughed up blood. He was curled on the floor, every fiber of his body throbbing in pain, his manacled wrist dangling from the marble Affinite's control. He forced a smile to his cracked lips. "That the best you've got?" he croaked. "You've become soft, Kerlan."

Kerlan's smile did not waver, but his eyes promised death. He motioned at the marble Affinite. A second piece of debris sculpted itself around Ramson's unshackled wrist, dragging his other arm into the air, lifting him so that he knelt before Kerlan. His dagger clattered to the ground, the sound reverberating across the empty hall.

Tap . . . tap . . . tap.

It took Ramson a moment to realize where the noise was coming from. Kerlan watched him with an amused smile, his gold fountain pen rapping against his ring.

Tap . . . tap . . . tap.

The sound sent a shiver through Ramson.

"I don't know how you define 'soft,'" Kerlan said, raising his pen so that it caught the light of the chandelier overhead. He pressed the end with his finger. With a click, a ring of tiny, sharp blades shot out from the tip, glinting like teeth. "Perhaps you'll let me know how this feels."

He slammed the pen into Ramson's chest, right where he'd seared the Order of the Lily insignia.

Ramson screamed. Kerlan laughed and twisted the pen, the razor-sharp blades burrowing into Ramson's flesh. And then he tore it out.

Ramson fought to stay conscious. It felt as though his flesh were on fire, and the pain sent fuzzy edges of darkness shooting through his vision.

He was shaking as he threw up, his tears mingling with sweat. Kerlan's maniacal laughter rang in his ears.

I'm going to die, Ramson thought.

But even as his body began to slump, he scanned the area around him, his brain working frantically to find anything that could help him.

A shadow flitted in the hallway behind Kerlan.

There was a soft *whoosh* and a whisper of a thud. The marble Affinite staggered forward. Blood poured from his mouth.

The Affinite crashed to the floor, eyes still open, the metal hilt of a dagger protruding from his back. The marble cuffs around Ramson's wrists, cracked and crumbled away.

Kerlan and his bodyguard turned. Seizing his opportunity, Ramson grabbed his dagger from where it had fallen and slashed at Kerlan.

His vision was blurred with tears, blood, and sweat, and his aim was weak; his blade bit into Kerlan's flesh, leaving only a shallow scratch. Kerlan stumbled back, his face contorting in a snarl.

The bodyguard roared, leaping and raising both fists. Ramson threw himself forward. Pain exploded in his chest as he rolled beneath the man, springing to a crouch by the wall behind him.

The bodyguard raised his fists again. This time, Ramson had nowhere to go.

A surge of wind blasted at him, so strong that even the huge bodyguard staggered, raising his hands to shield himself. A small dark blur shot at Ramson. He felt an arm lock around his abdomen, and then they were sliding across the debris-cluttered floor, propelled by the gale.

Hands gently laid him on the floor, and a face came into view. Slender and sharp, with short black hair and midnight eyes. He'd seen this face only across a crowded arena, and then in the murky shadows of a bar in Novo Mynsk, when he'd bought her contract afterward.

"Windwraith," Ramson croaked. "Linn."

"Ana," Linn said. "Have you seen her?"

He had so many questions—had the Windwraith held her end of the Trade? But his head swam. "The Coronation ceremony," he managed. "I told her I'd hold off these Affinites."

She cast him a doubtful look. "You?" she intoned, and with the suppleness of a professional acrobat, she sprang to her feet. Daggers flashed in her hands. A leather belt strapped across her waist held a wicked assortment of throwing knives.

Wind exploded before Linn, knocking Kerlan back, screaming, against the bodyguard. The bodyguard raised a hand again, turning his face from the gale.

Linn flicked her wrist.

The bodyguard howled in pain. Blood seeped from his midriff, where a small knife had embedded itself in his flesh.

Suddenly, the wind died and a terrible silence fell upon the hallway.

Linn made a noise, like a small animal in pain. Ramson saw the white flash of a cloak against the wreckage of the hall. The yaeger had returned. He was blocking Linn's Affinity. He strode out from behind a pillar, his eyes pinned to Linn.

Linn flung two knives at the man. He blocked them easily with his swords.

Beyond the pain of his bleeding wounds, hope fluttered in Ramson's chest. He realized that none of Kerlan's Affinites were trained fighters like Linn.

Over twenty paces from them, Kerlan clutched his expensive doublet, his face pale as a sheet. Interesting, Ramson thought, that a man who aimed to inflict so much pain could bear so little. Kerlan motioned to his bodyguard, who was bleeding profusely from his own wounds. The bodyguard stooped and wrapped a giant arm around Kerlan's waist.

Abruptly, they turned and hobbled away.

Linn's hands went to her thighs, and two more knives appeared in her fists. She crouched by where Ramson lay, her eyes trained on the yaeger. The man waited across the hall by a broken marble pillar.

Kerlan and his bodyguard's fading footsteps were smothered by another sound: a rhythmic rumbling that echoed across the domed ceilings and broken marble façades. Ramson recognized these—he had heard them many, many years ago, at the Blue Fort. These were the footsteps of an army. He racked his brain for the security protocols of the Salskoff Palace. In the case of an attack, the Palace guards held the first line of defense until the reinforcements came. And the reinforcements were not just any ordinary guards. These were the Empire's elite fighters and strongest warriors.

The Whitecloaks were coming.

"Can you move?" It took Ramson a moment to realize Linn was addressing him.

He pushed himself up, and his chest felt like it was on fire. A groan escaped from deep in his throat. "Yes."

Linn plucked something from her waist: a small leather

pouch, camouflaged among all the weapons. The contents inside clinked gently as she slipped it into Ramson's hands. "Bring these to Ana. They are the evidence she needs."

"You don't expect me to leave you to fight alone?"

"Go," she replied, without looking back at him. The yaeger advanced on them, swords held at his sides, reflecting the light from the chandelier above.

Ramson climbed to his feet, the broken pieces of marble and crushed flooring crunching beneath him as he stood. His chest bled where Kerlan had stabbed him, but the wound wasn't deep enough to kill him.

He would live—at least until he reached Ana.

He glanced back. Linn remained in the same defensive stance, her knives steady in her hands, her gaze focused with sharp intent on the approaching yaeger.

It was a fight between a sparrow and an eagle.

For a moment, Ramson thought of calling back to Linn with a Kemeiran blessing. But blessings and prayers were for the fainthearted, and Ramson had never believed in leaving your fate to the gods.

Besides, he would thank her in person after all of this.

Ramson turned and sprinted down the ruins of the Hall of Deities.

38

A stunned silence filled the Grand Throneroom. All around, expressions of confusion and shock were mirrored across the faces of Imperial Councilmembers and guests alike. Ana stared at Luka, struggling to process his words.

Only, instead of the sunken and gaunt shell of a man her brother had been a second before, Luka was sitting up straight, his face alight with triumph. And he was looking back at her. His grin widened to a full-on conspiratorial beam as he put a finger on his lips, and then, just for that moment, they were small children again, protecting each other from a world of cruelty. It was their act of defiance. Their secret.

The Throneroom burst into cacophony. Imperial Councilmembers stood in their seats, some leaning over the mahogany banister, calling out to Luka and Morganya, whose expression was frozen in a look of horror. The remaining guards at the dais appeared just as dazed as they raised their hands to placate the crowd.

We won.

The thought stunned Ana so much that she could only stare at the scene unraveling before her. Morganya would be tried for treason and murder; the poisons that would indict Morganya and the antidote that would save Luka's life were in the apothecary's wing.

The guards holding Ana looked just as uncertain; they shifted their stances, lowering their blades slightly from the now-heir to their empire.

Ana wrapped her Affinity around them and pushed. She straightened and stepped forward. The din quieted, and every pair of eyes in the room watched as she walked across the aisle to the dais.

A cry sliced through the air. "Stop her!" Morganya stood by the throne she only moments earlier was confident was hers. She had one hand clamped across the back as though she wanted to both protect it and to hide behind it. "Guards!"

"No!" Luka commanded. He was trying to stand, and it hurt Ana to see him struggle. "My sister is the heir to this empire, and she will be treated as thus."

Morganya whirled to him. "Kolst Imperator," she said. "I appreciate your love for your sister, but you cannot deny what she is! The Blood Witch of Salskoff!" She turned to the crowd. "Or were you not all there that day in the Vyntr'makt, when she slaughtered eight innocents out of her monstrous bloodlust?"

There were gasps around the room; a few guests and Councilmembers cried out.

"You're right," Ana said, and the entire room turned to watch her as she closed in on the throne, one step at a time. "I've done terrible things, and the world made sure to remind me of my monstrosity. But so have you, Morganya." She slowed, facing her aunt across the dais. "Don't you see? We're the same. But someone once told me that our Affinities don't define us. What defines us is how we choose to wield them."

Luka's eyes shone with pride.

"We both know this empire is broken. But we cannot fix it through fear or revenge." Ana thought of Sadov's words, of how they had carved themselves deep inside her. Of how she had grown to believe them, and to believe she *was* what the world told her she was. *Monster. Deimhov.* Her voice was a cracked whisper as she said, "Please, mamika. Choose to be good. We could help our people . . . together."

For several moments, Morganya stood frozen, as though carved from stone. And then her eyes narrowed. Her voice echoed across the hall, calm and cold. "I have no idea what you are talking about, Anastacya."

A strange pressure descended upon Ana's body, locking her in place so that she couldn't move. A darkness rolled across her mind like fog.

A flesh Affinite with control of the mind.

They were mirror images of each other, her and her mamika, Ana realized. Both born to gruesome Affinities. Both vilified by the world.

There is good and bad in everything.

Morganya had made her choice.

With all her strength and fury, Ana hurled her Affinity at Morganya.

Morganya's lips parted in a cry. She stumbled and fell, clinging to her throne. Within the space of a second, she seemed to have transformed back into a broken, frightened girl. "Please," she sobbed, and reached a shaking hand toward Luka.

"Guards!" Luka had pushed himself to his feet and was gripping his throne to hold himself upright. "Take Countess Morganya to the dungeons for questioning. As your Emperor, I order you to follow the orders of the Crown Heir. We will overturn this castle to find the evidence of the poison Morganya has been using."

Chaos fell upon the Grand Throneroom as Councilmembers and guests began shouting over each other at the sudden turn of events. But Ana kept her gaze on the dais.

She alone caught the look Morganya gave Luka. It was a look that promised death.

Sudden fear gripped Ana. She knew, from some primal instinct in her gut, that something was about to go horribly, unfathomably wrong.

Ana burst into a sprint toward the dais. "Luka!" she shouted. She didn't know why she was calling his name. She only knew that she had to get to him.

Her brother turned to her. His smile slipped when he caught her panicked expression.

"Luka!" Ana focused on Morganya's crumpled frame, hurling all the strength of her Affinity at the woman, pinning Morganya down and willing her not to move.

The knot of panic loosened just slightly inside her chest. Ten more steps. She pressed harder on Morganya. *You will not hurt him.*

In the corner of her vision, a figure moved. From the shadows of Luka's white-gold throne snaked a hand. Fingers, pale and long and hauntingly familiar, twisted around an object—but this time, it was not a whip.

Sadov was smiling as he plunged his dagger into Luka's chest.

Time stopped. The world—the blood, the bodies, the screaming—blurred into the background. There was only Luka, and the copper tang of his blood in the air, magnified by her Affinity.

Her brother fell, his face serene but for the spark of surprise in his eyes.

Someone was screaming. No, *she* was screaming. Her Affinity was expanding, sweeping around her outside of her command. People toppled out of her way like figures on a chessboard.

Ana flew up the steps of the dais and flung herself down next to her brother. Her hands shook as she gathered him gently into her arms. Blood stained the blue carpet beneath him; blood dripped onto her hands and legs; blood seeped into the soft fabric of her dress.

Blood. Her Affinity, her gift and her curse.

"Luka." Ana's voice broke. His eyes found hers, misted with pain but clear as a field of grass beneath the sun. He exhaled with a horrible rattling sound. Ana placed a hand over the wound in his chest, willing the blood back, back, back into his body. "Shhh," she whispered. "I'm here, bratika. Shhh."

Luka opened his mouth. She lowered her head to his lips. "Brat," he whispered, his voice faint. "I've . . . missed you."

She was crying. "There's so much I have to tell you. We'll . . . we'll fix this. And everything else. We'll fix it together, Luka."

"You . . . came back," he rasped.

"I'm back," she sobbed, cradling him in her arms and touching her forehead to his. And then she raised her head, screaming. "Healer! We need a healer—*now!*"

"Ana," Luka wheezed. "Sistrika. I'm . . . tired."

"Hold on," Ana begged. "Help is coming— *Healer!*" Her voice cracked. *"Please!"* She turned back to Luka. "Hold on. I'm here. Sistrika's here."

His eyes fluttered; he struggled to keep them open. He made a small motion as though to shake his head. "Not sistrika," he whispered, and his eyes suddenly widened, burning with intensity. He drew a deep breath, straining. *"Empress."*

"Luka," she wept.

"Promise . . . me."

The words cut through her heart. "I promise."

A smile warmed Luka's face, like the sun coming out after the rain. His body seemed to relax. He gazed at her with that fondness, that light in his eyes, and for a moment they were children again, grinning at each other with a silent promise. "I'll tell Papa and Mama . . ."

He never finished the sentence. A serene look passed over his face, and just like that, he fell still, his spring-grass eyes trained on her as though he'd just been about to tell her a secret.

39

Ana held her brother tightly, burying her head in the soft crook of his neck the way she used to when she was a child. Her tears wet the fabric of his white silk doublet. She thought she would stay like this forever; she thought she would never get up again.

"She killed the Emperor!" Morganya's scream pierced the air.

Slowly, bit by bit, the world seeped back in. The bloody carpet beneath her feet. The shrieks of the panicked and the dying. The crimson soaking her dress.

Ana set Luka's head onto the carpet, smoothing his hair and closing his eyes. A ghost of a smile was etched on his face.

A strange redness crept into the world; it swirled at the edges of her vision like a living, breathing fog. Everything began to smell like blood.

Ana straightened. Her chest was a hollow hole. There was no grief there. Not yet. Once she let her sorrow in, she would be pulled under its waters and never surface again.

No . . . that empty space inside her flickered with rage. Smoldering. Churning.

The redness roiled, tendrils snaking toward the pulsing

blood in the room. A delicious darkness spread within her. Ana leaned toward it.

Her world erupted in crimson. She staggered back, squeezing her eyes shut and gulping in ragged breaths. Slowly, like silhouettes in a fog, the world came into focus in her mind, mapped by blood. It grew stronger and sharper, and when it settled, she felt as though she had been looking at the world through a darkened window . . . until now.

Everything was vivid, visceral. Her Affinity was sight, smell, sound, touch, and taste, all combined into one. She could see each and every drop of blood spattered on the floor, glistening as bright as stars in the night sky. She smelled the liquor swirling in the veins of all the guests; tasted the adrenaline and fear churning within; heard the desperate pounding of their hearts.

A twisted sense of peace settled over her. She reached out, and her attention caught on a figure slowly backing away behind her. His blood was as cold as darkness; it smelled of rot and tasted like death.

Without moving, without even opening her eyes, she dragged him toward her as a child might drag a rag doll. She felt his scream in the vibrations of his veins.

He cowered before her, his Affinity crushed beneath her power. Ana opened her eyes. "Sadov," she murmured.

He stared up at her, the dagger in his hand still coated in Luka's blood.

A mere flick in her mind and he was dangling before her, limbs splayed out like a butterfly on a board. *Where should I start? Where will it* hurt *the most?*

Fear rippled across Sadov's features. "N-no, Kolst Pryntsessa," he whispered. "P-please . . ."

She smiled at him. "'You little monster,'" she crooned, tightening her grip on him so that he cried out in pain. "Isn't that what you always said to me?"

He screamed, his face turning red from her hold on his blood. Foam bubbled from his mouth. With his face contorted in pain, he truly looked like a creature from hell, a deimhov from a nightmare.

"You wanted a monster," Ana hissed. With a *crack,* blood began to drip from Sadov's nose. "Here I am."

She'd never thought she would savor the utter terror that warped his face at this moment, that she'd feel a burst of delight at each drop of blood that fell to the floor.

Through the red haze of her Affinity, she felt someone else watching her. The gaze was familiar and unfamiliar at once. Morganya's pale eyes were trained on her, and it suddenly felt as though she were a child again. There was a kind of approval shining from that gaze.

Approval. Something churned in Ana's stomach. She stared back, Sadov dangling before her like a marionette, struggling for air. All the while, Morganya merely watched.

Morganya was not going to stop Ana if she killed Sadov. No—Morganya *wanted* her to kill Sadov.

An image flashed before her: a square of silver and snow, a crowd, and a crimson pool seeping into the cobblestones. Eight crumpled figures, limbs twisting in unnatural angles. They formed a circle around her, radiating like enormous petals of a gnarled flower.

Ana dropped to her knees and screamed. It stretched, long and thin, threatening to shatter her mind like glass.

It's all right, sistrika. I'm here. Bratika's here.

In her mind, she was back in her room, and Luka had wrapped his arms around her shoulders, murmuring soothing words.

The memory shifted, and he lay dying in her arms, crimson spreading across his tunic.

Promise me, he'd said.

He hadn't only been asking her to promise to become Empress. No—Luka had always thought bigger than that. For her entire life, her brother had watched over her, saving her . . . saving her from what? Not from death. Not from the wrath of the world. Not even from Sadov, or from Morganya.

Luka had been protecting her from the darkness of her Affinity; from the version of herself she could have—and could still—become.

To kill Sadov, to take her revenge . . . that was the choice that would make her a monster.

Promise me.

The world dulled. The red receded. She released Sadov and he crumpled to the floor. The fury, the bloodlust, and the blinding rage that had consumed her withdrew like a receding tide, leaving her raw.

Ana collapsed. As though from a distance, she heard Morganya calling orders. *Kill her,* her aunt cried. *She is a dangerous Affinite. She could have murdered us all.*

Sadov crawled away from her, trailing blood and whimpering. All around them, guests were fleeing through the doors, and the remaining Councilmembers lingered in the safety of the farthest corners of the Throneroom.

A shadow fell upon Ana. The face was familiar; large eyes against pale skin and a bald forehead. Those eyes gazed into hers, as inscrutable as ever.

She felt a cold glass vial being tilted to her lips; sweet, honey-like liquid poured down her throat. This was not Deys'voshk. It was a different kind of poison. Ana struggled. The gray eyes became stern. Tetsyev clamped a hand on her nose. She had no strength left to resist.

Her mind was becoming muggy.

A numbing sensation was spreading from her stomach to her abdomen and into her limbs.

"It is done, Kolst Imperatorya." Tetsyev's voice was distant as he drew back. "The Blood Witch will die."

The poison worked fast. It spread through her veins like ice, freezing her muscles.

Several steps from her, Luka lay on the dais, peaceful even in his death.

I love you, Luka, she thought. *I'm sorry.*

A figure approached. Morganya's eyes brimmed with tears, and they spilled down her face as she knelt next to Ana. She put a hand to Ana's cheek; her fingers were ice-cold to the touch. Slowly, Morganya lowered her lips to Ana's face, pausing a breath away.

"You pitiful creature," Morganya whispered, caressing her hair. "Tetsyev did the humane thing. He's always been more softhearted than I, my talented alchemist. I would have saved you for Sadov's dungeons."

Ana wanted to reach up and claw Morganya's eyes out. Her arms would not move.

Morganya's breath warmed Ana's neck. She was laughing softly. From a distance, anyone would think she was kneeling over Ana's body, grieving.

"I might have taken you in," Morganya murmured. "After

all, we are purging the world of the monsters that oppressed us—that treated us like vermin." She paused, and her voice became mockingly sad. "You look at me with such hatred. You think me the villain. But what you don't understand is that sometimes we must commit terrible deeds for the greater good. My acts are sacrifices that I am willing to make to pave a better world, Little Tigress."

Ana could only stare at her aunt, her mind trying to make sense of Morganya's words. Only now did she realize that her aunt hadn't done these things out of spite, or pure evil. In Morganya's mind, she was making the right choice.

"You chose the wrong side," Morganya continued. "And now you will pay for it by dying alone, dishonored and disgraced. The whole room watched you torture Vladimir; I am the heroine who saved them from a deimhov. And the dark legends of the Blood Witch of Salskoff will carry on." She leaned in and placed a soft kiss on Ana's forehead. Her lovely face crumpled again as she lifted her head, tears glistening on her cheeks for the world to see. "Pyetr," she said hoarsely, backing away to the dais. "Is she . . . ? Could you . . . ? I cannot bear to look at her."

There was so much more Ana needed to do; so much more she should have done for her empire. But her strength was giving out. A strange sense of peace settled over her, as though her body were falling into slumber. Her head lolled to the side and she waited for the darkness to close in. If this was dying, it wasn't so terrible.

A light breeze brushed Ana's face as Tetsyev knelt by her side, his white robes fluttering. He put a finger to her neck to check her pulse. To her surprise, he, too, dipped his head in respect and mourning. The softest whisper came from his lips: "It's a paralysis poison." And then, straightening, Tetsyev turned to Morganya. "The Blood Witch is dead."

Her mind was heavy, but surprise cut through it like a blade. A paralysis poison.

She wasn't dying.

Could it be? That Tetsyev had saved her life? That everything Tetsyev had told her held true?

A shout sounded somewhere outside. Sharp, quick footsteps rang in the silence of the vast hall, growing closer and more frantic.

"No!" someone yelled. Ana knew that voice. It was familiar, in a way that made her want to reach out to its owner and touch him, even with just a hand on his shoulder, or be near enough to feel his presence.

Ramson crashed to his knees by her side. "No." His voice cracked, and the raw emotion in it stirred something within Ana. Never had she seen Ramson so unguarded, the stricken look on his face shifting to anguish as he gently pulled her into his arms. She felt the touch of his skin, the warmth of his breath as he lowered his head to hers, clutching her and bent over her as though a part of him had broken.

"Kapitan!" Morganya cried. "Arrest this criminal."

"No!" Ramson roared. He stood, folding Ana into his arms and lifting her. "Imperial Councilmembers, I have irrefutable evidence that the Countess is a murderer and traitor to the Crown of Cyrilia."

His voice was drowned out by footsteps as the guards, emboldened by Ana's still body, closed in on him.

No, Ana begged. *Put me down and run, Ramson.*

A deep voice spoke, cutting through the scuffle. "I will take the Princess."

The guards closing in fell back.

A familiar figure approached. His gray-peppered hair fell into his lined face, and his eyes—the same steady gray of storm clouds—were immeasurable wells of sadness. Gently, ever so gently, Kapitan Markov took Ana in his arms.

On the dais, a squad of guards lifted Luka's body. Tetsyev stood by Morganya's side, whispering. Morganya's eyes followed Ana. "Take the Princess's body to the dungeons. My alchemist has some work to do on her."

For a moment, Markov's face contorted with rage as Ana had never seen before. But he reined in his anger and turned to Morganya with a stoic expression. "Yes, Kolst Contessya."

"Kolst Imperatorya," Morganya corrected. "Your Glorious Empress."

Out of the corner of her eye, Ana saw two remaining Councilmembers glance at each other. She recognized one of them as Councilman Taras.

"Kolst Imperatorya." Markov's tone cut like steel. "And the criminal?"

"Take him to the dungeons," Morganya commanded. "Schedule an execution. I want the world to know what happens to traitors of the Crown."

No, Ana wanted to scream. But her body was a prison.

The last she saw of the Grand Throneroom was Morganya standing at the dais, a smile curling her lips as she watched Ramson struggle against the guards. Tetsyev stood by her side, in her shadow. Sadov leaned against the throne, wiping blood from his face.

Markov shut the great doors and carried Ana away into the silence, his steps as somber as a funeral drumbeat.

40

The stars were visible from the highest tower of the Salskoff Palace. Linn's steps were light yet growing heavy, her breathing becoming frantic as she sped through the marble-white halls. She hurtled up a set of stairs, three at a time, her winds guiding her at her back.

Footsteps pounded behind her, closing in.

Linn leapt over the landing—and her stomach clenched as she stumbled into the watchtower. Two guards spun around; their surprise barely registered on their faces before she'd dealt two kicks to their temples and they crumpled to the ground.

Linn spun around, forcing herself to take controlled, rhythmic breaths. It was difficult not to give in to her intrinsic need to gulp down frantic lungfuls of air, but she knew she only had seconds before her pursuer appeared. She needed to be in a state to fight, and her heartbeat was too fast right now.

She took in her surroundings: white marble walls with narrow windows. Good for observing and shooting, and to limit the range for incoming arrows. Moonlight spilled through a single door, leading to a balcony outside that stood over the Palace walls.

A shadow fell across the floor. Linn spun.

Her pursuer's eyes were molten silver; his white cloak flapped behind him in the slight breeze that stirred between them. Linn clutched her last remaining dagger tightly.

The yaeger stood, as though he had been carved from rock and marble—and Linn recognized the precision in his stance, the years of training etched into the corded muscles of his back. Only his eyes flickered like a ripple across a moonlit pond. "I am not your enemy."

"You are not my friend," Linn replied.

"I do not wish to hurt you."

"I've heard that before."

His eyes shifted to her empty weapons belt and the gash across her midriff. It was shallow, but Linn had left the blood to make it look worse than it was. The best advantage in a fight was to be underestimated. "You are wounded, and you are out of weapons. You will not win this fight." He took a step closer. "My men are storming into the Grand Throneroom as we speak. The Blood Witch is a murderer and a monster. She will not triumph. Please, come quietly and save yourself."

Their gazes held for two, three seconds. Linn remained quiet.

The yaeger's arm shifted slightly. Linn forced herself to flinch. To appear afraid.

Within the blink of an eye, she lashed out. Her throwing knife was a silver blur. It struck the marble wall, a hand's throw from the yaeger's face, and clattered to the ground.

The yaeger's eyes flickered with an emotion Linn could not read—it might have been surprise, or anger, or even admiration.

Slowly, with infinitely precise movements, the yaeger

unbuckled his shoulder straps and shrugged off his white cloak. His eyes fastened on her as he drew two swords from their sheaths. "You have chosen," he said. "Shame. I would have preferred not to kill as talented a fighter as yourself."

"You won't," Linn said quietly. Every muscle in her body was tense with anticipation.

A hard, impregnable wall clamped down upon her Affinity. Linn's insides churned; for a moment she thought she would throw up. It was as though one of her senses had suddenly been shut off—as though she had lost her ability to smell, or taste, or hear, or see. The winds that had been whispering at her back suddenly died. The silence was unbearable.

Linn reined in her nausea. *Action, and counteraction.*

Linn slashed her arm out, feinting. The yaeger flinched and shifted to his left. In that fraction of a second, Linn sprang backward, spinning and plucking two daggers—one in each hand—from the unconscious guards. In an extension of the same motion, she flung them at the yaeger, one after the other in rapid succession.

By the time she heard the *plink* of a dagger against his blackstone sword, Linn had already turned and was sprinting toward the open door. She heard the soft sound of metal slicing through flesh, followed by a grunt. At least one of her blades had found its mark. It was far from a killing blow, but anything that slowed him down would help her right now.

Linn burst into a night of wind and stars. Up here, high above the shelter and protection of any walls or buildings, the Cyrilian winter winds whipped at her face and snatched at her hair. She reached out to them, but felt nothing. Her Affinity was gone.

Beyond the balustrade, the city of Salskoff glimmered with

torchlight and festivities. The Tiger's Tail snaked all around the Palace, its frothy white water visible from even up here. A wave of dizziness and fear twined around her as she looked down at the tiny, faraway lights, at the vast emptiness of space and air and nothingness in between. Even the thick Palace walls below the watchtower were too far down—Linn might have aimed to jump had she had her winds.

She sensed him before she heard or saw him. He came from the darkness, a white blur in the moonlight, swords glinting as they slashed. Linn ducked and spun at the last moment. She'd intended for his momentum to carry him into the balustrade, but instead of careening off balance, he stopped suddenly and twisted in her direction, jabbing a blade at her.

Linn reeled back, throwing her weight into her upper body and then her head. Even as she flipped backward, she felt the sharp bite of his blade on her side. Her landing was slightly off; she took a step to adjust her balance, and then the yaeger was upon her again, his two swords cutting this way and that, his eyes calculating her every step and move.

She was going to lose. She had neither blade nor Affinity on her side, and even if she'd managed to cut him earlier, he had cut her right back.

Her moves were slowing, and every duck and dodge was more difficult than the last. She'd barely avoided the slice of one blade before another was bearing down upon her. She was becoming sloppier, her nerves fraying fast as she anticipated blow after blow after blow.

The second sting of his sword was deeper than the first, and Linn nearly gasped aloud. She stumbled, the pain blotting out all rational thought and training for a fraction of a second. That was all the yaeger needed. Out of the corner of her eye, she saw his foot kick out; she leapt back, too little and too slow.

The yaeger's foot slammed into her abdomen, sending her reeling. The cold marble balustrade slammed into her back: a firm reminder that she was out of space.

The yaeger stepped toward her. Linn leaned back, trying not to think about the fact that half of her body was hanging over empty air. *A wingless bird,* her Wind Masters had called her after she had stopped flying. *How can a bird be afraid of heights?*

She shrank against the banister. Sweat drenched her clothes, her wounds were bleeding, and her breath was ragged and shallow. A lump of panic rose in her throat as she assessed her options: a precarious fall behind her, and a fight she could not win in front of her.

The yaeger frowned. His jaw hardened. "I told you, I wished not to kill as fine a warrior as yourself. Such talent is already difficult enough to come across in this world."

Linn shivered. "We Kemeirans believe that everything in life was meant to be; that there is a fate behind every event and every meeting." She had no idea why she was telling him this, but the words of her homeland and her Wind Masters brought her comfort in her last moments. "Perhaps . . . perhaps you will be the death of me."

His eyes narrowed. She could glean no emotion from them whatsoever. "Why do you not seek to kill me?" he asked.

"Action, and counteraction," she whispered. "That is our belief—that every action has a counteraction. You attacked, and I defended. You had no intention to take my life, therefore I had no right to take yours. And now, I am paying for that choice with my life." She would die without a blade in her hands and without the wind in her face, cornered like a coward.

Linn squeezed her eyes shut, trying not to shake. She had thought of death many times, but not like this. No—she had always pictured a glorious death, a warrior's death, plunging from the skies by the side of her fellow windsailers as a Kemeiran should.

A breeze stirred behind her, rippling the folds of her clothes and cooling her sweat-soaked back. *Courage,* it seemed to whisper. *Courage.*

The empty space behind her seemed to expand. And suddenly, she realized that she could still fight with the winds at her back and the stars above her head.

Something like regret flashed in the soldier's eyes. "I am truly sorry," he said.

"Don't be," Linn said. She arched her back and kicked off. Using her arms to grip the balustrade, she swung herself over.

And then she was falling.

It was terrifying and exhilarating at the same time: the wind roaring in her ears, the world tumbling all around her, and the knowledge that there was nothing and no one to catch her below and save her. Her scream was trapped in her throat, and for the first time in a long time, she felt a slip of her old self stir. She flung out her arms. Her instincts kicked in, and she pivoted so that she was falling feetfirst.

She was in free fall. The feeling of weightlessness, of uncertainty and freedom in every breath she gasped, was utterly frightening and familiar at once.

She felt as though she were . . . flying.

The white crenellated Palace walls rushed up to meet her.

Linn slammed onto the ground, flexing her knees and staggering her fall to catch her balance. The momentum was still too strong.

Her hand flew out, and she felt a jolt as her palm hit the ground, followed by a sharp streak of pain in her wrist. Linn cried out, but through the daze of pain and blur of tears, she was somehow running, somehow pushing herself forward with each step toward the edge of the wall.

A shout rang in the night. Linn kept running.

Ten, fifteen steps. The moon slid behind the clouds, cloaking the night in utter darkness.

I am shadows and wind. I am the invisible girl.

The pressure on her Affinity lifted, clearing like fog above a lake. A feeling of serenity passed through her, followed by elation as her winds roared to life by her side.

For a moment, Linn wanted to slow her steps, to turn and look at the watchtower above.

Instead, she put on a burst of speed and ran for the edge of the walls.

Twenty, thirty steps. The wind was a pack of invisible wolves, darting by her side and howling in triumph.

Thirty-nine, forty steps—

Linn leapt. And then she was airborne, her winds roaring all around her, reacting to the slightest of her pulls and pushes and carrying her light body. A delighted laugh burst from her mouth as she flung out her arms, letting childhood instincts take over. For a glorious moment, she was in Kemeira again, soaring beneath the eternal blue skies and between mist-cloaked mountains.

The moon slid out from behind the clouds, bathing her

in its cool fluorescence. The white waters of the Tiger's Tail churned below her, its waves reaching up as though to greet her. Out of the corner of her eye, she saw a dark figure outlined against the balustrade of the watchtower. Watching her.

Action, and counteraction.

Linn kept her gaze on him for a moment longer, pulling on her winds to slow her descent. Even as she hurtled toward the Tiger's Tail, a part of her realized that the soldier had spared her life today. And she couldn't help but wonder whether she'd become entwined in a new strand of destiny with this cold enemy, this fierce warrior—for better or for worse.

Linn curled into herself as tightly as she could. And plunged into the icy river.

41

The first thing she felt was the cold. And then came scent: the unmistakably musty smell of damp stone and stale air.

Ana shifted a hand and felt a cool, hard surface beneath her. Her head spun, and her body felt sluggish, as though she had just woken from a deep sleep. Her muscles were stiff, but she could feel the effects of the paralysis potion fading already.

She opened her eyes. The darkness was absolute, but she recognized this place. There was nowhere else in this world that carried such a strong stench of hopelessness and taste of absolute fear. Papa had always told her that this was a place full of demons.

But Ana had learned that demons were not the creatures to be feared the most. Humans were.

She drew a deep breath and shifted her focus to her Affinity. It leapt to her command and the room lit up: the walls and floors riddled with specks and splatters of blood, old and new layers superimposed like coats of paint.

She wriggled her fingers and toes. Nobody had bothered to

shackle her, or inject her with Deys'voshk . . . because she was supposed to be dead.

And Luka. Luka was gone.

Despite what she told herself—that she needed a plan, that she needed to get out of here, that she needed to save Ramson and find Linn—the tears came. It was as though her sorrow were a flood, crashing through her strongest will and iron strength, pouring out. She lay on a table in the cold, dark dungeon, clamping both hands on her mouth to stay silent as she cried. With each long, drawn-out sob, she curled into herself like she would never breathe again.

She was pathetic. Luka had survived a year of Morganya's torture, of being slowly drained of life, and even toward the very end he had been able to resist her in his own way.

Get up, brat, he'd say to her right now. *Our empire needs you.*

Her empire needed her. She had no right to grief, not now.

Ana clenched her jaw and curled her fists. Her body still shuddered with silent sobs, but her mind cleared.

Promise me.

Somewhere far off, a door clanged. Footsteps reverberated through the deserted corridors. Ana suppressed a shudder and lay frozen in place. Those sounds evoked an unspeakable fear in her: the anticipation of thin white fingers curling around prison bars, a sadistic smile on a sallow face, and the promise of Deys'voshk against her lips.

Holding her breath, she reached out with her Affinity. Someone had entered the dungeons and was heading her way. He walked briskly but calmly—the measured steps of a person familiar with these dungeons. He slowly drew closer, his blood glowing brighter like a candle.

A soft murmur. Someone was saying her name. The voice was so familiar, she thought she was hallucinating.

A figure stepped before her cell, the far-off torchlight illuminating the silvers and whites that peppered his hair. By the time the cell door clicked open, she had scrambled to her feet.

Ana fell into her kapitan's firm embrace. Through her tears, she breathed in the scent of his shaving cream and armor metal.

"Kolst . . ." Markov's deep voice cracked; he couldn't finish the word as he sank to his knees and drew a circle over his chest. A salute; a show of respect.

Ana held back tears as she drew him back up, touching her fingers to his weathered face, tracing tears from the lines that had deepened around his eyes. Kapitan Markov had been like a second father to her, after Papa had turned from her. "I've missed you so much, Kapitan."

More footsteps sounded sharply down the hall again, and Ana tensed, grasping for her Affinity.

Two men rounded the corner, throwing bright torchlight into her cell. For a moment, Ana could only stare at them.

Lieutenant Henryk saluted. Shame heated his cheeks—their thoughts both inevitably turned to when he had tried to arrest her earlier in the evening—but he kept his gaze firmly on hers.

And next to him . . . next to him was—

"Hello, Witch," Ramson said softly. His face was bruising in various places, and his shirt was torn open at the collar. Someone had hastily bandaged his chest, but blood was already soaking through the gauze.

She remembered the Throneroom, the way he had burst

in, the devastation on his face. The shadow of that grief still clouded his eyes. He looked so fragile.

Ana's throat ached, but she forced herself to stay where she was. "Hello, con man," she whispered.

Ramson looked as though he were about to say something else, but Kapitan Markov cut across him. "You'll address her as *Empress,*" the old guard said sternly.

Ana noticed that Ramson stood a bit straighter. "Yes, sir."

Among them, there was one person still missing. "Linn," Ana said, looking at Ramson. "Where is she?"

"She was fighting the Whitecloaks when I left her," Ramson said. "She gave me a pouch and told me to hand it to you—said it was evidence. Kapitan, did you happen to take any prisoners from last night?"

Desperation twined around Ana when the kapitan slowly shook his head. "Please, Kapitan," Ana whispered. "She's my friend. Will you ask your guards to search for a Kemeiran girl?"

"I will, Kolst Imperatorya," Markov said gravely, "but I do not think you can stay here for the results of my search."

The implication of his words left her breathless with dread. "Morganya," Ana said quietly. "What happened? What has the Imperial Council decided?"

Markov hesitated. "There is no . . . Imperial Council anymore," he said at last. "Morganya has seized complete control of the Court and dismissed the Council. The remaining Councilmembers have pledged their loyalties to her."

The inevitable truth loomed like a shadow. Ana was back where she had started, with no army, no power, and no title. "I've lost." The words numbed her lips.

"No, Kolst Imperatorya!" Henryk's fists were clenched.

"A few of the Councilmembers believe Morganya committed treason and usurped the throne. You need to go back. Announce that you are alive, sentence Morganya, and take back the Court."

"Do you really think that matters?" Ramson spoke suddenly, his anger a quiet undercurrent. "If Ana goes back now, she'll be killed. Pardon me," he added. "The Princess. The Heir. The Empress. Whatever you want to call her—*it doesn't matter.* This is a coup, and Morganya has solidified her power already; the majority of the Cyrilian Court sides with her. We've been outmaneuvered. But there is one advantage we hold over her—everyone believes Ana is dead."

He was right, Ana realized. This was a war that Ana could not win with brazenness and the strength of her Affinity. This was a long game, and Ana needed to outscheme, outwit, and outmaneuver Morganya.

Ana held a hand up, and the three men fell silent, their attention on her. "I must leave," Ana said. "But I will not disappear. Morganya plans mass murder and a reign of terror. She *must* be stopped." Yuri's defiant face appeared in her mind's eye, his hair as bright as fire. "I have a small group of allies in the south of the Empire. I will travel there and begin my campaign. I will gather support; I will gather an army. And once I am ready to prove to this empire—to this world—that I am worthy of being heir . . . I will return."

Markov gave a slow nod. "How you have grown, Little Tigress," he murmured.

"Kapitan, Lieutenant," Ana continued. "If you support me, then I need you to stay here. If I am to win, and if I am to return, then I need allies close to my enemy. I need you to be my eyes and ears within the Palace, within the Imperial Court. Can you do that?"

Henryk gave her a sharp salute. There were tears in his eyes. "We will not fail you, Kolst Imperatorya."

"You must go," Markov said, and Ana could tell how much of an effort it took for him to say those words to her.

Ana met his eyes. "I will return, Kapitan," she whispered. "And I *will* see you again."

Guided by Henryk's torchlight, they made their way to the secret passageway in the back of the dungeons. The narrow cell door stood ajar from their earlier entry.

Markov took Ana's hand and squeezed. "Deys blesya ty, Kolst Imperatorya."

"Deys blesya ty," she replied.

A grating sound reverberated throughout the dungeons. With a grunt, Henryk straightened. The door to the passageway gaped from the wall, darkness beyond.

Ramson tapped two fingers to his forehead in a sharp salute and slipped in. Ana followed, placing a hand on the entrance to steady herself.

She glanced back. Markov and Henryk stood behind her, the torch flickering like a beacon in the darkness. Only one year ago, she had run through this door, afraid and alone and completely lost. Ahead of her lay darkness, uncertainty, and a long, long path she'd have to fight her way through. Behind was a crumbling empire, a people in peril, and a world divided.

Promise me.

Ana turned and slipped into the darkness that welcomed her like an old friend.

42

The stars had reeled a full cycle above her head, and the faintest edges of blue had begun to crown the horizon in the east. In the distance, the Salskoff Palace was barely visible beyond the white-tipped forest that stretched in all directions beneath the hills. It glowed a faint, predawn gold, thick tendrils of morning mist clinging to its spires and crenellated walls.

Ana exhaled, her breath fogging in the air before her. From their vantage point atop the hill, she could barely make out the curved back of the Kateryanna Bridge, linking the castle to the sleeping town below. Salskoff spread out under the watchful gaze of its Palace, the Tiger's Tail winding protectively around it.

"Quite beautiful from up here, isn't it?" By her side, Ramson wore a placid expression as he gazed at the sight before them. "I suppose that's what it must look like to the gods, or Deities, or whatever. Who cares about the petty battles that humans fight? There's a whole world out there for them to look at."

"That's why it's up to us to fight our battles. Not the Deities."

"That's what I've always said. Gods, I should become a priest."

A snort burst out from Ana. "You? A priest? It's not the end of the world yet, Ramson."

He shot her a grin, and Ana realized that, despite everything, Ramson had managed to make her laugh. "Then we should get moving, to stop the end of the world. If you *really* don't want to see me become a priest."

Ana glanced back at her home. A weight seemed to settle on her shoulders again. For so long, she'd been trying to make a life in a place that had not been a home for a while. And for so long, it had remained distant yet visible, close yet just out of reach. Her heart was heavy as she steeled herself for the inevitable.

Ramson clasped a hand over hers. He tilted her chin with a finger so that she was gazing into his warm, clear eyes. "Have courage, Princess."

She shut her eyes briefly, leaning into his light touch. "I'm afraid, Ramson. I feel like I've been fighting for so long, and yet . . . I'm back where I started."

"That's life," he said quietly. "This isn't one of the fairy-tale stories you read in your childhood, where the hero always wins in the end. You'll have many battles to fight, and you won't win them all. And at the end of every single day, you'll always face the same choice: keep fighting, or give up."

Our choices. A breeze stirred, and she seemed to hear her brother's words in the whispers of the pines around them. Far above their heads, an eagle's sharp cry pierced the silence.

Luka had named her heir. But that title meant nothing if she couldn't prove herself worthy of it.

Ana lifted her head. "I've made my choice already. I'm going to journey south to find Yuri and the Redcloaks."

Ramson drew back. "You're joining the rebellion?"

A cold wind stirred around her, and she thought of Yuri's

parting words. *The future lies here, with us. In the hands of the people.*

“For now,” Ana said, drawing her cloak tighter around her. Morganya had eliminated any and all checks and balances against the monarchy and her reign. And the Redcloaks . . . they didn’t seem to want a monarchy at all. “The winds of this world are changing, Ramson, and I . . . I need to find out where I stand. But first, Morganya needs to be stopped, and I need an army. I’ll begin working to gain the support of the other kingdoms. And seeing as Bregon is our most neutral ally, I’ll start there.” She paused, and dared herself to meet his eyes. “I could use the help of a Bregonian soldier.”

He held her gaze. “I could think about it. But I have a question.” A sly look was working its way into his eyes. “What’s the Trade, Witch?”

She almost exhaled in relief; her heart fluttered with joy. “How about, in return, I won’t choke you on your own blood?”

“Incredible. What have I done to deserve such an opportunity? The gods have truly smiled upon me.”

“Don’t count your blessings yet.”

“Fair enough,” he said, and shifted, his gaze on something behind her.

Above the treetops, outlined in the dawn sky, a snowhawk was descending toward them. Ramson held out his arm, and the bird landed with a rustle of its snowy wings. Ramson fished out something from his pockets and held it toward the snowhawk; the bird clasped it with a quick clack of its beak.

“What are you doing?” Ana asked. The thing in the snowhawk’s beak resembled . . . hair. Midnight-black hair.

“Linn,” Ramson said simply, giving the bird an affectionate

pat. "If Kapitan Markov doesn't find her, then she must be out there somewhere. When Fisher finds her, he'll lead her to us."

Ana looked at the lock of hair, curled in the bird's beak, and sent a prayer to the Deities that her friend was safe. That, one way or another, they would find each other again.

"Fisher," she repeated. "That's an interesting name for a Cyrilian snowhawk."

A ghost of a smile lit Ramson's lips. "It's an old friend's name," he said softly. "He was a wayfinder, just like this bird."

Ana studied the snowhawk. It stared right back with intelligent golden eyes. Legends said that snowhawks were blessed with the touch of the Deities; that Winter had blown a breath upon the frozen land and created these birds out of nothing but wind and snow.

Ramson thrust his arm into the air. With a mighty flap of its wings, the snowhawk shot into the sky. *Be swift,* Ana thought. *May the gods that watch over Linn watch over you, too.*

As though in response, a soft wind stirred and kissed her cheeks.

"They're magical, you know," Ramson said as they watched the bird grow smaller and smaller. "At least, that's what Bregonian legends said."

Ana looked at him in surprise. "Cyrilian ones, too."

"They say Affinites and snowhawks and moonbears and a lot of legendary creatures are remnants of the Deities, reminders that the gods once walked this world."

"I didn't know you believed those kinds of tales."

Ramson leveled his gaze to her. His eyes were bright in the early-morning light, his cheeks tinged red from the cold, his hair mussed from the winds. "I could be persuaded," he murmured.

Something about his open, piercing stare and the honesty of his tone brought back the boy who'd stood before her on the night of the Fyrva'snezh. Ana found herself drawn inexorably toward him, taking in the curl of his hair at the nape of his neck; the strong, chiseled edges of his jawline; the crooked curve to his lips. They parted slightly as Ramson let out a soft breath and dipped his head toward her, his eyes tracing every angle of her face. Something about the way he looked at her, like nothing else around them existed, made her heart beat faster and her breaths come shorter.

That feeling—like she was falling and flying at the same time—made her afraid.

Another gust of wind pressed at her back, more insistently, and out of the corner of her eye, she saw the Palace again, looming in the distance. It was a reminder that she couldn't afford to think of anything else right now. Not when she had an empire to save.

Ana turned away abruptly. The cold rushed in to fill the space between them. "Well," she said, swallowing. "Here we are."

She sensed Ramson's gaze still on her, softer now and more distant. "Here we are," he echoed.

Ana kept her gaze straight ahead, on the Palace. She was, once again, a girl in a threadbare cloak, with nothing to her name and nowhere to run to. Yet somehow, in a year, it felt as though everything had changed.

I unsee you, Little Tigress.

It was she who had changed, Ana realized with a burst of

surprise that tasted sweet in the wintry air. She was no longer the frightened girl of twelve moons past, who had so desperately sought a way to fix herself, her monstrosity. If the line between good and evil was drawn by choices, then she would choose to wield her Affinity to fight for those who could not.

Ramson was right. This wasn't a fairy-tale story where the good triumphed in the end. There were real people suffering in her empire right now, in the shadows of the laws that claimed to protect them. There was evil and darkness here—oppressors and those who perpetuated violence with hatred and greed in their hearts.

But there was also the good; there was the light of this world that came in shattered, piercing fragments, whether it was a small earth Affinite making flowers out of barren soil, or a fire Affinite's secret chokolad treats, or a wind Affinite tilting her face to the skies, telling her that there was something worth saving—in her and in this world.

This world—this beautiful broken world that harbored so much of the gray—was the only one they had. And it was one she would continue to fight for.

But first, she had to prove to her people that she was worthy of being their leader. That, no matter her title, she would not stand by and watch innocents die under a regime of terror. That, in her flesh and bones and soul, she was Anastacya Kateryanna Mikhailov, blood heir of the Cyrilian Empire.

GLOSSARY

Affinite: person with a special ability or a connection to physical or metaphysical elements; ranges from a heightened sense of the element to ability to manipulate or generate the element

blackstone: stone mined from the Krazyast Triangle; the single element immune to Affinite manipulation and known to diminish or block Affinities

bratika: brother

chokolad: cocoa-based sweet

contessya: countess

copperstone: lowest-value coin

dacha: house

dama: lady

deimhov: demon

Deys: Deity

Deys'voshk: poison that effects Affinites and is used to subdue them; also known as Deities' Water

Fyrva'snezh: First Snows

goldleaf: highest-value coin

guzhkyn gerbil: pet rodent from the Guzhkyn region in southern Cyrilia

Imperator: Emperor

Imperatorya: Empress

Imperya: Empire
kapitan: captain
kechyan: traditional Cyrilian robe typically made of patterned silk
kologne: scented perfume
kolst: glorious
kommertsya: commerce
konsultant: consultant
mamika: "little mother"; term of endearment for "aunt"
mesyr: mister
pelmeny: dumplings with fillings of minced meat, onions, and herbs
pirozhky: fried pie with sweet or savory fillings
pryntsessa: princess
ptychy'moloko: bird's milk cake
Redcloak: rebels; a play on the colloquialism "Whitecloak"
silverleaf: medium-value coin
sistrika: sister
sunwine: mulled wine made in the summer with honey and spice
valkryf: breed of horse; a valuable steed with split toes and an incomparable ability to climb mountains and weather cold temperatures
varyshki: expensive bull leather
Vyntr'makt: winter market; outdoor markets usually established in town squares prior to the arrival of winter
Whitecloak: colloquialism for "Imperial Patrol"
yaeger: rare Affinite whose connection is to another person's Affinity; they can sense Affinites and control one's Affinity

ACKNOWLEDGMENTS

I began learning the English language at the age of seven, when I was plucked from my birth town of Paris and dropped into an American international school in the dusty gray city of 1990s Beijing. I've come a ways since that first day, when I was lost and the words that my teachers and classmates spoke flowed over my head like water, out of my reach.

Books changed everything for me, transporting me to a hundred different worlds within their pages, allowing me to live a thousand different lives. I began reading in earnest, and slowly, with each turn of a page, a dream began to form. I wanted to be an author; I wanted to shape the worlds and change lives with the power of my words. Today I'd like to express my profound gratitude to every person who has touched my life in this process and shaped this book—you have all made my dream.

To my wonderful agent, Peter Knapp, who pulled me through the doors and set me on this incredible journey, and continues to be a champion in every way. Thank you for changing my life on that dreary gray November morning in Beijing.

To my incredible editor, Krista Marino, whose razor-sharp mind and pen have caught all the plot holes and fashion faux pas in this book—I am so blessed to be working with you. You continue to push me with every revision to make this book into the best version of itself. I'm (selfishly) glad you missed your flight to Paris last December and I got to have that second call with you.

To Delacorte Press—visionary publisher Beverly Horowitz and assistant editor extraordinaire Monica Jean, publishers Barbara Marcus and Judith Haut, and the entire team at Random House Children's Books, who have already made me feel like a part of this giant, amazing family: Felicia Frazier and Mark Santella in sales; Angela Carlino, Alison Impey, Ray Shappell, Regina Flath, and Ken Crossland in design; fearless copyeditors Colleen Fellingham and Alison Kolani and managing editor Tamar Schwartz (who will probably have to copyedit this paragraph again—I'm so sorry); Tracy Heydweiller, production manager; Mary McCue and Dominique Cimina in publicity; the amazing marketing team, John Adamo, Jenna Lisanti, and Kelly McGauley; Kate Keating, Elizabeth Ward, and Cayla Rasi in digital marketing; and Adrienne Waintraub, Lisa Nadel, and Kristen Schulz in school and library marketing. This book exists thanks to all of you!

To the team at Park Literary, including Abby Koons and Blair Wilson, whose tireless work allows this book to continue traveling all over the world.

To my first-ever beta readers and critique partners on Absolute Write, who read iterations of my opening chapters between 2014 and 2017 and whose comments helped my writing grow by leaps and bounds.

To my first critique partner and writing friend, Cassy Klisch, whose daily texts inspired me to keep going and whose critiques of the early versions of this book motivated me to finish. I cannot wait to see your books on shelves one day soon, too.

To my early beta readers and dear friend Heather Kassner,

whose Twitter DM changed my life that autumn day and whose magical, whimsical, gorgeous words continue to inspire me. We will have our Happy Hour one day, and a photo that is not my head Photoshopped on your mom.

To my beloved writing friends: Becca Mix, viral sensation and meme master, whose obnoxious but endearing cheerleading for me makes my mornings, and from whom I continue to learn understanding and humility and how to get along with cats. Katie Zhao, the true Dragon Warrior, possible long-lost cousin, and beastly writing machine, whose work ethic inspires and motivates me, whose books are exactly what young Amélie needed to read and will inspire an entire generation of kids. Molly Chang, Typo Queen, who continues to hold my hand throughout the publishing journey, taught me the magic of tax deductions, and shares my great love of hotpot. Hopefully when this book is out I'll have time to watch all the Chinese dramas. Grace Li of Sparta, whose breathtaking prose continues to be a source of inspiration (and burning jealousy), who murders my favorite children and laughs about it. #2Blood2Furious coming your way, 2020. Andrea Tang, the wickedly smart *jiejie,* whose witty real-life rom-com stories and bantering book children give me life. Fran, my sweet agent sister (and so close to debut sisters!); Aly, Lyla, the entire summer 2018 retreat group, and so many amazing online friends I have yet to meet—thank you all for your friendship and support, for the late-night life talks over Barefoot wines and screaming over Twitter.

To my closest confidants, keepers of my secret dream from early on: Amy Zhao, evil twin and best maid, who read early versions of this book and supported me throughout, who was role-playing on Virtual Hogwarts and our various Kalaskre sites with me way back in middle school, whose abs are a source of envy, and whose gym sessions were often my only breaks during deadline-riddled months. Crystal Wong, who read an early version of this book and caught numerous typos, whose friendship got me through NYU and Orgcomm, and who continues to push me through every grueling work day: here's to the future Real Housewives of Midtown West and Santa Monica. Betty Lam, who shared a love of YA fantasy books with me at UCLA, who read the first few chapters and gave me amazing feedback, and who is still waiting to find out what happens (sorry!).

To my ISB friends—Jack, Sara, Jessica, Kevin, Alex, Darren, Alan—whose humor and support and shenanigans have gotten me through half my lifetime and who have continued to show up for me this year. I'm blessed to be surrounded by such intelligent and worldly human beings as some of my greatest friends. (Except for you, Jack.)

To my author and writer friends who stayed by my side during the good times and the bad: when darkness falls, the shadows leave, and you are left with those made of light. This book wouldn't be here today without you.

To the authors who reached out to me and offered me their guidance and wisdom, thank you for that phone call, for that email, for that message. I hope you know it meant the world to me.

To Clement—the Ramson to my Ana, the Pewp to my Millie, the love of my life. Thank you for being my biggest rock in all the ups and downs of life, for picking up the housework and doing the dishes when I wanted to get some extra writing done, for cooking and feeding me when I was on deadline, for cheering me on with every small piece of news I sent your way, for loving me at my best and worst times. I read about so many fairy-tale princes and storybook heroes, but you're the real thing (albeit a sports-loving, beer-drinking, bro-speaking version). I love you, and I continue to fall more in love with you with each passing day.

To my little sister, Weetzy—my best friend, my soul sister, my co-conspirator, who has woven stories with me since we were old enough to speak, who read all my terrible novels growing up and got mad at me for my bad writing, who sat with me side by side during hot Beijing summers and wrote all those unfinished novels about fairy princesses and girls with magical powers. Life would be a lot lonelier without you; thank you for always being there for me, and know that I will always be here for you.

Last, and most of all, to Mama and Papa—for being the most wonderful family and giving me the best upbringing I could ever want. I am blessed to have two fiercely intelligent and loving role models who taught me kindness, dedication, humility, and perseverance; who gave me the opportunity to dream. Every summer vacation, every museum trip, every book you bought me, every story you told me, every life lesson you gave me, every drop of incredible knowledge you shared with me has shaped me into who I am today and bled into this book. I hope I've made you proud.

THE PRINCESS AND THE CON MAN LIVE TO FIGHT AGAIN.

TURN THE PAGE FOR A SPECIAL PREVIEW OF THE SEQUEL TO *BLOOD HEIR.*

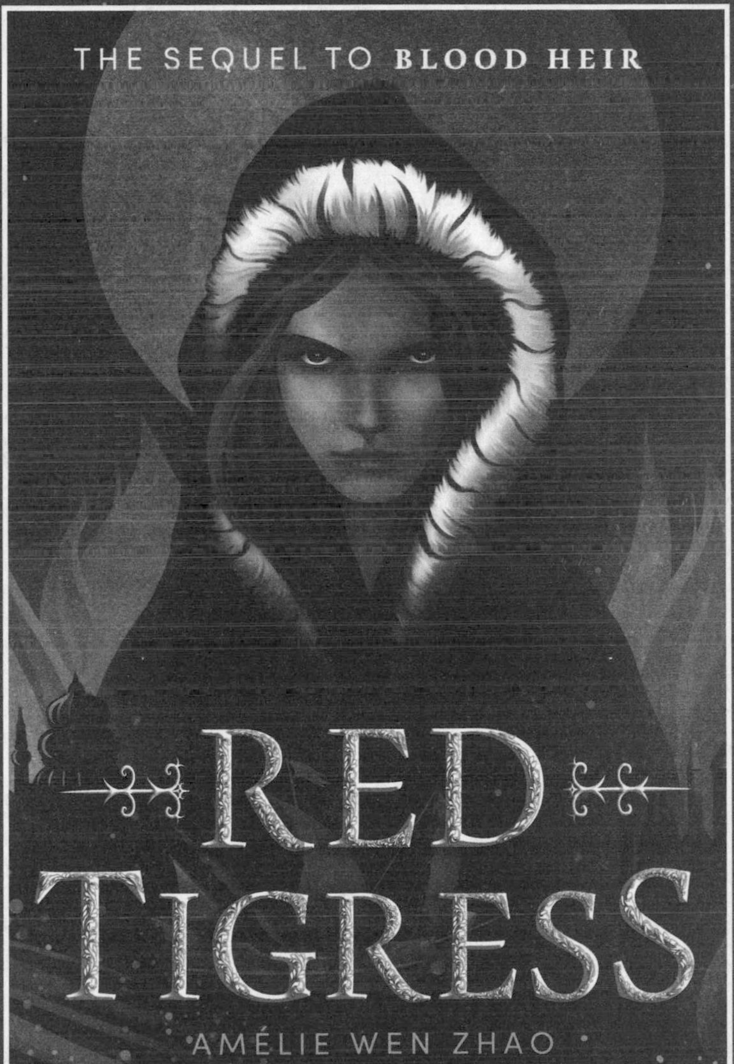

1

Novo Mynsk reeked of death.

It always had, but to Ramson Quicktongue, the city had also held the stench of power and corruption, of murder and survival, swirling together in an intoxicating redolence that corroded one's soul. It was no different now, save for the eerie darkness and the silent snow that blanketed the streets.

Ramson navigated the narrow alleys of his childhood haunts with quick, precise steps. The last time he'd been here had been with Anastacya Mikhailov during the Fyrva'snezh at his former master's mansion. It had only been a little over one moon since the celebration of the First Snows, but now, that world felt almost utterly unrecognizable.

In just four weeks, Novo Mynsk had transformed into a ghost town, abandoned by most of its residents as they fled the new regime. Streets that had once glistened with torchlight and writhed with bejeweled bodies and raucous revelers had been replaced by shuttered stores and empty windows. Bodies littered the streets in areas where gangs had scrapped over bits of food, and snow had covered them, leaving only glimpses of clothing or a protruding boot as macabre grave markers.

It was not an unfamiliar sight over his travels from town to ravaged town with Ana. Since Morganya had ascended the throne, much of Northern Cyrilia had fallen to her control. From pieces of newspapers and torn posters in abandoned villages, Ramson and Ana had learned of the Imperial Inquisition, a wide-scale hunt for non-Affinites who were accused of any affiliation with Affinite trafficking. Led by newly established Affinites fiercely loyal to the Empress, it was a movement that had come to define Morganya's regime.

The south, though, remained free from the tightening grasp of Morganya's rule. That included Goldwater Port. According to Ana, the Redcloaks had established their base there, as it was one of the last standing free havens for Affinites and non-Affinites alike. It was to there that Ana traveled to begin her resistance movement with the Redcloaks.

And it was there, Ramson had slowly begun to think, that he could fight for some semblance of a life again after all this was over. He'd once been the Portmaster; under his former master Alaric Kerlan's rule, he'd built a city teeming with commerce and crime and underground networks, the kind of place he'd dreamt of calling his own one day.

He hadn't told Ana explicitly where he was going tonight, because it wasn't *explicitly* a task for her—their—mission. Rather, Ramson had felt the silent call of this place as soon as he'd set foot in Novo Mynsk, the phantom pull of a connection he hadn't quite managed to sever yet.

He'd come to find out, for himself, what had happened to Alaric Kerlan and the Order of the Lily. And he'd come to bid goodbye to the wreckage of his past once and for all as he turned down a new path.

The tapping of his freshly sharpened misericord against his hip came to an abrupt stop when Ramson turned the last corner and slowed. He found that he was suddenly glad for the sharp knife at his waist.

The Kerlan Estate stood alone in the middle of a snow-covered street, half-buried by the snow, its battered golden gates yawning wide. Gone were the rows of liveried guards; gone were the diamond-glass lamps spilling halos of light onto lush lawns; gone were the brightly lit windows that had burned incandescent even in the darkest nights.

Ramson touched a leather-gloved hand to the broken railing of the gate and hesitated.

Even now, the sight of the Kerlan Estate did not fail to elicit a muddy swirl of emotions in him. He'd known pain here—so much pain, still seared into his flesh in the shape of the brand of the Order of the Lily. He'd seen growth, sharpened by that hunger and fear and driven by the knowledge that he had to do whatever he needed to in order to survive. And he'd tasted happiness, fleeting as bursts of color in the Empire's gray skies, in the blood trades he'd made and the honors he'd gained, paid for with the lives of other men as he upheld Alaric Kerlan's rule.

Ramson's heart pounded in his throat as he hurried up the path. When he reached the mansion, he saw that one handle of the giant mahogany double doors had broken; the other seemed to have been hacked clean off by a serrated blade of some sort. The wood creaked as he pushed them open and stepped inside.

The Kerlan Estate looked as though it had been mauled. The marble walls had been stripped of their gold-framed paintings, and the lapis lazuli vases had disappeared, along with the many other items Kerlan had deemed "exotic." Someone had shattered the glass ceiling, and one of the crystal chandeliers had plunged into the middle of the banquet hall, creating a mess of glass and crystal that glinted in the moonlight. Drifts of snow carpeted the hallways, and Ramson's breath plumed before him in the subzero temperature.

When Ramson turned a corner and almost tripped over the dead man, his alertness pricked.

The body was half-buried in the snow; he could only make out a sleeve and a blackened hand. Ramson knelt by the corpse, sweeping off the freshly fallen snow to reveal the man's left arm. Just as he'd suspected, a tattoo of a lily of the valley was inked on the inside of the man's left wrist.

He had been a member of the Order.

Instead of feeling fear or grief or even pity, Ramson

examined the frozen hand with a clinical curiosity. Skin, blackened evenly, suggested internal bleeding. Farther up, on the forearm, raised flesh: evidence of a rash.

He had been poisoned.

Ramson pushed away more snow, revealing the dead man's face.

It was twisted in pain, bruised to a hideous purple and sunken with time, yet perfectly preserved by the cold. Ramson studied the face for several more seconds before deciding it wasn't a man he'd known in the Order. The corpse of a low-ranking grunt, a nobody, left to rot once winter swept its snows away.

And though their common master was nowhere to be seen, his voice tided over Ramson in phantom echoes.

I suppose you'll die unknown and irrelevant, your unmarked body rotting with the sewage of the Dams.

Ramson stood sharply to his feet, the whispers dissipating as his senses picked up on something else.

In one motion, he drew his blade, swung his arm out, and pivoted.

A startled cry; his blade connected with soft flesh, exposed throat. And . . . long, wavy hair.

Ramson closed his fist around a handful of hair and pulled the intruder's face into the moonlight. His apprehension turned to surprise. "Olyusha," he said as the woman struggled against his grip. "Damn hells."

“Let me go,” she said with a gasp, but Ramson only drew her closer, angling the misericord against her delicate neck.

“I don’t think so,” he said. Hells, he hadn’t been planning on running into anyone here—but as Ramson Quicktongue well knew, things rarely went according to plan. “Should’ve known this was your handiwork. Nightshade?”

“Oleander,” she rasped. “You’ve gotten rusty, Quicktongue.”

“Try anything and we’ll see just how rusty my skills are with a blade.”

He’d first known of Olyusha as an Affinite working at the Playpen, specializing in poisons and needles tipped with toxins. And though she didn’t know this, he’d used her as a bargaining chip against Bogdan, the affable yet stupid Penmaster of the Playpen, the infamous club where Alaric Kerlan had run shows featuring indentured Affinites.

That she was here, amidst buried corpses showing signs of poisoning . . . Ramson had an inkling he was very close to sniffing out the truth of what had happened to the Order.

Olyusha hissed, but he felt her swallow against his blade. “Then perhaps we’ll both join the corpses at our feet,” she sneered. “Let me go. I didn’t come here to kill you.”

“So why *are* you here?” Ramson asked pleasantly, digging his blade into her skin in a way that he knew would be uncomfortable but would not cut.

“To warn you. Kerlan wants you dead, and he’s set a high price on your head. The whole Order’s probably out for your blood, Quicktongue." She paused. "What's left of them, anyway."

At that, he glanced up, a thread of caution tightening inside him. The hallways stretched empty in front of and behind them. "And why would you want to warn me? We're cut from the same cloth, Olyusha, so spare me the 'out of the goodness of my heart' act."

"Because I need you." The sharpness in her tone became tinged with desperation at her next words: "Bogdan is gone."

This was news to Ramson. "What do you mean?"

The few times he'd run into Olyusha after her stint at the Playpen, she had been soft-spoken and doe-eyed, clinging to the gold-emblazoned sleeve of Bogdan. The Penmaster had rescued her from a lifetime of performances served under a forced contract—and he'd married her. It was Ramson who had helped cook Kerlan's books so that Kerlan would never find out.

"He's missing. That's why I came here to find you." Olyusha's throat bobbed against his blade. "Now let me go, and I can explain."

So there *was* something she needed from him. Ramson shifted tactic in an instant. "A Trade, then," he said. "You know I never give without taking, Olyusha."

"Fine," she said, and he stepped back, pushing her far enough from him that he was out of range of any needles or sharp, poison-laced objects she might try on him. She straightened, massaging her throat, and he noticed that her hands shook as she swept back her tresses. She suddenly looked small, tucked into her coat, which had lost some of its sheen and was now covered in a layer of gray. Ramson remembered her dressed in the finest of furs and silks, pearls gleaming in her hair as she turned her head and laughed.

Ramson tapped his misericord on the marble floor. It echoed hollowly. "You can start by telling me what happened to the Order," he said. "What you mean by 'what's left of them.'"

Olyusha sniffed. "I forget how long you've been out of it all, Quicktongue. After Morganya took the throne, Kerlan forced me to kill everyone associated with his trafficking business. He is intent on burying proof that it ever existed, for fear of the Inquisition." Her eyes flashed. "Then he left with a handful of top-ranking members. He's decided to refocus his efforts on his new Trade with Bregon."

The name of Ramson's birth kingdom sent a shock wave through him, even as his ears perked at the news. "What Trade? And why Bregon?"

"He said it was a new development with Affinites. Besides that, I don't know."

Ramson took a moment to digest this information. It didn't make sense. Bregon had never shown interest in its Affinites—magen, they were called—who, in Ramson's memory, had been largely left alone and unidentified. "And how do you know this?"

“Because,” Olyusha said, “he took Bogdan with him. I haven’t heard from him in weeks.”

Her voice had grown quiet; her large eyes shone wet in the dark. At last, Ramson connected the dots. “You want my help to find him.”

“He promised it would be a quick job. He told me he’d be back within the moon.” Olyusha swallowed. “I think . . . I think something went wrong.”

He was getting sidetracked—he’d only come here out of habit, to find out what had happened to the Order and his former master. Perhaps it was indeed better to let sleeping wolves lie.

Ramson began to turn away. “I’d love to help, Olyusha, really,” he said, “but with Kerlan demanding my head, I think I have better things—”

“He’s in Goldwater Port.” The words froze him, reeled him back. Slowly, Ramson turned to face her again. She was looking at him closely; at his reaction, she continued, “He told Bogdan that he would take it over, rebuild from there. No doubt he’s leveraging the trade routes to Bregon that you’ve established.”

Liquid cold spread through his veins, and suddenly, all the plans he’d been spinning for himself the past few weeks seemed to dissipate into smoke before him. Goldwater Port had been center to any prospects of a future he’d dreamt up for himself.

Only, Kerlan had gotten there first.

He heard Olyusha speaking as though from very far away.

"I thought that would get your attention. Here's my proposal: an alliance to take down Alaric Kerlan together, once and for all. Find him, find Bogdan, and bring my husband home to me. And in return, you'll have my protection. Someone watching your back from the enemy's side. Whoever from the Order is looking for you, I'll get to them first."

Ramson was silent as he considered, his thoughts already running ahead, weaving situations and possibilities and weighing the pros and cons. He'd wanted to leave Kerlan alone, to let the Order fade away as a part of his past that he wished to bury—but it seemed they had come looking for him, instead. And by taking Goldwater Port, Kerlan had seized the most valuable asset between them, backing Ramson into a corner.

Through the broken windows, moonlight spilled onto the floor. Even in the empty house, Ramson thought he could feel his old master's presence, like a shadow looming behind him.

This was all a game to Kerlan; it was Ramson's turn to make a move.

He was tired of playing the pawn.

"Well?" he heard Olyusha say at last. "Do we have a Trade?"

"I'm inclined to say so," he said. "Though don't expect me to shake with you on it." He'd witnessed the tricks she hid up her sleeves, how one drop of her poison could paralyze a man.

Olyusha's smile didn't meet her eyes. "I knew from the start that you wouldn't save Bogdan out of the goodness of your heart unless there was something in it for you. Seems

I was right."

"Am I really that predictable?"

Olyusha shrugged. "I'm not one to lay any claims as to how well I know you, Quicktongue," she said, picking at one of her nails, "but Bogdan and I would not have survived for so long in Kerlan's Order without someone watching over us. Of course, you might have done those things to buy yourself insurance . . . but I do think that you have the propensity to be good, in your own terrible ways."

The words stirred an echo of a memory. A girl, standing beneath the softly falling snow of a new winter, her eyes brighter than the moon. *You could be good. Make the right choice, Ramson.*

Olyusha's voice dragged him from the memory. "Before we part, I have one more gift for you," she said. "I know someone in Goldwater Port. Kerlan hired her for a few shipping jobs before, specific to Bregon. She'll have more information."

Ramson listened carefully to the name Olyusha gave. It didn't ring a bell, which surprised him. Perhaps there were still secrets that Goldwater Port carried, buried deep beneath its sands by the man who'd made Ramson the person he had been, the person he still was.

It was time for Ramson to beat his own path.

He turned, tipping his cap at Olyusha. "Goodbye, Olyusha," he said. "You sit pretty and focus on murdering our ex-colleagues. By the time you're done, I'll be back with your idiot husband."

He heard her give a throaty laugh, the sound echoing over the clip of his boots as he walked away. "I'm not giving up on you just yet, Quicktongue." A pause, and then: "When you do find Kerlan, promise me you'll give him my regards."

"I don't make promises," Ramson replied. "That way, I can't break them."

Yet even as he spoke, he could feel the sharp edges of a vow burrowing deep into his heart.

Jonah had once told him to live for himself. *Thing is, Ramson,* he'd said, his raven-black eyes sharp with intelligence and uncanny wisdom for his twelve years, *you can achieve everything in this world, but if it's for someone else, it's pointless.*

Yet as Ramson walked through the snow, the Kerlan Estate behind him with its empty-eyed windows and broken, gaping mouth of a door, he realized that the path in front of him was still far out of reach, blocked by a shadow that grew larger and clearer with every step he took.

Alaric Kerlan represented everything Ramson despised about himself, his life, and this world. As long as Kerlan lived, he could never be free.

And right now, if Kerlan was establishing a new criminal empire in Goldwater Port, using the trade routes Ramson had built to get to Bregon, then he was the obstacle that stood in the way of the glimpse of the future Ramson hoped for. One that involved planting the roots of the resistance in the south with Ana, and then making some semblance of a life for himself after the war was won.

Ramson tilted his face to the sky, his breath unfurling before him in a cloud as he spoke. "I'll find my own path, Jonah," he said aloud. "But first, I'm going to hunt down Alaric Kerlan. And I'm going to kill him."